NEST OF SALT

NEST
OF
SALT

Stories
by
Matthew V. Brockmeyer

BLACK THUNDER PRESS

ISBN: 978-1-7353085-0-0
PUBLISHED BY BLACK THUNDER
PRESS

Printed in the United States of America
Suggested Retail Price (SRP) $8.95

"There is no exquisite beauty . . . without some strangeness."
—Edgar Allan Poe, *Ligeia*

"The instruments of darkness tell us truths."
—William Shakespeare, *Macbeth*

CONTENTS

THE WITCH'S YULE

A Fable

Max knew if you believed in something hard enough it would come true. That you could be anything you wanted to be. You just needed a little magic.

Slipping his wolf cap over his head, Max silently crept on all fours into his brother's bedroom, looking for the magic he needed.

His brother, Eight Ball, was sprawled on a bare mattress on the floor, still wearing his sneakers and sleeveless jean jacket, snoring softly. Lately he'd been staying up for four or five days in a row and then passing out and sleeping for two. It had become a pattern, as reliable as the fattening and shrinking of the moon. Max knew there wasn't a chance in hell he'd wake up right now. He'd tried to wake him before, and had never been able. When Eight Ball was out, *he was out.*

Max scurried round the mattress, over the candy-bar wrappers, empty soda bottles and dirty clothes—black shirts and bright blue jeans—strewn across the floor. A pizza crust lay forlornly on a greasy plate, half-hidden behind a pile of filthy socks and porn mags. Max poked at the crust, looking for mold. Wrinkling his nose, he gave it a quick sniff before snatching it up. Eyes darting about the dim room as he gnawed on the hard crust, he spied what he was looking for: three blackened glass pipes resting on a cinder block beside a battered old lamp.

The first one he picked up looked empty as can be, nothing in it but a scaly, black crust. The second one maybe a hit or two if he was lucky. But the third one was just perfect, with a dark little frozen pond in the bubble at the end, tiny glaciers poking up from the abyss.

The flame from the torch lighter hissed loudly, the potion bubbled, rich blue smoke swelled up, and then Max was a wolf again. A real wolf. Running free through the forest, dodging the giant redwoods, over fragrant duff and past massive prehistoric ferns, the night sky infinite above him, his old friend the moon rising impossibly giant and full, bathing the dark forest in its beautiful, eerie glow. Bats twisted and darted above him, the glowing eyes of owls gleamed from trees, and the green eyes of racoons peered from beneath the shelter of ancient roots.

Galloping with his nose to the ground, he caught a feral, musky scent and quickened his pace to track the animal smell. Then he spotted it, up ahead, passing through the shadows and into a column of moonlight: a small, hairy creature with long muscular back legs. It darted around a rock outcrop and he followed, so close now he loomed above it. Panicked, the creature sprung to the right, slender ears pinned to its downy shoulders. Max pounced, all claws and fangs, relishing the blood and purity of the thing as it struggled and kicked against the cold stillness of the night.

—

Max awoke in the hollow of a redwood stump, naked and bloody, cradling a dead rabbit in his arms, its pelt soft and fragrant with the scent of earth and blood.

Panic rippled through him for a moment as he thought of his wolf hat. He shot his hands to his head, relief flooding through him when his hands fell on the battered old thing, his oldest and most cherished possession: a gray faux-fur cap with big, floppy wolf ears and a long tail, so old and worn now he'd had to patch it up with pieces of old leather and black denim.

He stretched and languidly pulled himself from the warm, dry duff, yawning as he rose. Shafts of morning sunlight cascaded down from between the tall trees and the dew-laden earth glimmered. Grasping the rabbit in his mouth he sprang from the stump, dropped to the ground on all fours and trotted off. He knew someone that would treasure this prize from the forest: Miranda the Good Witch of the Eastern Forest.

In the past he had taken his prizes to Mary Ellen's house, leaving them there on the doorstep for her and her family. But no more.

They never appreciated them.

He'd watch from the forest as her mother would open the door and shriek, kick the dead little critter off the stoop and slam the door. Her father coming out later only to put it in a trash bag, suspiciously gazing about as he hauled it to the garbage cans beside the house. That house that had always looked like a gold gilded castle to Max. That had been a many, many moons ago. When Max was just a little wild-thing pup learning the ways of the forest.

No one had ever found Mary Ellen's body. Max didn't think they ever would.

As he plodded through the redwoods, up the eastern hills, the sky turned gray and a smattering of snow began to drift lazily down, dusting the ground in white. Up, up he went, through a grove of hemlock and alder and tangles of huckleberry, till he came to a clearing of rattlesnake grass and bull thistle, in the center of which sat a little house made of red-and-white-striped peppermint candy, perched on concrete blocks.

Max knew it wasn't really made of candy, but that's the way he always pictured it. The way he saw it in his heart. And anyway, anything could be real if you believed hard enough, and could manage to dig up a little magic.

Pale, mildewed gourds hung from rotting red strings in the trees, rustling softly in the crisp winter breeze. Past a rusted engine and a pile of tires, up to the door he went, pawing at it happily. It swung open and there she was: Miranda, the Good Witch of the Eastern Woods, a wizened old woman with a riot of graying-red hair framing her gaunt face, mouth stretched in a warm smile of rotten teeth, wearing a fringed Harley Davidson shirt and acid-washed jeans.

"Oh, Wolfie," she said. "You brought me a rabbit. Thank you. But where are your clothes, silly boy? You can't be running around in the buff! Going to get yourself in trouble. Now get in here."

She stretched the door open and Max scampered in past her. The room was dim and very warm. The scent of cooking fat and strange plants hung heavy in the air. Clumps of herbs hung from the rafters. Max recognized some of them: dandelion, wheat straw, weed. A woodstove rumbled in the corner, waves of heat rolling off it, the amber glow from the cracks in its door casting strange shadows about the dark room. A greasy black kettle steamed away atop it. Jars of beans and seeds, corncobs, crumpled leaves and roots, were everywhere on makeshift shelves of scrap wood and old bricks.

"I got some clothes for you, boy, tucked back here somewhere," she said, disappearing past a hanging tapestry and into a back a room, returning a moment later with a red-flannel shirt and a faded pair of blue overalls. "Gonna be a little big on you, but they'll do the trick."

Max slipped on the shirt and stepped into the overalls, pulling the straps up over his shoulders.

"Fit you pretty nice, actually." The old woman said nodded her head approvingly as she appraised him. "Yes. Very nice. And don't ask who they belong to neither. A lady don't kiss and tell. Sit. Sit. Sit down. Make yourself comfortable while I tend to this rabbit."

Max sat at a small table of rough-hewn redwood planks. It was ancient and pockmarked, covered in grease stains and gouges, cluttered with overflowing ashtrays, mason jars and clusters of tiny flowers. In the center sat a digital scale and box of plastic baggies.

The old woman mumbled something Max couldn't make out, reached up and tugged at a tangle of leaves hanging from the rafters. "Eat this here sorrel, boy. Just picked it this morning. Still wet with dew." She pushed a clump of clover-shaped leaves at him. Max frowned and turned his head away. "Go on now. My momma used to say, 'Eat something with roots in the ground every day, always keep sickness at bay.'"

Max dutifully took the green clovers and put them in his mouth, but grimaced at the sour taste and spit them out.

"Stop that, boy. You eat them like I told you." She scooped the rabbit up by the hindlegs and pulled a gleaming, square-bladed cleaver off a rack by the sink. "Running around in the snow naked. Need to get your immunities up!"

She took the rabbit to the counter, laid it out gently, then brought the cleaver down with a bang against the middle joints of its back legs. She held up a furry paw. "They say these things are lucky. Keep one in your pocket and it will attract moneys. Put one under your pillow and you'll dream of your true love." She tossed it to Max, who sniffed it and gave it a quick, tentative lick before sliding it into the bib pocket of his overalls.

Pushing the other foot aside, she deftly rolled the fur down off the thighs, working at the flesh with her long, strong fingers, the knuckles swollen and gnarled. Pale blue veins snaked up her wiry and muscular arms as she labored.

"I knew your father, you know. He was a wild thing just like you. Used to come scampering to my door, too, looking for warmth and love. Just like you." With a hard yank she pulled the fur so that it slipped up, turning inside-out over the head, leaving its pink body naked and shiny, its shimmering black guts bulging from its belly. She scooped the viscera and dark organs out and into a bowl, talking quietly the whole time. "A mother and a lover and a healer is what I been to all the wild things. Ravens, racoons, wolves and men folk, all the same in their own ways. It's a blessing I suppose." Lifting the cleaver, she brought it down on the neck, severing the skin, hair and head from the pale sinewy body. "Your momma still live in that trailer in the bottoms?"

Max nodded, yipped.

"That orchard of plum trees still back there?"

He nodded, drifting along lazily to the rhythm of her

words. Her voice was like a comforting balm and Max's head swam at the thought of those plumbs: the scent of the flowers in the spring, so thick with petals they'd fall like snow, the sound of the bees screaming inside, and later the trees covered in engorged fruit hanging hot and ripe in the summer sun, dripping with sugary syrup.

She pulled the pelt right-side out again and stuck her hand inside, making a puppet of it, wagging the rabbit's head at him, the creature's black eyes staring out lifelessly, ears hanging limply to the sides. "What say I make you a nice soft scarf from this here critter? Keep you warm out there while you running wild."

Max cooed.

Placing the pelt aside, she took the carcass to the sink she gave the flesh a good rinse off, then laid it splayed out on the redwood counter. Lifting a back leg, with a sharp tug she cracked it free of the joint, then brought a knife to the hip and sawed it free in two swift motions. Then the other, and the front legs as well. She cut the belly flap away along the rib cage, setting it aside, and then cracked the backbone in half, separating the chest cavity from the thick meat of the hindquarters.

With a rusty pair of pliers, she cranked open the gas on the stovetop, scratched a wooden kitchen match into fire and lit a burner, sliding a greasy cast-iron pan over the licking blue flames. When the grease in the pan began to spit, she threw the thighs and legs in. They crackled and sizzled, the rich aroma of frying flesh filled the trailer. Max squirmed in his seat, drool filling his mouth and flowing over his lips.

She smiled at Max. "And now for the magic! Everything needs a little magic."

Reaching up into a cabinet, she retrieved a gleaming red-white-and-blue box of Captain Crunch from the shadows. Cackling, she pulled a handful of cereal out from within the wax-paper folds, ground it between her palms, mumbling something about the sweetness of the earth as she sprinkled the crumbs atop the frying rabbit parts. They stuck and clumped to the sizzling flesh, and with a ladle she spooned hot grease up over the Captain Crunch crust, the sugar caramelizing and browning. She set a plate before Max, then brought the skillet over and slid the rabbit out atop it.

"Eat what you kill, boy. That's the way of the wild."

Max lifted a leg and sucked the stringy meat from the bone, grease running down his chin, the sweet, peanut-buttery taste of the cereal offsetting the gamey tang of the feral creature in a heavenly and most delicious manner. Licking and gnawing on the bone, he felt his eyes flicker and roll back in his head in ecstasy before he grabbed another leg.

The old woman eased herself down in a chair opposite him and watched him eat with a crooked grin. "Yes, child, yes, eat your fill." She pulled a slender glass pipe from a black-leather pouch, dropped a diamond-like shard of meth in the tiny hole at the bubble end, and set it to boil with a flame, slowly inhaling the vaporous fumes. "Eat, eat. Then rest. You are safe here, little wild one. Safe and loved."

—

Max lay curled on a blanket beside the woodstove, warm and sated.

The witch had visitors at her table: an old scarecrow of a man in dirty tan overalls, drinking Coors Light, and a fat woman knitting. Not as fat as his mother, but a big, plump woman nonetheless, with several chins and thick flesh pleasantly swaying from her arms as she brought a loop of yarn up and over the needles.

The old man had a grumpy, vexed look on his face Max didn't like. He seemed irritated, kept tapping his fingers on his knee. After slurping down his beer, he crushed the finished can in his hand, dropped it to the floor, yanked another from the cardboard twelve-pack beside him, and cracked it open with a jerk of his claw-like fingers.

"Thrice the brinded cat hath meowed," he grumbled, casting beady eyes about the shadows of the room.

The fat woman yawned, pulled a loop of yarn tight and

clacked her long needles. "Thrice and once the hedge pig whined."

Miranda cleared her throat. "Harpier cries, 'Tis time. Tis time.' I now call this meeting to order. What is our main point of business today?"

The old man slammed his beer on the table, foam frothing up over the metal lip and down his bony knuckles. "I think we all know why we're here. Let's not pussyfoot around it!"

The tiny, bristly hairs on Max's neck stood up and he lifted his head, teeth bared and eyes narrowed at the old man, and let out a long, low growl. The witch reached down and stroked his head, softly whispering to him. "Shhh, shhh, It's okay, boy. He's with us. He's a friend."

Max lay his head back down upon his folded hands, but kept his eyes warily fixed on the old man who went on talking in his grumbly manner.

"Geek Jimmy has been flooding the market with cheap and inferior product. It's brought prices down, and put the heat on all of us."

The fat woman, never taking her gaze off the tubular pattern of knotted black yarn that hung from the long metal spikes in her fingers, then spoke. "It's true. On the street grams are going for fifty bucks now, and eight balls for one fifty. And that awful shit has been causing troubles in the community. We all know what happened with Toadstool Donnie the other day. An absolute tragedy. He wouldn't have behaved that way if it wasn't for a bad batch of inferior quality. People don't do things like that on our product. Ripping that poor woman's face off like that, terrible, and totally unprovoked."

"And," the old man shouted, a burst of spittle erupting from his mouth and hanging down off his bottom lip, "he's brought in undesirables. Outsiders. Filthy trash from Sacramento who got no right being here."

Miranda nodded solemnly, took a hit off her glass pipe and leaned back in her chair. "Then we have an agreement over our problem?"

"Aye," said the old man, glugging down a beer then wiping his foamy lips with the back of a dirty hand.

"Aye," said the fat lady, knitting needles clicking away.

"And it is fire shall be this deed without a name?"

"Aye."

"Aye."

"So be it. With a song, Holy Mother, turn the goat around from this Thursday and the next six days, forty-four celebrations in a year, up, stop, I return you with the curses and all these that makes him powerless."

—

That night, Miranda sat Max in front of the woodstove.

As she ran a flame beneath her glass pipe, Max thought she looked more beautiful than he'd ever seen her, her orange-and-gray hair shiny and clean and thick. In the flickering firelight Max could see she was wearing lipstick, her lips thick with it as if they were engorged with blood. And she wasn't wearing jeans, but a red dress. The skin of her shoulders looked soft and pale and there was a peculiar smell to her, something deeply floral and earthy, yet spicy and sweet, too. Like a peppermint stick buried in the deep, wet earth.

Gently grasping his chin, she lifted his face up to hers and blew a steady stream of smoke into it. He closed his eyes and inhaled deeply, the scent plasticky like new toys and fresh paint and turpentine on a hot summer day. His eyes fluttered back open and he smiled at her, warm and content, his heart pounding.

She cocked her head and fixed her gaze deep into his eyes, stroked his cheek, then placed her fingers on his wolf hat, easing it slowly off him. He started and drew back, sensitive over having this most intimate part of himself touched, his nakedness revealed. She shushed him and smiled, told him it was all right, and gently removed the hat, running her fingers through his hair.

"Listen to my words, Max." She'd never called him that

before. Always Wolfie or boy, never his real name. The name his father used to call him. "What is it you want, Max? What do you want from this life most of all?"

He shivered, his soul stirring within him, shook his head.

"It's okay," she said. "Talk to me, Max. You can do it. Use your words and tell me what you want."

He gave a furtive glance to the woodstove, words welling up inside of him, his voice croaking out roughly. "Warm. I want to be warm."

Her face broke into a huge smile. "Good. Warmth. You want warmth. What else, what else do you want?"

"Food. Hot food. Good food."

"Warmth and food, yes, yes, yes. Good. And what do you want most of all? Out of anything in the world?"

Max searched the emptiness of his heart, looking for clues in a black, black room. He felt a great heat well up inside of him, his eyes growing wet and heavy with tears. "Love," he finally managed.

"You want love?"

He nodded.

"You want to be loved?"

"I want a mommy who loves me," he said, and like a log jam breaking, a torrent of hot tears broke from his face.

"Oh, Max, I can be that. And give you all you wish for." She pulled him to her chest and rocked him as he wept, big aching sobs. "Shhh. Mother Miranda's here. Shhh. You're going to be warm and fed and loved from now on. Shh. Shh. But, Max?"

She gently eased him away by the shoulders to look him in the eye again. "Max? Are you listening?"

He sniffled, nodded, wiped the tears from his eyes.

"Max, I need something from you. You'll help Mother Miranda, right? Help avenge her against those that would give harm?"

He nodded.

"Say, 'Yes,' Max. You have to say it. Say, 'Yes'".

"Yes."

"Good. Now listen closely. Listen closely to my words, Max. Fire burns. And fire's bright. The knives are sharpened to cut, from the house to the table to eat, from the table to a bowl, from a bowl to a spoon, from a spoon to a head in the soil to put them deep. Do you understand?"

Max nodded, lost in shadows, his eyes half-shut.

"Thrice to fire and thrice to mine and thrice again to make up nine," she said and with her wizened fingers she turned the pipe stem to Max who, trance-like, pressed his lips to it and inhaled as she ran a flame beneath the bubbling potion, the beast within his heart swelling and filling like the ripening of the moon.

—

Gasoline and rags, the skunky scent of propane and the coldness of the awkward heavy cylinder. Smoldering smoke, blinding, burning his lungs. The tall trees and darkness of the forest, baby mice. Tiny little pink maggots of things, no bigger than the pad of his index finger, blind and squirming in the feather-like redwood fronds.

Max watched fascinated at the cluster of tiny baby mice, pink and hairless, spilled free from the nest he'd accidentally uncovered running through the woods. The mother darted back and forth, panicked, heading first along the edge of a thick redwood root, then, encountering the ridge of an exposed rock blocking her path, back again, in a senseless headlong rush. Max gently pushed the babies to their nest, shifted the duff back around them, scooped up the mother and lay her gently with her children.

His clothes reeked of gasoline. The sleeve of his flannel shirt was scorched and hung from his arm in ragged black strips, his hand soot-covered and seared, badly burned and blistering at the wrist, the ears of his wolf hat singed and smoking. He could smell the smoke in the air now, see the first large flames springing up in the distance, and so he started back off, continuing onward through the forest.

He crossed over a small promontory, thick with colt's

foot and huckleberry, then slid downward out of the hills and to a group of suburban homes, their eaves strung with Christmas lights glowing red and green. He leapt a fence, darted across a front yard, and paused in the shadows of a hawthorn hedgerow to glance about, then began to scurry across the road, when a voice called out to him, freezing him in his tracks.

"Max?"

Max turned and there was his brother Eight Ball, in his jeans, denim jacket, and Metallica *Ride the Lightning* t-shirt, standing beneath the street lamps in a circle of light that broke the darkness and shadows of the tall redwoods.

"Max, where have you been? Fuck, man, I've been freaking out, looking for you everywhere." Eight Ball stepped forward, held out his hand. "Well, come on, man. Let's go. Let's go home."

Max stared at his brother's open hand.

Home? What did it even mean?

He loved his brother. The thought of him ached at his heart like a swollen, infected splinter. But he had a new home now. A place of warmth and abundance, security and purpose, so different than that cold barren trailer he'd come from.

His brother took another step forward, imploring with a shake of his upturned palm. "Max, let's go."

Max wavered, unsure what to do, caught between conflicting impulses. He reached up and grasped the rabbit's foot in the bib pocket of his overalls, thinking the talisman might give him some direction. Eight Ball smiled at him and he could see their father in his eyes, in his lopsided grin. His brother was his everything. His kin. It had always been them against the world. Max took a hesitant step towards him.

But then a great explosion cracked the night in pieces as the propane tank at Geek Jimmy's house went up, and a ball of flame rose over the trees. Car alarms went off, dogs erupted into barking, and lights turned on in the windows of neighboring houses. Max's instincts kicked in and he bolted towards the shadows of the trees and the safety of the forest, sailing through the darkness and chaparral for what felt like over a year and in and out weeks and through a day and into the night of Miranda's house of candy where she had cold ginger ale and Campbell's Chicken Noodle Soup waiting for him. And the soup was still hot.

—

One night, Miranda had a party for Max.

The old man was there in an aluminum lawn chair, drinking his Coors Light, and the fat lady, too, knitting away in a rocking chair. They all sat in the front yard around a rusted fifty-gallon barrel with a roaring fire inside it and Max was allowed to eat all the hot dogs he wanted.

Miranda served a beautiful and magical punch: Grape Kool Aid with orange and tan dried mushrooms and old brown poppy heads floating in it. The old man had brought a pig on a leash, a huge beast of a thing, covered in coarse black hair. It snorted and rooted at the earth with its snout as Miranda took Max by the hand and led him to the fire.

"Do you know what day it is?" she asked him, the orange and amber light of the flames flickering across her face.

Max shook his head.

"It's the solstice, the shortest day of the year. Yule. A celebration of the wild hunt! And you're our new hunter, Max. So today we celebrate you! It's all for you, Max, all for you, King of the Wild Things! And to show the best of our delights, I'll charm the air to give a sound, while you perform your antic round!"

She pressed play on a battered cassette player and Mötley Crüe's "Shout at the Devil" came blaring out. The old man banged a tambourine in time to the beat and Miranda shrieked joyously, screaming along and waving her fist in the air. "Shout! Shout!"

The pig went apeshit, snorting and stomping, and the beat of the music, the squeal of the guitar and pounding of the drums, billowed up inside of Max, filling him with the urge to dance. He romped about the fire, gyrating and spinning, kicking his legs and throwing up his arms.

The flames whirled and pranced, now purple and green, the smoke curling in on itself and massing, congealing and taking form, and from the conflagration an image appeared: a great black goat. Curled horns blossomed from its lean head, its glaring eyes yellow and phosphorescent. The ashen beast rose up on its hind legs from the barrel and turned slowly, lifting and twitching its tail.

Max stood before it in awe. Transfixed. Mesmerized. Stunned still.

Miranda came from behind and whispered hot into his ear.

"Kiss it," she said. "Don't be scared. Kiss the black goat's ass!" and she gave him a little shove.

Max took a tentative step forward, pursing his lips, the smell of smoke and goat overwhelming him, gamey and feral, musky and barnyard, hay and earth and fire. His head spinning, eyes slipping shut, he bowed forward and let his lips press against the hindquarters of the great goat.

A cheer erupted and pandemonium broke out: the pig now gone completely wild and racing in circles around the burn barrel, the fat lady bellowing, "Shout! Shout!" and rocking so hard and fast the battered old chair seemed to be pulling itself up and lifting from the muddy ground with each pendulous swing.

Miranda had a ratty old broom, just a crooked stick with a wisp of straw tied to the end, and she cradled it in her arms, spinning and spinning in a mad dervish as the old man rose up from his chair and straddled the hog, riding it like a horse, waving a can of Coors Light over his head, grunting and howling, the giant pig bucking and stomping, leaping upwards and hanging still in the air, legs gracefully splayed.

Max's jaw dropped open as he witnessed the impossible: the fat lady's rocking chair swinging up off the ground, like a kite caught on a sudden breeze, the pig's racing feet no longer touching the earth as it made its rounds about the fire, but hovering over the ground, lifting into the night.

He turned to Miranda who now straddled her crooked broom and held a beckoning hand out to him. "Come, Max, come, my wolf boy, ride the night skies of yule with us!"

And Max took her hand, filled with a strange sense of trust and adoration, of love and hope. He grasped her around the waist, pressed his cheek into her back, shutting his eyes for a moment as her scent of earth and smoke and fire and flowers and grease enveloped him.

They rose up and when Max opened his eyes again they were high above the tops of the redwoods, the town of Arcata tiny and toy-like below them, the black bay stretching out to the sea. The old man rode along beside them, straddling his grunting hog, sucking down the last of a Coors Light and tossing the can over his shoulder. The fat woman, still knitting, rocked as her chair traversed the skies, the night awash in spilled stars leaking across the darkness above and about them.

The moon rose from behind the forested hills, red as blood and fat and bloated as the belly of a carp, and all was well and all was good and all were happy and all were fed and all were warm and all was perfect on this day of the witch's yule.

THE GYPPO'S CLOTHES

Why am I wearing the gyppo's clothes? Because I was robbed. Drugged and thrown in a pile of rotting filth, top coat gone, shirt tore open, pockets pulled out and ripped from my trousers, shoes missing. A disastrous affair.

It all began in Seattle with the telegram that fell into my lap like an albatross tumbling dead from the sky.

It arrived as I was receiving a shave from the barber in the lobby of the hotel I had procured for myself some weeks prior.

"Is there a Blackwood here?" a bellboy's voice cut through the fog of cigar smoke. "An Alexander Blackwood?"

I motioned him forward and examined the thin yellow paper as the barber ran a razor up my neck, wiped the soap and hairs on a towel, and then proceeded to wax and style my mustache. It was from my sister. My father was ill. It was serious, and I was to return to our ancestral home in San Francisco at once if I cared to see him again alive.

I immediately went and packed my belongings, checked out from my lodgings and secured passage on a steamer headed south to San Francisco. I was lucky in that the Selja—a freight ship looking to ferry a few passengers— was pulling out that evening. With both the current and wind being in our favor, it was to be but a three-day voyage from Seattle to San Francisco.

The Grand Trunk Pacific dock was an impressive pier, the largest on the West Coast, and that fateful evening it was packed with masses of shuffling humanity. I tugged my luggage through the crowded dock, the sailors and barkers,

Chinamen with long black ponytails, a gaggle of short South Americans draped in brightly colored cloth and carrying crates of strange fruit.

And then . . . then I thought for a moment I saw him there. My father. Not a man who looked like him, but him, himself, in his signature green frock coat and bowler, snow-white mutton chops. I startled and gasped as he turned and locked eyes with me. Though my mind knew it could not be him, my heart beat as if otherwise and my ears rang as a tinge of guilt ran through me, for I had been to Seattle on a family business trip and it had not gone well.

Some foolish investments with some shady men had squandered the investment I had been entrusted with, and, if truth be told, shamed, I had dreaded returning to my family in San Francisco, and had been putting it off for some time.

But then there was a shove to my back as the great crowd heaved around me and when I blinked the figure was gone. I chalked it up to the melancholy malaise that had recently fallen upon me and the stress of a failed business trip and pushed forward.

The vessel appeared sound enough. It wasn't a regular passenger ship, but a cargo vessel with a few spare quarters below deck, so it hadn't the comforts and amenities I was used to, but a cot and dry room was all I really required.

The captain, a gruff-looking bearded man with a downturned face and watery, jaundiced eyes, gave me a nod and a grunt as I boarded.

Strange dreams plagued my sleep that night as that rusted hulk crashed through the waves. Visions of my father supine, my fair sister Samantha kneeling at his side. I would awake, fevered, slick with sweat, heart pounding, a terrible feeling of guilt surging behind my ribs, the hull groaning against the sea, the crash of the slapping ocean swirling in the darkness.

On the second day of our journey, we took port for the night in the small town of Arcata, cradled in the shelter of the Humboldt Bay. Restless and anxious, nerves vexed, I craved some respite in the form of drink and female gaiety and company. Walking along the deck, the moon was high and full, the night bright with its light: glinting the black waves of the bay, streaking the rusted bars of the ship's rails, and seeming to beckon with its eerie glow on the tiny port landside. As I plodded down the gangway off the ship, the captain called out to me, almost as if he could sense my carnal pursuit.

"Where ye be headed, good sir?"

"Just a stretch of the legs. Perhaps a dram or two."

He nodded knowingly, stroked his grizzled beard. "Watch your Ps and Qs and be sure and be back well before morning. We leave at first light, with or without you."

"Aye, Captain," I replied with a tip of my hat, and stepped off into the fog and night.

Since there was only one house of ill repute in all of Arcata, and rumor swirled that the sheriff often camped outside it waiting to grab unwary travelers, I decided to jump a stage to Eureka, a city a few miles to the south, which boasted of a large, waterfront red-light district.

Eureka was quite a bustling port. After strolling the streets for a bit and taking in the tone of the town, I finally settled on an ornate seaside mansion aptly named The Palace.

Coming into the parlor my coat was checked by a boy and the proprietress—a mammoth woman whom everyone called "The Empress"—offered an assortment of lovely ladies to me. A pale, skinny redheaded lass immediately caught my fancy. With a grin she led me up a flight of stairs and to a small room where she quite efficiently and passionately employed her generous labors in a most satisfactory way.

Feeling a warm relief, a lifted heaviness from my burdened soul, I returned to the parlor for a cigar. However, catching some commotion in the saloon area, I decided to make my way there.

Satiated carnally, I was now hungry for drink, conversation and human interaction after spending two days sequestered in my cabin. The saloon was quite opulent, rich wooden walls, sturdy tables and chairs all about, a long redwood bar with a great multitude of spirits displayed behind it. A tiny man of what appeared African descent sat before a piano in the corner, plucking out a most delightful tune.

At the far end of the bar a crowd encircled a boisterous bulldog-faced fellow holding court, sending the gathered mass into bouts of laughter with his exhorts.

I bellied up and ordered a draft of beer, then asked the fellow beside me what the fracas was about.

He grinned and cocked his head. "Writer over there. Always gets them wound up. Mad character by the name of Jack London."

"Jack London?"

"Aye, tis him."

"Why I've read his work. The one about the poor fellow who lights a fire beneath branches covered in snow. He's quite famous and well regarded in San Francisco, I can tell you. Fancy seeing him here."

"Ya, he's got a farm not too far south from 'ere. Comes up ta drink away his problems when it all gets too much for him down there. He may be able to tell a story, but he's a terrible farmer. Full of daft ideas that never work."

"That so, is it?"

"Aye, and the fellows love to give him a good ribbing over it."

"So, Jack," a portly fellow with his thumbs tucked in his suspenders shouted, "What's your next book to be about?"

The stocky blonde man took a hearty chug of his beer and waved a dismissive hand. "Bwaa. I only write for the money. It's tilling the earth, working the land, producing crops. That's real work. That's what I care about. Bollocks to writing."

Sure enough a voice called out, "Couldn't raise a crop a beans to fruition is what I hear. What kind of farmer can't even grow beans? Nothing but fodder for the bugs."

"Ha ha, what I tell you," the gent beside me proclaimed with a wink.

"Very good," I replied, and since the fellow had piqued my curiosity, followed with, "Say, what's your story, mate? You live here in Eureka?"

"Aye, at times. I'm what they call a gyppo. An independent logger. Travelling to the logging camps when they need a strong man willing to work, who knows his way around a choker and a cant hook."

I engaged the gyppo for several minutes. His name was Misolf and he told me about the nature of logging, which was a huge source of commerce in this region. The demand from San Francisco was seemingly limitless, what with the earthquake and fire only five years past. He told me briefly of the innovations in the field, the steam donkey and lumber trucks. It was quite interesting and made quite the backdrop, what with Jack London's proclamations of how hard work with one's hands cleansed the soul, and the benefits to being in nature.

Another rowdy drunk shouted something about London's recent failures on the farm. The crowd was roaring with laughter, and Jack screaming back at them. "Hear hear, yes, it's true we lost those beans to them damn beetles. But listen up, we learned. And more than that, we're making a socialist and equal commune. All workers together."

A commotion broke out as a large man dressed ridiculously in red, white and blue overalls, a frilly blouse and a matching bowler pushed through the crowd shouting. "Take your socialist hedonism back to the old country. In America we're capitalists, damnit! You dirty Marxist."

"Damn right I'm a Marxist. Karl Marx was a genius and man of the people."

"Aren't you proud to be American?"

"By God, I'm more American than you! Patriotism is more than dressing like a clown, good fellow. In this land of the free I plan on using my freedom for the socialist cause. No reason the two can't go together."

The big man spit. "You're a traitor is what you are. A traitor to your country."

London took a long pull off his ale, tilting his dog-like

head back and finishing it before resting the empty mug on the bar and leisurely turning to face the large man in the flag outfit, who'd stepped up even closer now and was mere feet from him. "Hope you can use your fists as well as you can run that fat mouth, because I will not stand to be slandered."

Then there were no more shouts, no more laugher. The room was silent. Even the little piano player had ceased playing and was now standing up on his stool, craning his neck to look about.

"Aye, my fists are always ready for Marxist scum."

"So be it. Then with fists will this argument be settled."

Suddenly there was a great cheer and a scurrying of people moving chairs and tables away, clearing room, while a tall black man in a top hat rushed to shut and lock the front doors, extinguishing the glowing-red exterior gas lamps.

I was swept back with the crowd, laughing. It was quite the spectacle as Jack and the other man stripped off their shirts and began to flex in that opened circle of men. Wagers were soon circling in hushed tones.

"I got five on the writer. He's a wily rascal."

"Give me two on the big guy."

As the two men raised fisticuffs, one of the whores slipped up beside me, a raven-haired little beauty wearing a negligee that was really nothing more than a lace-trimmed smidgen of silk. Clutching my arm and pressing her chin to my chest, she gazed up at me with large, black-rimmed eyes, blinking deliciously long eyelashes. "Come upstairs, handsome?"

It was then, with a seismic rush, that I remembered the Captain's warning. To be back well before dawn.

I gazed at the clock above the bar and saw that it was fast approaching midnight. Who knows how long it would take to catch a coach, and if I was forced to walk it could take hours.

"I'm afraid I have to be going," I said to the girl who was now running her fingers up the inside of my thigh in a manner I must admit I found both desirable and delightful.

"Oh, but you must stay for the fight. One more drink

for the road?" she said, presenting a tall cocktail glass she seemingly pulled from nowhere. London and the fat man were circling each other now, hunched with hands raised. The gyppo was laughing excitedly and slapping his hands together.

"Well one more can't hurt, can it?" I replied, for the elixir truly did look wonderful and I'd suddenly developed quite a thirst, my mouth going sandy dry.

As the big man threw a punch and London dodged, I imbibed. It was sweet and cold with a strong and bitter after taste and drinking it was the last thing I remember of that night.

—

I awoke with my father hovering over me, gazing down with a stern face, concern in the wrinkles of his eyes and set of mouth.

"Alexander? Alexander can you hear me?"

"Yes, father," I said through the trails of mist that stretched between us.

"I'll meet you at the house in the woods, Alexander. Meet me at the house in the woods."

Panic swelled up in me, for I knew not what house he was speaking of. "What house in the woods, Father? Where? Where is this house you speak of?" I shouted, only to blink and have his visage blur and change and become someone else entirely. It was the gyppo.

"Oi! Alexander, are you alive?"

"Where . . . where am I," I asked, suddenly aware of the stench of sewage and horse manure. "What happened?"

"Ere, mate, looks like ya've 'ad quite the rough night. Near ready to ring the undertaker I was."

I peered around. I was in some back alley, lying in a pile of refuse. My coat and hat were gone, my pockets turned inside out and rent. Standing, I realized my feet were bare. Thieves had taken even my shoes.

And the ship! The Captain warned they'd be off at

dawn. "What is the time?"

The gyppo squinted and looked to the sky. "Coming on high noon here, I believe."

Panic and shock paralyzed me a moment. I stood there gaping.

The gyppo laughed. "Just count thy blessings and thank your luck star to be alive and in one piece. Say, friend, care to take your luck to the forest? Dolbeer and Carson Company is looking for some gyppos right now to pull in a harvest before the fall storms. They're in a pinch for workers this late and are hiring right now. One week of hauling logs down off the hill to the camp."

"What?" I said, still trying to comprehend this most heinous situation I found myself in.

"A job, mate. One week of work hauling trees off the hill. I've got an extra pair of boots that should fit you, and strong trousers and a spare coat." He patted his two large canvas duffle bags. "A good gyppo is always prepared for two! Just pay me rent on 'em at the end of the week. Stick with me, I'll show you the ropes and chains of choke hooking."

My mind churned. I was penniless. I had not even money to send a telegraph home requesting funds. I suppose I could beseech the Western Union to let me send a telegraph like a common beggar, but the thought of troubling my dear sister, and the humiliation, after having already squandered so much of the family fortune, made the idea of trying to earn my wages palatable, if not entirely appealing.

That, and hearing that London fellow talk of the satisfaction of work done with one's hands. Truth be told, I wished to learn more of this logging business as well. See it from the bottom tier so to say. Perhaps I could glean some insight for future investment that would make this miserable trip at least somewhat worthwhile. Find something to bring back to my ailing father.

Damn it all, maybe an adventure was in order.

"All right then. I thank you most kindly and will take you up on this offer."

"Damn if you don't talk funny, mister," he said,

rummaging through his bag and procuring a set of sturdy work clothes and pair of boots. Okay. Let's get going, the train is waiting. The old Whiskey Express!"

—

The Whiskey Express was a rickety, jarring little train the lumber camps used to ferret their men to the whore houses of the Eureka waterfront and back. As it worked its way up a winding track into the eastern redwood hills, I pondered my fate. What in God's name was I doing in this strange man's clothes headed off into this desolate land? It was certainly below my station.

The men on board were a sullen bunch. An old timer with a white beard sat in the back, singing low and mournful.

"When the wind is howling, take heed mister lumberjack, there are voices in the wind."

The smoke and mist drenched hills felt apocalyptic, the forest like a forlorn battlefield of massive stumps, trampled underbrush and wood fires, as if a great war had occurred there not too long ago. Ash floated lazily in the air which stank of burning coal and woodfire. One almost expected to see bodies lying on the blackened ground amongst the huge moss-covered stumps, blackened ground.

At the base camp there was a long queue of disheveled, tired looking men awaiting to board the train back to Eureka. Disembarking, I asked the gyppo, "If they are in such need of help, why are all these men leaving?"

"Those men are fellers and cutters. They fell the trees and cut them into sections, but no will work to bring them down from the hills. That's the low work, left to us, the choke hookers. The mutts. Bad luck mixing felling and hooking they say."

Harsh voices then rang out, screaming, "Make way! Make way!" and two men carrying a badly-bloodied third by the arms and legs came pushing up to the open train door. "Easy now. Get him on the train. Careful, careful."

He appeared to have suffered some contusion to the

top of the head, his face was covered in a sheet of blood, his hair thick and nappy with it. As they laid the man down in the aisle, the gyppo asked.

"What happened to 'em, then?"

Clutching a grisly, blood-soaked rag to the man's head, one of the men said, "He was settin' the chokers on the candy side, hookin' on to a big blue-butt, when the fucking riggin' slinger says, 'Let 'er go.' Stupid cock sucker. Happened quick. Just like that."

A smattering of the men around us crossed themselves and kissed their fingers, the gyppo just shook his head sadly. A murmur went up among the crowd. "Always in threes. It always happens in threes." They looked amongst each other, as if to ascertain whom would be next. I shivered as the danger of this hasty and ill-conceived jaunt fell home.

The gyppo, sensing my ill ease, pat me on the back and steered me away from the sight. "Don't listen to their nonsense, mate. They'll drive you mad with their craziness. Just keep an open eye and a be awares. You'll be fine."

But as I turned away, the wounded man's eyes locked on mine. I could see where his skull was cracked open and his brain—a tannish-brown mass of wrinkles like sleeping worms—shimmered there. He groaned, spitting up blood, lifted a hand and pointed a trembling finger at me and spoke with an awful, gurgling whisper, "Your father awaits in the house in the woods."

I shuddered, blinked, and then he was just lying there again, looking quite still and dead as the gyppo pulled me away and into the camp.

—

The gyppo and I were put into a crew of seven, with a Boss, which made eight of us, a lucky number they said, that couldn't be divided by three. Superstitions seemed to abound here in this desolate and tore apart wasteland.

Our crew was as follows:

The Donkey Punch, a grizzled old-timer with a long

beard, who wore a sideways looking cowboy hat that made him appear like a caricature of one of those 49ers from the last century. His sole job was to man and maintain the steam donkey, a loud and dangerous mechanical wench used to pull the huge trees down off the hillside.

Finn and Connor, an Irish pair of brothers with coal-black hair and wary faces. Conner was the knot bumper who waited at the landing for the logs and unhooked the chokers, telling the Donkey Punch when to lay on the power and put her in gear. Connor was the rigging slinger who sent the signal down to his brother. They had some code and language between them they could transmit down the hillside with a series of whistles, shouts and hand movements. It was amazing actually, the way they communicated.

And then there were the choke hookers. A sad-faced Portuguese fellow by the name of Alfonso who was the most superstitious of the lot, and Sal, a pudgy and squat local boy who was constantly complaining. Rumor had it he'd once been a cutter but had been demoted down to choke hooker due to his ill temper.

Then the gyppo, and myself, whom they called the brush monkey, as I was new and inexperienced, and would be given the most menial of chores.

And of course, the Boss.

The Boss was a brutish-looking man with mean eyes and fiery red hair. I never did learn his name. We just called him the Boss. He had this tooth that hung out the side of his mouth. A long, pointed fang.

Alfonso claimed the Boss once had a rotten tooth, and after he'd pulled it loose from his head, he'd thrown it into the mud where a black dog had stepped on it. That's what caused the dog's fang to grow from his mouth, that black dog's foot. The Portuguese man crossed himself as he said this and shivered, explained it was the sign of an open door to the devil.

—

Our first day was a long journey through a maze of roads that weren't much more than rutted paths to the far outskirts of the logging operation. The Boss rode a mare ahead of us while we followed on foot, leading a couple donkeys laden with our wares and supplies: bedding and food, ropes, pullies and tools, the Donkey Punch's equipment and lubricants.

As we marched along Sal came up beside the gyppo and myself, muttering. "Fookin two-bit, hardtack operation they got running. Making us American white men walk along with dirty foreigners while the Boss is perched on a hay burner up there."

"Oi!" Finn yelled from behind us. "We'se can hear ya, ya bloody gobshite bastard. You think the Irish aren't white, do 'ya?"

"I know you ain't no native son of America. That much I reckon, what an Irishman is, I don't know. Though I might have heard certain words for it."

The Boss jerked his reins, rearing his horse up, and spun it around, causing us to leap back out of the way.

"AYE! You want to fight and argue? Do it on your own time! Here we work together to get the job done. The man you curse today may be the one who saves your worthless life tomorrow. Now, you got complaints about how this operation is handled, you best shove them deep up into your asses where they can remain quiet and hidden, before I do it for you! Now keep your mouths shut, there's still many a mile to be covered."

He turned his steed back to the path and we walked on.

—

Eventually we came to the base of a mountainous hillside rising up into the mist. There was a steam donkey there, a big teakettle-looking thing with wheels and gears not unlike those on a train. It was anchored to a redwood stump whose diameter was at least twice the length of the tallest of us. Two rusted cables thicker than a man's forearm twisted out from it and snaked up the hill.

The Donkey Punch was immediately at the machine, greasing and testing the gears, muttering to himself. He was to sleep down there in a little shack beside the machine, the rest of us were to make camp at the top of the mountain where the last of the monstrous logs awaited us.

The trek up the mountainside was grueling. Following the labyrinthine path of those cables upwards, upwards, upwards, the grade impossibly steep. The mere misstep could send one plunging straight down and at times even the donkeys appeared nervous, braying and refusing to budge unless whipped most unmercifully. Finally, we rounded the top and came to an immense flat plateau of felled logs, just as the sun was slipping behind the western valley.

I stood there panting, watching as the sky darkened, and Alfonso came in close, slipped me a bulb of garlic. "Keep this on you, will protect you," he said in a halting, tentative whisper.

"Protect me from what?"

"Nosferatu. Undead haunt this forest."

The gyppo, panting as we scaled the mountain, whispered angrily, "Listen to his nonsense, not!"

But I took the papery mass and put it in my inside pocket, close to my heart.

—

Getting those logs down off the steep hillside and to the road was quite the operation. Harrowing and hard labor.

The gyppo and I would use our cant hooks to roll the logs to the edge where Alfonso would pound in the drive grab and Sal would slip on the chokers, hollering to Conner to send the signal to let her go. The steam donkey would pound and screech, the cable going so taunt it sang, and that massive round of wood would rip through the dirt and duff, and on we'd go to the next one. By evening I was sore and more tired than I'd ever been.

—

On our second day at the camp the skies filled with dark clouds and it began to drizzle rain. A strong wind whipped through the ferns and around the moss-covered stumps.

"Storm's coming," Sal said to the Boss. "We best break camp and head back."

"Nonsense," the Boss barked, that big fang gleaming in his mouth. "We work till the last of this timber is pulled to the road. Sun, rain or whatever weather the good Lord deems us worthy of."

"It's dangerous and not what I signed up for."

The Boss stormed up to Sal, fists at his side, his face a knot of anger. "You signed up to work and by God you will, have you a problem with that?"

"I'm a white man and a native son of Eureka. Yes, I have a problem, just this year I was a cutter, working my way to faller, now I'm in the rain with you hooker scum. I won't stand for it no more—"

Quick as a lightning strike, the Boss whipped out a fist and delivered a strike to his face. Sal fell backwards, landing on his back in the duff.

"Now," the Boss said, looming over the fallen man, "you've had a taste of my right, don't make me give you the left as well. What do you say, then?"

Sal just lay there staring, rubbing his jaw.

The Boss took a threatening step toward him, kicking dirt and redwood needles into his face, body tense like a coiled rattlesnake. "Can you hear me now, you wall-eared cock sucker?"

Sal nodded.

"Then what the fuck do you say then?"

"Yes, Boss."

"Good. Now get back to work!"

Cursing under his breath, Sal pulled himself to his feet and set to gathering the choker cables, casting furtive glares to the Boss who'd gone to barking orders up to the gyppo.

And the day went on.

—

On the third day the drizzle turned to rain. Pouring rain. Roiling sheets of water cascading down from a black sky. We huddled by the woodstove in the cook area, a sort-of lean-to of roughhewn redwood planks, nursing our coffees and waiting for the Boss.

"It's madness to stay here any longer," Sal said.

"The third day," Alfonso intoned. "Our third day. The rain is a sign."

Sal turned to him. "But we spent a day hiking 'ere, so it's no really our third, but our fourth day."

"No, our third day here. Always in threes."

"That makes no sense. We got here before dusk, so this is our fourth day here."

"Our third day awakening in this place."

Finn, sitting sullen on a stump beside his brother, shouted at them. "Can ye please give us some quiet! Listen to ya! You're both daft as can be. What's it even matter?"

Well, it's the principle to me," said Sal.

"Threes. Always in threes," Alfonso muttered forlornly.

"For fuck's sake, can ye please shoot your mouths!" Connor hollered.

The Boss then came storming up. "What's this then? Let's get to work."

Sal began to grumble, but it was Conner who stood up and spoke. "Sir, I'm no afraid 'a 'ard work. You knows that. But the men all agree, to continue in this weather is madness."

The Boss stood steaming a moment, eyes filled with fire, that sharp tooth pressed hard into his chin, then seemed to relent and look away, smiling.

"Conner, you're a good man, and I understand your hesitation. But we must work on. The Tyee wants the last of this down, and he's willing to make it worthwhile to us." He slapped his hands together. "Okay, men, give me your ears with no prejudice. First: double pay. Double pay because of the rain, and if we get the last of these logs down, every last one of them . . ." He looked around, locking eyes with each of us in line. "A bonus of fifteen dollars to each and every one of you. Now what say you? Do we have a deal?"

Sal banged his coffee cup down and held his chin up. "Twenty dollars each."

"Ah, now, you know I can't agree to terms without the—"

Conner took a step forward. "Twenty-dollar bonus each or we all walk out of here now."

The men looked around at each other, grimly nodded.

The Boss took a deep breath, put his hands on his hips and gazed down at his muddy boots, shaking his head. "All right then. Agreed!" He rubbed his hands together briskly, as if to create heat. "Ya fookin hooking bastards run a hard bargain, ya do. Now come on, let's get this timber off the hill."

—

The earth had turned to a cloying muck of mud and clay with the rain, making each step a torment of hard work. The logs refused to roll in the mushy mess and the gyppo and I were forced to rely on brute strength to push them to Alfonso and Sal.

Things felt dream-like and weird working in the storm like that. With the rain slamming down and the pounding of the steam donkey, I struggled to hear the screams of the Boss barking orders. Seeing his mouth open and close with no sound, I felt as if I was a mute as he glowered at me, waving his hands frantically. Stumbling through the water and mist I suddenly realized what he was telling me, *GET OUT OF THE WAY!!* and leapt to the side just as the haul-back cable sprung tight and a great log came swiveling around.

As I fell to the earth I blinked and then opened my

eyes to see that log come barreling towards Sal, who opened his mouth in surprise before it slammed into him, crumpling him and pulling him along as it slid across the earth, scraping away all the mud and duff, chaparral and ferns.

And then it was as if the mountain itself grew sick and vomited, for the whole front of the hillside trembled for a moment and then fell away in a great avalanche of mud and timber and kicking donkeys. A landslide. There was a rumble, a whoosh, followed by a great echoing *thump* that shook the ground beneath us. Then a sudden stillness.

My mind struggled to comprehend the enormity of it. One moment there was a steep slope of stumps and battered ferns, piles of brush, cables, burros; the next there was nothing but slick mud dropping down into fog and clouds. The steam donkey was silent, buried in a sea of wet earth, the only sound the patter of rain.

The gyppo, Conner and Alfonso stood beside me, on the edge of the chasm, staring downward. The Boss stood on the higher ground above us. Sal, Finn and Punch were gone.

Alfonso looked to us, from one to the next, his long, sad-featured face now ashen and riveted with horror. "We've got to help them!" Cupping his hands to his mouth he screamed into the abyss of rain. "Sal! Finn! Punch! Can you hear me?!"

"Damn fool," the Boss said, "they're buried beneath a ton of earth and lumber. Even if they did survive the fall and mud, there's not a chance they could hear you beneath it all."

"We have to try to help them."

"Help them how? Do you not notice the goddamn road is gone? Have you given any fucking thought as to just how the hell we're going to even get out of here?"

Conner spun around and stormed up the hill towards the Boss, an angry finger extended. "YOU! This is all the fault of you and your greed. You killed my brother, damn you."

The Boss held his palms out and took a step back. "Whoa there. It's no fault of mine. I killed no one. You all came on your own free will and accord."

Conner glared at him, the muscles in his neck throbbing, and charged forward, hissing and putting his face a finger's length from the Boss's. "And you killed Sal. I saw it. Leaving him on the lee side of the timber when you knew that log was coming."

The Boss grabbed him by the collar of his coat and pulled him even closer, so that their noses were pressed together. "That damn fool wasn't paying attention. The bush monkey either. He's goddamn lucky to be alive, that one there," he said, pointing at me. "Why God chose your brother and Sal over 'im I know not. Blame God if you need to pin blame somewhere," and he pushed Conner away from him.

Conner grunted and groaned, turned, and put his hands to either side of his head, letting out an anguished scream.

Alfonso crossed himself. "Don't forget Punch. This was going to be his last season in the hills. Had a nice piece of grazing ground right on the Van Duzen he was looking to settle down on."

The Boss scrubbed his face with his palms, then slapped his thighs. "Now listen, men. There's no time for blame and anger. What we need to do is make a plan to get off this mountain. If we're not careful, this whole face is liable to fall right the hell off. We no can skirt too close to the slide. We'll have to take the backside down, then circle around when we get to the bottom. When we get back to the road we can look for survivors before heading back. Are you with me, then?"

All eyes turned to Conner, who slowly turned, let his hands slip down from his head, took a deep shuttering breath, and finally nodded.

—

We walked all through that day, the Boss leading us down the steep hills where the forest was virgin and pure. The trees loomed from impossibly high heights, like nothing I'd ever seen before. A forest prehistoric, like a land of dinosaurs with ferns that stretched up over a man's eyes. The rain slackened and it grew icy cold, our breath leaving us in great white clouds as we lumbered downwards. A smattering of snow began to drift down and dust the ground and the wind came whipping through those mammoth redwood trunks with a sad, moaning sound.

"The windy goo," Alfonso whispered.

"What heathen trash talk now?" the gyppo said.

"A spirit of loneliness and hunger in the woods."

"Aye, I feel like a spirit of loneliness and hunger myself in these woods," the gyppo replied back with a sigh.

It would be the last thing I ever heard him say.

—

It was when we made camp that we noticed the gyppo was no longer among us.

Everyone tried to remember the last time they had seen him, how far back. His last words, about being a spirit of loneliness and hunger, echoed in my head and I struggled to remember how far back we'd been when he uttered them. Two miles? Three?

We shouted into the forest and discussed going back for him, Alfonso crossing himself and whispering how we couldn't leave him out there with the windy goo. But the Boss scoffed at his superstitions and decided it was imminent we make camp and start a fire to dry our soaking clothes and warm our bodies. We were all shivering uncontrollably, a marked pallor on our countenance.

"Liable to freeze to death if we don't. Dead men can rescue no one," the Boss said, his lip curling over that dog fang snaggle tooth. "Besides, he'll surely see the light of the fire and come to us."

Conner reluctantly agreed. Still being just a bush monkey among them, my opinion wasn't sought, though I trembled at the thought of my friend lost out there in that vast forest.

Soon we had a raging fire going that surely could be seen for miles as the darkness fell around us, yet as we dried our clothes and made up pallets for slumber by the fire's edge, the gyppo was not to be heard from.

—

I awoke to a terrible screaming that was over so quickly I wondered if maybe I had dreamt it. But sitting up and gazing about I could see the others were awake, too, staring across the fire at each other. Except for Conner. He was gone, his bedding a disheveled mess, footsteps in the snow snaking away into the darkness.

A groan punctured the night, followed by a distant, strangled-sounding, "Help . . ."

"It's Conner," Alfonso whispered.

The Boss was up, tearing a strip of bedding and wrapping it around a stout branch he retrieved from the wood pile we'd accrued, then setting it alight in the fire. "Right, probably wandered off to take himself a piss and fell in some damn hole. Come then, men. Let's find him."

We followed the torchlit footsteps as they weaved through the huge shadowed trees, watching as they grew erratic and then turned quickly. We all gasped when another pair of footsteps appeared there in the snow, followed by a great gout of blood and a ragged path like that of someone dragging themselves away. The Boss cast his torch into the shadows and there, curled under a rotting log, was Conner.

He lay on his back, his eyes clasped shut, a look of agony etched across his face, and with great horror and a rising gorge I realized there was only a bloody stump where his right arm should have been.

The Boss thrust the torch into my hands and dropped to his knees, pressing his palms to Conner's wound, trying to slow the blood which seeped out, but I could see from the Irishman's deathly-white complexion and blue lips that too much had already been lost.

"What happened to you, man?" asked the Boss as he

tore a strip from Conner's shredded coat and wrapped it around the stump.

"I 'eard the voice of my brother, calling for me. Calling for me to help him. I . . . I followed the sound to a figure, only it wasn't my brother at all. T'was that other fellow. The gyppo. He was smiling at me with this awful, terrible lear. Then he attacked me. Cut my bloody arm off with an axe, and then . . . then, sitting there right before me, his eyes huge and ugly, he began to eat it. Eating me own bloody flesh right before me. Only . . . only it wasn't the gyppo anymore. It was . . . it was something else. Something horrible. So horrible."

Alfonso gasped and crossed himself. "The windy goo. The spirit of loneliness."

"Shut your goddamn mouth," the Boss hissed at him. When we turned back to Conner he was dead. No mistaking it, he'd gone completely blue and still, eyes now open and peering out at nothing, mouth hanging open.

The Boss pulled his compass from his pocket and peered at it. "All right. We walk through the night. Head eastward around the base of the mountain and we will surely hit the road by daybreak. There's no missing it, even in the dark. Come along." He stood, grabbed the torch from me, and started off, Alfonso and I behind him.

—

Dawn was turning the black sky the gray-blue of gun metal when we came upon a rough skid road. Alfonso crossed himself, knelt, and kissed the path.

It was the first time I saw the Boss smile, his thick lips turning up, that dog tooth hanging there, but then his eyes went angry again and a huge frown encompassed his face as he muttered, "No, no, no . . . It can't be."

"What," I cried. "What is it?"

"Look, you damn fools, don't you see where we are?"

"It's impossible," Alfonso said.

I ran forward in disbelief and found myself staring

down at the sheer face of mud and rock that had once been the path down off the mountain. We were somehow back where we'd started, though we'd gone nothing but downward. Down, down, down, only to be back at the top again. Alfonso was right, it was simply not possible.

The Boss looked to be going insane, pulling at his hair, foaming from his mouth, darting into the woods yelling, "But where did we start? Where did we start?"

Gazing about in disbelief, my heart froze and my breath caught in my neck, for there was the gyppo! He was high up in the branches of a fir tree, smiling down at us. His eyes were impossibly white against the dark, drying blood that covered his face and he clutched Conner's severed arm in his hands, ripping huge bites out of it with his grinning mouth.

When he noticed me staring up at him, he waved, tossed the arm behind him, and dropped forward, falling from the branches. Tumbling down he stretched out his arms and a leathery black membrane erupted from his back, spreading into huge wings like that of a bat. He took to the air, swooping first upward, then down to where Alfonso stood staring in awe.

The bat-thing that was the gyppo came down behind him and wrapped him cocoon-like in its wings. Its body had changed into something animalistic: squat, with a thick mat of dark hair, but it still had the face of the gyppo. It smiled at me, eyes now glaring red orbs, and from its mouth came two huge fangs, massive tusks that it sunk into the neck of Alfonso.

Frozen in horror I watched breathlessly as the thing then spread it wings and flew off into the mist, Alfonso howling and screeching in its terrible grasp.

I turned and there was the Boss, coming at me angrily, screaming. "It was you, wasn't it? You all along. You killed them all. Killed them and ate them."

"What are you talking about?" I stammered, backing away from him. "Have you gone mad?"

"Look at you! You're covered in their gore and blood."

And when I looked down, to my shock and surprise, he was right. There was blood and pieces of flesh all over me. I could taste it like rusted iron in my mouth, the sickening scent flooding my nose.

"You're a sick dog, you've got to go down," he hollered, and came at me.

He was going to kill me. I saw it in his eyes. I . . . I had no choice.

As he swung a fist, I darted forward and the most primal instinct of self-defense came over me.

I bit him.

Opened my mouth and brought my teeth down on his neck, right where I could see that pulsating tube of blood rising up from his heart, and I tore it open and felt its warmth pour over me as we fell together to the cold, snow-covered earth.

He beat at me and struggled, but I held fast, and soon the fight went out of him and he lay there with only the occasional spasm as his life's blood left him.

Lifting myself off his quivering body, whom should I see standing there in the swirling snow and mist, but my father. He stood before a quaint log house, smoke belching from its stone chimney. It was like something from a fairy tale.

He was wearing his green frock coat and bowler, and he beckoned me with a wave of the hand, then turned and entered the front door. I followed after him, entering into a large and spacious room, in the center of which sat a long table, draped in a lace-trimmed linen cloth, all made up for dining: gold-trimmed plates and utensils, thick cloth napkins, a candelabra with thirteen flickering candles. The room was quite warm, with a fire roaring in the hearth and I took off my work coat and hung it on a brass rack beside the door.

My father sat down on one side of the table, I on the other.

"Are you not well, Father?" I asked. "I heard you were ill."

He said nothing to me, just remained sitting there, seeming to stare straight through me with a fixed look to his crevassed face.

The door slowly began to creak open, and there in the swirling snow stood a strange and terrible creature with a gleaming white animal skull for a head—adorned with a massive rack of antlers—and a bestial, emaciated body.

I know not why, but the sight did not terrify me like one might expect. I felt completely tranquil and at ease in the presence of this hideous beast. Perhaps it was the dream-like nature of the scenario, but I just accepted it all as the strange thing approached and took a seat at the head of the table.

My father unfolded a napkin and placed it on his lap as a whistling and singing erupted from a back room. A door swung open and there was the gyppo, arms laden in silver platters overflowing with an abundance of food: oysters and trout still with their heads on, sliced meats and tiny cakes.

"Chow down, gentlemen," he proclaimed, setting the platters before us on the table and disappearing into the back room only to promptly reenter bearing more gleaming trays, some open and filled with pastries and fruit, glistening brown roasts sliced to reveal pink insides, other platters with ornate covers atop them, their opulent insides hidden from sight.

A dark-red wine of equally sweet and bitter measure was poured and we sipped at it as we feasted long into the night, embarking on an orgy of feeding, filling our mouths in a near frenzy state with strange fruit and many cuts of meat.

Sugary syrups and thick fat dripping from my chin, I ate on, my jaws beginning to ache, till satiated and drunken, bedeviled and exhausted, I pushed my chair back and lazily watched as the creature and my father fed still, slurping down oysters and cracking open crabs, seemingly insatiable, the gyppo now bringing out a fully roasted pig with an apple between its jaws.

I found the scene inexplicably amusing, and began to laugh uproariously as I sat back and stretched my feet before me. The warmth of the fire so strong I opened my shirt, and my belly so swollen I unfastened the top button of my trousers, I chuckled on, so cozy, content and satisfied that I vowed to take a nap right there and then at the table, only to wake and find myself here, in this godforsaken jail cell.

Yes, yes, yes, I hear their whispers and taunts. Angry proclamations and threats of hanging.

Tales of how they found me naked in the snow, covered in gore and laughing hysterically. They claim there is no truth to my story, that it is either the delusions of a lunatic or a clever attempt to disguise my crimes with madness.

They claim there never was any gyppo, or moreover, that I am, in fact, the gyppo upon whom I blame the slaughter.

But I know the truth. I know who I am, and I know why I wear the gyppo's clothes.

THE TALE OF THE FEARLESS VAMPIRE KILLING BROTHERS

"Just remember this," Abe told his brother, digging his knife blade down the wooden stake, shaving the tip to a sharp point. "It's not human. If you begin to think of it as human, even for a moment, you put this entire operation in danger. And we must avoid its keeper at all costs."

Johnathan gulped and nodded as Abe tested the tip with the pad of his finger. He crossed himself, and handed his brother a heavy wooden mallet. "Are you ready? Once we start there is no going back."

Johnathan blinked his large blue eyes. "Yes. I'm ready. Let's do this."

Abe palmed him a bulb of garlic, and the two set forth into the gathering twilight.

The somber hoot of an owl rang in the distance. The rustling leaves of the tall oaks were beginning to yellow. Autumn was approaching, the nights growing steadily longer. The sky above them was a riot of color, burgundy and orange to the west where the sun sunk into the horizon, a growing darkness to the east where night crept.

Yes, now was the time to strike.

The house, once such a happy place, was preternaturally quiet and ominous as they slunk through the shadows, past the creature's keeper, who lie sprawled on a sofa, snoring softly, and down the hall to the creature's lair.

They stopped a moment before the heavy wooden door,

hearts hammering in their chests, their breath coming in quick gasps, before Abe pressed a sweaty palm to the door and pushed it slowly open, careful to not have it squeak and possibly alert the keeper.

And there it was, curled up in a tangle of sheets, its thumb in its mouth: the slumbering monster of the night. Tangle of raven-black hair, skin unnaturally soft and sallow.

In sleep it looked so peaceful. Innocent. It was hard to comprehend the agony and torment the foul creature conjured.

The creature had first appeared nearly three years ago, its unholy presence bringing an awful change to their lives, and since then nothing had been the same. The nights were filled with dreaded howling, and during the day evidence of its rampage was clear: walls ink splattered in strange patterns and crude drawings. Beloved objects destroyed. Loved ones changed forever. It was time to put an end to this madness.

As they eased toward it, the creature stirred and turned onto its back, exposing its small, pale chest to them. A good omen.

Abe ran a tongue over his parched lips and lifted the stake, holding it firmly over the creature's heart, then nodded to his brother, who brought the mallet up, over his head, and with a grunt, sent it smashing down onto the top of the stake. The tip buried itself into the pale skin, black blood bubbling up as the monster awoke with a nerve-shattering shriek.

"Again!" Abe screamed, struggling to hold the stake in place as the thing thrashed and howled. "Hit it again!"

Panicked, Johnathan pounded the stake, the creature's ribs cracking as the heavy piece of sharpened wood sunk in deeper, blow by blow, blood now spraying out and splattering their faces, till the stake had pierced it through and stuck it to the mattress.

The creature let out a long shuddering breath, quivered, and went still.

They had done it. The deed was done. Abe sighed with

relief, wiping blood from his face with the back of his hand, when the door went flying open and light filled the room.

It was the beast's keeper! They turned and gasped as she stormed towards them, shrieking, "Boys! My God, what have you done to your brother?"

BLIND CLOWN CHAOS

Scott's skull-thumping, nearly-blinding hangover didn't make the sight of all those clowns any fucking easier, that's for sure. Gazing through slit eyelids into the blistering sun, he saw them everywhere: handing out balloons to children, setting up some sort of elaborate stage for magic tricks, pouring out of a large white van with the words *AZATHOTH BLIND CHAOS Clowning and Miming* scrawled on the side in swirling Day-Glo letters. Christ, what was worse, a clown or a mime? If one of these clowns started pretending he was stuck in a box, Scott thought for sure he was going to puke.

It was graduation day at his kid's elementary school, Jake's last day of fourth grade. Scott knew he had to get up early for this shit last night, but couldn't tear himself away from a guilt-endowing binge watch of *The Walking Dead*, looking over in surprise at the clock to see that it was two o'clock in the morning and he had managed to drink two bottles of Pinot noir and uncork a bottle of zinfandel. Now he was paying the piper.

As Jake scurried out of the mini-van and ran across the meadow to a gaggle of his friends circled around an extremely tall clown twisting balloons into weird shapes, Scott moaned softly and slid on a pair of RayBans. His wife, Cindy, sidled up beside him and gave him a poke in the side.

"How you feeling there, big guy?" she asked, digging her finger into his ribs and cocking her pretty face at that funny angle she affected when mocking and teasing. "You look a little ragged around the edges."

"Huh? Me? Naw, I'm fine. Just wondering about all the

fucking clowns everywhere."

"It's odd, isn't it? Marsha never mentioned clowns at the parent enrichment meeting. Clowns are so gaudy. I would have gone with a bluegrass band. Yeah, and maybe some pony rides."

"Hillbillies and piles of horse shit. Classy."

"What would you have done? Wine tastings? Open bar?"

"Honestly, I *could* use a mimosa."

"Just try to keep it together. Okay, sweetie?" She gave him a quick peck on the lips and wandered over to Bob and Nadine who were strolling across the parking lot towards the meadow. Damn, that clown twisting up balloons was *tall*. He had to be on stilts or something. Was he staring at Scott? Leering at him from across the open field of screaming children?

Bob rolled up with an open palm extended for a bro shake and a man hug, slapping Scott's back a bit too hard as he started talking rapidly. "S'up, my brother? Dude, I was literally just thinking of you. You gotta come over and check out my new surround sound, it's literally the dopest system. Put on *Apocalypse Now* with The Doors and all those helicopters, literally insane, bro."

Scott didn't know what was worse: this nightmare of a hangover, the clowns, or the way Bob was incorrectly using the word "literally" over and over.

"*The horror, the horror,*" he mumbled, trying to not make eye contact with the freaky clown who was now nodding at him and pointing.

"Ha ha! Right. Fucking Brando, man. Hey, you wanna go puff a fatty real quick?"

Oh God, did he. Anything to ease the jackhammer going off in his alcohol poisoned brain. Cindy was going to be bent when he came back reeking of weed, but fuck it, half the parents here were stoned. Shit, half the teachers and staff as well.

They walked away, down the long dirt driveway that led up to the school, and ducked into a patch of woods in the hillside. Bob fired up the doobie and handed it to Scott. One hit and he felt better, the pressure in his head easing up, the sweet, candy-tasting flavor of Blue Dream calming his belly.

"Fuck, man," Bob said between puffs. "What's up with all the clowns? That shit literally freaks me out."

Not again, thought Scott, please don't use that word again, it was *literally* driving him fucking crazy. That's when the shots rang out and the screaming started.

"The fuck?!" yelled Scott and they were racing up the driveway, a rapid volley of gunfire echoing through the valley.

In the meadow was a horrible scene of mind-melting carnage.

Clowns encircled the field, and they'd traded their balloons and slide whistles for assault rifles. They were popping off rounds at anyone who broke the parameter. He saw Claudia—the principal—dart toward the edge of the clearing. A clown in a satiny, blue, puffy suit and a painted-on frowny face stepped up behind her with a sawed-off shotgun and fired into the back of her skull. The top of her head disintegrated into a fountain of impossibly-red gore as she slammed face first into the ground, her body twitching and jerking.

The tall clown was chasing a toddler in bib overalls around with a large hunting knife, swatting and toying with him like a cat with a baby rabbit, before finally swooping him up by the ankles and—as he dangled helplessly—slicing open his throat from ear to ear, the wound opening like a gaping mouth to spill out a torrent of blood that quickly covered the kid's face. In the center of the meadow—amid the chaos of screams, bloodshed, and rifle fire—a group of clowns were forcing screaming children and parents to their knees, barking orders at them to *Get down! Get down!*

Scott saw Cindy and Jake among them and sprinted forward on raw instinct, desperate to save them. A clown leaped in front of him, laughing wickedly, his giant eyes jaundiced and yellow against the fish-belly white of the grease paint smeared across his face. As Scott went to scream a stream of liquid came spurting out of a large plastic flower on the clown's lapel, splashing him in the face.

And then all was darkness.

—

Scott came to slowly, strange sounds—like underwater screams—filling his head. He tried to move and realized his wrists were bound behind him. He tried to speak and realized he was gagged. He looked around groggily, the shapes and sounds about him beginning to come into focus. It was dark and there was chanting. He was tied to a chair on the edge of the meadow. Other parents were there, too, all tied to chairs and gagged just like him. As his eyes adjusted, he saw the clowns stood in a circle, gripping torches and chanting strange words. *Azathoth, Azathoth, blind clown of chaos awaken. Blind clown of chaos awaken.*

Then he choked and tried to scream, for lying before him was a pile of limp and bloody bodies, tiny bodies, the bodies of children, stacked atop each other, their eyes blank and wide. And there, in the center of the field, was his beautiful wife Cindy, the girl he sometimes thought about in the morning when he woke up, wondering how he had gotten so lucky as to get her. She was naked and bound to an altar, arcane symbols painted on her in what appeared to be blood. Before her stood a clown draped in embroidered robes and wearing an elaborate headdress. He stretched his arms open to the night sky, his face—made-up in a horrid pattern of green and yellow lightning bolts—lifted upwards, screaming, *"Azathoth! Azathoth!"*

The clown lifted a squirming body and set it atop Cindy's heaving belly, and when Scott saw that it was Jake, his son, his boy, his life and his light and his everything, he jerked so violently against his restraints that the chair tipped over. He hit the ground hard just as the clown cleaved open his son's chest with a gleaming knife, hacking through the tiny ribcage, and—reaching in with puffy-fingered, gloved hands—ripped out his still-beating heart. He lifted it to his horrible face and sunk his teeth into it, a stream of blood dripping down off his chin.

And then the sky went white with light and all was still for a moment. It was as if all the air in the meadow were suddenly sucked away, upwards, with a great gust of wind, and then dropped back down again with a loud *whooomp*.

Looming from the depths of the sky was a mammoth being, peering down at the earth like a man might gaze into the workings of an ant hill. But its eyes—framed in giant diamond patterns of alternating reds and blues—were clearly sightless, covered in milky-blue cataracts and leaking a syrupy yellow liquid. It turned its head blindly from side to side, as if to ascertain who had called it from the great depths of space and why. Its nose was a massive and rotten blood-red ball, flaking off tufts of crimson skin which crashed to the ground with wet, slopping thuds. From either side of its head sprouted tufts of pumpkin-orange hair, streaming out to sharp points.

And then existence itself was forever gone as the dreamer awoke and all that was and had ever been was forgotten as the dream of existence evaporated with Azathoth's awakening, most literally.

CHARYBDIS

Pete's big brother was a total fucking dick, no two ways about it.

Even his stupid name: Ace. Naming himself after the guitar player in Kiss, his favorite band. What a dickhead thing to do. His real name was George, but he hated when anyone called him that. Uttering it was sure to get Pete a punch on the arm, or worse, even though Ace loved to call him Dog Turd.

They lived on this weird dead-end street of dilapidated houses that backed up to the highway. No one went down there unless they had to. Between the highway and Pete's house was a swampy and overgrown no-man's land of poison oak and Scotch broom with a concrete storm drain running through the middle. That was their hang out, where they were now, huffing glue and laughing while Pete watched from above, hidden in the hillside bushes. Maggot was spray-painting OZZY across the culvert while Froggy and Ace lay by the entrance, passing a brown-paper bag back and forth as lumber trucks full of logs rumbled by on the highway.

They thought they were some kind of gang, called themselves the Rip Ass Raiders, and all wore these denim jackets with the sleeves cut off, the backs bleached white with RIP ASS RAIDERS written in black magic marker across it, and a goofy skull that was supposed to be scary, but totally wasn't.

They constantly ragged on Pete, calling him Dog Turd and little kid, wouldn't let him hang out with them, even though he was almost thirteen, as old as they were when they started their dumb-ass gang.

Pete cocked his head and tried to focus on what they were saying. They were talking about Jodi Perkins, this eleventh grader whose boobs had doubled in size over the summer.

"Fuck yeah I broke into that stupid bitch's house," Ace said. "Skipped school Friday and hit that shit."

"Bullshit," Froggy said with a dismissive wave of the hand. "You're so full of shit your eyes are brown."

Maggot, a chubby blonde kid with teeth so bucked he looked like a cartoon drawing of a horse, shouted over the whoosh of passing cars while scrawling 666 in dripping red paint. "Yeah, you expect us to believe that crap?"

Ace ran a comb through his hair. "You think I'd come back empty handed?"

"What you got, Ace?"

He shook a cigarette from a pack, dramatically lit it. "Check it." He tugged a piece of white cloth from his pocket, held it aloft, cigarette clenched between his teeth. It was a pair of girl's panties with frilly pink trim. "Got em out of her hamper." He clenched them to his face, inhaled deeply. "Ah, yeah, smell that sweet cherry."

He tossed the panties to Maggot, who put them to his nose with a fierce sniff, his face screwing up comically.

It was all too much for Pete. *They were smelling her underwear! Where her butt had been! GROSS!!!*

He struggled not to laugh, holding a hand over his mouth, but he couldn't stop himself and the laughter come rippling up from his belly, bursting out. He ducked and turned, but they had heard him.

"Dude, it's your brother," Maggot said.

"The fuck I tell you about spying on us, Dog Turd?"

Running away down the trail, Pete chanced a quick look back over his shoulder to see his brother leap up, grab a fist-sized rock, cock his arm, and hurl the thing at him.

Pete stared dumbly as it sailed through the air, watching it spiral, wondering if he should dodge to the left or right, as it came crashing down square on the top of his head.

Stars exploded behind his eyes and he went sprawling, hitting the ground hard, face first, dirt going up his nose and into his mouth, his lip cracking open. He lay there groggy for a moment, reached up and touched his throbbing head. His hand came back bloody. He could hear them all laughing at him--the stupid-ass Rip Ass Raiders--their guffaws echoed in his ears as he lifted himself off the ground, dizzy and suddenly nauseous, and took off in an unsteady sprint down the path, his brother's voice booming from behind him.

"Take that, Dog Turd, and don't let me catch you spying on us again! Rip Ass Raiders rule!"

—

Back at the house, Pete climbed up on the kitchen counter and rooted deep into the empty cupboards. Food had become a hard commodity to come by lately and he was constantly hungry. His mother drank away her hunger, and his brother seemed to have other means, probably dealing pot and living on fast food. There were always telltale McDonalds wrappers in his room.

In the far left corner he uncovered a forgotten jar of peanut butter with a few brown smears still left in the corners where a knife hadn't been able reach. He scooped it out with his finger, stuffing it greedily into his mouth.

His head pounded and he could feel blood beginning to trickle down behind his ear.

Stupid fucking Ace.

He went to the bathroom, took Ace's toothbrush from the chipped mug on the counter, held it over the toilet, peed on it, then shook it off and put it back.

Take that fucker.

As if he ever even used the thing anyway: Mr. Green Teeth.

He thought about his brother and his friends sniffing that girl's stolen panties. It was weird, and gross. But something about it sent a tingling sensation down his spine.

He remembered that stack of nudie magazines he'd once spied in his brother's room and cast an eye down the hall to the bedroom door. There was a KEEP OUT sign tacked to it, and he'd attached a hasp and locked it with a padlock.

Pete laughed. Stupid jerk. All that and he kept his back window wide open. He'd always open it to smoke pot, blowing the smoke outside so their mother wouldn't smell it when she got home from the bar and have a "complete and utter freak out". Then he'd be too stoned to remember to shut it again.

Pete went outside, feeling a little better with the peanut butter in his belly, an odd giddiness swelling in his brain. He even had a little skip to his step as he slipped around the side of the house and to Ace's open bedroom window. Gripping the inside ledge, and kicking his feet against the side of the house, he scurried up and inside.

The room was like a dank cave, musky with the scent of weed, old socks and teenager, the walls covered in dayglow posters for Kiss, Blue Oyster Cult, Deep Purple.

Pete crept to the bed, lifted the mattress, and found what he was looking for: a stack of glossy porn mags. He slipped the bottom one out, thinking it would be the one his brother was least likely to notice. *CHERRY*, a 4th of July special with two naked girls kissing beneath a huge American flag.

With trembling hands, he rolled it up and stuck it in the waistband of his jeans, a cool sheen of sweat breaking out on his neck, then let himself back out through the window.

Slipping down to the ground he could hear the laughter of his brother and his friends as they walked up the trail towards the house. *Shit, time to skedaddle.*

He got on his bike and started pedaling furiously, headed as far away as he could get, for the one place he knew he could be alone in: the abandoned K-Mart.

—

The K-Mart was right on the highway, on the outskirts of town. He remembered going there on happier days to buy Halloween costumes and school supplies, new shoes and a winter coat. But just like the store itself, those times were over and a thing of the past.

The entire perimeter was sealed in a heavy chain-link fence topped with barbed wire. The boarded-up front of the store faced the highway and there was a massive, desolate parking lot there, a kind of creepy asphalt waste land that could easily be seen from the 101, so you'd never want to be seen there or you'd get in big trouble. But the back of the store, where the big concrete loading dock extended out, butted right against a little strip of forest that had grown up beside one of the many sloughs that circulated through the barren outskirts before leaking its waters to the bay.

Pete completely avoided the busy highway and followed a back route out along the slough, pedaling along a thin path where hobos went to drink, wasters went to get wasted and teenagers went to fuck. His heart hammered at the thought of the glossy magazine pages tucked into his pants. He walked the final stretch, pushing his bike, ears sharp for anyone lurking around. The cops had made a big deal about clearing out the vagrants and druggies a few weeks ago, staging big raids. Since then he hadn't seen a single soul around.

He stashed his bike beneath a scrub oak that had grown up by the chain-link fence, covered it in a bunch of leaves to hide it, then plodded off to the place where someone had cut a short, jagged line through the bottom half of the fence. Prying the edge upwards, he pulled himself under, through the dirt and broken glass, to the asphalt on the other side.

He jogged up to the concrete loading ramp, then scrambled to the top of the steel railing. There was a boarded-up window there, but the plywood was loose on the corner and it was easy to squeeze through.

It was cool and dark inside the cavernous building, lit only by snatches of sunlight slanting in through the cracks of the boarded-up windows. Shelves and racks still divided the space up into sections, but they were all bare of products, most of them smashed and pushed over. The floor was filthy, covered in dust and cigarette butts, bottles of all shapes, sizes and colors. A pair of women's panties. In the corner, below where someone had spray-painted HEATHER BROWN IS A WHORE, was an old mattress.

Unbuttoning his pants, he sat on the edge of the mattress and unfurled the magazine, spreading its thick glossy pages out on his lap where a square of sunshine cascaded in from a small smashed window high up on the wall that hadn't been boarded over. His hands trembled. Ever since he'd first glanced at the magazines a week ago, he'd dreamed of being alone with one, and sure enough the pictures were doing something to him. There was the nakedness of the women, the brazenness of them spreading their legs and exposing their most hidden, secret parts, but it was the looks on their faces that really flushed Pete. The lurid expressions of want in their half-shut eyes and panting lips. A sheen of cool sweat broke out on his forehead as he stroked himself to the point where he felt like he might burst, when there was a noise from behind him: a shuffling, scraping sound.

He shot up, the magazine tumbling from his lap, and quickly buttoned his pants.

Was someone there? Had someone seen what he was doing? Embarrassment and shame ripped through him.

Nothing moved, everything was still.

Could have been a rat.

He rolled up the magazine and got ready to bolt when there was a disturbance in the light and in from the broken window flew the most amazing thing he'd ever seen: a huge black insect, like a fist-sized beetle, hovering on blue-veined transparent wings. Its shell was an iridescent, glowing silver with what looked like shimmering black symbols carved into it. Beneath the shell hung hundreds of tiny black tentacles that squirmed and twisted, seeming to taste the air.

Spikey, skeletal legs spread from it as it gracefully

landed on the wall, tucking in its wings. And then, miraculously, it began to grow. Very slowly, so slow that it was hard to even see, but it was definitely growing.

Pete rubbed his eyes and blinked, not sure if what he was seeing was real, as the symbols on its back began to slowly rotate and morph together, forming new shapes, as if it was spelling out some code or spell.

The creature's head swelled, turned milky-white and began to spin toward him. Pete gasped: it was the face of a beautiful woman with her lips puckered at him, like a lurid China doll, and the glowing shell on its black split down the center, revealing two quivering pink lips, a glistening pearl perched where their swollen, flower-like folds met in a pyramid shape. The lips glimmered, sleek and wet, pulsating hungrily, then slowly parted, spreading open. And inside . . . inside was the universe.

All the stars of all the galaxies were in there. Far off planets, constellations, comets and asteroids blaring past with fiery tails. Infinite space in all its magnificence, worlds beyond his comprehension. He blinked and laughed as the thing stretched and grew even larger. He felt himself slipping away, his mind transfixed on the wonders the creature showed, when hands grabbed him from behind and threw him against a concrete pillar.

A dirty, bearded man in a tattered coat pressed against him, pinning him to the pillar, his foul, awful-smelling breath hot in his ear saying, "I saw you there, boy. Saw what you were doing. You like that? You like touching yourself?"

Pete struggled and screamed, kicking and hollering for help, though he knew there was no one who could hear him. Then he gasped and stopped screaming for he saw something utterly insane that his mind struggled to comprehend. From over the man's shoulder he saw that the beetle-thing had grown impossibly large, much taller than the foul-smelling man pressing himself against him. The creature seemed to loom over them, worlds being born and dying inside the pink lips of its gaping maw, and it was stretching four of those skeletal arms out towards them.

With a quick snatching motion, the thing grabbed the man, two arms grasping him by the shoulders and two by the ankles, pulling him up, off the ground, to the yawning universe hole in its back.

There was part of a strangled cry, just the beginning of a scream, before the dirty man's head disappeared, the pink lips closing around his shoulders, his arms and legs flailing frantically. The thing began to slowly pulse, swelling and shrinking, and Pete realized that it was chomping on the man and swallowing him down.

Pete stared transfixed and lost in wonder, torn by curiosity and the urge to run as the man's filthy shoes disappeared into the thing. It was like he was of two minds, one logical and screaming for escape, the other feeling some strange affection for the strange insect-thing that had just saved him.

Indeed, as the lips closed in on themselves and the shell resumed its position, he felt an odd sense of warmth emanate from the thing. While every sensible atom in his body screamed to run while he had the chance, he found himself approaching the strange, huge insect, marveling over the thousands of tiny tentacles that squirmed beneath the shell's edges, and stroking it lovingly.

It cooed back sweetly.

—

It was late when Pete got back to his neighborhood, pedaling his rusty bike down that dark, dead end street. The sun had fallen to the edge of the horizon, casting everything in soft pink and amber light, and Ace was waiting for him, squatting behind the overgrown bushes by the front walk. As Pete hopped off his bike and started toward the house, Ace leapt out, delivering a hard punch to Pete's stomach, knocking the air right out of him, before Ace pushed him to the ground and pinned his arms down with his knees.

"You take my *CHERRY*, you little creep?"

"Naw, naw. I didn't take nothing. Promise."

"Liar. I told you to stay out of my room. Now I'm going to teach you a lesson."

He cocked his fist, poised to strike, when Pete shouted, "Don't hit me! Please. I'll show you something I found. Something, something amazing. I'll take you there, show you. Just don't hit me!"

"What you going to show me?"

"It's a . . . a bug. A crazy bug!"

"A fucking bug?" Ace laughed. "You think I care about a stupid bug?"

Pete's mind reeled, trying to think of something his brother might want. "No, no, there's more. Weed! A whole bunch of weed!"

Ace's face softened. "Weed?"

"Yeah, a whole bunch. Someone must have stashed it and I found it. I'll show you where it is!"

"You better not be fucking with me, or your ass is grass."

"I'm not. I'm not."

"Where's this weed you're talking about?"

"At the old K-Mart. I'll take you there and show you."

—

"This place is fucking cool," Ace said, strutting through the abandoned store. "How come you never told me about it before?"

Because it's the only place I could ever be away from you, Pete thought, as he said, "I was going to. Honest."

"Hey! There's my *CHERRY*. I knew you took it you little creep."

Pete desperately scanned the walls, looking for the big beetle. He didn't see it anywhere, and an icy sliver of fear raced down his throat as his brother approached, pounding a fist into his palm. "So, where's the weed, little man? You didn't bring me all the way out here for nothing, did you?"

As panic gripped him, he began to stammer, "I, ah . . .

ah." Then he saw it, up by the ceiling, in the corner of the room. It had constructed some kind of nest, with little cocoons. "Over there!"

Ace turned and walked into the corner, kicking at bits of rubble and an old soda bottle. "Where, I don't see shit here." The thing was directly above him, but it wasn't doing anything. Just sitting there. The markings on its back dull and still. Maybe it was sleeping. Or dead. Could it have given birth to those cocoons and then died? That's what happened to the spider in that book *Charlotte's Web*.

Ace spun around. "What the fuck, you little shit? Where's the weed? You fucking with me?"

"No, no, it's over there. I swear I saw it."

Ace shook his head, spun, and with a lightning-fast motion smashed his fist into Pete's surprised face. There was a crunching sound that echoed deep into the back of Pete's skull, then a rose of pain bloomed behind his eyes as a torrent of hot blood poured from his nose. Stunned, he stumbled back and fell down.

Ace pushed up the sleeves of his flannel shirt. "Kid, I'm going to mop the fucking floor with you." And that's when the creature struck.

Four nimble insect legs shot out of the shadows, clamping onto Ace and yanking him up into the darkness, stuffing him into that hungry mouth that fed into another universe before he even had time to scream.

—

"Can I have Ace's room if he never comes back?" Pete asked his mother as she stumbled into the kitchen in a dirty bathrobe and poured herself a glass of Kool Aid from the fridge.

It'd been over a week since Pete had taken his brother to the abandoned K-Mart. Since then he'd also taken Maggot and Stumpy to see the beetle-thing. The Queen Mother as he liked to think of her, for the cocoons had cracked open, adorable little baby bugs squirming out and snuggling against her. It was a beautiful and marvelous thing to see.

Pete's mother lit a cigarette and splashed some gin into her Kool Aid. "The fuck is wrong with you, Petey? Your brother's run off and all you think about is his room? Don't you miss your brother? Don't think he's coming back? What kinda way to be is that?"

Pete just looked at his feet, delicately touched his still-sore nose, ran a finger over the new ridge where it now went out of line. His mother took a long sip of her drink, then swatted him across the back of the head, hard. "Hey, I'm talking to you, boy. I said, 'Don't you miss your brother?'"

"Yeah, Mom. I miss him."

"Besides, if that kid ain't around and the social worker shows up, my welfare could be in trouble. We need to find him."

"You know, sometimes kids go to the old K-Mart on the other side of town to hang out."

"Yeah? Would you go there for your momma? Go find your big brother and bring him home?"

"We could go together. I could take you there. I . . . I heard they still got stuff in there." Pete's mind raced. What would it take to lure his mother to the old K-Mart? "I heard there's still jewelry in the cases."

"Jewelry?"

Pete smiled. "Yup. Jewelry and all kinds of stuff. Things you wouldn't believe!"

"Yeah? Maybe you ought to take your old momma out there for a looksee. You're a good boy, Pete."

"Thanks, Mom," Pete said, smiling and thinking of the Queen Mother in her nest, those pink lips to other worlds so hungry.

Finding her was the greatest thing that'd ever happened to him. Ace's room and all his stuff were a sure bet for him now!

NEST OF SALT

I'd saved up all summer for the dress: a pink Betsy Johnson baby doll. A special dress for a special night with a special boy.

I knew my mother would never approve of the lowcut and lace ruffle trim, the way it hung from my slender shoulders like a nightie or negligee, so easy to slip out of. She'd probably say something crazy, like it was demonic or the devil's dress and make me get down on my knees and pray with her.

So, I'd had to hide it from her. First stashed in the cellar with the board games we stopped playing after Dad died, then into my school backpack, where I planned to secret it away to my BFF Brenda's house, and finally get to wear it.

Brenda and I had been friends since we were little girls, she only lived a few blocks away. Ever since I can remember, I'd been skipping and running through those streets of Myrtletown, over the cracked sidewalks and past the crumbling Victorians and the little corner market to Brenda's house.

That day, the early-autumn sun high and bright, the first fallen leaves littering the sidewalks, my mind was just a swarm of butterflies, so wrapped up in thoughts of the pink dress in my backpack, and my date with Robby Jenkins that I didn't even see Pastor Willard standing there on the corner—wearing his three-piece baby-blue polyester suit and daisy yellow button-up shirt, a large wooden crucifix hanging on his neck from a leather thong, hair slicked back from his

long slanting forehead, staring at the sky and whistling—
until I nearly slammed into him.

"Why, Gretta," he said, catching hold of my left hand.
"So good to see you."

Mother had joined his congregation when dad died.
After the funeral she'd gone kind of Jesus crazy. Said my
sister and I need Lordly direction without a father to guide
us.

"Hello, Pastor," I said, startled and pulling back. He
gripped my hand harder, his thumb creeping down to my
fingers, resting there on my ring finger and easing itself back
and forth.

"I see you're not wearing your purity ring, Gretta."

Mom had forced my sister and me to take part in this
ridiculous chastity ritual where we married ourselves to
Jesus and swore to stay chaste until marriage. Afterward
they gave us these stupid silver rings that had *PURE IN THE
BLOOD OF THE LAMB* engraved on them.

I thought it was nonsense: it was the nineties not the
fifties.

Out of all my friends I was the only one who was still a
virgin, and I was nearly eighteen and going to graduate in the
spring. No one wanted to graduate high school a virgin.
Robby and I had been going steady months now,
unbeknownst to my mom, and I was ready. The ring, my
crazy religious mom, it was a total embarrassment. I slipped
the stupid ring off my finger every morning as soon as I got
on the school bus.

"Yeah," I said. "I had to take it off for cheerleading
squad. We're not allowed to wear any jewelry during practice.
Must have forgot to put it back on. I've got it right here," I
swung my backpack off and as I pulled my hand free to reach
into the zippered front pocket where I kept the ring, he
snatched it back and yanked me hard towards him.

I gasped and he said, very slowly, "You know, Gretta, I
understand what it's like to lose a . . . *family member.*"

I could smell him. Not the cologne he stunk of, but
him, a rotten unwashed odor like the locker room in the gym.

And when he talked, although his front teeth were square and white and perfect, I could see that his molars were craggy and black, rotten to nubs.

"And I want you to know," he continued, "I am here if you ever need me. Feel free to look upon me as a . . . well, as a father." He let go of my hand and I fell backwards a step, then fumbled for the ring, finding it in a clutter of pencils and erasers and slipped it onto my finger.

"Yes, yes," he said, licking his lips. "You must wear your ring. In sexual sin we violate the sacredness of the God-given body, the body that was made for God's love, not man's. A body made for the pleasure of The Lord, not those dirty boys sniffing around like stinking dogs." He lifted his hand and caressed my cheek. "Can I get an 'Amen,' Gretta?"

"Uh, amen?"

"And a 'Hallelujah'?"

"Hallelujah," I whispered.

"Hallelujah," he whispered back. "I'll see you in church on Sunday, Gretta. Be a good girl. Be not tempted by the demons of Babylon. Go with Jesus, in the blood of the lamb."

He plucked up the wooden crucifix that dangled from his neck, puckered, and brought it to his lips.

—

"That pastor is, like, so creepy, I can't even take it," I said as I smeared a streak of baby-blue eyeshadow across my closed left lid. Brenda sat cross-legged on the silly princess canopy bed she'd had since she was ten, Sasha Macfadenburgh laying on her belly beside her flipping through a glossy, thick-paged copy of *COSMOPOLITAN* and smirking.

My mom thought I was having a sleepover there, but I was really just waiting for Robby Jenkins to pick me up for our date. I was wearing my new dress and feeling very pretty as REM purred about losing their religion on the radio.

"It says here to give both him and you a thrill, get his dick cold with a piece of ice!" Sasha said, turning her face to Brenda. "Oh. My. God. Can you imagine? It'd be, like, all cold and stuff when it's inside you." She made a pinched face and shook her head, her blonde pigtails bobbing crazily.

Brenda laughed and looked up at me, catching my eye in the reflection of the mirror. "Hey, *Gret-ta*," she called—that's how she said my name when she was going to tease me, two syllables, not the breathless *Gredda* she said when she needed to talk or wanted something from me, or the cheerful and plain Gretta she used when she would call to see what I was up to, had been that way ever since we were little girls. "You going to use the ice on Robby Jenkins tonight, *Gret-ta*?"

I hated the way she acted around Sasha. All grown up and know-it-ally. Mocking everything, including my virginity. Another reason I was ready to lose it.

"Gross," I said, wiping the eyeshadow away with an alcohol pad, thinking that blue was much too garish. Something plainer would bring out my eyes. Maybe a light gray. I glanced at Brenda and Sasha on the bed together, giggling, the two of them blonde and perfect beneath a huge purple and yellow Backstreet Boys poster, exchanging knowing looks, and a pang of jealousy and loneliness rippled through me. Both Brenda and I had been towheads as children. There are all these pictures of us together in kindergarten and first grade, both with shimmering platinum locks, but while hers had patinaed and thickened into a golden yellow hue as we grew into teenagers, mine had thinned and dulled into a mousy brown that matched my eyes.

"But you are going to go all the way with him, aren't 'ya, *Gret-ta*?" Brenda asked, giggling away and burrowing into Sasha like a playful kitten.

"Ohhh, tonight's the night is it?" Sasha said, raising her eyebrows up and down, giving a little shake of her head that set those pigtails in motion again.

Heat rose up into my face, but it was a good feeling. I felt ready, I wanted to do it, to be like them. Stupid chastity pledge.

"Maybe," I said teasingly, turning to the side and

looking at my reflection over my shoulder, admiring how the light-gray of the new eyeshadow really did highlight my eyes, which I always thought had a beautiful, sleek shape to them, even if they were an ordinary mudpuddle brown. "But we won't be using ice or anything gross. I want it to be romantic."

"Romantic!" Sasha shouted before they burst into thick peals of obnoxious laughter, so hard the bed bounced.

"Yes!" I said, twirling before the mirror, making sure there were no wrinkles in my dress. "Romantic."

"I heard Robby tell his football buddies where he's taking you, sure sounds romantic," Sasha said, unwrapping a sliver of mint gum from its foil wrapper and curling it into her mouth.

"What's that supposed to mean?" I asked, her words worming their way into my blood and turning it cold.

"Nothing, it just sounds romantic," she said, smacking the gum beneath her molars, eyes focused on her magazine now, giving the page a careless turn.

"Well, where's he taking me?"

"It's a surprise! I can't tell. You'll love it, though. Trust me."

I shot a look at Brenda, she just shrugged.

The REM song ended and there was a brief moment of silence, punctuated by the low grumble of a car rolling to a stop outside the house, before three quick bursts of a horn ripped through the night and a Spice Girls song sprang to life, startling me so that I that gave a tiny shuddering jerk.

Sasha caught my unease, grinned, and winked. "Looks like Prince Charming is here in the romance vehicle. You ready, Princess?"

—

"Where are you taking me?" I asked as Robby eased his Mustang off the pavement and down a twisting dirt road.

He grinned that squinty-eyed smile of his, his head a

big square on that thick jock neck. "Someplace special. You'll love it."

The sky was cloudless and star filled, the moon fat and bloated and bright, and in the glimmer of that moonlight you could see the leaves of the tall oaks that lined the road turning yellow and curling in on themselves, some tumbling into the wind. Robby turned up the radio—*The Cure: Robert Smith crooning how the raging sea had stolen the only girl he ever loved*—and tapped a beat on the steering wheel with his fingers as he stretched his arm out so that I could curl into him, ensconced in his warmth, his man/boy smell of jock sweat and Polo cologne, and rest against the slow rise and fall of his breathing as the world swam by outside. The trees grew taller as we drove, oaks giving way to redwoods that obscured the sky with their dark silhouettes and there was a moment of almost utter darkness as their branches loomed out above us before the sky suddenly opened up revealing ocean.

A tiny private meadow tucked away above the sea.

It was magnificent.

Robby eased the Mustang to a stop as the road puttered out into a thin path that curled down to that grassy spot, a hidden little enclave overlooking the black lapping waves.

Robby squeezed my shoulder, turned off the engine and removed the keys. The hot engine ticked against the cool ocean air. "You like?" he asked.

"It's magical."

Everything was perfect.

He reached behind him and pulled a stack of folded blankets from the backseat. "Come on, let's go sit by the edge."

We trotted down the path and to the field, spread a blanket out by the rim of the cliff and curled up against each other, laying the other blankets over ourselves and staring up at the impossible depth of the stars, the pregnant moon reflected in the tall waves that crashed on the rocks far below us.

He leaned towards me and we kissed for a moment. Softly and innocently, tongues darting out for just a moment to playfully taste each other. Then pulled away and gazed into each other's eyes. I took a deep, shuddering breath, smiled and laid back against the blanket, my head upon the cold earth as he lay beside me, the sky so vast and open above us.

He nuzzled my neck, kissing softly upwards to my ear, making the hairs on the back of my neck go stiff and my insides soft and hot.

"Do you know why I chose this place?" he whispered.

"No, why?"

"Because a girl was murdered here."

"What?"

"Yeah. Back in the fifties. Forty years ago this night, actually. I thought it'd be neat. Kind of romantic and scary."

"Robby, you're not serious."

"I totally am. They called her the Lady of the Rocks, 'cause, like, after he killed her, he threw her over the cliff, thinking the water would carry her away. Only she landed on one of those real tall rocks, and just laid there till someone noticed her a few days later. They never did find out who murdered her."

"Stop. Just stop it." I pulled away from him and sat up.

"What? It's local history! It's interesting. I thought you would think it was cool. You like all that history stuff."

"It's scary. If it's even true. And you're freaking me out with it. I don't like it."

"It's supposed to be scary. I figured if you were scared, you'd want me to protect you. You know. Be close to me. Isn't that romantic?"

"Taking me to where a girl was killed? How is that romantic?"

"Well, how's it not romantic?"

"Robby, was a girl really killed here?"

"Yeah, October 13th, 1956. Forty years ago today. I told you. The Lady of the Rocks."

"Okay, I want to go. Take me back to Brenda's."

"Aw, come on, don't be that way."

"I just don't . . ." but I was interrupted by a moaning sound above the crashing of the waves. Almost like a fog horn, but more human. More feminine. "Did you hear that?"

"No. What?"

Again, this time a whimpering that seemed to come from behind us and to the side. "There it is again! It's like a crying sound."

"I don't hear nothing. Probably just the wind."

I stood up and peered around, shivering against the cold air. "It's cold, Robby. Come on, let's go back to the car."

He put his hands behind his head and kicked his feet out. "I ain't going nowhere."

"Robby, come on! I'm going back to the car." I stormed away towards the path.

And that's when I saw her.

A girl, not much older than me. Lying there battered and naked in the tall sea grass, smears and splashes of black blood covering her pale skin, her eyes turning up to look at me. She reached an arm out, a blood drenched hand, and murmured, "Help me."

Wounds, like black toothless mouths, gaped across her bare breasts and down her side, oozing dark liquid, before a shadow rose up over us, blocking out the sea and the stars and the moon, making everything but me and her darkness, as if we were caught together in some other plane of existence, some dream realm, suspended in time, and then the roof caved in. That darkness, that black shadow that had captured us, came crashing down with a heavy *whoompf*, knocking the air from my lungs, sending me falling back onto the wet grass breathless and dazed. I gasped for air, and when I found it began to scream.

Robby was beside me in an instant, kneeling in the grass to grasp my shoulders, flustered, asking, "What is it? What's the matter?"

"I . . . I saw something. I . . ."

"What? What'd you see?"

I looked around. There was nothing there. Nothing but grass shimmering in the blue light of the moon. Not even an indentation that someone had been there.

"I . . . I don't know."

Tears welled up from my gut, I tried to catch them, stop them, but a dam burst inside me and suddenly I was crying uncontrollably.

"Take me back to Brenda's, Robby," I managed between sobs. "Please, just take me back to Brenda's."

—

By the time we got back to Myrtletown I was calm, though I felt sick to my stomach.

"You okay?" Robby asked as he pulled up a few houses shy of hers, in the shadows of a couple tall, swaying palm trees.

"Yeah, I'm just . . . feeling mixed up."

"Look, I'm really sorry. I know you wanted this night to be special. But we can go somewhere different. It's not too late. Someplace you'd like to go to."

"I just want to go lay down."

"Come on, baby. It's still early. Let's go get a hamburger. Relax."

"Sorry, Robby, not now."

"But I thought tonight was the night."

"I don't know if I feel that way anymore. I'm not sure I still even want to go there."

"But why? You were so ready."

My mind was reeling. I stuttered, looking for any excuse I could. "I . . . I promised Jesus, Robby. Okay. I just don't think I want to do it anymore."

"You promised Jesus? Are you fucking serious? You told me that was all your mother. That you didn't believe any of that crap."

"Yeah, well, maybe I do," I shouted, swinging open the door, totally lying because I just wanted out of the car and any excuse would do. "Goodnight, Robby," I said, slamming the door behind me as I got out.

He stared at me a moment through the window, shaking his head, then slammed his palms against the steering wheel and took off, tires spinning and leaving black smears and a rank smell of burning rubber behind.

—

The next day, a storm rolled in.

I watched from my bedroom window as the dark clouds gathered in the gloomy distance, herded by the wind like black sheep, then roiling over the neighborhood and breaking open into a deluge of pouring rain, so transfixed that I started when the phone rang and my sister called up to me, "Gretta, phone!"

I went downstairs. My mother sat mesmerized and slack-jawed before the television, watching a preacher pace across the stage, waving a bible, sweat streaming over his pink, angry face. "De-mons, are real! They are not some metaphor to teach you a lesson. They are evil at work, try-ing to burrow their way into your godly soul."

My sister Trish sat smirking in the kitchen, dangling the receiver by its cord. "It's a boy," she said in a teasing, singsong voice.

"Just give me the phone, Trish," I said, grabbing it from her hand and slinking down the hall as far as I could stretch the cord.

"Hello?"

"Gretta, hey, it's me. Robby."

"Hi, Robby," I whispered, cupping my hand against the receiver to shield my voice from the spying ears of my mother and sister.

"I'm sorry about last night."

"It's okay," I said, though I was still a mess. I couldn't get the image I'd seen out of my head. That girl, naked, covered in blood, reaching out to me and pleading for help.

"But, look, I've been thinking. Maybe we shouldn't see

each other anymore."

The air turned to ice and my lungs froze. "What do you mean?"

"Well, I like you a lot. I do! It's just, you know, not really working out. Is it?"

I didn't know what to say and found myself opening and closing my mouth uselessly, finally managing to get out, "It's not?"

"No. And the way we're always sneaking around, afraid your mom is going to find out about us. It's a pain."

"Robby, I can change. I'll tell my mother about us. I'm not afraid. I—"

"Gretta, look, I've got to be honest with you. Last night, after you left, I . . . well, I was kind of upset, and a little hurt, and I . . . I really don't know how to put this, so I'll just say it. I hooked up with Sasha McFaddenburgh. I didn't mean to, didn't plan it. Neither of us did. It just happened. And, well, we're going out now."

I clasped my eyes shut, feeling the bitter sting of tears. *That slutty bitch.*

"Gretta, you there?"

"Yeah, I'm here."

"You okay?"

"Uh huh, I'm fine. I . . . I, uh, I gotta go. My mother needs me."

"I'm sorry, Gretta. I—"

"It's fine. That's fine. I gotta go. I'll talk to you later," and I was back in the kitchen hanging up the phone, struggling to breathe, an emptiness lurching open in my belly.

"Who was that boy?" my mother asked from the sofa in a monotone voice.

"Nobody, mother. Just a boy from school asking about homework."

—

Monday at school was a nightmare. My heart felt like a fragile thing in my chest, I kept catching glances and sniggers, covered mouths and whispers. It was a torture.

Brenda finally caught up to me in the bathroom after second period.

"What happened between you and Robby, Gretta?" she asked. "Everyone's calling you Gretta the Frigid. Saying you started to cry and pray to Jesus when Robby tried to kiss you."

I slammed my books down on the sink. "That's not what happened."

"Well, what happened? You seemed all gung-ho and ready."

"He took me to a place where a girl was murdered."

"Uh, creepy."

"Yeah, and I . . . I think I saw something."

"What?"

"I don't know. A girl, in the grass, naked and covered in blood. It was horrible."

"You, like, really saw a naked girl?"

"Yes. No. Oh, I don't know. I think it was a ghost."

"A ghost?"

"Yeah, a ghost."

"You wouldn't fuck Robby Jenkins because you saw a ghost?"

"It was more than that. Just that he even took me to that place. I told you I wanted it to be romantic. Special."

"Yeah, well, you know he's going out with Sasha now."

"I know."

"And you're cool with that?"

I nodded my head. What else could I do?

I didn't even bother going to cheerleading practice that day. The thought of seeing Sasha's smug face, those mean eyes. Dealing with her beside me in the dressing room, having to perform with her out on the field. It was all too much for me.

—

Sitting before the television, bathed in its projection-tube-blue light, an old quilt draped over my head, I watched a thin scarecrow of a man ride a pig about the screen, one eye a milky cataract-blue, the other brown like mine, moaning how some of them want to use you and some of them want to abuse you.

My sister came down the stairs and slipped up beside me.

"The big game's today. Aren't you supposed to be cheerleading?" she asked.

"I quit the squad."

"You quit?!"

"I don't want to talk about it."

The bare-chested scarecrow withered and snarled, the low notes of the dark melody filling the space between us, before she finally asked, "What are you watching?"

"Marilyn Manson."

"He is so ugly."

"I think he's beautiful," I said, reaching out to touch the screen, relishing the feel of the electric static tingle my fingertips.

"Gross. How can you say that?"

"There's something true about him. He's not a fake. A phony. You wouldn't understand."

"You know, Mom says we're not allowed to watch this channel. She says MTV is strictly off limits."

"Yeah? What are you going to do? Rat me out?"

"Not if you let me watch Beverly Hills 90210."

I laughed, stood, and tossed her the remote. "Be my guest," I said, heading to the door.

"Where you going?"

"To the library."

—

Down in the dusty depths of the library basement, I scrolled through microfiche. A blur of headlines and dates stream by on the screen. I slowed, October 10th 1956, October 11th,

12th, 13th and then, there on October 15th, I find what I'm looking for: The Lady of the Rock.

Missing teenage girl found murdered north of Clam Beach . . .

It was all true. Everything Robby had said.

Mary Mack, sexually assaulted and stabbed to death, tossed from the cliff's edge . . .

Below the article there's two pictures, side by side.

One is of an oval-faced girl with high cheek bones and a shy smile, hair a perfect black and shiny bob. She's showing off a what looks like a new dress, a leg kicked back teasingly in a pirouette, lifting the hem with one hand and waving the other. She looks so alive and happy.

The other is a grainy picture of a blurry figure atop a black rock jutting up from the ocean. Nothing more than a pale smear against darkness, really. But I peer closer, trying to make out just what I'm seeing. Though the details are impossible to make out, she's obviously naked, arms flung out to either side, her legs crossed and slightly curled, so that she almost gives the illusion of a mermaid, a thing of the sea unnaturally washed to the shore. I try to make out the features of her face, to tie this abandoned body to the picture of the happy girl beside it, but it's just grain, a few thick black dots implying shadow that seem to slowly spin as I stare harder and harder, willing my mind to make sense of the image, to find clarity in it, and I'm growing dizzy, my head feels gaseous and bubbly, effervescent like a soda pop, and then I'm falling, falling, falling to the ground in a heap and the librarian is there, asking me if I'm all right, if she should call an ambulance.

"I'm fine," I tell her, standing up and brushing myself off. "Just fine."

—

After midnight and swirling black water snaking around the sink as I rinsed my hair, quiet, quiet quiet so as not to wake my sleeping mother. Then the scissors, cutting it off above the shoulders, curling the ends to get that perfect bob. Rit dye into the washing machine with my Betsy Johnson dress. Black, black, black. And afterwards, blacking each bit of lace with a thick permanent marker, the industrial scent of its ink making my head feel hazy and distant.

—

"Oh my God!" Sasha says as she and a couple other cheerleaders pass me in the hall. "Halloween's not for three more weeks!"

I just ignore them, their laughter and squealing, their long swaying hair and whispered insults of *freak* and *Gretta the Frigid*. I've got my headphones on and I just concentrate on the Nine Inch Nails song on my disc player, thinking Brenda had a head like a hole. Supposed to be my best friend and now she doesn't even look at me. Pretends I'm not there.

I swing open my locker. There's a mirror hanging in there, and I stop and stare at my reflection: my Egyptian eyes framed in a now shimmering black bob of hair, my ebony dress with the blacker-than-black lace which makes my shoulders and neck look so bare and pale and soft.

I feel perfect.

I lift a pallid hand and lay a finger on the reflection of my face, as if to test if it is even real, a reflection and not a window.

For the first time in my life I feel like I am perfect.

I am the person I'm meant to be.

And I think, fuck this place, fuck these people. They could never understand me.

I take that black permanent marker and coat my lips in stinky ink. So perfect, kissing the mirror, leaving a flawless stain of puckered lips.

The bell rings shrilly, an awful sound that signals first period has begun, and the last stragglers duck into their classrooms. The hall is now empty. I just let my text books tumble from my fingers to the floor, and walk away, locker door open and swaying as down the hall I go and out the heavy industrial doors to the outside world.

—

That ocean facing meadow was easy to find, even if it did take me hours to get there.

My legs aching, calves on fire and blisters swelling on my feet, I sit on the cliff edge, watching the surf lurch out and smash against the rocks only to be pulled back frothing into the sea again. The squeal of seagulls and the dank salty scent of the ocean, and I could feel her there with me, shadowlike. An ephemeral presence, a kind of static lingering behind the sounds of the sea and the wind, like fingers of fog falling down the crevices of the surrounding hills she's behind me, placing a hand upon my shoulder.

"I've been waiting for you," I said.

"I know," she replied. "I'm sorry I scared you. Sometimes it's hard for me to . . . communicate."

"That's okay," I say, and she's sitting down beside me, wearing that same black dress I'd seen in the microfiche picture. She's flush with life, cheeks rose-colored, lips ripe and crimson, raven hair clean and shiny. We stare out at the horizon for what feels an eternity before she holds out her hand to me, and I take it.

—

I remember certain things.

I remember secrets told and promises given. A nest there in the tall sea grass. Me swearing I would avenge her, and her promising she'd never leave me, that we'd be together for eternity. I remember the taste of sea salt on her lips. Her hands running through my hair, her arms holding me as we rolled in the matted grass and the sun tumbled into the Pacific with a murmur of purple fire and the black of night fell upon us, the stars spinning like mad and my head alive like a circus, a calliope of exploding sensations as her hand slipped up between my legs, her curious fingers finding my secret places and her mouth on my chest and her eyes always boring into mine, hungrily watching my reaction to her touch, and we were together and one in every sense of the word.

—

They found me wandering along the road that night. Lost and disorientated, my black babydoll dress dirty and torn, mumbling to myself, not making any sense.

At least that's what they told me.

I don't remember any of that. I only remember waking up in my bed, feverish and nauseous. My first thought was wondering why I was wearing this ridiculous, long white nightie—the kind I used to wear when I was a little girl—not the oversized T-shirt I usually slept in. I looked around, dazed, my mother was beside me in a chair looking frantic.

"She's awake again," my mother said. "Gretta, Gretta is that you?"

"Careful," a deep voice called out. "It could be the demon again. Identify yourself."

I blinked and there was Pastor Willard at the foot of the bed, wearing some kind of weird purple robe over his tacky leisure suit, that big wooden crucifix dangling from his neck on its black leather tong.

"Mommy," I said. "What's going on?"

The pastor held a battered black bible towards me. "I said identify thyself!"

"Pastor, it's me, Gretta. What is going on?"

"Oh, thank God," my mother cried, taking me in her arms and rocking me, her chest hiccupping with sobs as she stroked my hair. "I was so scared. Scared I lost my little girl."

She was whimpering and squeezing me, suffocating me, and I could feel the snot from her nose dripping onto the top of my head.

"Jeeze, I'm fine. Stop." I said, pulling away.

"You are not fine. Look at you. Your hair, what happened to your hair?"

"It's black. I like it this way."

"Trish told me you were watching the MTV. You must have gotten a demon from that terrible television. *What* was I thinking letting them attach that cable to the house? *A cable straight to Hell.*"

The Pastor cocked his head and pointed at me dramatically. "And out in cars with boys sinning. We know what's been going on. Sneaking around full of lust. You've strayed from the herd and been tempted, let a demon into your heart. Now we must cast it out."

My head was pounding and I was dizzy. "You don't know what you're talking about. I didn't do anything with Robby Jenkins. Can you guys just leave me alone? I don't feel well."

"Leave you we will not."

"Why are you talking ridiculous Yoda shit," I laughed. "Seriously, I feel like I'm going to puke, so just leave me the fuck alone. Okay?"

"Hear the profanity? It's the demon!" the Pastor shouted. "Demon! Thing of sin! Leave this girl's body!"

I thought about Mary and laughed. "I know who you're talking about and she's not a demon. She's my friend and I love her."

"I can see the lust in your eyes, fornicator!"

"Listen to you, *Pastor*, you don't think all the girls see you eyeing them up? Staring at our tits. That we don't see the bulge in your pants when we're too close to you, see you sniffing at us like a dirty dog?"

The Pastor stepped back, his face twisted in anger and revulsion. "Foul beast. Liar. Whore of Babylon. Let us pray."

My mother fell down to her knees, hands clasped before her, head bent, and mumbled while the pastor stretched out his arms to either side and tilted his head skyward, saying loudly, "And all who dwell on earth will worship it, everyone whose name has not been written before the foundation of the world in the book of life of the Lamb who was slain."

Then suddenly I remembered. Like waking up from a

dream, it all came back to me and I remembered all the things Mary had told me about the night she was murdered. All the hot whispering in my ear about who had done it and how I was to avenge her.

"It was you!" I shrieked. "You killed her. Raped and killed Mary Mack. Didn't you?"

He thrust his bible at me again. "And they have conquered him by the blood of the Lamb and by the word of their testimony, for they loved not their lives even unto death."

I turned to my mother, kneeling at his feet, rocking with her hands clasped before her face. "Mom! Don't listen to this guy. He's sick. He's a killer. He killed a girl forty years ago."

He's leaning over the bed now, shoving his bible right into my face. "King of lies! Your web of deception mocks you. I'm only forty-five years old. How could I have killed someone forty years ago?"

"Bullshit. Utter bullshit, you fucking hypocrite!" I scream. Bolting upright, I bat the bible out of his hand and shove my palms into his chest as hard as I can. He stumbles back, a look of surprise crossing his stupid face, trips over his feet and falls onto the floor as I bound from the bed after him in my best cheerleading leap, using the footboard as a vault so that I'm so high in the air above him my black hair brushes the ceiling. I come down hard, landing with my knees on either of his arms. I can feel a creak as his shoulders give and both his arms dislocate. He bellows in pain and I cackle in his face.

"Dirty shaman, I know what you've done."

And I can feel her there with me, beside me, guiding me, her breath hot in my ear. "Do it. Do it! *Do it!!!*"

And I can hear my mother behind me, screaming, "No! No! *Noooooo!*" as I lift the wooden crucifix hanging from his neck—that same cross I'd seen him press his foul lips to—bring it up over my head, and slam it down into his left eye, squirming it back and forth so that it sinks deeper and deeper. Blood and bits of eye spray up as he writhes helplessly, and my mother is pulling at my shoulders, screaming at me to get off of him, tearing my stupid nightie as she claws and yanks at me.

I swing out an arm and backhand her across the face, knocking her away, then bring my palm down with all my might onto the top of the crucifix. It sinks in with a cracking sound, propelled like a hammer-driven nail through his eye socket so that a deeper, darker, black blood gurgles out now, the horizontal beams snapping off the crucifix and Jesus falling free and one more time I bring my palm down on that wooden spike and I can feel it burst into the soft tissue of his brain and he erupts into spasms, his legs kicking and arms flailing briefly, before he is suddenly still and silent.

My mother sobs hysterically, curled fetal-like, hands clasped in prayer. *"Worthy is the Lamb who was slain to receive power and wealth and wisdom and might and honor and glory and blessing."*

The pounding of the cross has caused a wound in my palm and I prod at it a moment, watching my blood spill out and mix with that of the Pastor's, before slowly rising. I step over my mother and through my bedroom door, the nightie now gore-streaked and hanging from my aching frame in tatters, my black hair—damp with sweat and blood—cascading down over my eyes. Walking down the dim hall I see my sister's door ajar, catch her eye peering from behind it, watching me, ready to slam the door shut.

I smile at her. "Don't worry about telling on me. It's okay. I love you." And then I'm down the steps and out the front door and into the night.

—

Mary's waiting for me, in our nest of salt, by the cliff's edge.

I run to her, laughing, crying with joy and sorrow and the knowing of the abyss. We're spiraling about, arms around shoulders, hands in our hair and our lips together and tongues entwined. Below us the surf crashes black against the jagged ancient volcanic rocks. She looks at me, the infinite ceiling of stars reflecting in her eyes, and says, "Now we can be together forever."

We turn and look out over the ocean, where the night sky meets the sea, the forever of the horizon beckoning and winking.

THE PET

When he placed the order, Devon Newton thought of the pet as an early Christmas present to himself. It had been expensive, he'd blown his whole savings on it, converting the money to bitcoin to perform the transaction, and now he didn't have money for rent. A part of him wondered if it was a rip-off scheme, it did sound too good to be true, and he nervously questioned if the pet would even arrive. But a few days later, he got a message from the shipping yard: a crate had arrived for him.

In order to pick the pet up from the shipping yard, he had to borrow his mother's pickup truck. He had arranged to meet her at noon in the greasy-spoon diner where she worked as a waitress. He swung open the door to the Redwood Café and was greeted by the din of forks scraping over plates, muffled conversations, and rattling coffee mugs.

He was a big man, over six feet with a sizeable girth around his middle, but he stooped—bent at the back—and hung his head low, so that he appeared much smaller than he really was. He pushed his thick, Coke-bottle glasses up his nose and shuffled up to the counter where his mother was setting a side order of glistening sausage links in a puddle of grease down before a customer.

"There you are, Devon. Late as usual."

"Hello, Mother." He absent-mindedly dragged a finger under the back of his ear, brought it under his nose where he could take a quick sniff of the musky-cheesy aroma.

"Quit slouching and stand up straight, Devon. And for God's sake stop sniffing your fingers. It's a disgusting habit."

"Yes, Mother."

"Christ, sometimes I'm glad your father is dead so he doesn't have to see what a pathetic slug his son has become." She took a rag and began to run it in circular motions over the counter. "Mrs. Harper says that you're late with the rent again. That true?"

"I'm going to pay it now."

"It was due last week. You're thirty-two years old, time to start acting more responsible. You spending all your money on dirty magazines and movies again?"

"No, Mother."

"You remember you get those checks every month because your poor father died busting his ass for this family. Show a little goddamn respect."

"Yes, Mother."

"All right. Here are the keys. I want it returned with a full tank of gas. And be sure to have my grass cut by this evening. Come here and let me give you a kiss. You're a good boy." She planted her wet lips on his cheek, where they left a bloom of deep-crimson lipstick.

Devon went to the shipping yard and loaded the crate into the back of his mother's rusted-up Toyota pickup. The crate was made of roughhewn wood and rather ugly: there were splintered chips in it from rough handling, crude air holes drilled into its sides, and Malaysian stamps and writing scrawled all over it. It did not look like something that was going to change his life forever and turn him into a new person.

Devon took the crate home and in the privacy of his bedroom pried it open, utterly floored and amazed at what lie inside. It was exactly like the seller on the deep web had promised.

Whoever had amputated her arms had legs had done an excellent job. The skin at the nubs was smooth and blemish free. It was amazing really, no scars at all. They must have performed plastic surgery afterwards. You would have thought she was born without a tongue; it was impossible to tell that someone had cut it out. And you could only tell that her eyelids had been stitched together over her sightless eyes if you looked really close and saw the fishing-line sutures holding them together.

He pushed up his glasses, ran his index finger back and forth over the back of his ear, and put his thick, sausage-link finger under his nose, inhaling deeply and marveling at his new pet. She was beautiful, with long raven-black hair and delicate skin the color of coffee with only half a spoonful of cream. He lifted her from the box and sat her beside him on the bed. She began to make terrified gurgling noises and to flail her stumps, but he stroked her back and soothed her. "It's okay. It's okay. I won't hurt you. You're home now. You're nice and safe." This seemed to calm her and she actually leaned into him and cuddled against him. He wrapped his arms around her and cried. It was the first time he had ever held a naked woman.

Before the crate arrived, he had imagined tying the pet up. Maybe suspending her from the ceiling somehow with a ball gag in her mouth and a dog collar on her throat, like he had seen in all those BDSM movies. But now he knew he would never do something like that, for the emotions that ripped through his heart were awe, pity and love.

Devon had always wanted to be a slave master. That's why he'd started searching the deep web for a pet. He frequented all the BDSM websites and even put some ads up on Craigslist as a dom looking for a sub. He got a few replies but only one woman—a pretty, older redhead—had agreed to meet with him. They had met at a coffee shop but after five minutes of talking to him she had started laughing and stood up.

"Sorry, honey, but you're no dom," she replied before walking out and leaving him with the check.

Of course, he fucked the pet occasionally. That's why he bought her in the first place, after all. But their relationship was not one built on sex, but rather tenderness. Most of the time he spent with her was brushing her lustrous hair till it shone and glimmered, delicately applying lipstick and eyeshadow to her winsome and arresting face, singing softly to her as he spooned soup into her mouth and changed her diaper, and just holding her in his arms at night while he slept, happy and content for the first time in his life.

"Cassandra," he said, his eyes brimming over with tears. "That's what I'll call you. Cassandra. My sweet, sweet Cassandra."

He began to walk taller and stopped slouching. Got a real job at the hardware store: stocking shelves with hammers and drills, boxes of nails and screws. One day he found himself canceling his membership to all the BDSM sites and packing a big box with all of his pornographic magazines and DVDs, hauling it to the dump. He didn't need that stuff anymore. In fact, it made him sick.

Then, Christmas day, sitting in church beside his mother, the sunlight shimmering down purple and blue from the tall stained-glass windows, he realized that the pet had been a gift from God.

Look at all Cassandra had done for him. She had turned his life around and made him whole, given him meaning and purpose. He smiled and looked out at the congregation. He wanted to give the pet a gift, to show how much he loved her, how much she meant to him. He would get her a companion, someone to be with when he wasn't there. Yes, another pet. A pet for the pet. This time, maybe he would just make his own.

A TRUE CHILD OF WODEN

A breath of autumn wind, heavy with the salt and scent of the sea, blew up the cliff face as Kvasir led his younger brother Baldr down the steep path to the hidden cove where the Faining ceremony was to take place.

Tonight was the night Baldr would officially be taken into the sect and made a member of the Frenrir's Wolf tribe. A night of great auspiciousness, promising immense ceremony, wonder and awe.

The ocean spread out below them as infinite and blue as the sky which stretched out above, and their leather boots fought for traction in the sandy earth as they made their way down to the beach. The fresh tattoos on Kvasir's face—runes that marked him as a man of knowledge—stung from the salty sea air.

As they traversed the path along the cliff edge, past the shimmering green lupines and clumps of gum weed, Kvasir noticed a possum rotting in the sun to the side of the path, two ravens picking and pulling at its glimmering guts. The birds cawed at them briefly, tugging on a ropey strand of intestine, before beating their glistening, black wings and taking flight. Kvasir turned to his brother.

"This is a good omen, Baldr. They are Huginn and Muninn, pets of father Woden. They will bring him word of your acceptance into the sect."

Baldr nodded gravely.

Though they were young— Kvasir sixteen and his brother only thirteen— the boys were tall and lean. Their hair was as pale and yellow as the sandy shore that lay beneath them.

They finally stepped down onto the beach: the secret cove Geirskogul had told him of. The surf beat loudly and rhythmically against the land, a few fishing boats dotted the horizon in the distance. It was a magical place where earth, sky and sea met. A place where the mysteries of Asatru would be revealed.

"All of this you see," Kvasir explained to his younger brother, "all of Midgard, was once Ymir, born from venom. Father Woden made the earth from the flesh of Ymir and the ocean from his blood. We truly are the sons of Woden."

Baldr nodded his head solemnly, his blue eyes staring out at creation.

Kvasir couldn't really remember his real father. His earthly father who had left over a decade ago on a voyage and never returned.

Kvasir could remember him in a foggy and nondescript way, a memory of a memory.

He could remember the dirty Caterpillar baseball hat he always wore, the scent of menthol cigarettes and liquor. The funny drink he made: Seagram's 7 and Mountain Dew, how he called it a Hillbilly Highball. Kvasir could remember being held on his lap and cradled in his strong arms, back when Kvasir's name was Kevin. He could remember his father telling him tales of his travels as a long-distance truck driver. The voyages to distant lands. Places with exotic names like Kentucky and Mississippi. He would tell him tales of a great salt lake and mountains that stretched up a mile into the sky. And Kevin would curl up, pressing himself against his father's big barrel chest, feeling safe and loved, and drift off to sleep. His little brother, then known as Brian, gazing over the edge of the bassinet at them, eyes wide in wonder. Now it seemed a time before time. A dream nearly forgotten.

—

It was still early and the rest of the sect would not arrive on the beach until the sun had set. It was October 9th, Leif

Erickson day: an auspicious and important day. Kvasir sat his brother in the sand and explained the importance of this day.

"You see, brother, most of the world thinks that Christopher Columbus was the first European to find this great land where we dwell. But that is a lie. Leif Erickson was here five-hundred years before Columbus. They tell you this lie because Columbus was Catholic and a worshiper of Jesus, the king of the Jews, while Erickson was a worshiper of Woden. Christianity has erased our heritage, our old true culture. Erased the world's true cultures wherever it spread. Christianity is the root of all evil. You understand this, right? You understand our mission?"

Baldr nodded his head. "I understand, brother."

The surf beat against the beach, sea birds screeched.

It was hard to believe it was only months ago Kvasir had discovered Fenrir's Wolf. How different life had been back then. How different he had been.

Just a skinny, sixteen-year-old black-metal fanatic, wearing his black-metal uniform: overcoat hanging limply off his shoulders like sad raven's wings, a belt made of sharp bullets, spiked wrist bands. Ubiquitous VENOM T-shirt with the sleeves cut off. He dyed his long hair black and let it hang over his face. He sometimes wore corpse paint: white-and-black makeup to make himself look lifeless and dead. Often he used his own blood to adorn his forehead with an inverted cross.

He loved European bands like Bathory, Mercyful Fate and Celtic Frost, but his favorite shit was the Norwegian stuff, like Darkthrone, Gorgoroth and Mayhem. Cold. Grim. The grinding guitar and other-worldly, screeching vocals, like something from a nightmare. A sound like the bleak darkness he felt in his heart.

He kept a poster of Mayhem's bootleg album *Dawn of the Black Hearts* above his bed. On it was a grisly photograph of the singer Dead after he had shot himself in the head. At night, when he heard his mother stumble into their apartment, drunk from a night at the bars, the sounds of her fucking some stranger reverberating through the thin walls, he would put on his headphones, his Walkman drowning out the moans and grunts, and stare at that poster, his gaze going from the black spiderweb of inverted crosses in the band's logo, to the dark spray of the singer's blood on the wall, to the fat, bright-red puddle of brains where they'd fallen out of his skull and onto the pillow before him, and he'd always end up fixating on that mysterious look in Dead's lifeless eyes, a searching gaze, as if he was looking past something, through the veil, and Kevin's mind would churn in darkness, reveling in it and wondering what death really like.

But everything changed the night he saw Fenrir's Wolf play.

While Mayhem had brought him only thoughts of death, Fenrir's Wolf brought him life.

—

It was a typical black metal show in the basement of the Veteran's Hall in Eureka. He'd been to lots of them, the little apartment complex where he lived was only a few blocks away. There were a bunch of bands on the lineup. A couple local ones, one big one from Seattle. And this band he'd never heard of before: Fenrir's Wolf.

Everyone was milling around in their black attire, lots of corpse paint, Doc Martens and spikes, and then he saw what at first looked like a couple of dreadlocked hippies getting on the stage and setting up big goat-skin drums.

Dreadlocks and anything even slightly colorful stood out that night, but only a quick glance showed these were no peace-loving hippies but some kind of strange crust punks. They wore knives. Big ones, bowie knives. And they had tall, mud-splattered work boots, like a lumberjack would wear, and there was something fierce about them, their movements and their tattoos. Their arms were intricate patchworks of ink, and they had tats on their faces as well. Each of them had a line of markings below their eyes. Triangular, letter-like patterns he would later learn were *futharks,* runes signifying their places within the tribe.

The lights dimmed and the two drummers, standing shoulder to shoulder, began to pound away on the tall upright drums with large wooden mallets. They wore homemade-looking vests of patched together sheep's wool and leather, banging out this tribal rhythm, like the sound a galley slave would beat in the belly of a ship, as a muscular, bare-chested man, black-leather gauntlets clamped on his swollen forearms, a thick dread-locked beard spilling down over his chest, stepped to the microphone, croaking out a demonic-sounding chant through the mane of knotted hair that cascaded over his face and shoulders like giant spider legs.

Thus it is well seen that Sigi has slain the thrall and murdered him; so he is given forth to be a wolf in holy places, and may no more abide in the land with his father; therewith Woden bare him fellowship from the land.

An acidic roar, a cacophony of noise, erupted as a woman on the side of the stage plugged a battered electric guitar into a Marshall half-stack with a burst of feedback and ran the side of her pick over the strings. And then, there it was: that graveyard sound he loved so much. That buzz-saw tremolo of guitar, the notes coming so fast they sounded like one screeching noise, a sound like an engine revving or a million black insects beating their wings at once, her right hand playing lightning-quick plucked notes while her left's fingers snaked up and down the neck to let out an eerie, satanic-triad riff.

So dark, so powerful, and coming from this blonde goddess.

She turned from the amp and strode slowly across the stage, her steps sure and graceful, the guitar and her like one being, this awesome, evil noise just spilling effortlessly from her. She wore tall suede boots that reached to her knees, a short skirt of animal pelts, and a leather corset secured with dozens of tiny brass buckles.

And my god how she was beautiful.

Like something beyond this world. Both ethereal and majestic, fierce yet lissome. The sides of her head were shaved short, the rest of her thick blonde hair hanging in long ropey dreads that fell past her waist, and as the dim light caught her, Kevin could see bits of bone and rock sewn in there. She strutted to the microphone, eyes ablaze above the row of ancient symbols tattooed across her cheeks, and let out a ravishing war cry that made the hairs on Kevin's arms stand erect. Visions of Valkyries and banshees filled him.

The music was like a revelation: a combination of this new, stark, black-metal sound with the ancient and tribal, pure and primitive. How the drummers were even keeping up with the wicked guitar tremolo was a mystery, their mallets a blur as they replicated the double bass pounding most metal drummers used their feet to produce. The singer growling strange poetry, and like a shaman, hunching and drawing up spirits, then throwing his arms up and head back with a howl and releasing ancient ghosts into the night.

Kevin stood in rapt awe their entire set, utterly mesmerized.

Afterwards, the lights up, the air cooling as the crowd thinned out, he wandered over to the little merch table they had set up in the back shadows. The two drummers sat there on folding chairs, looking bored and ignoring him. They had a couple T-shirts for sale, that typical black-metal style of spasmatic tree-roots spelling out their name. They also had some cassette tapes, which Kevin really wanted, but had no money for. He wouldn't be getting paid from his part-time job at the record store till tomorrow. He'd paid to get in the show that night with change he'd managed to save, embarrassingly having to count the seven-dollar entrance fee with quarters and dimes.

Then a voice came from behind him, "How'd you like the show?"

He turned, and there she was: the Viking guitar

goddess. He was struck dumb for a moment, unable to form or even conceive words. She was even more gorgeous and fierce there in the light before him than onstage. A face like an angel, adorned with leather and bones and tribal tattoos. It was as if he was walking in the forest and came into the presence of a true wild thing, a bobcat or wolf. It was exhilarating yet scary at the same time. But she had a kind smile, and warm eyes that sparkled when she squinted, giving him a sense of inclusion and security, as if they were both in on some amusing inside joke.

"It was . . . amazing," he stammered.

"Oh yeah?" she said, cocking her head, as if she wasn't sure she believed him. "You wouldn't just say that, would you?" Her voice had a slightly foreign lilt to it and he saw what looked like a hawk's skull woven into one of her thick dreads.

"No! Totally amazing. I mean it."

"Then why don't you buy a shirt? Get a tape? If you thought it was *so amazing.*"

Kevin let his long black hair fall down over his face. "I totally would. I'd love a tape actually, but you know, I'm fucking broke. I don't get paid till tomorrow."

"Yeah?"

"Yeah. I work at the record store in Old Town. The Works."

"Ohhh, in the music business, huh?"

Kevin laughed and kicked at the ground with the toe of his Converse All Star. "Yeah. I just mainly sweep up and unpack boxes."

"So glamorous!"

"Yup. Quite the glamorous life. I'm hoping to make the big move from scraping gum off the floor to stocking used disco albums."

She threw her head back and laughed. She smelled of sweat and earth and woodsmoke and exotic herbs. "I like you. What's your name?"

"Kevin."

"Nice to meet you, Kevin who works at the record

store." She held out her hand. "They call me Geirskogul."

"Geirskogul. Very cool," he said, taking her hand and glancing quickly from her sparkling eyes and back to his shoes before letting go.

"Here you go, Kevin." She reached over and grabbed a cassette and a couple stickers, held them out for him. "Since you're in the music business and all."

He took them, shaking his head in gratitude, casting timid glances, a humble smile cracking his face. "Stoked on this. Thank you so much. I really loved the show."

"Yeah? Well, here," she snatched a flyer off the table, pressed it into his chest with a smirk. "We're playing on Saturday. At a campground in Orrick. It's a free show, so you don't need money, but, you know, donations are appreciated."

She gave him a sly wink and, feeling himself flush from his feet to the top of his skull, he ducked his head, studying the black-and-white flyer, hoping she wouldn't see how flustered he suddenly was. He didn't recognize any of the bands, but it looked metal as fuck with a very Nordic vibe: axes and horned-helmets, shields and spiked hammers.

"Cool," he managed. "I'll try to make it."

"Hope to see you there, Kevin."

—

The tape was beyond his expectations. Something about those drums and that black-metal guitar sound that was absolutely mesmerizing. So raw and primitive, yet structured and complex at the same time. The sound hollow and cold but rich with a thick primal essence.

And the haunting low growl of the singer. Completely and utterly terrifying and menacing.

It was difficult to make out the words, but from what he could decipher they were epic poems of Norse gods, the eternal struggle of life and death, trickery and magic, Loki and Thor. He'd loved Vikings when he was a kid and his dad used to entertain him for hours with tales of Scandinavian mythology.

He listened to that tape nonstop for the next three days and begged his mother to let him borrow the car. Begged, pleaded, cajoled. Nearly got down on his knees and cried.

She just sat at the kitchen table, eating scrambled eggs and smoking Kools, complaining about her hangover.

"Please," he said. "I'll bring it back full of gas. I promise."

"Kevin, you already said you'd take your little brother to the movies on Saturday. Remember? Now what kind of mother would I be if I let your brother down?" She put the butt of her Kool to her lips and sucked on it, shaking Tabasco sauce out, over her eggs. "Christ, my aching fucking head. They say protein and peppers are a hangover cure, you know."

"Look, Mom, I'll take him Sunday. That's cool, right, Brian?" he called to his brother who lay on his belly in front of the television, his chin nestled in the crook of his palms, watching Beavis and Butthead. "Cool if we see *Curse of Michael Myers* Sunday, buddy?"

"Well, I kind of wanted to see *Judge Dredd*."

"Okay, *Judge Dredd*. Fine. Just Sunday, not Saturday. Okay?"

"Yeah. Okay with me."

"See, Mom?"

"I don't know. This weird music you like, always dressed all in black. Ever think of wearing some colors? You were such a cute little boy. Now you look like some kinda zombie monster."

"Come on. I'll fill up the tank, *and get you a pack of Kools*."

"Pack of Kools, huh?"

"That's what I said."

"Tell you what, two packs of Kools and you got yourself a deal. But don't forget about taking your brother to the movies Sunday. And that tank better be full, mister!"

—

Before leaving for the show he put on full corpse paint: his face streaked white with makeup, black rings under his eyes, and an inverted cross with 666 scrawled above it. He also wore a cape.

Getting gas he felt very awkward, the other customers giving him amused looks and sly smiles as he stood outside his mother's station wagon filling up, his cape billowing about, his face that of an angry mime, but the attendant was cool as fuck: flashed him the devil horns and said, "Keep on rocking, buddy."

Driving into the woods with clouds darkening above him and that Fenrir's Wolf tape blaring on the stereo, he felt pulled by destiny as lightning crackled against the horizon.

By the time he made it to the campground it was raining. Pouring. He could barely see past the clacking windshield wiper doing double time smearing the pelting rain across the glass. The roads were a muddy mess. Pulling in there were a cluster of police by the entrance, their lights spiraling red-and-blue in the gray deluge of the storm.

As he snaked his way through the maze of pitted roads, it seemed there were an army of cars and vans leaving. *The fuck?* he thought, *Where's everybody going?* He checked the rumpled flyer again. Right time. Right place.

The road thinned around a bend and he had to pull over to let a black VW bug covered in Metallica stickers pass. He rolled down his window, shouted out into the storm, "Is this the way to the show?"

A bucktoothed, long-haired guy, cigarette hanging out the side of his mouth, hung his head out the window of the VW. "Show's cancelled, dude! Best turn around when you can, it's a fucking mud pit down there."

"Fuck!" Kevin muttered, slamming his palms against the steering wheel. His heart sank, all this shit for nothing. He slowly eased the station wagon back on the road, keeping an eye out for anywhere to turn around, when he saw her, Geirskogul, up ahead, talking to the two drummers he would

later learn were brothers from Australia who went by Skuld and Skogul.

It was as if the rain couldn't touch her, had no effect: she stood with her head cocked and chin up, one hand on her hip, the other grasping the handle of sticker-covered guitar case, booted feet planted firmly in the mud.

He inched up beside her, reached across and rolled down the passenger window. "Hey, what's up?" he shouted over the clack of the windshield wipers. "I heard the show was cancelled."

She turned, tossing her long, wet dreads over her shoulder, and ducked her head into the station wagon window, her face lighting up into a big smile when she saw him.

"Kevin! You made it. Yeah, sorry to say: show's cancelled. First some fuckers called the cops complaining, now this." She held her face up to the rain and stretched out her hands, like, *what can you do?*

A heat rose over Kevin at the thought that she recognized him and even remembered his name, and then the singer of the band was strutting up through the mud behind her, shirtless in the cold and rain, water dripping from his long, dreaded beard. He placed his arm around Geirskogul's waist and she looked up at him.

"Any luck?" she asked.

He shook his head grimly.

"Maybe Kevin here can help. Kevin, this is Gungnir. Gungnir, this is Kevin who works at the record store. *He thinks we're amazing.*"

Gungnir nodded and raised his palm. "Hail and joy to you, Kevin."

She ducked her head back into the window, rested her elbow on the sill and put her chin on her palm. "So," she said, raising her pretty eyebrows up to stare straight into his face. "We're in a bit of a pickle. Our friend's band Black Plague, well, their ride broke down. So we're helping them haul their equipment, and now there's no room for all of us in our van. One of us needs to find a ride back to our squat in Honeydew." She gave him a sly grin and a half wink, bobbed her head. "What do you think? Could you give a girl and her guitar a lift down the road aways?"

How amazing was this?! He'd drive to the depths of hell and back for this girl, this black metal guitar goddess. "Yeah, I guess. Sure. No problem," Kevin said.

She pulled open the door and tossed her guitar in the backseat, but as she bent forward to get in, Gungnir placed a hand on her shoulder, stopping her. "No."

She turned to him, "What's up?"

"You go with Skuld and Skogul. I'll go with Kevin."

"Yeah?"

"Yes."

"All right," she said, giving him a kiss as he impassively stared down at Kevin, face like an ancient chiseled monument.

She glanced at Kevin, "You boys have fun. I'll see you in Honeydew," then trotted off into the rain.

Gungnir slid into the passenger seat. He was a large man and looked cramped there, all muscles and dreads and beard, tattoos slick with rain.

Kevin put the car into gear, looked both ways into the storm before pulling out. "Bummer the show got cancelled," he said with a furtive glance. "Was really looking forward to seeing you guys again. Show last week at the armory was fucking insane good."

Gungnir just grunted, squinting ahead.

There was a cop in a light-blue poncho at the end of the drive, standing in the rain and directing the cars to turn around. Gungnir twisted slightly away, hiding his face. "Fucking pigs."

They turned, headed back out the twisting dirt road in silence, and soon were on the highway, coasting along 101 South through the redwoods.

Finally, Gungnir broke the awkward silence. "How do you know Geirskogul?"

"I don't really. Just met her at the show last week," Kevin said awkwardly.

"You like her, huh?"

Kevin glanced over at the huge man. He was staring straight ahead, somber, but Kevin could see his wide nostrils flaring. "Uh, yeah. You know. She's cool."

"Cool, huh?"

"Uh, yeah."

"You just seemed a little upset when I got in the car instead of her, is what I'm saying."

"What? No, man. As a matter of fact, I really wanted to meet you. I got your tape and I've been listening to it non-stop. I fucking love your voice and how you sing." Kevin pressed play on the tape player, grinding guitar and savage screaming came ripping out of the speakers. "See?"

"Mind if I ask you something personal?" Gungnir asked, turning to face him for the first time.

"No problem. Ask away."

"Why do you have that Jew's cross on your fucking head?"

Kevin coughed. Swallowed. Tried to focus his attention ahead. "The cross? The black cross on my forehead?"

"Yeah, the cross of the Jew Jesus."

"Well, it's inverted."

"Uh huh. Yeah? It's still a symbol of a Hebrew Messiah."

"But it's upside down, so, it's, like, satanic, man."

"Satanic? As in praising Satan?"

"Uh, yeah."

"Did you ever think by giving praise to Satan you are recognizing Christianity's Abrahamic domination over you? You're not really rebelling, but just giving them more power by acknowledging their gods."

"Huh. I don't know. I guess I never thought about it that way."

Then went back to silence. Headlights came up behind them, slipped past, trees silhouetted in the storm darting by.

"What is it that you like about metal music, Kevin?" Gungnir asked. "About black metal music in particular?"

"I don't know, man. I guess, like, the hardness. The

intensity."

"Exactly. The intensity, the *purity* of it. You like it because it's pure. There's a distilled essence to it. No bullshit. That's what you like, isn't it?"

Kevin thought about it, staring out at the storm, slipping through the tunnel of dark trees, and nodded. "Yeah, I guess so. It's stripped down, bare, no bullshit."

Gungnir smiled and gave his shoulder a friendly squeeze. "I thought so. You're a seeker of purity, Kevin. Just like me. But you've gotten sidetracked in their web. That's how thick their bullshit and dominion is: by trying to escape it you risk being tangled even further in it. I know. I've been there."

Kevin nodded. He couldn't deny what the guy was saying. Worshipping Satan *was* giving credence to Christianity, when he thought about it. He relished the rebellion and evil creepiness of it all, but it was really just the back of the same coin.

The tape ended with a squeal of haunting guitar feedback and then there was only the sound of the rain slashing down and the wipers softly clacking and squealing. The little town of Rio Dell slipped by them on the right, pointed rooves poking from the fog, and then they were passing Pacific Lumber, mountains of redwood logs waiting to be turned into lumber for decking and lawn chairs.

Gungnir ran a hand down his beard. "Us . . . we seek purity by going to the ancient religion of our own blood. Woden and Tiwaz, the European gods of old. This is our *true* origin, what that blasphemous Christianity wiped out. And the pure essence of that . . . is nature." He held a burly hand out, palm upwards, to the redwoods and ferns speeding by outside. "We find solace in the trees and the forest. But not in some bullshit hippie way. The forest contains multitude of darkness. It's a place of wonder, but also of struggle, of blood and bone. But where the true essence of life reveals itself. Turn off here."

Kevin slowed and took the Honey Dew/South Fork exit, the Eel River twisting below on their left, and veered onto a thin strip of blacktop snaking its way into the redwoods.

"My dad used to tell me stories about the Vikings," Kevin said.

"Really?" Gungnir asked. "Well I'd love to hear them!"

"I can only remember little bits now. He died when I was eight."

"I'm sorry to hear that, Kevin," Gungnir said, placing a hand on his shoulder. "I'm sure he was a good man."

They bumped along over the cracked asphalt for a while, and then Gungnir directed a thick finger off to a dirt road slinking up into the foggy hills on the right. "Up here. The road without a name!" The old station wagon bounced and heaved over the ruts, groaning up the steep incline.

"How far we going?" Kevin asked.

"Don't worry, you'll be home for dinner tonight."

They bounced along the muddy road, through the tall trees, past passages of clear cut, over hills.

"Easy," Gungnir said as they slid into a turn, then slipped past a busted-up gate and shotgun blasted sign, up a long driveway and down through tall alders and a tangle of whitethorn and to a tiny redwood-shingled cabin on a small flat surrounded by hundreds of black-plastic containers. Green garden hoses and thin lines of black tubing lay everywhere in a thick spider's web.

"Old pot farm," Gungnir said. "Owner gets busted, then never pays the land taxes and the county seizes the land, leaves these little cabins to just sit here and rot. Lots of 'em around ready for the squatting. Come inside a minute, kid, there's something I'd like to ask you." The big man winked at him before cracking open the door and lumbering out.

"Sure," Kevin said, as he shakily killed the engine and darted out into the rain after him. Gungnir hulked bear-like across the muddy abyss and to the cabin door, throwing it open and waving Kevin in.

It was musty and dank inside, lit only by the gray light breaking through the dirty windows. Gungnir stepped in and shut the door behind him, motioning to a tree stump by a wooden table of rough-hewn redwood slabs. "Have a seat. And here," he threw him a towel, "Dry off. You might want to wipe that shit off your face, too, it's wet and running everywhere." As Kevin toweled off his hair and scrubbed the corpse paint off his face, Gungnir went and squatted by the woodstove in the corner and began to make a fire.

Kevin looked around, there were candles and animal skins stretched everywhere. Drums and tambourines. An altar-like shelf of stones and amulets and a large steers horn. Jars of beans, bags of rice stowed in the corner beside a pile of Army field rations, pumpkins and odd-shaped squashes, big five-gallon glass carboys filled with cloudy liquid. Soon the fire was roaring, filling the place with warmth and strange shadows.

"Nice, huh?" Gungnir said. "People just use these places to grow weed and make money, not realizing they're living in paradise. What do you need money for if you can live here in nature, surviving off the land?"

Gungnir produced two mason jars from a shelf, pulled the cork from a large jug with his teeth, and filled them with a thick amber liquid with bits of plant matter floating in it. "Mead, made from local honey. Infused with damiana I harvested myself down in Texas." He lifted his glass with a beefy hand, the nails chipped and dirt crusted. "May Woden's wisdom light your pathways and part your shadows. Skål!"

Kevin nervously raised his glass and tapped it against Gungnir's, who let out a deep, growl-like laugh and tilted his glass up, swilling the elixir sloppily, liquid spilling down his thick beard, before slamming the jar down and filling it again.

Kevin sipped his cup cautiously. It was very sweet and fruity, but with a strong herbal flavor to it: minty and spicy, hickory like. He smiled at Gungnir. "It's really good. Thank you."

"You're most welcome, Kevin. And thank you so much for the ride, which is what I wanted to talk to you about. So, you have a valid driver's license, I assume?"

Kevin nodded.

"All up to date?"

Kevin continued to nod.

"See," Gungnir said, "problem is: none of us do, and some of us have some certain legal, ah, . . . issues we're dealing with it, making law enforcement a thing we're to avoid, if you know what I mean. So we could really use a driver. Someone to help us haul equipment. We can't pay you much, but you'd obviously get into all the shows, travel, meet a lot of girls, hear great music. But we offer you more than that, Kevin." He set his elbows on the table and leaned his big square forehead close. Kevin could smell his sweat and the fruity tang of the mead on his breath. "We offer you brotherhood. We're a family, but our beliefs are no joke. I must warn you, to us Valhalla, Woden these aren't just metaphors, they're real. And you must adhere to our ways if you decide to travel with us. Do you understand?"

Kevin nodded and swallowed, overcome as he realized something like this is what he'd craved ever since his father died. To be a part of something, accepted. To have a man like Gungnir to guide him. Someone to look up to.

Rain pattered against the roof and the fire crackled as the logs shifted, the room very warm now, the mead hot in his belly and gaseous and light in his brain.

Suddenly the door burst open and Geirskogul, Skuld and Skogul came barging in, laughing and screeching, rain drenched, water dripping from their dreads.

"Kevin!" Geirskogul shouted, her face lighting up when she spied him, holding up a dead racoon by the tail, shouting, "Behold the road kill-blessings Woden has bestowed! Found this poor little fellow on the side of the highway. He'll make a lovely stole!"

"Well, all right, the mead's already out!" Skuld exclaimed grabbing a glass, Skogul following suit.

Geirskogul had her big bowie knife out, and was sawing away at the tail of the racoon, tearing it loose, and wrapping a thin leather string around the fleshy base. "Come here, Kevin. I got something for you."

Kevin awkwardly got up from the table, pausing as she got down on her knees before him.

"Turn around," she said. "Go on, I'm not gonna bite ya."

Kevin turned and she pushed aside his cape, grasping his bullet belt, pulling him to her before winding the leather thong around the belt, yanking it taunt so that it hung down between his legs, then using her teeth to knot it off.

"There you go," she said. "Now you're a wild thing!"

Kevin beamed, the tail sprouting from him like something he was born with, and vowed to never take it off as long as he lived.

—

Kevin began driving their van for them, helping haul their rudimentary equipment up on stage, set it up and tear it down, working their little table selling merchandise.

Their shows were more like tribal gatherings than concerts, drawing Woden worshipers from throughout the Pacific Northwest, with a cross section of crust punks, goths and black-metal heads. It was a very underground scene, but surprisingly large. A huge network of different pagan communities that would come together for all sorts of festivals, parties and gatherings. They would play in the woods when they could, at National Parks, campgrounds or old hippie communes, and when they couldn't do that they'd play at Bowling Alleys, bars and community centers.

They started calling him Kvasir, taught him about the Gods of old. The Norse and Germanic Gods: Woden, Freyja, Frigg and Baldr. A change overcame him. He no longer thought of death and the devil anymore. He felt positive and full of life. He took down the black and white posters of the Norwegian black metal bands and replaced them with colorful images of nature and the gods of his new religion. Woden and Frigg. Thor, Loki, Balder, and Heimdall. He cut his long dyed-black hair to where it was growing in pale and golden.

Skuld and Skogul came to him one evening with some carved wooden drums, rawhide tops bound and stretched taut with thick rope and steel o-rings. "Oi, come with us, mate," Skogul said, offering him a small black hand drum.

They took him deep into the forest, over moss-covered logs, and down a ravine thick and downy with ferns. They sat by a running creek, and to the sound of water slipping over stone Skuld began to pound out a rudimentary beat, Skogul joining along, nodding his head in time. Kevin followed, slapping his hand against the percussive hand drum on each downbeat, letting his eyes slip shut as the rhythm filled him. Soon Skuld and Skogul were doing little rolls, filling the empty spaces with flourishes they traded back and forth, the sound like a giant creaking insect, echoing through the shadows of the tall redwood trees and Kevin was transported away to a primordial time and place.

They started taking him out with them all the time to get lost in their weird tribal rhythms. Sometimes to the beach, sometimes they'd hike high up into the mountains.

He really liked Skuld and Skogul. They were quiet, seemed to speak more with their eyes and their drums than with their mouths. But there was a sense of kindness to them. They never left each other's side, and their sense of brotherhood and the simple and obvious endearment they had for each other moved Kevin.

He began to gain a respect for the concept of family and a feeling of affection began to swell in him. He tried to spend more time with his own brother, take him places and talk to him more. He grew kinder to his mother and helped her by keeping their tiny apartment clean.

One day Gungnir approached him and laid one of his huge hands on his shoulder. "Kvasir, finding you was a great blessing, you've been such a help, and I want to thank you." He slipped him a few hundred-dollar bills. "Let this plunder be a token of our affection and gratitude," and he wrapped Kevin in his bear-like embrace, patting his back affectionately.

It was the most money Kevin had ever had at once. A

month's-worth of work at the record store. He spent the entire thing on groceries for his family. He felt so proud bringing them in the door to their apartment, setting those brown paper bags filled with food on the counter. He cooked them all green beans stewed with garlic and slivered almonds, pork chops fried in garlic butter and brown sugar-- smothered in a jar of homemade apple sauce Geirskogul had given him--his mother happily exclaiming about how his father had loved to cook just like him. He put a big metal tin of Hawaiian Punch on the table, punched a triangular hole in the top with a church key, and told his brother he could have as much as he wanted.

That was an amazing night, pride swelling in his chest as he watched his mother and brother feast on the bounty he'd brought home.

His mother licked grease from her lips and sat back in her chair, a beatific look of satisfaction on her face as she lit a Kool. "I have to admit," she said, "I like the direction you've taken this summer. Whatever you've been up to its been making you a good boy. No, not a good boy. A man. A good man. Your father would be proud."

Those words rang in his ears, reverberating like some great bell, and when his brother slurped down the last of his punch and let out a long deep burp, they all burst out into glorious laughter together.

—

It was a heady time.

Fenir's Wolf recorded an album in a dingy little basement studio and had a thousand compact discs burned. They made the covers themselves, Geirskogul drawing an amazing black-and-white picture of deer's skull, the antler's twisting into a tree-like maze of fractals that had Fenir's Wolf hidden within it.

The drawing spoke so much to Kevin, how the name, like the band itself, was hidden and only those who knew where to look could find it, puzzle out the mystery. It made such perfect sense: this music was only for the worthy. The initiated who could understand it for the magic that it was. There was a secretive, outlaw spirit to the whole thing, with a palpable sense of menace.

It was Kevin's job to fold each CD cover and slip it inside a plastic case with an oak leaf they'd gathered from the forest. He was sitting at the redwood table in the little cabin they squatted in, sweating as the fire blazed in the woodstove, a mountain of plastic CD cases on his left, a mound of xeroxed covers and a pile of oak leaves on his right, when the entire band somberly walked in the door, staring daggers at him. He was used to Gungnir's grumpy-bear demeanor, but it was odd to not have Skuld and Skogul smiling and waving at him, affectionately calling him brother in their thick Aussie accents.

"Hey, guys," he said, trying to sound casual. He pressed a folded paper cover into the plastic guides, tucked an oak leaf on top, shut the case and set it on the pile and reached for another as they circled him, faces stern: Gungnir in the center, massive arms folded over his swollen chest, Geirskogul beside him in a pale-blue peasant's gown, Skuld and Skogul to the side in their furry vests with bone buttons.

"Kvasir," Gungnir said, his voice grim and betraying no emotion. "We have talked amongst ourselves of you and it has been decided. We want to make you one with the tribe, officially bring you into the fold."

Kevasir's breath caught in his throat, and he felt a great smile break across his face.

Gungnir lifted a palm-facing hand. "Be not glad yet, young one. You will be tested. There will be a ritual which you cannot fail. Do you understand?"

"Yes," Kvasir said, knowing he must speak the affirmation.

Geirskugul narrowed those alluring eyes of hers and grinned devilishly. "A sacrifice of blood and fire is demanded. Prepare yourself."

—

They blindfolded him and drove him far, far away, pouring chunky ceremonial mead down his throat the entire time. The honey wine had a dirty, earthy taste to it, and he guessed it was the psychedelic mushrooms he'd heard them talking about, for his mind was soon spinning. He reminded himself he was a warrior and to remain focused. He could do this. Pass this test into manhood.

The old van bumped along gravel roads for what felt like ages, going uphill. He could hear the slosh of liquid beside him and the stink of gasoline was overwhelming. Finally they stopped. He heard the door slide open and then he was pushed stumbling out blind into the cool night air. Frogs creaked loudly. From somewhere very, very far away a dog barked. And, oh yeah, he was definitely tripping, strange kaleidoscope patterns filling his head.

He could sense them circling him, faintly hear their footsteps and breaths. Then one came very near, he could smell the sour breath and sweat of Gungnir. "Heil og sael, Kvasir."

"Heil og sael, Gungnir," Kevin said back.

"Kvasir! What are the nine noble virtues?"

His lips felt too thick, his tongue too large to speak, and his mind swam through a sea of colors and stars, but he could do this. "Gungnir, spear of Woden," he said, "the nine noble virtues as stated in the Havamal are courage, truth, honor, fidelity, discipline, hospitality, self-reliance, industriousness, and perseverance."

"Correct," Gungnir said, and Kevin could sense him stepping away from him.

Then there was that sweet voice of the Viking guitar angel, Geirskogul, whispering, her breath hot in his ear. "What should you never reproach one for, according to the wisdom of Woden?" she asked.

He hesitated for a fraction of a second, then spoke. "Love. For beauty ensnares with desire the wise, while the foolish remain unmoved."

Then so close her lips brushed against his ear, "Very,

very good, Kvasir," her hand against the back of his neck, fingers snaking up seductively into his hair for the briefest moment before slipping away.

Skuld's playful voice, tinged with that Australian accent, "How did Loki appease the vengeance of Skadi, then, eh?"

"With laughter. He made her laugh."

"Righto, he did."

And finally Skogul asking, "And how many days did Father Woden hang from the cosmic tree Yggdrasil?"

"Nine days. Woden hung upside down from Yggdrasil nine days with no food or water."

There was clapping and cheers and his blindfold was ripped from his face.

Kevin blinked into the night. They were standing in the middle of a dirt parking lot before an old white-clapboard church. Kevin stared at the rickety, paint-peeling steeple looming up into the stars, a vertiginous sensation filling him. His mind swam in a puddle of mushrooms and mead. It was as if everything was embroidered on some slowly turning tapestry, the moon and stars, the earth, the church. Then the leering faces of Fenir's Wolf were everywhere as they closed in, thrusting a squirming, struggling rodent-like creature at him.

Gungnir grasped the thing's two front paws, spreading them apart so that its soft down chest bloomed like a white flower. Skuld and Skogul each yanked on a leg, stretching the wriggling beast out to its full length.

Geirskogul sidled up beside him, pressing her body against his, reaching down to grasp the handle of her knife and slowly sliding it free of its sheath. "Spill its blood," she said, taking his hand and pressing the knife handle into his palm, gently closing his fingers over it. "Kill it."

A slow chant of "Kill it, kill it, kill it," went up amongst them as Kvasir slowly lifted the knife, the sharp edge shimmering in the starlight, and held it poised above the squirming creature.

It was a rabbit. A big old jack rabbit with long ears and

huge yellow eyes that blinked fearfully into the night as it jerked its head back-and-forth. It wrinkled its nose as it turned its face and looked at him, eyes narrowing. Its tiny pink tongue darted out, licking its lips, and then it spoke. "What are you doing?" it asked as it craned its neck to peer at its captors with those strange yellow eyes. "You don't really trust these people, do you?"

Kvasir blinked and ground his teeth.

"Don't listen to the rabbit," Geirskogul said, her face fierce and eerie in the strange light of the weird psychedelic night. Reality seemed to be slowly melting around her, dripping in molten droplets like hot candle wax, spilling to the ground about her feet. "Do it," she said, eyes half shut, her full lips wet and parted. She laid her open palm against his chest, pressed. "Do it. Stab the bunny. The Blot Ceremony demands a blood sacrifice."

His heart hammered beneath her outstretched fingers and the scent of her wafted up, filling his nose and face— sweet and fruity, yet savory and raw, deeply sexual and filled with pheromones and musk—and an electric jolt surged through him as he gripped the hard shaft in his sweaty palms. He shuddered and thrust the blade down into the soft furry belly of the bunny. The pink skin parted easily and the knife slipped into the warm wet insides. He gasped and with a moan jerked the blade free, then brought it back again, the rabbit thrashing and jerking. And again he brought the knife down, and again, until finally the bunny went limp and still, head and ears hanging flaccid and lifeless.

Geiskogul squealed with delight and ran her hand over the gash, slipping a finger inside the rabbit. Pulling her blood drenched finger from the belly, she smiled seductively and touched it to her tongue. "Welcome to the tribe," she said to Kevin and smeared a streak of rabbit's blood beneath his eyes.

"Oi, welcome to the family, mate!" Skuld said, giving him a hug before grabbing a red-plastic gasoline can and skipping towards the church.

"Welcome, brother," Skogul said, smiling his funny

crooked grin and wrapping an arm around his shoulder.

Gungnir produced a thick wooden branch, its end wrapped tightly in gas-soaked cloth, pressed it to Kevin's chest. With the strike of a match the torch burst into flame. "Now, as a symbol of erasing the false god forced upon us, in veneration of Woden, our true ancestral father, we will burn this church to the motherfucking ground. Go ahead, brother, go forth and set it alight."

Kevin looked up to see Skuld splashing gasoline against the church door and spilling it around its foundation.

He took the torch, the world swirling about him, and stalked to the church, the earth upending itself and melting around him. He stooped and touched the flame to the black puddle before the church's doorway and a ball of flame erupted from the stillness of the night, roaring and knocking him backwards into the arms and laughter of Fenir's Wolf who danced and cheered as the fire crackled and embers spun upwards into the dark skies.

And it was all howling and singing and crazy feral frolicking and mead and mushrooms and comets and black rainbows to other lands beyond our own.

And then they were back at the cabin. Candles flickered about the small room like dancing fireflies, constellations throwing off amber waves of light and shadow as Gungnir took the ceremonial horn from the shelf and filled it with mead.

Kevin was perched up on a tall chair like a king upon a throne, blood running down his face, Geirskogul curled on his lap, one hand pressed against his chest, the other tapping an ink-stained needle into the flesh below his eyes.

Skuld and Skogul were smoking a joint—the earthy, skunky scent like that of a primordial forest, a land beyond time—and the pale smoke hung like antediluvian mists, curling about them.

Gungnir raised the sacred horn vessel in a toast. "To Kvasir, who is now one with us. Welcome."

Skuld and Skogul lifted their fists, bellowing with agreement, "Here! Here!" and emotion washed over Kevin, his eyes growing hot and swollen, tears spilling down and mixing with the ink and blood.

"Does it hurt?" Geirskogul asked, craning her neck to look into his eyes, her face so gorgeous, her lips so close to his.

He shook his head. "No, it doesn't hurt at all." And she smiled, dipped the tip of the needle in a pot of ink and pierced him again, and he wondered what it would be like to kiss her. Taste the lips of this fallen angel, this earthly Valkyrie, so wild and feral and pure in her beauty. If he could kiss her, just once, he felt he could maybe die happy, that all the suffering and bullshit of this shitty life would be worth it.

—

His mother cried when she saw the tattoos.

She was at the kitchen table reading a tabloid and drinking coffee. He came in with an arm full of groceries, set them on the counter, and she looked at him, coffee mug frozen halfway to her mouth. "Tell me they're not real."

"They're real, mother."

She let out a hiccupping cry and, sobbing, ran from him and to her bedroom, slamming the door behind her.

But his brother liked them, popping up from his position prone on the rug before the television and running over. "Cool!" he exclaimed. "Do they mean something?"

He showed Brian what each symbol meant, the björk symbolizing spring and new life, the reio symbolizing his journey, how together they deemed him a poet and wiseman, and watching his brother's rapt face, eyes wide with wonder, he realized that for so long in trying to replicate his father he'd only been trying to replicate the hole in his heart his father had left. He'd been trying to give more emptiness instead of filling the void. He understood that now, and yearned to heal that wound, to be there for him.

As they sat there at the kitchen table, he told his little brother all the ancient tales of the old gods and their drama and ways, just as their father had once told the tales to him.

He felt whole and complete, keeping a culture alive and being the conduit for scriptures and esoteric histories. This sense of completeness and sentimentality filled his eyes with heat and tears and, overcome, he grabbed his brother and wrapped his arms around him, pressed his cheek against the top of his brother's head and told him how much he loved him. Told him things were going to be different from now on, and that from now on Brian would be known as Baldr.

And then he told him everything else, things he had promised he would never tell another living soul.

—

It wasn't the first time he had asked that his brother be taken into the fold. He'd mentioned it before and the response had always been the same: No. He was too young.

Apparently, they'd debated over whether to even bring Kvasir into the tribe. In the end they said it was his passion and love of music that had convinced them, but he was as young as they were willing to go. Anyone younger couldn't be trusted with the secrets of the sect. Their rituals and hidden ways. But this time Kevin felt emboldened to push it further, to give his plea more strength. He was, after all, now an official member of the tribe, the scabs on his face still fresh and painful.

They were sitting around the woodstove, Gungnir drinking mead, Geirskogul lying beside him, strumming a small lyre, Skuld and Skogul in the shadows, tapping their feet and passing a joint back and forth.

"We've told you before," Gungnir said. "Your brother is too young for the tribe. Let it be, you are disturbing the tranquility of the mead hall."

"But I've taught him well. He knows all our beliefs and customs. Everything."

"Everything?" Gungnir asked, his face hardening as Geirskogul stopped playing and set the harp aside. Skuld dropped the roach he was hitting and crushed it with the toe of his boot. Kevin hesitated and for a long moment there was only the sound of the fire crackling, before Gungnir spoke again.

"I asked you a question, boy."

Kevin looked at his shoes, scratched his leg. "Yes. Everything." The implication was clear. He'd told of that which was not to be mentioned: the burning of the churches, their most sacred rite. But it wasn't to a stranger. It was to his own brother! His own flesh and blood. They had to understand that.

Gungnir began to tremble. He stood, went to the shelf and placed the horn upon it, his nostrils flaring. Fear and doubt flooded Kevin's blood. *Was telling his brother a mistake?*

But then Geirskogul sat up and spoke. "Hasn't Kvasir always been loyal? Hasn't he been true to the tribe. I say we bring his brother in, give him what he wants." She strode to Gungnir, rested her hand on his shoulder and whispered into his ear.

Gungnir nodded, arms crossed across his broad chest, fair-haired Valkyrie whispering in his ear, his eyes locked on Kevin. "All right. We will discuss it amongst the band, and let you know when we come to a decision. Until then no more talk of it."

Geirskogul smiled at Kevin, her eyes sparkling, but brows and lips sharp, predatory and hawk-like.

"Thank you," Kvasir said. "Thank you."

—

Kvasir didn't hear from them for a couple days and began to grow worried. *Had he gone too far?* They wouldn't kick him out of their tribe, *would they?* Or maybe just abandon him?

He knew they could pack up and leave at any moment, it was their nature. They often talked about all the different places they'd lived and left— Austin Texas, Telluride Colorado, Madison Wisconsin— and there had been talk of them hitting the road again. The thought of them leaving him behind made his heart grow cold and still.

But then his mother was telling him he had a phone call and Geirskogul's heavenly voice was telling him congratulations, he was going to get what he wanted. There was going to be a big party, an Althing Gathering, with other tribes of Woden worshippers coming from all over, and for the blot ritual there would be a goat they would kill and roast. It was to be on a secluded beach, far up the coast, in Southern Oregon. He was to come early. And bring his brother.

—

Kvasir and his little brother sat waiting on the beach, watching as the sun slipped down into the ocean, a brilliant ball of molten red melting into the vast waters. As darkness crept over the cove and there was still no sign of anyone, he worried for a moment that they were in the wrong place, that he'd somehow misread the instructions Geirskogul had given him, but then he heard the faint beating of distant drums and saw a procession of torches slinking down the cliff-side trail.

They were led by Geirskogul and Gungnir who marched with the noble manner of royalty, Skuld and Skogul following behind beating a somber dirge on dark drums hanging from their shoulders. There were many others that Kvasir did not recognize, a dozen or so, bearded men, women in peasant blouses and leather pinafores. As he and his brother rose, they encircled them. Two five-gallon carboys of mead were placed in the circle, long torches stuck in the sand illuminated the scene with orange and red coruscating light. The pounding of the drums ceased and an eerie quiet fell upon them, punctuated only by the crashing of the waves.

Gungnir stood arms crossed with his stern, bear-like demeanor, while Geirskogul paced back-and-forth before him.

Her beauty always unnerved Kevin and made him feel foolish and childlike, but tonight there was a very intense fierceness to her, a cold and grim look in her eyes that chilled him deeply. He tried to appear strong, lifted his chin and spoke steadily. "Heil og sael, Geirskogul,"

"Heil og sael, Kvasir," she murmured back, slowly unsheathing her knife.

"Where's the goat?" he asked. "I thought we needed a blood sacrifice for the Blot."

"Oh, we have our goat," Geirskogul said, spinning forward and stretching an arm out, the knife point mere inches from his face. "Kvasir! Do you remember the nine noble virtues?"

Was this some kind of test? He could sense his little brother growing uneasy beside him and placed a hand on his back to reassure him. If this was a test, he would pass. He was Kvasir, the wise one.

"Geirskogul, chooser of the slain, the nine noble virtues as stated in the Havamal are courage, truth, honor, fidelity, discipline, hospitality, self-reliance, industriousness, and perseverance."

"Correct," she said, leering, her white teeth catching the light of the torches and staining her mouth an orange and amber hue. "But what is the greatest commandment in the law?"

"The greatest commandment is the proscription of oath-breaking."

"Very good, Kvasir. Very good indeed."

Kvasir felt relief. *Had he passed the test?*

Geirskogul stepped back and continued pacing, gently slapping the belly of the knife against her palm. "So, Kvasir, did you not take an oath of loyalty to this tribe?"

"Yes."

"Did we not make you part of our family?"

"Yes."

"Did we not name you and mark you so that you were reborn as one of us?"

"Yes."

"When you wanted to bring your brother into the tribe did we not tell you, 'No'? That he was too young? That he couldn't be trusted with the secrets of our sect?"

"Yes, but he's no stranger, he's my—"

"Shut your mouth, traitor!" and she flashed out her knife and nicked his cheek. The cut stung and a trickle of blood wept out. For the first time he felt doubt and real fear flood through him.

"But you insisted, she continued. "You were sworn to secrecy and you told him of our doings. An outsider! You have broken your oath!"

Kevin struggled not to weep, but could feel the tears and snot rising up in him, and he wondered if maybe he should throw himself at her feet and beg forgiveness. Mercy. But no, he had to be strong. Had to adhere to the ways of Woden, be a warrior. This had to be some kind of test. They were testing him. He had to remain steadfast and stalwart.

"But he's not an outsider. He's my brother. My blood. My family."

Geirskogul was shaking her head sadly, testing the tip of her knife against her finger. "Family, huh?" she said, and laughed, cocked her pretty head so that her dreads streamed down behind her like a cloak. "*We're* supposed to be your family. I'm just curious, you know. What the fuck were you thinking? How could you have done this to us? Forced us to this point? Wasn't I pretty enough for you? Weren't Skuld and Skogul brothers enough for you? Wasn't Gungnir enough of a father for you? I found you, I cultivated you. I tried to make you one with us. But what do you do? Revert back to your family? Your mommy and little brother? We're supposed to be your new family! Us. You took an oath and made a bond. And you know, Kvasir, I blame you for this.'

"For what?"

"For what's about to happen."

Brian began to shake and whimper now. "Kevin, I want to go home," he said. "I'm scared."

"It's okay," Kevin replied. "This is just a test."

"Oh, it's a test all right," Geirskogul, said. "But it's also a Blot Ceremony demanding sacrifice and blood." And she shot out a hand, grasping Brian by the wrist and pulling him to her as she brought her knife to his neck, holding it threateningly there. Kevin lunged forward, desperate to do something, anything, but Gungnir was there, holding him back with one of his massive hands.

"Help me, Kevin," Brian whimpered.

"Silence," Geirskogul said, slipping a hand up over his mouth. "There's going to be a sacrifice. An outsider has been told our rituals and must die. Now, Kvasir, you can either participate and live, or fight it and join him. But either way he dies. So, what's it going to be?"

Gungnir pressed a bowie knife into Kevin's hand. "Do it, Kvasir. Slay the rabbit."

"Come on," Geirskogul whispered, grasping Brian tight and licking her lips. "You know you want to do it. Just like the bunny. And then we'll be together forever. Nothing can break a bond like that. Do it for me. Do it to prove you love us. Your new family."

Kevin looked about at the leering faces all around him. Searching for any glimmer of sympathy or kindness. He saw Skuld there, but he just nodded his head as if to say, "Go on, then," and started a slow beat on the drum. Not knowing what else to do, Kevin stepped forward, tears streaming down his face, and shakily raised the knife. He stared at his brother's heaving chest, avoiding his wild pleading eyes, and with a grunt struck out, slicing Geirskogul across the wrist of her knife hand.

She cried out in surprise, dropping her knife, and Brian struggled free.

"Run, Brian, run!" Kevin screamed, spinning and slashing at Gungnir, who stepped back and laughed at him, batting the knife away.

"Good for you, Kvasir!" Gungnir said, a huge smile plastered across his bear-like face. "A noble and unwinnable fight is a sure way through the gates of Valhalla."

Then Kevin's nose exploded as Gungnir's fist slammed squarely into it, sending him sprawling into the sand. A million hands reached out, everyone grabbing him and hauling him off the ground, spinning him so that he was upside down, and he watched in horror as Geirskogul came dragging his brother screaming down the beach towards him by the hair.

She knelt in the sand and grabbed Kevin by the face, squeezed his cheeks, blood and snot streaming and bubbling from his shattered nose. "Oh, you stupid, sad little boy. I brought you in and it looks like I'm going to have to take you out. But first, I want to give you what you wanted." She pulled Brian closer. "You want your brother to know our ways? To grasp the mysticism, understand the scripture of the All Father? Well there's a price to drinking from the well of Urd."

"No," Kevin pleaded, gurgling through all the blood and phlegm. "Please don't hurt him. I'll do anything."

"It's too late for that, Kvaisr," she said and with a gleeful glint in her eye she jerked her knife up, the tip catching Brian's left eye, and dug it in. Brian howled and shrieked, desperately clawing at his face as she laughed and carved, pulling the orb free, grasping it up and slicing away the deep-red muscles and tendons. She stepped to one of the big bottles of mead, leaving Brian in a weeping ball in the sand, and plopped the eyeball into the vessel. It bobbed and floated there in the oily liquid, a trail of nerves and tendons hanging from it. "Now hang him from a tree. Let him experience Yggdrasil and the connection of the nine worlds. Then he will know our ways."

"Sorry, mate," Skuld whispered to Kevin as he and Skogul grabbed Brian up, "just the way it goes." They dragged Brian screaming across the beach to where a massive Cyprus tree jutted from the rock and sand. Kevin could see them, shadowy figures, duct-taping his squirming brother upside-down in the tree's branches like a spider wrapping a struggling fly in its web.

"As for you, Kvasir," Geirskogul said, wiping a streak of blood from her knife with a finger before running it down her tongue. "Oh, wise one, since there are no questions you cannot answer, your sacrifice will be to the Mead of Poetry, so that the tribe may drink of it and share in your knowledge."

She grabbed a fistful of his hair and jerked his head

back, held his chin in the cradle of her palm, the sharp blade of her knife pressed to the soft skin of his throat. "Goodbye, my love," she said, "sorrowfully slipping from us like a sparrow's flight through the mead hall," and she kissed him. Brought her lips slowly to his, soft and moist, parting to let her tongue gently slip into his bloody mouth. She tasted of ambrosia, nectar, of stars and space and mystery, of the sea and sand and wonder and all the mysteries of life, and, intoxicated by her kiss, for one brief instant he felt strangely fulfilled, oddly content, and he smiled as she ran the blade across his throat, opening it wide with the ease of opening a window on a fine spring day to let the breeze in.

Blood poured from the gash, splashing down into the carboys, mixing with the mead: a dark crimson rose blooming in the pale-yellow liquid, and when he was drained, they heaved him away, throwing him—gurgling and quivering—to twitch in the hard sand by the ocean's edge.

Gungnir stepped into the circle with his ornamental horn. He tilted a blood streaked carboy over it, spilling bloody mead into the vessel and then raising it to the heavens, and shouting, "The traitor has been punished and the outsider banished. Let the Sumbel begin! To my brothers and sisters, it is with valor that we celebrate this night! May we all die with our knives bloody and reunite in Valhalla so that we may drink and fight and fuck together again and again for all eternity!"

A great cheer rose up from the crowd as Gungnir drank, the mixture of blood and honey wine spilling from the corners of his mouth and dripping down his thick dreadlocked beard. The others surged forward to fill their cups and make glorious toasts, to swear their allegiance to the gods of old as Kvasir's body lay lifeless and still in the sand, growing cold and pale, as his brother squirmed in the distance, crucified, upside down, to the cosmic tree that connects the nine worlds.

And so it was that the old ways returned to the world and the ancient tales became truths once again.

MALL SANTA

Fuck that bitch, Trish thought as the light changed from yellow to red. She stomped on the gas, sending her Civic careening through the intersection, horns blaring. Her wheels skidded on the ice and the little car lilted out of control. Undaunted, Trish downshifted, cranked the wheel, and swerved through the light. Chomping on a stale piece of gum while hanging her middle finger to all the honking assholes, she whispered over her shoulder to Jenny—bundled in her car seat in the back, yanking at the hair of a naked Barbie doll.

"Don't worry, honey, I'll get you there."

Trish had to get her to the mall before Santa left.

She screeched into the Bayshore parking lot, a busy hive of headlights and shoppers. The fan to the heater was broken—Ronnie insisting he'd be the one to fix it, like being a technician assistant at Auto Lube made him a master mechanic—so it was freezing in the car. Her breath came out in pale, wet clouds as she eased the vehicle to a crawl, and began searching for a spot that wasn't a fucking mile away from the entrance. The clock was ticking.

This was her chance at a new beginning. She'd already posted on Facebook that she was on her way, and she'd be humiliated if she didn't get there on time. Becca, Annie, and Monica had already posted pictures of their toddlers on the lap of the mall Santa, and the amount of likes and comments they had received was fucking nuts. A good picture of Jenny on the lap of jolly St. Nick could give her a big boost, get her the respect she deserved from the other mothers at the preschool. Snobby bitches.

And then, right by the main entrance, a shiny minivan pulled out of a spot.

Rock star parking!

Trish waited, clacking her gum against her back molars, fingers nervously tap-tapping on the wheel to the beat of a Lady Gaga song, when—*motherfucker!*—an SUV cut in front of her and stole the space.

Fucking bullshit!

She slammed her palm against the horn and flipped her off, and as the yuppie-wannabe, bleach-blonde cunt pulled out her own toddler from the backseat, the stupid bitch smiled and shrugged, blew Trish a kiss.

—

The festive red-and-green Christmas lights of the mall bloomed like an oasis of light against the night as Trish hustled across the frozen parking lot. Jenny was perched on her hip, little arms clutching her neck. A small flurry of snow fell from the sky, glowing in the tall lights, dusting the rows of cars. People were leaving in droves and she had to push her way through them to get in the entrance.

When the first parent—Jessica Knicks, a quiet mousy lady—had asked to be her friend on Facebook, Trish thought nothing of it. She hadn't thought much about the other mothers at the daycare. But then more requests began to trickle in, and the other mothers' posts started appearing on her feed, and she'd noticed something, a sort of hierarchy of who had the cutest photos, who looked the nicest. Her own posts got a distinct lack of likes. And sometimes an odd comment could be taken so many ways: a simple "nice," no capital letters, no exclamation points, no emoji. How was she supposed to take that? She didn't know whether to like it, give it a heart, or what.

One morning when she was dropping off Jenny, another mom—Angela—said to her, "I saw your party on Facebook. Cute photos," and there was a tone to her voice. The other mothers sounded fake as shit, all the time, because they were, but this had a tone of cattiness she hadn't heard since high school. And then later that night, curled up on the sofa with her phone, sipping a Bud Light tall boy, Trish went through her own posts with a new eye, and, *damn*, some of her shit was tacky. Not only blurry and out of focus, but down right trashy:

—Ronnie and his grease monkey buddies sitting around a keg, Ronnie crazy-eyed and probably high on meth, holding up an overflowing red-plastic cup, head craned so that the SS lightning bolts tattooed on his neck took up half the frame.

Delete.

—Ronnie's mom in a fringed Iron Maiden shirt, grinning crazily and missing more than a couple teeth as she swings a terrified Jenny by the arms.

Delete.

—Jenny sitting in the homemade baby pool Ronnie had fashioned out of an old refrigerator in their yard.

Definitely delete.

That's when it all began, the need for the perfect shot, one that conveyed the right amount of class, sass, and cuteness:

—Forcing Jenny to sit cherub-like on a tree branch, yelling at her, "Smile! A *real* smile, you're just grimacing!"

—Posing fashionably by a lake.

—Sitting childishly by a mound of raked-up autumn leaves.

—Gleefully putting a carrot nose on a little snowman.

It grew into an obsession.

Trish began to plan future posts. Lying in bed at night, staring at the water stain on the ceiling, she'd imagine Jenny in a pretty dress, planting nasturtiums and marigolds, swimming in a gleaming-blue pool in a new bathing suit—not hanging out of a broken-down refrigerator in one of Trish's old Guns N' Roses shirts.

The back end of the mall was dark. Only the dollar store remained open. The rest of the shops—Borders, Sunset Video, Pretzel Company—had all gone out of business.

When she saw the tree and lights and Santa atop his throne in the distance, she thought of her father and her heart did some weird thing: pounding in her chest and filling her face with heat. It was her father who had always taken her to see Santa as a little girl. She could still remember his logger smell of gas and trees. And her parents had always put that picture of her on Santa's lap on the refrigerator door, every year.

Something clicked. It all made sense. Facebook was like the refrigerator door, a place to pin what you wanted others to see.

Jenny was getting heavy and so she put her down.

The little girl yawned, rubbed her eyes, and said, "Mommy, I'm tired."

Trish licked her thumb and scrubbed at a smear on her daughter's cheek. "I know, baby. We just gotta see Santa real quick." She then took her by the hand and tugged her along the final thirty feet to the North Pole.

A small gaggle of parents waited in line between two giant candy canes, Santa waiting upon his throne. As Trish strutted up to the other moms, dragging Jenny along behind her, a tall, redheaded teenager-looking dude—wearing an elf suit much too small for him—stepped up and clicked a frayed-velvet rope barricade across the entrance.

"Sorry," the douchebag said with a hideous bucktoothed grin. He wore thick glasses, a Band-Aid on his chin. "Eight o'clock, no more visitors tonight. Santa has lots of work to do!"

Really? Trish thought, putting a hand on her hip.

She cocked her head, snarled at the gangly ginger elf and said, "What? You gotta be kidding me. Come on, dude, let me in."

"Sorry. Can't. See, the cash register's all locked up and shut down for the night. We open again at eleven tomorrow morning."

"Yeah?" Trish asked, waggling a finger. "Well, I can't be here tomorrow. Some of us have real fucking jobs. Unlike *you* people."

The elf frowned and squinted. "Us ... *elf* people?"

Trish was about to respond—to throw down some hardcore shit on this stupid elf-ass motherfucker—when she spotted the bleach-blonde bitch who had stolen her space. The woman stood just ahead of her in line. And the bitch was looking right at her, smirking, lifting a hand and giving her a tiny wave before turning her back on her.

"Fuck you, cunt!" Trish screamed, rage exploding within her like a lit-up gas-soaked rag.

"Ma'am, you're going to have to leave," the elf said, his stupid freckled face looking all serious and concerned.

"What the fuck are you going to do, you stupid ginger?" Trish ground her teeth, spitting the words out from a clenched jaw. "You gonna tell Santa on me? Put me on the naughty list?"

She could feel Jenny hiding behind her, clutching her leg.

"Mommy, what's happening?"

"This pea-brained ginger elf won't let us see Santa. That's what's happening, sweetie."

The elf crossed his arms and stood up straight. "If you don't leave right this instant, I'm calling mall security."

"Yeah, well *fuck you*, elf boy. I'm going, okay? I'm going."

She scooped Jenny up by her armpits, tucked her against her shoulder, and glared at the elf, then turned on her heel, striding away.

But then her ankle bent all wrong, her foot slipping sideways across the slick linoleum floor—wet from the melted snow. She tried to right herself, over compensated, and pitched forward. She hung in the air with both feet off the ground a moment before she fell, watching horrified as Jenny propelled from her arms. Her daughter floated upward and away, then slammed down squarely on the top of her head with a gut-wrenching *crack!*

Sprawled on her belly, Trish screamed and crawled to her.

Blood oozed from her daughter's head and into her curly locks of pale hair, her eyes blinking once then closing.

"Jenny? Jenny? Are you okay? Jenny?"

The little girl gave a low moan, but her eyes remained shut.

Trish looked about her at everyone slack-jawed and frozen in place: the gangly ginger elf, the bleach-blonde bitch, the other parents in line, even Santa up on his throne in his red cloak, white-bearded and god-like, everyone staring.

She shrieked, her breath hitching in her chest and coming out in sharp bursts.

"Isn't anyone going to help me?"

As if awoken from a daze, the elf jerked, then yanked a phone from his pocket and began frantically swiping a long pale finger across the screen.

—

The ambulance ride was like some strange dream, everything happening both too slowly and too quickly: Jenny strapped to a gurney, neck in a brace, still unconscious, but muttering under shallow breaths, the sound of the siren, the spinning lights reflecting patterns on everything outside the windows, the antiseptic and sterile smell of bandages and solutions, the paramedics' questions about past illnesses, allergies, previous surgeries, tetanus.

Then Jenny was on a stretcher, wheeled into the hospital, ushered through a maze of crowded halls, and put into a big machine to examine her head. They were looking for dark spots and bruising in the brain, fluid, swelling, inflammation, hemorrhaging, and other crazy things she didn't understand which sounded terrifying, *hydrocephalus* and *ventricles*, like strange words from science fiction movies.

Waiting for the doctor to return with the test results was agony.

Trish sat in that tiny white room—Jenny laying there with her mouth slightly open, head wrapped in bandages—with her mind racked with worry, brimming. She blamed herself for causing the scene, for being so careless, for being so obsessed with fucking Facebook and how she appeared to other people and what others thought of her. And she vowed to change, to be a better mom, to be a better person ...

But then the doctor returned, smiling, telling her that the MRI looked fine.

Relief flooded through her with a physical force, like a great rush of water cascading through her, then leaving her weightless as Jenny opened her eyes, blinking and asking for her.

"Am I all right, Mommy?"

Trish grasped her daughter's hand and smiled.

"Yes, you're fine," she said. And it was a fine moment. A beautiful moment. A tremendously heart-breaking moment. One of the greatest moments of Trish's life. And Trish thought to herself, *I should take a picture and post this on Facebook.*

THE HAPPIEST MAN IN THE WORLD

It was supposed to be a standard drug bust.

Your average pill-mill situation: corrupt croaker doctor handing out scripts of OxyContin and Xanax for cash and favors. The Sheriff's Department, where I was a deputy, were to assist the DEA—which was protocol since it was originally our case, and also a courtesy since we were the ones who had alerted them to it in the first place. I was sent mostly to observe, that and help catalogue and transport all the evidence, which was bound to be a huge haul. Word was there were piles of cash and pills laying all over, stacks of pre-signed prescription pads waiting to be sold, boxes of files. Every item was going to have to be catalogued. The doctor was apparently using too, and the place was supposed to be a real mess.

And then there was the basement.

Of course, we'd been warned about what might be in the basement, what horrors we might find, but it was more horrible than any of us could imagine.

The basement was where the abortions were performed. You see, it was a pill mill by day and unlicensed, underground abortion clinic by night. Mostly women in the third trimester with nowhere else to turn. The desperate and poverty stricken. Or very young girls, hiding their predicament, scared and alone. We'd heard the rumors and whispers. Nasty stories of hastily performed operations with dirty instruments, of how he'd give near term women Cytotek and have them miscarry in the toilet. How he'd scoop the squirming fetuses from the dirty water and snip their spines with a scissor.

I'd only been a sheriff's deputy a few months at that point. It'd been a tough few years for me. After Amanda's death, I'd been in a dangerously dark place. Still so painful to think about, yet it's never far from my thoughts. Lingering there like a festering kernel of lead in my brain, causing a gangrene of the soul.

Fuck, how it haunts me. That terrible head-on collision with that damn drunk asshole (three previous DUIs on his record, if the crash hadn't killed him, I swear to God I would have found him and done the job myself) on that horrible, horrible winter night, leaving me a widower at thirty-two.

The doctors all agreed it was a miracle I'd lived.

I can remember lying there in the hospital, surrounded by ticking machines, tubes and wires running everywhere, my body wrapped in bandages and held fast by armatures. Lost in a morphine drip, I just kept thinking, *Why? Why spare me? Why couldn't I have been killed, too?*

The shit I'd been through as a soldier, the chances I'd taken, walking through minefields and facing sniper fire in godforsaken desserts, only to come home and have my wife and unborn son taken from me by something as mundane as a car accident.

I didn't want to live without her. And for a while I seriously contemplated ways to remedy that situation. Going back to the house was hell, all the pictures of Amanda and I together, so many of her pregnant and showing off her bulging belly. I couldn't stand to look at them, and I couldn't bear to take them down either, to touch them. I'd been in the heart of battle, seen unimaginably horrible things, but nothing was worse than staring at a picture of Amanda with her swollen belly, me beside her, but not me, a former me, the me I used to be.

I'd avoid them when I could, but if one caught my gaze, I'd find myself staring for hours, imagining those wonderful times, reverie and nostalgia like a physical weight atop me, like one of those lead-filled blankets they drape over you during an X-ray.

Our golden retriever Daisy, (named by Amanda because her golden coat reminded her of the center of that simple yet lovely flower) was some consolation. Her warm, kind eyes, so obviously thrilled to see me, tail thudding against the floor in such a happy beat. But even she could be difficult to look at times, so filled with memories she was. It was hard to see her and not think of Amanda.

About a month after I got out of the hospital, my Uncle won his bid for sheriff. Won in a landslide, actually. The last guy had been wrapped up in some scandalous shit. Uncle Ross took pity on me, took me on as a full-time deputy. Not that I wasn't qualified. I was more than qualified. Former first-class officer combat veteran having served in Falujah and Kabul. But pity on me in that it was no secret I'd suffered a long series of trauma and tragedy, both on the battlefield and off, and bore the effects.

You hear it called the hundred-yard stare. Shit, I had that before losing Amanda. My stare had gone infinite.

It was like I was trying to see between things and beyond things: part of me trained to be aware of everything at once, part of me desperate to retreat to nothingness and give it all up. A conflict of will I carried burden-like on my shoulders and in my hard gaze.

—

But I digress, don't I?

It's so easy for me to get lost in the past. My memories are like some intricate, horrible maze. Let me get back to the bust.

His name was Dr. Fozie L. West. Late sixties, white-haired, bone thin. In the hours before the raid, sipping coffee with the DEA at the Sheriff's Office, we'd each been given a printout with his picture and a brief description. He looked like someone from a different time, a previous century. The 1920s maybe, with his tweed suit and long, grim face like H. P. Lovecraft or Albert Fish.

It was snowing when we converged on the clinic—a shabby building in a shitty part of town, surrounded by cheap motels, liquor stores and check-cashing joints. A crudely painted PAIN MANAGEMENT CENTER sign hung above the door. We quickly poured out, stomping across the fresh snow, and swarmed the place, the DEA barging in first, guns drawn, and us tailing behind.

We burst into a little anteroom where Christmas music was playing: Jingle Bell Rock. A startled secretary stared at us, stunned. A couple of dirty junkie-looking types sat in the corner by a small plastic Christmas tree, hooded sweatshirts and hooded eyes, obviously waiting for a fix. The place was filthy and reeked of cat shit and a swampy fetid odor coming from a huge fish tank, half-filled with green water and swarming with turtles. A DEA agent kicked open an office door and there was the doctor, trying to worm his way out of a small window, squirming, legs furiously kicking insect-like. An agent ordered him to freeze, and he slipped down to the ground and turned. There was a pistol in his hand.

Before anyone had a chance to even scream or holler a warning, he had the barrel of that gun up against his temple and was squeezing the trigger. The gunshot rang out like an explosion in that cramped office. He fell to the floor and the blood made an awful sluicing sound as it squirted up, out of his head, splashing the walls.

Pandemonium broke out. The secretary was screaming hysterically, the junkies running to the door. There were cries to call an ambulance, agents and sheriff's deputies racing about frantically. I was oddly calm, enveloped in an eerie sensation of detachment and curiosity, as if I was watching the chaotic scene from a distance. Time stretched and slowed, the hurried motions of the people around me playing out frame-by-frame as a high-pitched ringing filled my head, and I found myself wandering away from the madness of the front rooms and down a long corridor.

A rangy tabby cat mewled up at me as I slipped down the hall, an otherworldly push leading me into the depths of the clinic.

It was a confusing maze of passageways and rooms, medical waste bags strewn everywhere, flies swarming and buzzing over puddles of brown liquid on the floor, splatters on the wall, random boxes filled with cat shit and shredded paper. I came to a big industrial refrigerator, opened it and peered inside. More medical waste bags, an apple, yogurt containers, a half-eaten sandwich, and several tall glass jars filled with tiny white feet floating in a milky liquid.

Yes, feet. No bigger than the nub of your pinky, but perfectly formed: little ankles and toes. Dozens and dozens of them. All left. It was so surreal and disgusting. I gagged, but still felt this desire to keep moving and explore.

Onward I went, that crazy buzzing tone growing louder in my skull, past piles of trash and broken, discarded medical equipment, past a doorway where in a dark, tiny room a young girl lay on a gurney, groaning softly. She turned her head to me, a dazed-and-pleading look in her eyes. She held out a hand. But I kept walking.

Finally, I came to a black door adorned with a small, innocuous sign: BASEMENT.

I did *not* want to go down to that basement. The rational part of my brain was howling against it, but some strange force compelled me. Barely conscious of my own movements, in a foggy daze like a sleepwalker, that ringing in my ears rising a notch in tone, I pulled the door open and started down those dark steps and into the shadowy cavernous chamber.

The muffled cries of women moaning echoed from back rooms, and a new scent hit me, both antiseptic and sour, like cleaning products and death. Drawn forward, I passed stainless-steel tables where I saw unspeakable things in the pale-blue scintillating fluorescent light: piles of little body parts, fetuses like miniature, pale, discarded baby dolls, dismembered and sewn back together, some missing heads, some with their arms and legs switched and backwards. It was truly awful, beyond anything I'd ever seen in war.

And then . . . then I was before a small red door with an ornate brass handle.

I knew I shouldn't be down there. That I could potentially be polluting or even destroying evidence, that this was more than a crime scene, it was an abomination against nature and all that was good in the world. But a compulsion I couldn't name or control drove me to try and open the door, to twist and tug on the strange knob.

It was locked.

The door wouldn't budge, and I actually breathed a sigh of relief. For I didn't really want to go back there at all. In fact, I wanted out of that terrible dungeon of a place and my mind was screaming, "Get out! Get out! Get out now!"

But just as I stepped back from the door there was a creak, and I gasped, nearly choking on my own breath, as the door cracked open.

Out of no volition of my own, I reached out, opened the door, and found myself staring into the vastness of deep space: planets and stars, galaxies spiraling throughout luminous nebulas of purple and orange.

I wavered under the enormity of it, remembering myself as a child beneath the gaping maw of the planetarium, staggered by the vastness, and later as a soldier staring at the infinite desert sky, the constellations scintillating and glimmering, melting together.

But blinking, I realized it was just hundreds of candles. Yes, hundreds of candles in a dark room with black-painted walls. I took in a deep breath of air, let it slowly out through clenched teeth, jarred by that ringing which seemed to fill my entire body now, curling my toes and straightening the tiny hairs on the back of my neck.

My eyes adjusting to the dim amber light, I saw there was a star-shaped pattern painted on the floor in red, with strange writing and symbols around it, and before it an altar of sorts rose up, draped in black cloth, lit with elaborate steel candelabras.

I stumbled forward, the terrible feeling of being a living-marionette percolating inside me, and there, up on that black alter, lying deathly still in a pan of oily liquid, was a tiny pale fetus. Yeah, a little human baby fetus, all curled up in that iconic way, like the space baby in that movie *2001 A Space Odyssey*.

Some sick fuck had tattooed the little thing. Weird markings, triangles and crescent moons, writing in a bizarre alphabet. I was filled with a terrible sympathy for it: Such an innocent, cute thing, misused, tortured, left dead here in this strange chamber. It was beyond sick. I thought of Amanda and the child that had swam in her. My child. And suddenly I was choked with tears.

Sobbing, I stared down at it, and to my amazement, it stretched its arms—tiny hands curled into perfect fists—then yawned, as if awakening from a nap! It turned and looked up at me. It was alive! A fucking miracle.

Impulsively, I reached in and scooped it up. Once in my hands it appeared bigger than it had in the pan. More like an infant than a fetus. There was a weight to it, a heftiness and heartiness. It nuzzled against my palm and let out a soft coo. My heart throbbed with heat. It was a girl. A little girl. And, yes, she was much bigger than she had looked, filling both my hands.

A craziness filled my head. I don't know how else to describe it. A strange insanity. For I took her.

God help me, I took her.

—

At the time it seemed I was guided by empathy, by love. That it was my desire for a family that drove me to try and save her from the media and scientists and cops and Feds.

But I know better now.

Then, it felt like destiny: How I was so easily able to slip up the stairs, through those godforsaken halls and out that open door, with her cradled against my chest, hidden behind my thick Sheriff's coat.

No one even glanced at me.

But it wasn't destiny. That thing was controlling them, just as surely as it was guiding me.

By the time I made it to my patrol car the infant had tripled in size. More. I took off my parka and lay it on the passenger seat, nestled her there, wrapping her in the folds. Purple veins crisscrossed the tiny pale body and I could see dark fluid pulsing within them, and those weird tattoos gave off an unworldly glow. I noticed then, for the first time, that its eyes were yellow, with rectangular pupils, like a goat, its lips glistening and black.

How had I not seen that before?

Suddenly I didn't feel too good about this whole situation.

What the fuck had I done?

—

There was an old-fashioned basinet in the garage, a hand-me-down from Amanda's parents. A heavy, wooden thing from the sixties when they built things to last, covered in white frills and lace. I hauled it out, Daisy at my side, panting, her kind eyes curious, and put it in the spare room that was meant to be a nursery.

Placing the creature in it, it looked blasphemous there. Obscene, that tiny, ugly thing, skin like a green-and-yellow bruise, in that cute frilly bed made for a human baby.

Daisy approached, ever curious in that canine way of hers, sniffed at it, then whined and backed away, ears flat against her head, tail curled between her legs, and again I wondered, *just what have I done?*

A feeling of loathing settled over me, a sense of doom, the creature just staring at me blankly, its black lips sullen, yellow eyes cold as the depths of space. For the briefest moment I was actually filled with the urge to kill it, but then something inexplicable happened: it bat its huge eyes, and smiled warmly at me, cooing with laughter.

My heart lifted as the infectious giggles filled me and before I knew it, I was laughing too, bending down to stroke its cheek with the pad of my finger. It gave a soft, contented sigh, turned its head, and grasped my finger, kicking its pudgy little feet.

It's like a drug goes off in my brain and I'm awash in some kind of opiate high. I think, I have to name this thing, this glorious creature. It's like I am pierced with a radiant light, like a spear from a different dimension, and there's a name in my head. It just comes to me. Later I will learn what it means, but then I was ignorant. Alnilam: the brightest star in Orion's belt.

—

The next day I called in sick to work. My uncle answered the phone.

"What happened to you yesterday?" he asked in his gruff voice. "You just disappeared."

I told him that the clinic, the whole scene, just brought back so many memories of Amanda being pregnant that I had to leave. Just couldn't bear to be there. I apologized, said, "My anxiety is at maximum and my therapist says I should take some time off to try to work through this." Truth was, I hadn't seen my therapist in months. Hated her smugness and condescending attitude. It made me feel weak.

"Take as much time as you need," he told me.

—

She won't eat.

I've tried formula and milk. Warmed it and tried to feed her with a bottle. She just turns her little face away. Tried spooning baby food of all types into her mouth: vegetables, fruit, meat, from jars, tubes, little pouches, homemade recipes I researched and put in a blender. She just spits it out and clamps her lips shut. In desperation I tried bits of hamburger, doughnuts and cake. Even pizza. Nothing's worked. Not even a nibble. I don't know what to do.

But she's plump and healthy-looking. And keeps growing. No longer the size of a newborn, she's now a hefty infant. She's able to sit up, hold her head high and look around. She even squirms on her belly as if any day she'll begin to crawl. She even smells healthy, that fresh, clean, intoxicating baby smell.

I keep her in diaper. Though there's really no need, she hasn't once peed or had a bowel movement. Which also worries me.

—

Christmas.

I think she may be feeding on me somehow. Draining me. I feel weak and listless. My hair has begun to fall out, clumps coming loose from my head in the shower and clogging the drain. My gums ache and bleed.

This morning I lost a tooth. A canine on the upper right side. I could feel with my tongue that it was loose. When I jiggled it with my finger it slipped right out of my skull, long and slender, slightly yellow and dotted in blood. I was turning it before my eyes, studying it, a weariness deep in the center of my bones, when I heard a thudding crash followed by a high-pitched yelp.

How to explain the horror I saw after racing to the nursery? I don't know how. Alnilam, the baby, *that thing*, was out of her crib and on the floor, spilled out on her belly like a white puddle, gripping Daisy's snout in her fat little hands, pudgy legs kicking.

Daisy was still, but trembling slightly. She had gone completely white, unnaturally white, as if bleached, and a strange purple mist sluiced out her mouth and nostrils and into Alnilam's gently parted lips. The strange markings that adorned her body, *those weird tattoos*, glowed with a pulsating green light as she slurped the mist up, lifting her unearthly eyes to mine and grinning.

I screamed, pressing my palms against the sides of my head, as if my skull might crack apart if not held fast by my hands.

Alnilam burped and a giggle escaped her as she tossed the dog aside. I dropped to my knees, tears welling up, and took Daisy's head in my hands. Her lips were shriveled and dry, mummified, her eyes hollow and blank. She was stiff, and incredibly light, as if devoid of substance. I pulled her into my arms, rocking back and forth, clutching her to me and weeping.

Alnilam lifted herself up, cocked her head, and pointed a fat finger at me. "Da da. Da," she said, her voice a sweet singsong. Those words hit my heart like a wrecking ball and everything seemed to change.

Da da. Those elemental and ancient sounds. She saw me as her father. And when I looked at her, Christ, it was *so* easy to look beyond the preternaturally-pale shade of skin, the black lips, goat's eyes and glowing markings, to see a sweet, fat-faced baby girl. A cute little thing grinning innocently, clapping her chubby hands.

And how could I be upset? How could I be angry?

—

But later, digging Daisy's grave, wearily cracking open the cold earth with a mattock, beyond the strange influence of that baby thing, I made a grim decision: I'm going to kill it.

She was an abomination. Evil. She had to die.

Daisy was the last connection to my old world. To Amanda. To normality. Slipping her into that dark pit, spilling soil over her emaciated and bleached form, I realized why I was chosen. It was that empty part of my heart. That place Amanda had emptied with her death. That hollowness that yearned to be a father, a husband, to have a family.

That's why Alnilam had chosen me.

She needed someone wounded. Someone vulnerable to be her keeper. Someone desperate enough for a sense of family that they'd accept a demon into their life. She was using my hurt, my festering inner-wounds.

Yes, she had to die.

—

I approached the nursery slowly, my service revolver clutched in a trembling, sweaty fist, finger on the trigger. I had to be swift, without hesitation. I stepped into the room and raised the revolver, centering the sights on her.

She turned her strange goat eyes to me, those black lips yawning upward into a terrible grin, and my finger froze, locked, unable to squeeze the trigger. My hand quaked as she tilted her head, commanding me. I was helpless, under her complete control, as she demanded I lift my arm and put the barrel of the revolver to my head, pressing the cold metal to my temple.

And, yes, I admit, I found some peace in the thought of death. Welcomed it. I shut my eyes, took a breath, and gave in to her.

But she wouldn't even give me that condolence. She needed me and wouldn't let me die. Worse yet, it was then she let me know what she wanted. What she needed. What she feeds on. She had no need for flesh and blood as sustenance, no. She wanted souls. That's why she didn't want formula or baby food, dead stuff, pieces of meat and vegetable, fruit and milk. She needed something living, something with a consciousness and self-awareness. She craved to devour spiritual essence, and had taken mine to the brink.

And Daisy had a soul. That glint of love and empathy you see in a dog's eye, that's what Alnilam fed on, leaving nothing but a shriveled white shell, a worn-out body drained of life.

But what was the innocence and affection of a mere dog compared to that of a human child?

—

I found the first one standing just outside the park, staring forlornly towards the playground swings, a dripping ice-cream cone in her chubby hand.

She was a fat little thing in a pink sundress, with bushy-blonde ponytails bobbing on either side of her head, lapping sullenly on that vanilla cone. She couldn't have been more than four, her mother yapping away to a group of other young women in a gossip circle. Didn't even notice me take her by the hand and lead her away.

—

We've had to stay on the move. From California to Arizona to New Mexico and now Colorado. Looking for places where tourists come with their children. Living in cheap hotels beside third-rate amusement parks. I'm weary of the road, but constantly moving is the key to remaining undiscovered. Jurisdiction to jurisdiction, leaving no links, nothing for law enforcement to put together.

—

She's sick! My poor little Alnilam. I'm in an utter panic.

She's fevered, burning up. She just lays there moaning and there's something terribly wrong with her back. Her little shoulder blades have these nasty boils on them. They started as tiny welts, but have been growing and swelling, weeping a foul-smelling green puss. And I can see a weird movement in them, the swollen skin fluttering, as if there's something living inside them.

Can I take her to a hospital? Call a doctor?

Are these options even possible given our predicament?

I feel so helpless. She's all I have now. The thought of losing her is beyond soul crushing.

—

WINGS!!! SHE HAS WINGS!!!

This morning those nasty blisters on her back split open and out unfurled slick, slimy, beautiful black wings! All leathery and bat-like. Her fever was instantly gone and she was immediately back to her old happy self, laughing and giggling, flapping those wonderful new wings.

Oh, what a relief. My soul feels as if a terrible weight has been lifted from it. Thank God. Thank God my little Alnilam is all right.

—

She can fly. Actually fly. It's so amazing. Such an incredible sight.

I brought her back a toddler I found wandering around by the fountain at a shopping mall. A chubby little boy in OshKosh overalls with big blue eyes and a double chin. I led him into the room, and as soon as I shut the door behind us she spied him from the bed, lifting her head, those beautiful yellow goat eyes studying him as he plodded around clumsily.

Her pupils narrowed and those black wings fluttered to life and rose, beating softly, lifting her gracefully upwards. The little boy saw her and grinned, pointed a fat finger, mumbling nonsense, a bit of drool dripping off his bottom lip as she circled, as predatory and beautiful as the most American of bald eagles.

Then, in one swift and calculated motion, with the precision of a striking snake, she swooped down, catching his surprised face in her hands. He staggered back, nearly falling, but she held him fast, pulling him towards her, sucking his spirit from out his nose and mouth in a stream of purple mist. The little boy's ruddy complexion went pale, his rolls of fat shriveling and drying up, his wide eyes going blank and empty.

Then she released her grip and he toppled gently, nothing but a little husk of a child now. Alnilam laughed and swept across the room as I clapped my hands and whooped for joy, tears of happiness swelling in my eyes.

She's so amazing. The greatest daughter I could ever have asked for. An answer to my prayers. And I know within my heart, we have nothing but wonderful, wonderful days ahead of us. I'm just sure of it.

And now, right now, I'm the happiest man in the world.

A NOEL IN BLACK

The doors to the homeless shelter shut in ten minutes, but Caleb needed another drink. It was Christmas Eve 1970, and he was wandering the streets of Eureka, California in a tattered and filthy Santa suit, crimson hat perched atop his head, dirty beard pulled down around his neck, a streak of vomit running down his left leg.

When the Salvation Army gave him the costume, days ago—how many now? Three? Four?—it had been brand new and shiny clean, but he had gone AWOL as soon as he had begged up enough money for a good drunk. He couldn't believe how easy it was to get money begging in a Santa Suit during the holidays, especially when people thought they were giving to the Salvation Army. Too bad, he thought, that the racket had to end tonight. Fuck it, he was headed to the nearest bar and had a pocket full of money.

Bells on bob-tail ring, making spirits bright. Oh what fun it is to sing a sleighing song tonight.

Finally managing to make eye contact with the ape-faced bartender who was absent-mindedly pushing a dishtowel up and down a pint glass, Caleb waved a twenty in the air, a wry smile of *what the fuck?* on his face. Red and green Christmas tree lights flickered over the bottles and mirrors and off in the corner the Ghost of Christmas Past grinned its horrid smile. The bartender nodded acknowledgment and strutted over.

"Yeah? Whaddya want?"

"Beer and a whiskey."

"What kinda beer? What kinda whiskey?"

"The cheapest."

The bartender got him his drinks, took the twenty, and left his change in front of him on the bar.

Sipping the bitter medicine, Caleb noticed a woman a few stools down trying to draw his attention, a jet of blue smoke issuing from her cherry-red lips as she raised and lowered her thickly-pencilled eyebrows. He could tell she had done her best to look good tonight: lots of eye makeup, newer, hipper-looking clothes, but he could see the age in her face, recognized her need like a bad smell. Battered, needy women gave off a stink of desperation he'd learned to recognize over the years. Those years since he'd been back from the war. He'd had his fair share of these types. Always good for a warm bed and a hot meal, but too crazy to spend any real time with.

"Hey there, Santa. Buy a girl a drink?"

"Sure thing, honey." Caleb glanced at the barkeep. "Give the lady what she wants."

She slid down next to him as the grim-faced bartender mixed a rum and coke, speared a lime with a tiny sword and dropped it in the glass. "I've always had a thing for Santa," she whispered. "Coming in late at night to punish the naughty and reward the nice."

"Yeah, and what are you, darling? Naughty or nice?"

"I've always thought I was a little of both."

"Ha. What's your name, baby?"

"Sandra. They call me Sandy around here. But I think of myself as Sandra."

"All right, Sandra. What's your story?"

"Just a local girl, been in the same place too long. What about you, Santa? Don't you gotta lot of work to do tonight?"

Caleb laughed, that deep, reassuring laugh he'd mastered over the years, to put people—women especially—at ease. They talked for a while. Then Caleb ordered a pitcher of beer and a couple more shots and they moved to a corner booth. Sandra talked on and on, chain smoking Salems while he drank his beer and sipped his whiskey, watching as the room began to spin in slow, psychedelic and nauseating circles.

"You're awful quiet."

"I've been told that before."

"How'd you get them scars on your neck?"

Caleb put his hand to his neck, let it drift down to the dirty fake beard, and pulled the knotted grey and black mess of hair over to cover his throat. And that wicked Ghost of Christmas Past with sunken eyes and yellow teeth whispered, "Tell her." And so Caleb did.

"In the war."

"You were over in 'Nam, huh?"

"Yeah, two tours."

"And then what? You come back to have these damn hippies spitting at you? I feel for you, sweetie. My daddy died in France fighting Nazis. Now my brother is in the Navy while this country goes to shit. You got these bastards like that dirty Abbey Hoffman saying to steal everything. And this Charlie Manson Family killing movie stars." She laughed, shook her head and sipped her drink. "It's enough to make you sick."

They grew quiet. "So, you going to tell me about those scars, or what?"

"Well, I was a Kootchie Kootie. A tunnel rat. You know what that is?"

"Oh, yeah. You were one of those guys that go down in those gook holes?"

"Sure was. Infantry. 1st Reconnaissance Squadron." He sighed, not wanting to get into it, but once he started it was hard to stop. "I was working three clicks west of Duc Pho in the Quang Ngai province. I was down in a tunnel. Just me, my .45 and a flash light. Looking out for booby traps and rats and spiders, and this animal. . . it came out of nowhere. Fucking attacked me. Just latched onto my shoulder and wouldn't let go."

"Oh, baby. You was attacked by an animal down in

one of those tunnels?"

"Yeah. But when I killed it, when I shot it . . . " He couldn't tell her the rest. He couldn't tell her how after he had shot that thing, the muzzle blast a blinding light, the report deafening, after he had filled that monster full of holes and watched it drop, it had looked just like a little girl. Just a tiny, raven-haired girl, all shot up and bloody, when moments ago it had been a beast: a mess of lurching fangs and drool.

His mouth moved up and down silently. He couldn't say anything. Then, with an incredible effort, what he had managed to say was, "I think I brought something back with me. I . . . I . . . I don't know."

"You brought something back with you? You mean like that Agent Orange stuff, honey?"

"No, something different. Something, something. . ."

"What? In your head?"

He wanted to say, no, something in my blood: I brought back something in my blood that makes me a monster; but instead, he just nodded yes, his face a knot, visibly fighting to not break down in tears.

"Oh, baby, oh, baby, I understand."

The room was twirling now at a breakneck speed. He was going to be sick. He pulled away from her and vomited on the floor.

"Son of a bitch!" the bartender shouted. "Who's going to clean that up?"

Caleb hung over the edge of the booth, retching and dry heaving.

"Fuck you, Sam. He's a veteran! He fought for this country, got attacked down in one of them gook holes. What the fuck you ever done?"

"I don't care if he was on the beach at Normandy. Get him the fuck out of here!"

"You're a piece of work. A real piece of work, know that, Sam? Where's your sense of Christmas spirit?"

The bartender stomped up to her, eyes bulging, an accusing finger extended. "Get your cheap-whore ass out of here, bitch, and take your Santa Claus friend with you. Got me?" he grabbed her face in his hand and jerked her chin up so that he could look her in the eye. "This bar ain't no place for you anymore, Sandy. You make my customers sick. Everyone who's wanted to has fucked you, and none of them's too proud of it either. You'se don't belong here. Find some other place to haunt, you cheap skank." With that he tossed her head aside and stormed back behind the bar.

We wish you a merry Christmas. We wish you a merry Christmas. We wish you a merry Christmas and a happy New Year.

Sandra walked Caleb back to the motel room she rented by the month, holding him up the whole way while he leaned against her mumbling and pointing to ghosts she could not see. Once they were back at her room she helped him out of his Santa outfit and got him into the tub. In the heat of the steamy water he regained a semblance of consciousness, came back to himself. When he looked up he saw her through the mist, leaning in the doorway, staring at him. She had changed and was now wearing nothing but a silk kimono. He had to admit she didn't look that bad.

"How you feeling, Santa?"

"Good. I feel . . ." he paused, unsure what to say, how he actually felt. "Good."

She knelt down beside the tub, ran her finger over the surface of the water. "Thirsty?" she asked, holding up a tumbler of Scotch and water.

"As a matter of fact, I am."

Taking the glass into his hands, he took a sip. Handing it back to her she gave him a penetrating stare that he found hard to decipher and then leaned in to kiss him. She tasted of whiskey, cigarettes and peppermint. But it was good, the way she gently ran her tongue over his upper lip before she pulled away, and Caleb felt himself growing aroused.

"Now that you're all cleaned up, why don't we get you

to bed."

"Sounds good, baby."

"Dry yourself off. I'll be waiting." With that she disappeared out the door.

He got up from the tub and dried himself the best he could with the cheap, tiny towels the motel provided. When he entered the room she was already on the bed, prone on her back and naked. She may have had a butter face but her body was to die for, and she knew how to flaunt it. He started towards her but she held up her hand, palm out toward him, and exclaimed, "Stop right there, mister. The Santa suit. Put it on."

He gave her a questioning half grimace and then smiled. "You serious?"

"I told you: I gotta thing for Santa."

Smirking, he pulled on the dirty jacket and set the conical hat atop his head. "Better?"

"Oh, yeah, baby. I've been so naughty. I need to be punished."

With that she burst out in playful laughter, turned over onto all fours, and stuck her ass into the air, whispering over her shoulder, "Come and get it, Santa."

He approached the bed and, still standing, he pulled himself into her. She let out a deep moan and he began to move, slowly. He was still drunk as hell and the room was spinning slightly but he could feel that primal urge within to rock and rotate. He began to lunge faster, and faster, and then, suddenly, it was happening again.

Fuck. No. No. No. It was happening *again*. He could feel himself beginning to change as he thrust against her. A part of him wanted to run away, to bolt through the door and into the night so that he wouldn't hurt her. But another part of him wanted this. It felt good. It felt *so fucking good* to let go and let the animal inside him take over. Still pounding, Sandra moaning beneath him, he watched in wonder as his fingers—tightly gripping her bony hips—became claws and a thick mat of fur began to weave itself up his arms. Thrusting against her with all his might he lifted his face and began to howl as his mouth filled with sharp, gleaming fangs.

*Here comes Santa Claus, here comes Santa Claus, right down
Santa Claus lane!*

Margaret Ashton was the manager of the Lone Pine motel. She had been across the street visiting with her daughter and grandson in their two-story, cookie-cutter house, and was just walking back to the motel office when she heard the screaming in room 308. It was that cheap-tramp Sandy's room. Margaret had been waiting for an excuse to evict her and marched up to the door, ready to throw her out, Christmas Eve or not. But as she grew closer and heard the urgency to the screams, the gut-wrenching terror of the squeals, she grew hesitant and stopped.

The screaming stopped and the window exploded outward, showering her with glass and splintered wood. She fell back and slipped to the ground, watching in utter disbelief as the craziest thing she had ever seen in her life of fifty-six years came tumbling down atop her.

A wolf.

A huge monster of a wolf, with a snarling mouth of bloody fangs and drool. And it was wearing a red coat lined in white fur with a Santa cap perched atop its head.

From his bedroom window her grandson Tommy watched the entire thing.

Later that night homicide detectives would interview the little boy. Tearfully he would relate how he had seen his grandmother ripped to shreds by some kind of beast in a Santa suit. One of the uniformed officers standing idly in the background would then turn to his partner and whisper under his breath, "Looks like grandma got run over by a werewolf, walking home from his house Christmas Eve."

Oh Tannenbaum, oh Tannenbaum, lovely are thy branches.

God, the Easter Bunny, and the Ghost of Christmas Present watched as two-year-old Annabelle toddled out the door of her street-level apartment and onto the sidewalk, a thumb stuck in her mouth and dragging a Barbie doll along by the hair.

God looked like the guy from the Dos Equis commercials: an incredibly good-looking older gentleman with white hair, perfectly coifed, and a nicely trimmed beard, in a tuxedo. The Ghost of Christmas Present looked extremely bored and kept yawning. The Easter Bunny was an out-of-work writer who needed a shave, dressed in a pink bunny outfit.

"Cute kid," the Easter Bunny commented.

"I wouldn't get too attached," the Ghost of Christmas Present replied, disinterestedly stifling a yawn.

Annabelle's parents were fighting again and their voices echoed out from the apartment.

"Christ, how many Quaaludes did you take? You can't even look at me. Wake up, bitch, I'm talking to you."

"Fuck off, Henry. You always were a bore."

"You dumb piece of shit. I oughta slap the stupid right offa your face."

When the wolf came galloping down the middle of the street in its blood-soaked Santa suit the Easter Bunny turned to God and said, "You gotta be putting me on, man."

God rolled his eyes.

The wolf snatched the baby in its fangs and threw the child up into the night sky where she hung suspended in the moonlight for a moment, tiny arms and legs kicking, and then tumbled down, landing on the street with a thud. The beast leapt at her, sinking its sharp teeth into her neck and thrashing its head side to side until the tiny figure ceased to struggle and lay limp in its mouth.

"It's probably for the best," the Ghost of Christmas Past said.

"What? Why?" the Easter Bunny asked, scratching at the stubble on his face.

"You want to tell him, God? Or should I?"

God gestured with his hands, as if to say, "Go ahead. It's all you."

"If Annabelle had lived through this night, after being molested by her stepfather and stepbrother, she would have become a heroin addict by fifteen and a prostitute by sixteen. She then would have gotten picked up by a notorious serial killer who after raping her for days would finally kill her by trying to give her a lobotomy with a cordless drill. Her life taken like this, quickly and mercifully, is a blessing, a thing of joy. A Christmas miracle."

"Is this true?" the Easter Bunny asked God.

God grinned and nodded.

"You don't say much, do you?" the Easter Bunny asked God.

God just shrugged.

Deck the halls with boughs of holly, fa la la la la la la la la.
'Tis the season to be jolly, fa la la la la la la la la.

Father Mulligan was cleaning up after midnight mass when he heard the click-clack of claws on the wooden floor. He paused, chalice in one hand, ciborium in the other, and listened.

"Hello?" he called out, his voice echoing throughout the empty chapel. "Who's there?"

Beneath the pounding of blood in his ears he distinctly heard panting, like that of a large dog.

"Hello?"

Deep in the dark recess of the hall something stirred, moved, and then came slinking out of the shadows: a large creature walking on all fours, its eyes alight and flickering like yellow flames. The beast came forward slowly down the aisle, Santa hat drooping down one side of its head, a dead baby hanging limply in its mouth. The wolf approached the altar and came so close that the priest could smell it, a feral odor of blood and musk. It spit the baby to the floor where it landed with a horrible smack.

But the priest didn't run. He stood his ground, murmuring prayers beneath his breath. He knew why the beast was there, why this spawn of evil had come. It was here to punish him. Punish him for the things he had done to all those little boys. So many. First in Ireland when he had just been doing what had been done to him when he was an altar boy. Then, after coming to America, in Philadelphia, where for years the urban darkness of poverty and city life had let him run rampant. Not yet here in California, where he had been sent quickly by the diocese so as not to cause a scandal. But he had his eyes on a few of the boys in his congregation. Some of the poorer ones who he thought wouldn't tell.

Seeing the monster here was a blessing and death would be a mercy. He fell to his knees, kissed his stole, and lifted his neck to the beast. But instead of taking him by the throat, the beast spun him around by the shoulders so that the priest fell face first to the floor. With one quick jerking motion the monster shredded the priest's pants and mounted him. The priest cried out in pain and surprise as the wolf forcibly entered him and warm blood began to trickle down his leg.

God, the Easter Bunny and the Ghost of Christmas Present stood at the back of the chapel watching. The Easter Bunny had taken off his hood of rabbit ears and was puffing on an e-cigarette and furiously tapping away on an iPad mini. "Been blogging about this whole thing, and, yeah, a lot of people see that as offensive. I mean, what the fuck? You got a werewolf dressed like Santa Claus raping a child-molesting priest on Christmas Eve?"

The Ghost of Christmas Present laughed heartily. "Well, I hate to say I told you so, but . . ."

"You got nothing to say about this, God?" the Easter Bunny asked, momentarily looking away from his iPad.

God tilted his head to the left, his thin lips bending into a sad frown, and, raising his eyebrows in an, "Oh, well," manner, shrugged again.

Joy to the world, the Lord has come. Let Earth receive her king!

Gravy Brain Jane was out of her mind on LSD and had nowhere to go. She had a thousand tabs of purple sunshine on her but the connect had never shown and wasn't answering the phone. Exasperated and befuddled, her vision a swirling cyclone of light and darkness, she stumbled from the Greyhound Station to a small clearing in a copse of woods. She sat leaning against a tree, the branches dripping and melting around her, the sky a miasma of spiralling stars and galaxies. She giggled and mumbled her strange mantra. "No sense makes sense. No sense makes sense. No sense makes sense."

Charlie had sent a message from prison that she should deliver the acid here. If Charlie said it would work out, it would work out. She was sure of that. She had thought the other passengers on the bus would have been startled and scared by the X that Sandy and Squeaky had helped her burn into her forehead with hot bobby pins, but no one had noticed at all.

The Easter Bunny, who wasn't even wearing his rabbit outfit anymore, and was now just dressed in his usual black jeans and t-shirt, was pacing back and forth irritably. He turned to the Ghost of Christmas Present and asked, slightly argumentatively, "Well, where's God?"

"Oh, he couldn't make it. Had a concert to catch."

"A concert? What are you talking about?"

"Well, it was Skynard and you know how he loves 'Free Bird'."

"Typical."

Gravy Brain Jane giggled when she saw the beast slowly creeping towards her. She had been taught to love coyotes when the family was in the desert of Death Valley. Back on the ranch Charlie had taught them to break down the final walls society imposed on them by having them fellate the stray dogs.

"Hey there, beautiful," she said. The wolf just stared at her with its unblinking yellow eyes.

From their glimmer and spark she knew just what the creature wanted. It wanted what all men want and she had

NEST OF SALT

NEST
OF
SALT

Stories
by
Matthew V. Brockmeyer

BLACK THUNDER PRESS

ISBN: 978-1-7353085-0-0
PUBLISHED BY BLACK THUNDER
PRESS

Printed in the United States of America
Suggested Retail Price (SRP) $8.95

"There is no exquisite beauty . . . without some strangeness."
—Edgar Allan Poe, *Ligeia*

"The instruments of darkness tell us truths."
—William Shakespeare, *Macbeth*

CONTENTS

THE WITCH'S YULE

A Fable

Max knew if you believed in something hard enough it would come true. That you could be anything you wanted to be. You just needed a little magic.

Slipping his wolf cap over his head, Max silently crept on all fours into his brother's bedroom, looking for the magic he needed.

His brother, Eight Ball, was sprawled on a bare mattress on the floor, still wearing his sneakers and sleeveless jean jacket, snoring softly. Lately he'd been staying up for four or five days in a row and then passing out and sleeping for two. It had become a pattern, as reliable as the fattening and shrinking of the moon. Max knew there wasn't a chance in hell he'd wake up right now. He'd tried to wake him before, and had never been able. When Eight Ball was out, *he was out.*

Max scurried round the mattress, over the candy-bar wrappers, empty soda bottles and dirty clothes—black shirts and bright blue jeans—strewn across the floor. A pizza crust lay forlornly on a greasy plate, half-hidden behind a pile of filthy socks and porn mags. Max poked at the crust, looking for mold. Wrinkling his nose, he gave it a quick sniff before snatching it up. Eyes darting about the dim room as he gnawed on the hard crust, he spied what he was looking for: three blackened glass pipes resting on a cinder block beside a battered old lamp.

The first one he picked up looked empty as can be, nothing in it but a scaly, black crust. The second one maybe a hit or two if he was lucky. But the third one was just perfect, with a dark little frozen pond in the bubble at the end, tiny glaciers poking up from the abyss.

The flame from the torch lighter hissed loudly, the potion bubbled, rich blue smoke swelled up, and then Max was a wolf again. A real wolf. Running free through the forest, dodging the giant redwoods, over fragrant duff and past massive prehistoric ferns, the night sky infinite above him, his old friend the moon rising impossibly giant and full, bathing the dark forest in its beautiful, eerie glow. Bats twisted and darted above him, the glowing eyes of owls gleamed from trees, and the green eyes of racoons peered from beneath the shelter of ancient roots.

Galloping with his nose to the ground, he caught a feral, musky scent and quickened his pace to track the animal smell. Then he spotted it, up ahead, passing through the shadows and into a column of moonlight: a small, hairy creature with long muscular back legs. It darted around a rock outcrop and he followed, so close now he loomed above it. Panicked, the creature sprung to the right, slender ears pinned to its downy shoulders. Max pounced, all claws and fangs, relishing the blood and purity of the thing as it struggled and kicked against the cold stillness of the night.

—

Max awoke in the hollow of a redwood stump, naked and bloody, cradling a dead rabbit in his arms, its pelt soft and fragrant with the scent of earth and blood.

Panic rippled through him for a moment as he thought of his wolf hat. He shot his hands to his head, relief flooding through him when his hands fell on the battered old thing, his oldest and most cherished possession: a gray faux-fur cap with big, floppy wolf ears and a long tail, so old and worn now he'd had to patch it up with pieces of old leather and black denim.

He stretched and languidly pulled himself from the warm, dry duff, yawning as he rose. Shafts of morning sunlight cascaded down from between the tall trees and the dew-laden earth glimmered. Grasping the rabbit in his mouth he sprang from the stump, dropped to the ground on all fours and trotted off. He knew someone that would treasure this prize from the forest: Miranda the Good Witch of the Eastern Forest.

In the past he had taken his prizes to Mary Ellen's house, leaving them there on the doorstep for her and her family. But no more.

They never appreciated them.

He'd watch from the forest as her mother would open the door and shriek, kick the dead little critter off the stoop and slam the door. Her father coming out later only to put it in a trash bag, suspiciously gazing about as he hauled it to the garbage cans beside the house. That house that had always looked like a gold gilded castle to Max. That had been a many, many moons ago. When Max was just a little wild-thing pup learning the ways of the forest.

No one had ever found Mary Ellen's body. Max didn't think they ever would.

As he plodded through the redwoods, up the eastern hills, the sky turned gray and a smattering of snow began to drift lazily down, dusting the ground in white. Up, up he went, through a grove of hemlock and alder and tangles of huckleberry, till he came to a clearing of rattlesnake grass and bull thistle, in the center of which sat a little house made of red-and-white-striped peppermint candy, perched on concrete blocks.

Max knew it wasn't really made of candy, but that's the way he always pictured it. The way he saw it in his heart. And anyway, anything could be real if you believed hard enough, and could manage to dig up a little magic.

Pale, mildewed gourds hung from rotting red strings in the trees, rustling softly in the crisp winter breeze. Past a rusted engine and a pile of tires, up to the door he went, pawing at it happily. It swung open and there she was: Miranda, the Good Witch of the Eastern Woods, a wizened old woman with a riot of graying-red hair framing her gaunt face, mouth stretched in a warm smile of rotten teeth, clump of clover-shaped leaves at him. Max frowned and turned his head away. "Go on now. My momma used to say, 'Eat something with roots in the ground every day, always keep sickness at bay.'"

Max dutifully took the green clovers and put them in his mouth, but grimaced at the sour taste and spit them out.

"Stop that, boy. You eat them like I told you." She scooped the rabbit up by the hindlegs and pulled a gleaming, square-bladed cleaver off a rack by the sink. "Running around in the snow naked. Need to get your immunities up!"

She took the rabbit to the counter, laid it out gently, then brought the cleaver down with a bang against the middle joints of its back legs. She held up a furry paw. "They say these things are lucky. Keep one in your pocket and it will attract moneys. Put one under your pillow and you'll dream of your true love." She tossed it to Max, who sniffed it and gave it a quick, tentative lick before sliding it into the bib pocket of his overalls.

Pushing the other foot aside, she deftly rolled the fur down off the thighs, working at the flesh with her long, strong fingers, the knuckles swollen and gnarled. Pale blue veins snaked up her wiry and muscular arms as she labored.

"I knew your father, you know. He was a wild thing just like you. Used to come scampering to my door, too, looking for warmth and love. Just like you." With a hard yank she pulled the fur so that it slipped up, turning inside-out over the head, leaving its pink body naked and shiny, its shimmering black guts bulging from its belly. She scooped the viscera and dark organs out and into a bowl, talking quietly the whole time. "A mother and a lover and a healer is what I been to all the wild things. Ravens, racoons, wolves and men folk, all the same in their own ways. It's a blessing I suppose." Lifting the cleaver, she brought it down on the neck, severing the skin, hair and head from the pale sinewy body. "Your momma still live in that trailer in the bottoms?"

Max nodded, yipped.

"That orchard of plum trees still back there?"

He nodded, drifting along lazily to the rhythm of her

words. Her voice was like a comforting balm and Max's head swam at the thought of those plumbs: the scent of the flowers in the spring, so thick with petals they'd fall like snow, the sound of the bees screaming inside, and later the trees covered in engorged fruit hanging hot and ripe in the summer sun, dripping with sugary syrup.

She pulled the pelt right-side out again and stuck her hand inside, making a puppet of it, wagging the rabbit's head at him, the creature's black eyes staring out lifelessly, ears hanging limply to the sides. "What say I make you a nice soft scarf from this here critter? Keep you warm out there while you running wild."

Max cooed.

Placing the pelt aside, she took the carcass to the sink she gave the flesh a good rinse off, then laid it splayed out on the redwood counter. Lifting a back leg, with a sharp tug she cracked it free of the joint, then brought a knife to the hip and sawed it free in two swift motions. Then the other, and the front legs as well. She cut the belly flap away along the rib cage, setting it aside, and then cracked the backbone in half, separating the chest cavity from the thick meat of the hindquarters.

With a rusty pair of pliers, she cranked open the gas on the stovetop, scratched a wooden kitchen match into fire and lit a burner, sliding a greasy cast-iron pan over the licking blue flames. When the grease in the pan began to spit, she threw the thighs and legs in. They crackled and sizzled, the rich aroma of frying flesh filled the trailer. Max squirmed in his seat, drool filling his mouth and flowing over his lips.

She smiled at Max. "And now for the magic! Everything needs a little magic."

Reaching up into a cabinet, she retrieved a gleaming red-white-and-blue box of Captain Crunch from the shadows. Cackling, she pulled a handful of cereal out from within the wax-paper folds, ground it between her palms, mumbling something about the sweetness of the earth as she sprinkled the crumbs atop the frying rabbit parts. They stuck and clumped to the sizzling flesh, and with a ladle she spooned hot grease up over the Captain Crunch crust, the sugar caramelizing and browning. She set a plate before Max, then brought the skillet over and slid the rabbit out atop it.

"Eat what you kill, boy. That's the way of the wild."

Max lifted a leg and sucked the stringy meat from the bone, grease running down his chin, the sweet, peanut-buttery taste of the cereal offsetting the gamey tang of the feral creature in a heavenly and most delicious manner. Licking and gnawing on the bone, he felt his eyes flicker and roll back in his head in ecstasy before he grabbed another leg.

The old woman eased herself down in a chair opposite him and watched him eat with a crooked grin. "Yes, child, yes, eat your fill." She pulled a slender glass pipe from a black-leather pouch, dropped a diamond-like shard of meth in the tiny hole at the bubble end, and set it to boil with a flame, slowly inhaling the vaporous fumes. "Eat, eat. Then rest. You are safe here, little wild one. Safe and loved."

—

Max lay curled on a blanket beside the woodstove, warm and sated.

The witch had visitors at her table: an old scarecrow of a man in dirty tan overalls, drinking Coors Light, and a fat woman knitting. Not as fat as his mother, but a big, plump woman nonetheless, with several chins and thick flesh pleasantly swaying from her arms as she brought a loop of yarn up and over the needles.

The old man had a grumpy, vexed look on his face Max didn't like. He seemed irritated, kept tapping his fingers on his knee. After slurping down his beer, he crushed the finished can in his hand, dropped it to the floor, yanked another from the cardboard twelve-pack beside him, and cracked it open with a jerk of his claw-like fingers.

"Thrice the brinded cat hath meowed," he grumbled, casting beady eyes about the shadows of the room.

The fat woman yawned, pulled a loop of yarn tight and

clacked her long needles. "Thrice and once the hedge pig whined."

Miranda cleared her throat. "Harpier cries, 'Tis time. Tis time.' I now call this meeting to order. What is our main point of business today?"

The old man slammed his beer on the table, foam frothing up over the metal lip and down his bony knuckles. "I think we all know why we're here. Let's not pussyfoot around it!"

The tiny, bristly hairs on Max's neck stood up and he lifted his head, teeth bared and eyes narrowed at the old man, and let out a long, low growl. The witch reached down and stroked his head, softly whispering to him. "Shhh, shhh, It's okay, boy. He's with us. He's a friend."

Max lay his head back down upon his folded hands, but kept his eyes warily fixed on the old man who went on talking in his grumbly manner.

"Geek Jimmy has been flooding the market with cheap and inferior product. It's brought prices down, and put the heat on all of us."

The fat woman, never taking her gaze off the tubular pattern of knotted black yarn that hung from the long metal spikes in her fingers, then spoke. "It's true. On the street grams are going for fifty bucks now, and eight balls for one fifty. And that awful shit has been causing troubles in the community. We all know what happened with Toadstool Donnie the other day. An absolute tragedy. He wouldn't have behaved that way if it wasn't for a bad batch of inferior quality. People don't do things like that on our product. Ripping that poor woman's face off like that, terrible, and totally unprovoked."

"And," the old man shouted, a burst of spittle erupting from his mouth and hanging down off his bottom lip, "he's brought in undesirables. Outsiders. Filthy trash from Sacramento who got no right being here."

Miranda nodded solemnly, took a hit off her glass pipe and leaned back in her chair. "Then we have an agreement over our problem?"

"Aye," said the old man, glugging down a beer then wiping his foamy lips with the back of a dirty hand.

"Aye," said the fat lady, knitting needles clicking away.

"And it is fire shall be this deed without a name?"

"Aye."

"Aye."

"So be it. With a song, Holy Mother, turn the goat around from this Thursday and the next six days, forty-four celebrations in a year, up, stop, I return you with the curses and all these that makes him powerless."

—

That night, Miranda sat Max in front of the woodstove.

As she ran a flame beneath her glass pipe, Max thought she looked more beautiful than he'd ever seen her, her orange-and-gray hair shiny and clean and thick. In the flickering firelight Max could see she was wearing lipstick, her lips thick with it as if they were engorged with blood. And she wasn't wearing jeans, but a red dress. The skin of her shoulders looked soft and pale and there was a peculiar smell to her, something deeply floral and earthy, yet spicy and sweet, too. Like a peppermint stick buried in the deep, wet earth.

Gently grasping his chin, she lifted his face up to hers and blew a steady stream of smoke into it. He closed his eyes and inhaled deeply, the scent plasticky like new toys and fresh paint and turpentine on a hot summer day. His eyes fluttered back open and he smiled at her, warm and content, his heart pounding.

She cocked her head and fixed her gaze deep into his eyes, stroked his cheek, then placed her fingers on his wolf hat, easing it slowly off him. He started and drew back, sensitive over having this most intimate part of himself touched, his nakedness revealed. She shushed him and smiled, told him it was all right, and gently removed the hat, running her fingers through his hair.

"Listen to my words, Max." She'd never called him that

before. Always Wolfie or boy, never his real name. The name his father used to call him. "What is it you want, Max? What do you want from this life most of all?"

He shivered, his soul stirring within him, shook his head.

"It's okay," she said. "Talk to me, Max. You can do it. Use your words and tell me what you want."

He gave a furtive glance to the woodstove, words welling up inside of him, his voice croaking out roughly. "Warm. I want to be warm."

Her face broke into a huge smile. "Good. Warmth. You want warmth. What else, what else do you want?"

"Food. Hot food. Good food."

"Warmth and food, yes, yes, yes. Good. And what do you want most of all? Out of anything in the world?"

Max searched the emptiness of his heart, looking for clues in a black, black room. He felt a great heat well up inside of him, his eyes growing wet and heavy with tears. "Love," he finally managed.

"You want love?"

He nodded.

"You want to be loved?"

"I want a mommy who loves me," he said, and like a log jam breaking, a torrent of hot tears broke from his face.

"Oh, Max, I can be that. And give you all you wish for." She pulled him to her chest and rocked him as he wept, big aching sobs. "Shhh. Mother Miranda's here. Shhh. You're going to be warm and fed and loved from now on. Shh. Shh. But, Max?"

She gently eased him away by the shoulders to look him in the eye again. "Max? Are you listening?"

He sniffled, nodded, wiped the tears from his eyes.

"Max, I need something from you. You'll help Mother Miranda, right? Help avenge her against those that would give harm?"

He nodded.

"Say, 'Yes,' Max. You have to say it. Say, 'Yes'".

"Yes."

"Good. Now listen closely. Listen closely to my words, Max. Fire burns. And fire's bright. The knives are sharpened to cut, from the house to the table to eat, from the table to a bowl, from a bowl to a spoon, from a spoon to a head in the soil to put them deep. Do you understand?"

Max nodded, lost in shadows, his eyes half-shut.

"Thrice to fire and thrice to mine and thrice again to make up nine," she said and with her wizened fingers she turned the pipe stem to Max who, trance-like, pressed his lips to it and inhaled as she ran a flame beneath the bubbling potion, the beast within his heart swelling and filling like the ripening of the moon.

—

Gasoline and rags, the skunky scent of propane and the coldness of the awkward heavy cylinder. Smoldering smoke, blinding, burning his lungs. The tall trees and darkness of the forest, baby mice. Tiny little pink maggots of things, no bigger than the pad of his index finger, blind and squirming in the feather-like redwood fronds.

Max watched fascinated at the cluster of tiny baby mice, pink and hairless, spilled free from the nest he'd accidentally uncovered running through the woods. The mother darted back and forth, panicked, heading first along the edge of a thick redwood root, then, encountering the ridge of an exposed rock blocking her path, back again, in a senseless headlong rush. Max gently pushed the babies to their nest, shifted the duff back around them, scooped up the mother and lay her gently with her children.

His clothes reeked of gasoline. The sleeve of his flannel shirt was scorched and hung from his arm in ragged black strips, his hand soot-covered and seared, badly burned and blistering at the wrist, the ears of his wolf hat singed and smoking. He could smell the smoke in the air now, see the first large flames springing up in the distance, and so he started back off, continuing onward through the forest.

He crossed over a small promontory, thick with colt's

foot and huckleberry, then slid downward out of the hills and to a group of suburban homes, their eaves strung with Christmas lights glowing red and green. He leapt a fence, darted across a front yard, and paused in the shadows of a hawthorn hedgerow to glance about, then began to scurry across the road, when a voice called out to him, freezing him in his tracks.

"Max?"

Max turned and there was his brother Eight Ball, in his jeans, denim jacket, and Metallica *Ride the Lightning* t-shirt, standing beneath the street lamps in a circle of light that broke the darkness and shadows of the tall redwoods.

"Max, where have you been? Fuck, man, I've been freaking out, looking for you everywhere." Eight Ball stepped forward, held out his hand. "Well, come on, man. Let's go. Let's go home."

Max stared at his brother's open hand.

Home? What did it even mean?

He loved his brother. The thought of him ached at his heart like a swollen, infected splinter. But he had a new home now. A place of warmth and abundance, security and purpose, so different than that cold barren trailer he'd come from.

His brother took another step forward, imploring with a shake of his upturned palm. "Max, let's go."

Max wavered, unsure what to do, caught between conflicting impulses. He reached up and grasped the rabbit's foot in the bib pocket of his overalls, thinking the talisman might give him some direction. Eight Ball smiled at him and he could see their father in his eyes, in his lopsided grin. His brother was his everything. His kin. It had always been them against the world. Max took a hesitant step towards him.

But then a great explosion cracked the night in pieces as the propane tank at Geek Jimmy's house went up, and a ball of flame rose over the trees. Car alarms went off, dogs erupted into barking, and lights turned on in the windows of neighboring houses. Max's instincts kicked in and he bolted towards the shadows of the trees and the safety of the forest, sailing through the darkness and chaparral for what felt like over a year and in and out weeks and through a day and into the night of Miranda's house of candy where she had cold ginger ale and Campbell's Chicken Noodle Soup waiting for him. And the soup was still hot.

—

One night, Miranda had a party for Max.

The old man was there in an aluminum lawn chair, drinking his Coors Light, and the fat lady, too, knitting away in a rocking chair. They all sat in the front yard around a rusted fifty-gallon barrel with a roaring fire inside it and Max was allowed to eat all the hot dogs he wanted.

Miranda served a beautiful and magical punch: Grape Kool Aid with orange and tan dried mushrooms and old brown poppy heads floating in it. The old man had brought a pig on a leash, a huge beast of a thing, covered in coarse black hair. It snorted and rooted at the earth with its snout as Miranda took Max by the hand and led him to the fire.

"Do you know what day it is?" she asked him, the orange and amber light of the flames flickering across her face.

Max shook his head.

"It's the solstice, the shortest day of the year. Yule. A celebration of the wild hunt! And you're our new hunter, Max. So today we celebrate you! It's all for you, Max, all for you, King of the Wild Things! And to show the best of our delights, I'll charm the air to give a sound, while you perform your antic round!"

She pressed play on a battered cassette player and Mötley Crüe's "Shout at the Devil" came blaring out. The old man banged a tambourine in time to the beat and Miranda shrieked joyously, screaming along and waving her fist in the air. "Shout! Shout!"

The pig went apeshit, snorting and stomping, and the beat of the music, the squeal of the guitar and pounding of the drums, billowed up inside of Max, filling him with the urge to dance. He romped about the fire, gyrating and spinning, kicking his legs and throwing up his arms.

The flames whirled and pranced, now purple and green, the smoke curling in on itself and massing, congealing and taking form, and from the conflagration an image appeared: a great black goat. Curled horns blossomed from its lean head, its glaring eyes yellow and phosphorescent. The ashen beast rose up on its hind legs from the barrel and turned slowly, lifting and twitching its tail.

Max stood before it in awe. Transfixed. Mesmerized. Stunned still.

Miranda came from behind and whispered hot into his ear.

"Kiss it," she said. "Don't be scared. Kiss the black goat's ass!" and she gave him a little shove.

Max took a tentative step forward, pursing his lips, the smell of smoke and goat overwhelming him, gamey and feral, musky and barnyard, hay and earth and fire. His head spinning, eyes slipping shut, he bowed forward and let his lips press against the hindquarters of the great goat.

A cheer erupted and pandemonium broke out: the pig now gone completely wild and racing in circles around the burn barrel, the fat lady bellowing, "Shout! Shout!" and rocking so hard and fast the battered old chair seemed to be pulling itself up and lifting from the muddy ground with each pendulous swing.

Miranda had a ratty old broom, just a crooked stick with a wisp of straw tied to the end, and she cradled it in her arms, spinning and spinning in a mad dervish as the old man rose up from his chair and straddled the hog, riding it like a horse, waving a can of Coors Light over his head, grunting and howling, the giant pig bucking and stomping, leaping upwards and hanging still in the air, legs gracefully splayed.

Max's jaw dropped open as he witnessed the impossible: the fat lady's rocking chair swinging up off the ground, like a kite caught on a sudden breeze, the pig's racing feet no longer touching the earth as it made its rounds about the fire, but hovering over the ground, lifting into the night.

He turned to Miranda who now straddled her crooked broom and held a beckoning hand out to him. "Come, Max, come, my wolf boy, ride the night skies of yule with us!"

And Max took her hand, filled with a strange sense of trust and adoration, of love and hope. He grasped her around the waist, pressed his cheek into her back, shutting his eyes for a moment as her scent of earth and smoke and fire and flowers and grease enveloped him.

They rose up and when Max opened his eyes again they were high above the tops of the redwoods, the town of Arcata tiny and toy-like below them, the black bay stretching out to the sea. The old man rode along beside them, straddling his grunting hog, sucking down the last of a Coors Light and tossing the can over his shoulder. The fat woman, still knitting, rocked as her chair traversed the skies, the night awash in spilled stars leaking across the darkness above and about them.

The moon rose from behind the forested hills, red as blood and fat and bloated as the belly of a carp, and all was well and all was good and all were happy and all were fed and all were warm and all was perfect on this day of the witch's yule.

THE GYPPO'S CLOTHES

Why am I wearing the gyppo's clothes? Because I was robbed. Drugged and thrown in a pile of rotting filth, top coat gone, shirt tore open, pockets pulled out and ripped from my trousers, shoes missing. A disastrous affair.

It all began in Seattle with the telegram that fell into my lap like an albatross tumbling dead from the sky.

It arrived as I was receiving a shave from the barber in the lobby of the hotel I had procured for myself some weeks prior.

"Is there a Blackwood here?" a bellboy's voice cut through the fog of cigar smoke. "An Alexander Blackwood?"

I motioned him forward and examined the thin yellow paper as the barber ran a razor up my neck, wiped the soap and hairs on a towel, and then proceeded to wax and style my mustache. It was from my sister. My father was ill. It was serious, and I was to return to our ancestral home in San Francisco at once if I cared to see him again alive.

I immediately went and packed my belongings, checked out from my lodgings and secured passage on a steamer headed south to San Francisco. I was lucky in that the Selja—a freight ship looking to ferry a few passengers— was pulling out that evening. With both the current and wind being in our favor, it was to be but a three-day voyage from Seattle to San Francisco.

The Grand Trunk Pacific dock was an impressive pier, the largest on the West Coast, and that fateful evening it was packed with masses of shuffling humanity. I tugged my luggage through the crowded dock, the sailors and barkers,

Chinamen with long black ponytails, a gaggle of short South Americans draped in brightly colored cloth and carrying crates of strange fruit.

And then . . . then I thought for a moment I saw him there. My father. Not a man who looked like him, but him, himself, in his signature green frock coat and bowler, snow-white mutton chops. I startled and gasped as he turned and locked eyes with me. Though my mind knew it could not be him, my heart beat as if otherwise and my ears rang as a tinge of guilt ran through me, for I had been to Seattle on a family business trip and it had not gone well.

Some foolish investments with some shady men had squandered the investment I had been entrusted with, and, if truth be told, shamed, I had dreaded returning to my family in San Francisco, and had been putting it off for some time.

But then there was a shove to my back as the great crowd heaved around me and when I blinked the figure was gone. I chalked it up to the melancholy malaise that had recently fallen upon me and the stress of a failed business trip and pushed forward.

The vessel appeared sound enough. It wasn't a regular passenger ship, but a cargo vessel with a few spare quarters below deck, so it hadn't the comforts and amenities I was used to, but a cot and dry room was all I really required.

The captain, a gruff-looking bearded man with a downturned face and watery, jaundiced eyes, gave me a nod and a grunt as I boarded.

Strange dreams plagued my sleep that night as that rusted hulk crashed through the waves. Visions of my father supine, my fair sister Samantha kneeling at his side. I would awake, fevered, slick with sweat, heart pounding, a terrible feeling of guilt surging behind my ribs, the hull groaning against the sea, the crash of the slapping ocean swirling in the darkness.

On the second day of our journey, we took port for the night in the small town of Arcata, cradled in the shelter of the Humboldt Bay. Restless and anxious, nerves vexed, I craved some respite in the form of drink and female gaiety and company. Walking along the deck, the moon was high and full, the night bright with its light: glinting the black waves of the bay, streaking the rusted bars of the ship's rails, and seeming to beckon with its eerie glow on the tiny port landside. As I plodded down the gangway off the ship, the captain called out to me, almost as if he could sense my carnal pursuit.

"Where ye be headed, good sir?"

"Just a stretch of the legs. Perhaps a dram or two."

He nodded knowingly, stroked his grizzled beard. "Watch your Ps and Qs and be sure and be back well before morning. We leave at first light, with or without you."

"Aye, Captain," I replied with a tip of my hat, and stepped off into the fog and night.

Since there was only one house of ill repute in all of Arcata, and rumor swirled that the sheriff often camped outside it waiting to grab unwary travelers, I decided to jump a stage to Eureka, a city a few miles to the south, which boasted of a large, waterfront red-light district.

Eureka was quite a bustling port. After strolling the streets for a bit and taking in the tone of the town, I finally settled on an ornate seaside mansion aptly named The Palace.

Coming into the parlor my coat was checked by a boy and the proprietress—a mammoth woman whom everyone called "The Empress"—offered an assortment of lovely ladies to me. A pale, skinny redheaded lass immediately caught my fancy. With a grin she led me up a flight of stairs and to a small room where she quite efficiently and passionately employed her generous labors in a most satisfactory way.

Feeling a warm relief, a lifted heaviness from my burdened soul, I returned to the parlor for a cigar. However, catching some commotion in the saloon area, I decided to make my way there.

Satiated carnally, I was now hungry for drink, conversation and human interaction after spending two days sequestered in my cabin. The saloon was quite opulent, rich wooden walls, sturdy tables and chairs all about, a long redwood bar with a great multitude of spirits displayed behind it. A tiny man of what appeared African descent sat before a piano in the corner, plucking out a most delightful tune.

At the far end of the bar a crowd encircled a boisterous bulldog-faced fellow holding court, sending the gathered mass into bouts of laughter with his exhorts.

I bellied up and ordered a draft of beer, then asked the fellow beside me what the fracas was about.

He grinned and cocked his head. "Writer over there. Always gets them wound up. Mad character by the name of Jack London."

"Jack London?"

"Aye, tis him."

"Why I've read his work. The one about the poor fellow who lights a fire beneath branches covered in snow. He's quite famous and well regarded in San Francisco, I can tell you. Fancy seeing him here."

"Ya, he's got a farm not too far south from 'ere. Comes up ta drink away his problems when it all gets too much for him down there. He may be able to tell a story, but he's a terrible farmer. Full of daft ideas that never work."

"That so, is it?"

"Aye, and the fellows love to give him a good ribbing over it."

"So, Jack," a portly fellow with his thumbs tucked in his suspenders shouted, "What's your next book to be about?"

The stocky blonde man took a hearty chug of his beer and waved a dismissive hand. "Bwaa. I only write for the money. It's tilling the earth, working the land, producing crops. That's real work. That's what I care about. Bollocks to writing."

Sure enough a voice called out, "Couldn't raise a crop a beans to fruition is what I hear. What kind of farmer can't even grow beans? Nothing but fodder for the bugs."

"Ha ha, what I tell you," the gent beside me proclaimed with a wink.

"Very good," I replied, and since the fellow had piqued my curiosity, followed with, "Say, what's your story, mate? You live here in Eureka?"

"Aye, at times. I'm what they call a gyppo. An independent logger. Travelling to the logging camps when they need a strong man willing to work, who knows his way around a choker and a cant hook."

I engaged the gyppo for several minutes. His name was Misolf and he told me about the nature of logging, which was a huge source of commerce in this region. The demand from San Francisco was seemingly limitless, what with the earthquake and fire only five years past. He told me briefly of the innovations in the field, the steam donkey and lumber trucks. It was quite interesting and made quite the backdrop, what with Jack London's proclamations of how hard work with one's hands cleansed the soul, and the benefits to being in nature.

Another rowdy drunk shouted something about London's recent failures on the farm. The crowd was roaring with laughter, and Jack screaming back at them. "Hear hear, yes, it's true we lost those beans to them damn beetles. But listen up, we learned. And more than that, we're making a socialist and equal commune. All workers together."

A commotion broke out as a large man dressed ridiculously in red, white and blue overalls, a frilly blouse and a matching bowler pushed through the crowd shouting. "Take your socialist hedonism back to the old country. In America we're capitalists, damnit! You dirty Marxist."

"Damn right I'm a Marxist. Karl Marx was a genius and man of the people."

"Aren't you proud to be American?"

"By God, I'm more American than you! Patriotism is more than dressing like a clown, good fellow. In this land of the free I plan on using my freedom for the socialist cause. No reason the two can't go together."

The big man spit. "You're a traitor is what you are. A traitor to your country."

London took a long pull off his ale, tilting his dog-like

head back and finishing it before resting the empty mug on the bar and leisurely turning to face the large man in the flag outfit, who'd stepped up even closer now and was mere feet from him. "Hope you can use your fists as well as you can run that fat mouth, because I will not stand to be slandered."

Then there were no more shouts, no more laugher. The room was silent. Even the little piano player had ceased playing and was now standing up on his stool, craning his neck to look about.

"Aye, my fists are always ready for Marxist scum."

"So be it. Then with fists will this argument be settled."

Suddenly there was a great cheer and a scurrying of people moving chairs and tables away, clearing room, while a tall black man in a top hat rushed to shut and lock the front doors, extinguishing the glowing-red exterior gas lamps.

I was swept back with the crowd, laughing. It was quite the spectacle as Jack and the other man stripped off their shirts and began to flex in that opened circle of men. Wagers were soon circling in hushed tones.

"I got five on the writer. He's a wily rascal."

"Give me two on the big guy."

As the two men raised fisticuffs, one of the whores slipped up beside me, a raven-haired little beauty wearing a negligee that was really nothing more than a lace-trimmed smidgen of silk. Clutching my arm and pressing her chin to my chest, she gazed up at me with large, black-rimmed eyes, blinking deliciously long eyelashes. "Come upstairs, handsome?"

It was then, with a seismic rush, that I remembered the Captain's warning. To be back well before dawn.

I gazed at the clock above the bar and saw that it was fast approaching midnight. Who knows how long it would take to catch a coach, and if I was forced to walk it could take hours.

"I'm afraid I have to be going," I said to the girl who was now running her fingers up the inside of my thigh in a manner I must admit I found both desirable and delightful.

"Oh, but you must stay for the fight. One more drink

for the road?" she said, presenting a tall cocktail glass she seemingly pulled from nowhere. London and the fat man were circling each other now, hunched with hands raised. The gyppo was laughing excitedly and slapping his hands together.

"Well one more can't hurt, can it?" I replied, for the elixir truly did look wonderful and I'd suddenly developed quite a thirst, my mouth going sandy dry.

As the big man threw a punch and London dodged, I imbibed. It was sweet and cold with a strong and bitter after taste and drinking it was the last thing I remember of that night.

—

I awoke with my father hovering over me, gazing down with a stern face, concern in the wrinkles of his eyes and set of mouth.

"Alexander? Alexander can you hear me?"

"Yes, father," I said through the trails of mist that stretched between us.

"I'll meet you at the house in the woods, Alexander. Meet me at the house in the woods."

Panic swelled up in me, for I knew not what house he was speaking of. "What house in the woods, Father? Where? Where is this house you speak of?" I shouted, only to blink and have his visage blur and change and become someone else entirely. It was the gyppo.

"Oi! Alexander, are you alive?"

"Where . . . where am I," I asked, suddenly aware of the stench of sewage and horse manure. "What happened?"

"Ere, mate, looks like ya've 'ad quite the rough night. Near ready to ring the undertaker I was."

I peered around. I was in some back alley, lying in a pile of refuse. My coat and hat were gone, my pockets turned inside out and rent. Standing, I realized my feet were bare. Thieves had taken even my shoes.

And the ship! The Captain warned they'd be off at

dawn. "What is the time?"

The gyppo squinted and looked to the sky. "Coming on high noon here, I believe."

Panic and shock paralyzed me a moment. I stood there gaping.

The gyppo laughed. "Just count thy blessings and thank your luck star to be alive and in one piece. Say, friend, care to take your luck to the forest? Dolbeer and Carson Company is looking for some gyppos right now to pull in a harvest before the fall storms. They're in a pinch for workers this late and are hiring right now. One week of hauling logs down off the hill to the camp."

"What?" I said, still trying to comprehend this most heinous situation I found myself in.

"A job, mate. One week of work hauling trees off the hill. I've got an extra pair of boots that should fit you, and strong trousers and a spare coat." He patted his two large canvas duffle bags. "A good gyppo is always prepared for two! Just pay me rent on 'em at the end of the week. Stick with me, I'll show you the ropes and chains of choke hooking."

My mind churned. I was penniless. I had not even money to send a telegraph home requesting funds. I suppose I could beseech the Western Union to let me send a telegraph like a common beggar, but the thought of troubling my dear sister, and the humiliation, after having already squandered so much of the family fortune, made the idea of trying to earn my wages palatable, if not entirely appealing.

That, and hearing that London fellow talk of the satisfaction of work done with one's hands. Truth be told, I wished to learn more of this logging business as well. See it from the bottom tier so to say. Perhaps I could glean some insight for future investment that would make this miserable trip at least somewhat worthwhile. Find something to bring back to my ailing father.

Damn it all, maybe an adventure was in order.

"All right then. I thank you most kindly and will take you up on this offer."

"Damn if you don't talk funny, mister," he said,

rummaging through his bag and procuring a set of sturdy work clothes and pair of boots. Okay. Let's get going, the train is waiting. The old Whiskey Express!"

—

The Whiskey Express was a rickety, jarring little train the lumber camps used to ferret their men to the whore houses of the Eureka waterfront and back. As it worked its way up a winding track into the eastern redwood hills, I pondered my fate. What in God's name was I doing in this strange man's clothes headed off into this desolate land? It was certainly below my station.

The men on board were a sullen bunch. An old timer with a white beard sat in the back, singing low and mournful.

"When the wind is howling, take heed mister lumberjack, there are voices in the wind."

The smoke and mist drenched hills felt apocalyptic, the forest like a forlorn battlefield of massive stumps, trampled underbrush and wood fires, as if a great war had occurred there not too long ago. Ash floated lazily in the air which stank of burning coal and woodfire. One almost expected to see bodies lying on the blackened ground amongst the huge moss-covered stumps, blackened ground.

At the base camp there was a long queue of disheveled, tired looking men awaiting to board the train back to Eureka. Disembarking, I asked the gyppo, "If they are in such need of help, why are all these men leaving?"

"Those men are fellers and cutters. They fell the trees and cut them into sections, but no will work to bring them down from the hills. That's the low work, left to us, the choke hookers. The mutts. Bad luck mixing felling and hooking they say."

Harsh voices then rang out, screaming, "Make way! Make way!" and two men carrying a badly-bloodied third by the arms and legs came pushing up to the open train door. "Easy now. Get him on the train. Careful, careful."

He appeared to have suffered some contusion to the

top of the head, his face was covered in a sheet of blood, his hair thick and nappy with it. As they laid the man down in the aisle, the gyppo asked.

"What happened to 'em, then?"

Clutching a grisly, blood-soaked rag to the man's head, one of the men said, "He was settin' the chokers on the candy side, hookin' on to a big blue-butt, when the fucking riggin' slinger says, 'Let 'er go.' Stupid cock sucker. Happened quick. Just like that."

A smattering of the men around us crossed themselves and kissed their fingers, the gyppo just shook his head sadly. A murmur went up among the crowd. "Always in threes. It always happens in threes." They looked amongst each other, as if to ascertain whom would be next. I shivered as the danger of this hasty and ill-conceived jaunt fell home.

The gyppo, sensing my ill ease, pat me on the back and steered me away from the sight. "Don't listen to their nonsense, mate. They'll drive you mad with their craziness. Just keep an open eye and a be awares. You'll be fine."

But as I turned away, the wounded man's eyes locked on mine. I could see where his skull was cracked open and his brain—a tannish-brown mass of wrinkles like sleeping worms—shimmered there. He groaned, spitting up blood, lifted a hand and pointed a trembling finger at me and spoke with an awful, gurgling whisper, "Your father awaits in the house in the woods."

I shuddered, blinked, and then he was just lying there again, looking quite still and dead as the gyppo pulled me away and into the camp.

—

The gyppo and I were put into a crew of seven, with a Boss, which made eight of us, a lucky number they said, that couldn't be divided by three. Superstitions seemed to abound here in this desolate and tore apart wasteland.

Our crew was as follows:

The Donkey Punch, a grizzled old-timer with a long

beard, who wore a sideways looking cowboy hat that made him appear like a caricature of one of those 49ers from the last century. His sole job was to man and maintain the steam donkey, a loud and dangerous mechanical wench used to pull the huge trees down off the hillside.

Finn and Connor, an Irish pair of brothers with coal-black hair and wary faces. Conner was the knot bumper who waited at the landing for the logs and unhooked the chokers, telling the Donkey Punch when to lay on the power and put her in gear. Connor was the rigging slinger who sent the signal down to his brother. They had some code and language between them they could transmit down the hillside with a series of whistles, shouts and hand movements. It was amazing actually, the way they communicated.

And then there were the choke hookers. A sad-faced Portuguese fellow by the name of Alfonso who was the most superstitious of the lot, and Sal, a pudgy and squat local boy who was constantly complaining. Rumor had it he'd once been a cutter but had been demoted down to choke hooker due to his ill temper.

Then the gyppo, and myself, whom they called the brush monkey, as I was new and inexperienced, and would be given the most menial of chores.

And of course, the Boss.

The Boss was a brutish-looking man with mean eyes and fiery red hair. I never did learn his name. We just called him the Boss. He had this tooth that hung out the side of his mouth. A long, pointed fang.

Alfonso claimed the Boss once had a rotten tooth, and after he'd pulled it loose from his head, he'd thrown it into the mud where a black dog had stepped on it. That's what caused the dog's fang to grow from his mouth, that black dog's foot. The Portuguese man crossed himself as he said this and shivered, explained it was the sign of an open door to the devil.

—

rusted cables thicker than a man's forearm twisted out from it and snaked up the hill.

The Donkey Punch was immediately at the machine, greasing and testing the gears, muttering to himself. He was to sleep down there in a little shack beside the machine, the rest of us were to make camp at the top of the mountain where the last of the monstrous logs awaited us.

The trek up the mountainside was grueling. Following the labyrinthine path of those cables upwards, upwards, upwards, the grade impossibly steep. The mere misstep could send one plunging straight down and at times even the donkeys appeared nervous, braying and refusing to budge unless whipped most unmercifully. Finally, we rounded the top and came to an immense flat plateau of felled logs, just as the sun was slipping behind the western valley.

I stood there panting, watching as the sky darkened, and Alfonso came in close, slipped me a bulb of garlic. "Keep this on you, will protect you," he said in a halting, tentative whisper.

"Protect me from what?"

"Nosferatu. Undead haunt this forest."

The gyppo, panting as we scaled the mountain, whispered angrily, "Listen to his nonsense, not!"

But I took the papery mass and put it in my inside pocket, close to my heart.

—

Getting those logs down off the steep hillside and to the road was quite the operation. Harrowing and hard labor.

The gyppo and I would use our cant hooks to roll the logs to the edge where Alfonso would pound in the drive grab and Sal would slip on the chokers, hollering to Conner to send the signal to let her go. The steam donkey would pound and screech, the cable going so taunt it sang, and that massive round of wood would rip through the dirt and duff, and on we'd go to the next one. By evening I was sore and more tired than I'd ever been.

—

On our second day at the camp the skies filled with dark clouds and it began to drizzle rain. A strong wind whipped through the ferns and around the moss-covered stumps.

"Storm's coming," Sal said to the Boss. "We best break camp and head back."

"Nonsense," the Boss barked, that big fang gleaming in his mouth. "We work till the last of this timber is pulled to the road. Sun, rain or whatever weather the good Lord deems us worthy of."

"It's dangerous and not what I signed up for."

The Boss stormed up to Sal, fists at his side, his face a knot of anger. "You signed up to work and by God you will, have you a problem with that?"

"I'm a white man and a native son of Eureka. Yes, I have a problem, just this year I was a cutter, working my way to faller, now I'm in the rain with you hooker scum. I won't stand for it no more—"

Quick as a lightning strike, the Boss whipped out a fist and delivered a strike to his face. Sal fell backwards, landing on his back in the duff.

"Now," the Boss said, looming over the fallen man, "you've had a taste of my right, don't make me give you the left as well. What do you say, then?"

Sal just lay there staring, rubbing his jaw.

The Boss took a threatening step toward him, kicking dirt and redwood needles into his face, body tense like a coiled rattlesnake. "Can you hear me now, you wall-eared cock sucker?"

Sal nodded.

"Then what the fuck do you say then?"

"Yes, Boss."

"Good. Now get back to work!"

Cursing under his breath, Sal pulled himself to his feet and set to gathering the choker cables, casting furtive glares to the Boss who'd gone to barking orders up to the gyppo.

And the day went on.

—

On the third day the drizzle turned to rain. Pouring rain. Roiling sheets of water cascading down from a black sky. We huddled by the woodstove in the cook area, a sort-of lean-to of roughhewn redwood planks, nursing our coffees and waiting for the Boss.

"It's madness to stay here any longer," Sal said.

"The third day," Alfonso intoned. "Our third day. The rain is a sign."

Sal turned to him. "But we spent a day hiking 'ere, so it's no really our third, but our fourth day."

"No, our third day here. Always in threes."

"That makes no sense. We got here before dusk, so this is our fourth day here."

"Our third day awakening in this place."

Finn, sitting sullen on a stump beside his brother, shouted at them. "Can ye please give us some quiet! Listen to ya! You're both daft as can be. What's it even matter?"

Well, it's the principle to me," said Sal.

"Threes. Always in threes," Alfonso muttered forlornly.

"For fuck's sake, can ye please shoot your mouths!" Connor hollered.

The Boss then came storming up. "What's this then? Let's get to work."

Sal began to grumble, but it was Conner who stood up and spoke. "Sir, I'm no afraid 'a 'ard work. You knows that. But the men all agree, to continue in this weather is madness."

The Boss stood steaming a moment, eyes filled with fire, that sharp tooth pressed hard into his chin, then seemed to relent and look away, smiling.

"Conner, you're a good man, and I understand your hesitation. But we must work on. The Tyee wants the last of this down, and he's willing to make it worthwhile to us." He slapped his hands together. "Okay, men, give me your ears with no prejudice. First: double pay. Double pay because of the rain, and if we get the last of these logs down, every last one of them . . ." He looked around, locking eyes with each of us in line. "A bonus of fifteen dollars to each and every one of you. Now what say you? Do we have a deal?"

Sal banged his coffee cup down and held his chin up. "Twenty dollars each."

"Ah, now, you know I can't agree to terms without the—"

Conner took a step forward. "Twenty-dollar bonus each or we all walk out of here now."

The men looked around at each other, grimly nodded.

The Boss took a deep breath, put his hands on his hips and gazed down at his muddy boots, shaking his head. "All right then. Agreed!" He rubbed his hands together briskly, as if to create heat. "Ya fookin hooking bastards run a hard bargain, ya do. Now come on, let's get this timber off the hill."

—

The earth had turned to a cloying muck of mud and clay with the rain, making each step a torment of hard work. The logs refused to roll in the mushy mess and the gyppo and I were forced to rely on brute strength to push them to Alfonso and Sal.

Things felt dream-like and weird working in the storm like that. With the rain slamming down and the pounding of the steam donkey, I struggled to hear the screams of the Boss barking orders. Seeing his mouth open and close with no sound, I felt as if I was a mute as he glowered at me, waving his hands frantically. Stumbling through the water and mist I suddenly realized what he was telling me, *GET OUT OF THE WAY!!* and leapt to the side just as the haul-back cable sprung tight and a great log came swiveling around.

As I fell to the earth I blinked and then opened my

eyes to see that log come barreling towards Sal, who opened his mouth in surprise before it slammed into him, crumpling him and pulling him along as it slid across the earth, scraping away all the mud and duff, chaparral and ferns.

And then it was as if the mountain itself grew sick and vomited, for the whole front of the hillside trembled for a moment and then fell away in a great avalanche of mud and timber and kicking donkeys. A landslide. There was a rumble, a whoosh, followed by a great echoing *thump* that shook the ground beneath us. Then a sudden stillness.

My mind struggled to comprehend the enormity of it. One moment there was a steep slope of stumps and battered ferns, piles of brush, cables, burros; the next there was nothing but slick mud dropping down into fog and clouds. The steam donkey was silent, buried in a sea of wet earth, the only sound the patter of rain.

The gyppo, Conner and Alfonso stood beside me, on the edge of the chasm, staring downward. The Boss stood on the higher ground above us. Sal, Finn and Punch were gone.

Alfonso looked to us, from one to the next, his long, sad-featured face now ashen and riveted with horror. "We've got to help them!" Cupping his hands to his mouth he screamed into the abyss of rain. "Sal! Finn! Punch! Can you hear me?!"

"Damn fool," the Boss said, "they're buried beneath a ton of earth and lumber. Even if they did survive the fall and mud, there's not a chance they could hear you beneath it all."

"We have to try to help them."

"Help them how? Do you not notice the goddamn road is gone? Have you given any fucking thought as to just how the hell we're going to even get out of here?"

Conner spun around and stormed up the hill towards the Boss, an angry finger extended. "YOU! This is all the fault of you and your greed. You killed my brother, damn you."

The Boss held his palms out and took a step back. "Whoa there. It's no fault of mine. I killed no one. You all came on your own free will and accord."

Conner glared at him, the muscles in his neck throbbing, and charged forward, hissing and putting his face a finger's length from the Boss's. "And you killed Sal. I saw it. Leaving him on the lee side of the timber when you knew that log was coming."

The Boss grabbed him by the collar of his coat and pulled him even closer, so that their noses were pressed together. "That damn fool wasn't paying attention. The bush monkey either. He's goddamn lucky to be alive, that one there," he said, pointing at me. "Why God chose your brother and Sal over 'im I know not. Blame God if you need to pin blame somewhere," and he pushed Conner away from him.

Conner grunted and groaned, turned, and put his hands to either side of his head, letting out an anguished scream.

Alfonso crossed himself. "Don't forget Punch. This was going to be his last season in the hills. Had a nice piece of grazing ground right on the Van Duzen he was looking to settle down on."

The Boss scrubbed his face with his palms, then slapped his thighs. "Now listen, men. There's no time for blame and anger. What we need to do is make a plan to get off this mountain. If we're not careful, this whole face is liable to fall right the hell off. We no can skirt too close to the slide. We'll have to take the backside down, then circle around when we get to the bottom. When we get back to the road we can look for survivors before heading back. Are you with me, then?"

All eyes turned to Conner, who slowly turned, let his hands slip down from his head, took a deep shuttering breath, and finally nodded.

—

We walked all through that day, the Boss leading us down the steep hills where the forest was virgin and pure. The trees loomed from impossibly high heights, like nothing I'd ever seen before. A forest prehistoric, like a land of dinosaurs with ferns that stretched up over a man's eyes. The rain slackened and it grew icy cold, our breath leaving us in great white clouds as we lumbered downwards. A smattering of snow began to drift down and dust the ground and the wind came whipping through those mammoth redwood trunks with a sad, moaning sound.

"The windy goo," Alfonso whispered.

"What heathen trash talk now?" the gyppo said.

"A spirit of loneliness and hunger in the woods."

"Aye, I feel like a spirit of loneliness and hunger myself in these woods," the gyppo replied back with a sigh.

It would be the last thing I ever heard him say.

—

It was when we made camp that we noticed the gyppo was no longer among us.

Everyone tried to remember the last time they had seen him, how far back. His last words, about being a spirit of loneliness and hunger, echoed in my head and I struggled to remember how far back we'd been when he uttered them. Two miles? Three?

We shouted into the forest and discussed going back for him, Alfonso crossing himself and whispering how we couldn't leave him out there with the windy goo. But the Boss scoffed at his superstitions and decided it was imminent we make camp and start a fire to dry our soaking clothes and warm our bodies. We were all shivering uncontrollably, a marked pallor on our countenance.

"Liable to freeze to death if we don't. Dead men can rescue no one," the Boss said, his lip curling over that dog fang snaggle tooth. "Besides, he'll surely see the light of the fire and come to us."

Conner reluctantly agreed. Still being just a bush monkey among them, my opinion wasn't sought, though I trembled at the thought of my friend lost out there in that vast forest.

Soon we had a raging fire going that surely could be seen for miles as the darkness fell around us, yet as we dried our clothes and made up pallets for slumber by the fire's edge, the gyppo was not to be heard from.

—

I awoke to a terrible screaming that was over so quickly I wondered if maybe I had dreamt it. But sitting up and gazing about I could see the others were awake, too, staring across the fire at each other. Except for Conner. He was gone, his bedding a disheveled mess, footsteps in the snow snaking away into the darkness.

A groan punctured the night, followed by a distant, strangled-sounding, "Help . . ."

"It's Conner," Alfonso whispered.

The Boss was up, tearing a strip of bedding and wrapping it around a stout branch he retrieved from the wood pile we'd accrued, then setting it alight in the fire. "Right, probably wandered off to take himself a piss and fell in some damn hole. Come then, men. Let's find him."

We followed the torchlit footsteps as they weaved through the huge shadowed trees, watching as they grew erratic and then turned quickly. We all gasped when another pair of footsteps appeared there in the snow, followed by a great gout of blood and a ragged path like that of someone dragging themselves away. The Boss cast his torch into the shadows and there, curled under a rotting log, was Conner.

He lay on his back, his eyes clasped shut, a look of agony etched across his face, and with great horror and a rising gorge I realized there was only a bloody stump where his right arm should have been.

The Boss thrust the torch into my hands and dropped to his knees, pressing his palms to Conner's wound, trying to slow the blood which seeped out, but I could see from the Irishman's deathly-white complexion and blue lips that too much had already been lost.

"What happened to you, man?" asked the Boss as he

tore a strip from Conner's shredded coat and wrapped it around the stump.

"I 'eard the voice of my brother, calling for me. Calling for me to help him. I . . . I followed the sound to a figure, only it wasn't my brother at all. T'was that other fellow. The gyppo. He was smiling at me with this awful, terrible lear. Then he attacked me. Cut my bloody arm off with an axe, and then . . . then, sitting there right before me, his eyes huge and ugly, he began to eat it. Eating me own bloody flesh right before me. Only . . . only it wasn't the gyppo anymore. It was . . . it was something else. Something horrible. So horrible."

Alfonso gasped and crossed himself. "The windy goo. The spirit of loneliness."

"Shut your goddamn mouth," the Boss hissed at him. When we turned back to Conner he was dead. No mistaking it, he'd gone completely blue and still, eyes now open and peering out at nothing, mouth hanging open.

The Boss pulled his compass from his pocket and peered at it. "All right. We walk through the night. Head eastward around the base of the mountain and we will surely hit the road by daybreak. There's no missing it, even in the dark. Come along." He stood, grabbed the torch from me, and started off, Alfonso and I behind him.

—

Dawn was turning the black sky the gray-blue of gun metal when we came upon a rough skid road. Alfonso crossed himself, knelt, and kissed the path.

It was the first time I saw the Boss smile, his thick lips turning up, that dog tooth hanging there, but then his eyes went angry again and a huge frown encompassed his face as he muttered, "No, no, no . . . It can't be."

"What," I cried. "What is it?"

"Look, you damn fools, don't you see where we are?"

"It's impossible," Alfonso said.

I ran forward in disbelief and found myself staring

down at the sheer face of mud and rock that had once been the path down off the mountain. We were somehow back where we'd started, though we'd gone nothing but downward. Down, down, down, only to be back at the top again. Alfonso was right, it was simply not possible.

The Boss looked to be going insane, pulling at his hair, foaming from his mouth, darting into the woods yelling, "But where did we start? Where did we start?"

Gazing about in disbelief, my heart froze and my breath caught in my neck, for there was the gyppo! He was high up in the branches of a fir tree, smiling down at us. His eyes were impossibly white against the dark, drying blood that covered his face and he clutched Conner's severed arm in his hands, ripping huge bites out of it with his grinning mouth.

When he noticed me staring up at him, he waved, tossed the arm behind him, and dropped forward, falling from the branches. Tumbling down he stretched out his arms and a leathery black membrane erupted from his back, spreading into huge wings like that of a bat. He took to the air, swooping first upward, then down to where Alfonso stood staring in awe.

The bat-thing that was the gyppo came down behind him and wrapped him cocoon-like in its wings. Its body had changed into something animalistic: squat, with a thick mat of dark hair, but it still had the face of the gyppo. It smiled at me, eyes now glaring red orbs, and from its mouth came two huge fangs, massive tusks that it sunk into the neck of Alfonso.

Frozen in horror I watched breathlessly as the thing then spread it wings and flew off into the mist, Alfonso howling and screeching in its terrible grasp.

I turned and there was the Boss, coming at me angrily, screaming. "It was you, wasn't it? You all along. You killed them all. Killed them and ate them."

"What are you talking about?" I stammered, backing away from him. "Have you gone mad?"

"Look at you! You're covered in their gore and blood."

And when I looked down, to my shock and surprise, he was right. There was blood and pieces of flesh all over me. I could taste it like rusted iron in my mouth, the sickening scent flooding my nose.

"You're a sick dog, you've got to go down," he hollered, and came at me.

He was going to kill me. I saw it in his eyes. I . . . I had no choice.

As he swung a fist, I darted forward and the most primal instinct of self-defense came over me.

I bit him.

Opened my mouth and brought my teeth down on his neck, right where I could see that pulsating tube of blood rising up from his heart, and I tore it open and felt its warmth pour over me as we fell together to the cold, snow-covered earth.

He beat at me and struggled, but I held fast, and soon the fight went out of him and he lay there with only the occasional spasm as his life's blood left him.

Lifting myself off his quivering body, whom should I see standing there in the swirling snow and mist, but my father. He stood before a quaint log house, smoke belching from its stone chimney. It was like something from a fairy tale.

He was wearing his green frock coat and bowler, and he beckoned me with a wave of the hand, then turned and entered the front door. I followed after him, entering into a large and spacious room, in the center of which sat a long table, draped in a lace-trimmed linen cloth, all made up for dining: gold-trimmed plates and utensils, thick cloth napkins, a candelabra with thirteen flickering candles. The room was quite warm, with a fire roaring in the hearth and I took off my work coat and hung it on a brass rack beside the door.

My father sat down on one side of the table, I on the other.

"Are you not well, Father?" I asked. "I heard you were ill."

me. The warmth of the fire so strong I opened my shirt, and my belly so swollen I unfastened the top button of my trousers, I chuckled on, so cozy, content and satisfied that I vowed to take a nap right there and then at the table, only to wake and find myself here, in this godforsaken jail cell.

Yes, yes, yes, I hear their whispers and taunts. Angry proclamations and threats of hanging.

Tales of how they found me naked in the snow, covered in gore and laughing hysterically. They claim there is no truth to my story, that it is either the delusions of a lunatic or a clever attempt to disguise my crimes with madness.

They claim there never was any gyppo, or moreover, that I am, in fact, the gyppo upon whom I blame the slaughter.

But I know the truth. I know who I am, and I know why I wear the gyppo's clothes.

THE TALE OF THE FEARLESS VAMPIRE KILLING BROTHERS

"Just remember this," Abe told his brother, digging his knife blade down the wooden stake, shaving the tip to a sharp point. "It's not human. If you begin to think of it as human, even for a moment, you put this entire operation in danger. And we must avoid its keeper at all costs."

Johnathan gulped and nodded as Abe tested the tip with the pad of his finger. He crossed himself, and handed his brother a heavy wooden mallet. "Are you ready? Once we start there is no going back."

Johnathan blinked his large blue eyes. "Yes. I'm ready. Let's do this."

Abe palmed him a bulb of garlic, and the two set forth into the gathering twilight.

The somber hoot of an owl rang in the distance. The rustling leaves of the tall oaks were beginning to yellow. Autumn was approaching, the nights growing steadily longer. The sky above them was a riot of color, burgundy and orange to the west where the sun sunk into the horizon, a growing darkness to the east where night crept.

Yes, now was the time to strike.

The house, once such a happy place, was preternaturally quiet and ominous as they slunk through the shadows, past the creature's keeper, who lie sprawled on a sofa, snoring softly, and down the hall to the creature's lair.

They stopped a moment before the heavy wooden door,

hearts hammering in their chests, their breath coming in quick gasps, before Abe pressed a sweaty palm to the door and pushed it slowly open, careful to not have it squeak and possibly alert the keeper.

And there it was, curled up in a tangle of sheets, its thumb in its mouth: the slumbering monster of the night. Tangle of raven-black hair, skin unnaturally soft and sallow.

In sleep it looked so peaceful. Innocent. It was hard to comprehend the agony and torment the foul creature conjured.

The creature had first appeared nearly three years ago, its unholy presence bringing an awful change to their lives, and since then nothing had been the same. The nights were filled with dreaded howling, and during the day evidence of its rampage was clear: walls ink splattered in strange patterns and crude drawings. Beloved objects destroyed. Loved ones changed forever. It was time to put an end to this madness.

As they eased toward it, the creature stirred and turned onto its back, exposing its small, pale chest to them. A good omen.

Abe ran a tongue over his parched lips and lifted the stake, holding it firmly over the creature's heart, then nodded to his brother, who brought the mallet up, over his head, and with a grunt, sent it smashing down onto the top of the stake. The tip buried itself into the pale skin, black blood bubbling up as the monster awoke with a nerve-shattering shriek.

"Again!" Abe screamed, struggling to hold the stake in place as the thing thrashed and howled. "Hit it again!"

Panicked, Johnathan pounded the stake, the creature's ribs cracking as the heavy piece of sharpened wood sunk in deeper, blow by blow, blood now spraying out and splattering their faces, till the stake had pierced it through and stuck it to the mattress.

The creature let out a long shuddering breath, quivered, and went still.

They had done it. The deed was done. Abe sighed with

relief, wiping blood from his face with the back of his hand, when the door went flying open and light filled the room.

It was the beast's keeper! They turned and gasped as she stormed towards them, shrieking, "Boys! My God, what have you done to your brother?"

BLIND CLOWN CHAOS

Scott's skull-thumping, nearly-blinding hangover didn't make the sight of all those clowns any fucking easier, that's for sure. Gazing through slit eyelids into the blistering sun, he saw them everywhere: handing out balloons to children, setting up some sort of elaborate stage for magic tricks, pouring out of a large white van with the words *AZATHOTH BLIND CHAOS Clowning and Miming* scrawled on the side in swirling Day-Glo letters. Christ, what was worse, a clown or a mime? If one of these clowns started pretending he was stuck in a box, Scott thought for sure he was going to puke.

It was graduation day at his kid's elementary school, Jake's last day of fourth grade. Scott knew he had to get up early for this shit last night, but couldn't tear himself away from a guilt-endowing binge watch of *The Walking Dead*, looking over in surprise at the clock to see that it was two o'clock in the morning and he had managed to drink two bottles of Pinot noir and uncork a bottle of zinfandel. Now he was paying the piper.

As Jake scurried out of the mini-van and ran across the meadow to a gaggle of his friends circled around an extremely tall clown twisting balloons into weird shapes, Scott moaned softly and slid on a pair of RayBans. His wife, Cindy, sidled up beside him and gave him a poke in the side.

"How you feeling there, big guy?" she asked, digging her finger into his ribs and cocking her pretty face at that funny angle she affected when mocking and teasing. "You look a little ragged around the edges."

"Huh? Me? Naw, I'm fine. Just wondering about all the

fucking clowns everywhere."

"It's odd, isn't it? Marsha never mentioned clowns at the parent enrichment meeting. Clowns are so gaudy. I would have gone with a bluegrass band. Yeah, and maybe some pony rides."

"Hillbillies and piles of horse shit. Classy."

"What would you have done? Wine tastings? Open bar?"

"Honestly, I *could* use a mimosa."

"Just try to keep it together. Okay, sweetie?" She gave him a quick peck on the lips and wandered over to Bob and Nadine who were strolling across the parking lot towards the meadow. Damn, that clown twisting up balloons was *tall*. He had to be on stilts or something. Was he staring at Scott? Leering at him from across the open field of screaming children?

Bob rolled up with an open palm extended for a bro shake and a man hug, slapping Scott's back a bit too hard as he started talking rapidly. "S'up, my brother? Dude, I was literally just thinking of you. You gotta come over and check out my new surround sound, it's literally the dopest system. Put on *Apocalypse Now* with The Doors and all those helicopters, literally insane, bro."

Scott didn't know what was worse: this nightmare of a hangover, the clowns, or the way Bob was incorrectly using the word "literally" over and over.

"*The horror, the horror,*" he mumbled, trying to not make eye contact with the freaky clown who was now nodding at him and pointing.

"Ha ha! Right. Fucking Brando, man. Hey, you wanna go puff a fatty real quick?"

Oh God, did he. Anything to ease the jackhammer going off in his alcohol poisoned brain. Cindy was going to be bent when he came back reeking of weed, but fuck it, half the parents here were stoned. Shit, half the teachers and staff as well.

They walked away, down the long dirt driveway that led up to the school, and ducked into a patch of woods in the hillside. Bob fired up the doobie and handed it to Scott. One hit and he felt better, the pressure in his head easing up, the sweet, candy-tasting flavor of Blue Dream calming his belly.

"Fuck, man," Bob said between puffs. "What's up with all the clowns? That shit literally freaks me out."

Not again, thought Scott, please don't use that word again, it was *literally* driving him fucking crazy. That's when the shots rang out and the screaming started.

"The fuck?!" yelled Scott and they were racing up the driveway, a rapid volley of gunfire echoing through the valley.

In the meadow was a horrible scene of mind-melting carnage.

Clowns encircled the field, and they'd traded their balloons and slide whistles for assault rifles. They were popping off rounds at anyone who broke the parameter. He saw Claudia—the principal—dart toward the edge of the clearing. A clown in a satiny, blue, puffy suit and a painted-on frowny face stepped up behind her with a sawed-off shotgun and fired into the back of her skull. The top of her head disintegrated into a fountain of impossibly-red gore as she slammed face first into the ground, her body twitching and jerking.

The tall clown was chasing a toddler in bib overalls around with a large hunting knife, swatting and toying with him like a cat with a baby rabbit, before finally swooping him up by the ankles and—as he dangled helplessly—slicing open his throat from ear to ear, the wound opening like a gaping mouth to spill out a torrent of blood that quickly covered the kid's face. In the center of the meadow—amid the chaos of screams, bloodshed, and rifle fire—a group of clowns were forcing screaming children and parents to their knees, barking orders at them to *Get down! Get down!*

Scott saw Cindy and Jake among them and sprinted forward on raw instinct, desperate to save them. A clown leaped in front of him, laughing wickedly, his giant eyes jaundiced and yellow against the fish-belly white of the grease paint smeared across his face. As Scott went to scream a stream of liquid came spurting out of a large plastic flower on the clown's lapel, splashing him in the face.

And then all was darkness.

—

Scott came to slowly, strange sounds—like underwater screams—filling his head. He tried to move and realized his wrists were bound behind him. He tried to speak and realized he was gagged. He looked around groggily, the shapes and sounds about him beginning to come into focus. It was dark and there was chanting. He was tied to a chair on the edge of the meadow. Other parents were there, too, all tied to chairs and gagged just like him. As his eyes adjusted, he saw the clowns stood in a circle, gripping torches and chanting strange words. *Azathoth, Azathoth, blind clown of chaos awaken. Blind clown of chaos awaken.*

Then he choked and tried to scream, for lying before him was a pile of limp and bloody bodies, tiny bodies, the bodies of children, stacked atop each other, their eyes blank and wide. And there, in the center of the field, was his beautiful wife Cindy, the girl he sometimes thought about in the morning when he woke up, wondering how he had gotten so lucky as to get her. She was naked and bound to an altar, arcane symbols painted on her in what appeared to be blood. Before her stood a clown draped in embroidered robes and wearing an elaborate headdress. He stretched his arms open to the night sky, his face—made-up in a horrid pattern of green and yellow lightning bolts—lifted upwards, screaming, *"Azathoth! Azathoth!"*

The clown lifted a squirming body and set it atop Cindy's heaving belly, and when Scott saw that it was Jake, his son, his boy, his life and his light and his everything, he jerked so violently against his restraints that the chair tipped over. He hit the ground hard just as the clown cleaved open his son's chest with a gleaming knife, hacking through the tiny ribcage, and—reaching in with puffy-fingered, gloved hands—ripped out his still-beating heart. He lifted it to his horrible face and sunk his teeth into it, a stream of blood dripping down off his chin.

And then the sky went white with light and all was still for a moment. It was as if all the air in the meadow were suddenly sucked away, upwards, with a great gust of wind, and then dropped back down again with a loud *whooomp*.

Looming from the depths of the sky was a mammoth being, peering down at the earth like a man might gaze into the workings of an ant hill. But its eyes—framed in giant diamond patterns of alternating reds and blues—were clearly sightless, covered in milky-blue cataracts and leaking a syrupy yellow liquid. It turned its head blindly from side to side, as if to ascertain who had called it from the great depths of space and why. Its nose was a massive and rotten blood-red ball, flaking off tufts of crimson skin which crashed to the ground with wet, slopping thuds. From either side of its head sprouted tufts of pumpkin-orange hair, streaming out to sharp points.

And then existence itself was forever gone as the dreamer awoke and all that was and had ever been was forgotten as the dream of existence evaporated with Azathoth's awakening, most literally.

CHARYBDIS

Pete's big brother was a total fucking dick, no two ways about it.

Even his stupid name: Ace. Naming himself after the guitar player in Kiss, his favorite band. What a dickhead thing to do. His real name was George, but he hated when anyone called him that. Uttering it was sure to get Pete a punch on the arm, or worse, even though Ace loved to call him Dog Turd.

They lived on this weird dead-end street of dilapidated houses that backed up to the highway. No one went down there unless they had to. Between the highway and Pete's house was a swampy and overgrown no-man's land of poison oak and Scotch broom with a concrete storm drain running through the middle. That was their hang out, where they were now, huffing glue and laughing while Pete watched from above, hidden in the hillside bushes. Maggot was spray-painting OZZY across the culvert while Froggy and Ace lay by the entrance, passing a brown-paper bag back and forth as lumber trucks full of logs rumbled by on the highway.

They thought they were some kind of gang, called themselves the Rip Ass Raiders, and all wore these denim jackets with the sleeves cut off, the backs bleached white with RIP ASS RAIDERS written in black magic marker across it, and a goofy skull that was supposed to be scary, but totally wasn't.

They constantly ragged on Pete, calling him Dog Turd and little kid, wouldn't let him hang out with them, even though he was almost thirteen, as old as they were when they started their dumb-ass gang.

Pete cocked his head and tried to focus on what they were saying. They were talking about Jodi Perkins, this eleventh grader whose boobs had doubled in size over the summer.

"Fuck yeah I broke into that stupid bitch's house," Ace said. "Skipped school Friday and hit that shit."

"Bullshit," Froggy said with a dismissive wave of the hand. "You're so full of shit your eyes are brown."

Maggot, a chubby blonde kid with teeth so bucked he looked like a cartoon drawing of a horse, shouted over the whoosh of passing cars while scrawling 666 in dripping red paint. "Yeah, you expect us to believe that crap?"

Ace ran a comb through his hair. "You think I'd come back empty handed?"

"What you got, Ace?"

He shook a cigarette from a pack, dramatically lit it. "Check it." He tugged a piece of white cloth from his pocket, held it aloft, cigarette clenched between his teeth. It was a pair of girl's panties with frilly pink trim. "Got em out of her hamper." He clenched them to his face, inhaled deeply. "Ah, yeah, smell that sweet cherry."

He tossed the panties to Maggot, who put them to his nose with a fierce sniff, his face screwing up comically.

It was all too much for Pete. *They were smelling her underwear! Where her butt had been! GROSS!!!*

He struggled not to laugh, holding a hand over his mouth, but he couldn't stop himself and the laughter come rippling up from his belly, bursting out. He ducked and turned, but they had heard him.

"Dude, it's your brother," Maggot said.

"The fuck I tell you about spying on us, Dog Turd?"

Running away down the trail, Pete chanced a quick look back over his shoulder to see his brother leap up, grab a fist-sized rock, cock his arm, and hurl the thing at him.

Pete stared dumbly as it sailed through the air, watching it spiral, wondering if he should dodge to the left or right, as it came crashing down square on the top of his head.

Stars exploded behind his eyes and he went sprawling, hitting the ground hard, face first, dirt going up his nose and into his mouth, his lip cracking open. He lay there groggy for a moment, reached up and touched his throbbing head. His hand came back bloody. He could hear them all laughing at him--the stupid-ass Rip Ass Raiders--their guffaws echoed in his ears as he lifted himself off the ground, dizzy and suddenly nauseous, and took off in an unsteady sprint down the path, his brother's voice booming from behind him.

"Take that, Dog Turd, and don't let me catch you spying on us again! Rip Ass Raiders rule!"

—

Back at the house, Pete climbed up on the kitchen counter and rooted deep into the empty cupboards. Food had become a hard commodity to come by lately and he was constantly hungry. His mother drank away her hunger, and his brother seemed to have other means, probably dealing pot and living on fast food. There were always telltale McDonalds wrappers in his room.

In the far left corner he uncovered a forgotten jar of peanut butter with a few brown smears still left in the corners where a knife hadn't been able reach. He scooped it out with his finger, stuffing it greedily into his mouth.

His head pounded and he could feel blood beginning to trickle down behind his ear.

Stupid fucking Ace.

He went to the bathroom, took Ace's toothbrush from the chipped mug on the counter, held it over the toilet, peed on it, then shook it off and put it back.

Take that fucker.

As if he ever even used the thing anyway: Mr. Green Teeth.

He thought about his brother and his friends sniffing that girl's stolen panties. It was weird, and gross. But something about it sent a tingling sensation down his spine.

He remembered that stack of nudie magazines he'd once spied in his brother's room and cast an eye down the hall to the bedroom door. There was a KEEP OUT sign tacked to it, and he'd attached a hasp and locked it with a padlock.

Pete laughed. Stupid jerk. All that and he kept his back window wide open. He'd always open it to smoke pot, blowing the smoke outside so their mother wouldn't smell it when she got home from the bar and have a "complete and utter freak out". Then he'd be too stoned to remember to shut it again.

Pete went outside, feeling a little better with the peanut butter in his belly, an odd giddiness swelling in his brain. He even had a little skip to his step as he slipped around the side of the house and to Ace's open bedroom window. Gripping the inside ledge, and kicking his feet against the side of the house, he scurried up and inside.

The room was like a dank cave, musky with the scent of weed, old socks and teenager, the walls covered in dayglow posters for Kiss, Blue Oyster Cult, Deep Purple.

Pete crept to the bed, lifted the mattress, and found what he was looking for: a stack of glossy porn mags. He slipped the bottom one out, thinking it would be the one his brother was least likely to notice. *CHERRY*, a 4th of July special with two naked girls kissing beneath a huge American flag.

With trembling hands, he rolled it up and stuck it in the waistband of his jeans, a cool sheen of sweat breaking out on his neck, then let himself back out through the window.

Slipping down to the ground he could hear the laughter of his brother and his friends as they walked up the trail towards the house. *Shit, time to skedaddle.*

He got on his bike and started pedaling furiously, headed as far away as he could get, for the one place he knew he could be alone in: the abandoned K-Mart.

—

The K-Mart was right on the highway, on the outskirts of town. He remembered going there on happier days to buy Halloween costumes and school supplies, new shoes and a winter coat. But just like the store itself, those times were over and a thing of the past.

The entire perimeter was sealed in a heavy chain-link fence topped with barbed wire. The boarded-up front of the store faced the highway and there was a massive, desolate parking lot there, a kind of creepy asphalt waste land that could easily be seen from the 101, so you'd never want to be seen there or you'd get in big trouble. But the back of the store, where the big concrete loading dock extended out, butted right against a little strip of forest that had grown up beside one of the many sloughs that circulated through the barren outskirts before leaking its waters to the bay.

Pete completely avoided the busy highway and followed a back route out along the slough, pedaling along a thin path where hobos went to drink, wasters went to get wasted and teenagers went to fuck. His heart hammered at the thought of the glossy magazine pages tucked into his pants. He walked the final stretch, pushing his bike, ears sharp for anyone lurking around. The cops had made a big deal about clearing out the vagrants and druggies a few weeks ago, staging big raids. Since then he hadn't seen a single soul around.

He stashed his bike beneath a scrub oak that had grown up by the chain-link fence, covered it in a bunch of leaves to hide it, then plodded off to the place where someone had cut a short, jagged line through the bottom half of the fence. Prying the edge upwards, he pulled himself under, through the dirt and broken glass, to the asphalt on the other side.

He jogged up to the concrete loading ramp, then scrambled to the top of the steel railing. There was a boarded-up window there, but the plywood was loose on the corner and it was easy to squeeze through.

It was cool and dark inside the cavernous building, lit only by snatches of sunlight slanting in through the cracks of the boarded-up windows. Shelves and racks still divided the space up into sections, but they were all bare of products, most of them smashed and pushed over. The floor was filthy, covered in dust and cigarette butts, bottles of all shapes, sizes and colors. A pair of women's panties. In the corner, below where someone had spray-painted HEATHER BROWN IS A WHORE, was an old mattress.

Unbuttoning his pants, he sat on the edge of the mattress and unfurled the magazine, spreading its thick glossy pages out on his lap where a square of sunshine cascaded in from a small smashed window high up on the wall that hadn't been boarded over. His hands trembled. Ever since he'd first glanced at the magazines a week ago, he'd dreamed of being alone with one, and sure enough the pictures were doing something to him. There was the nakedness of the women, the brazenness of them spreading their legs and exposing their most hidden, secret parts, but it was the looks on their faces that really flushed Pete. The lurid expressions of want in their half-shut eyes and panting lips. A sheen of cool sweat broke out on his forehead as he stroked himself to the point where he felt like he might burst, when there was a noise from behind him: a shuffling, scraping sound.

He shot up, the magazine tumbling from his lap, and quickly buttoned his pants.

Was someone there? Had someone seen what he was doing? Embarrassment and shame ripped through him.

Nothing moved, everything was still.

Could have been a rat.

He rolled up the magazine and got ready to bolt when there was a disturbance in the light and in from the broken window flew the most amazing thing he'd ever seen: a huge black insect, like a fist-sized beetle, hovering on blue-veined transparent wings. Its shell was an iridescent, glowing silver with what looked like shimmering black symbols carved into it. Beneath the shell hung hundreds of tiny black tentacles that squirmed and twisted, seeming to taste the air.

Spikey, skeletal legs spread from it as it gracefully

landed on the wall, tucking in its wings. And then, miraculously, it began to grow. Very slowly, so slow that it was hard to even see, but it was definitely growing.

Pete rubbed his eyes and blinked, not sure if what he was seeing was real, as the symbols on its back began to slowly rotate and morph together, forming new shapes, as if it was spelling out some code or spell.

The creature's head swelled, turned milky-white and began to spin toward him. Pete gasped: it was the face of a beautiful woman with her lips puckered at him, like a lurid China doll, and the glowing shell on its black split down the center, revealing two quivering pink lips, a glistening pearl perched where their swollen, flower-like folds met in a pyramid shape. The lips glimmered, sleek and wet, pulsating hungrily, then slowly parted, spreading open. And inside . . . inside was the universe.

All the stars of all the galaxies were in there. Far off planets, constellations, comets and asteroids blaring past with fiery tails. Infinite space in all its magnificence, worlds beyond his comprehension. He blinked and laughed as the thing stretched and grew even larger. He felt himself slipping away, his mind transfixed on the wonders the creature showed, when hands grabbed him from behind and threw him against a concrete pillar.

A dirty, bearded man in a tattered coat pressed against him, pinning him to the pillar, his foul, awful-smelling breath hot in his ear saying, "I saw you there, boy. Saw what you were doing. You like that? You like touching yourself?"

Pete struggled and screamed, kicking and hollering for help, though he knew there was no one who could hear him. Then he gasped and stopped screaming for he saw something utterly insane that his mind struggled to comprehend. From over the man's shoulder he saw that the beetle-thing had grown impossibly large, much taller than the foul-smelling man pressing himself against him. The creature seemed to loom over them, worlds being born and dying inside the pink lips of its gaping maw, and it was stretching four of those skeletal arms out towards them.

With a quick snatching motion, the thing grabbed the man, two arms grasping him by the shoulders and two by the ankles, pulling him up, off the ground, to the yawning universe hole in its back.

There was part of a strangled cry, just the beginning of a scream, before the dirty man's head disappeared, the pink lips closing around his shoulders, his arms and legs flailing frantically. The thing began to slowly pulse, swelling and shrinking, and Pete realized that it was chomping on the man and swallowing him down.

Pete stared transfixed and lost in wonder, torn by curiosity and the urge to run as the man's filthy shoes disappeared into the thing. It was like he was of two minds, one logical and screaming for escape, the other feeling some strange affection for the strange insect-thing that had just saved him.

Indeed, as the lips closed in on themselves and the shell resumed its position, he felt an odd sense of warmth emanate from the thing. While every sensible atom in his body screamed to run while he had the chance, he found himself approaching the strange, huge insect, marveling over the thousands of tiny tentacles that squirmed beneath the shell's edges, and stroking it lovingly.

It cooed back sweetly.

—

It was late when Pete got back to his neighborhood, pedaling his rusty bike down that dark, dead end street. The sun had fallen to the edge of the horizon, casting everything in soft pink and amber light, and Ace was waiting for him, squatting behind the overgrown bushes by the front walk. As Pete hopped off his bike and started toward the house, Ace leapt out, delivering a hard punch to Pete's stomach, knocking the air right out of him, before Ace pushed him to the ground and pinned his arms down with his knees.

"You take my *CHERRY*, you little creep?"

"Naw, naw. I didn't take nothing. Promise."

"Liar. I told you to stay out of my room. Now I'm going to teach you a lesson."

He cocked his fist, poised to strike, when Pete shouted, "Don't hit me! Please. I'll show you something I found. Something, something amazing. I'll take you there, show you. Just don't hit me!"

"What you going to show me?"

"It's a . . . a bug. A crazy bug!"

"A fucking bug?" Ace laughed. "You think I care about a stupid bug?"

Pete's mind reeled, trying to think of something his brother might want. "No, no, there's more. Weed! A whole bunch of weed!"

Ace's face softened. "Weed?"

"Yeah, a whole bunch. Someone must have stashed it and I found it. I'll show you where it is!"

"You better not be fucking with me, or your ass is grass."

"I'm not. I'm not."

"Where's this weed you're talking about?"

"At the old K-Mart. I'll take you there and show you."

—

"This place is fucking cool," Ace said, strutting through the abandoned store. "How come you never told me about it before?"

Because it's the only place I could ever be away from you, Pete thought, as he said, "I was going to. Honest."

"Hey! There's my *CHERRY*. I knew you took it you little creep."

Pete desperately scanned the walls, looking for the big beetle. He didn't see it anywhere, and an icy sliver of fear raced down his throat as his brother approached, pounding a fist into his palm. "So, where's the weed, little man? You didn't bring me all the way out here for nothing, did you?"

As panic gripped him, he began to stammer, "I, ah . . .

ah." Then he saw it, up by the ceiling, in the corner of the room. It had constructed some kind of nest, with little cocoons. "Over there!"

Ace turned and walked into the corner, kicking at bits of rubble and an old soda bottle. "Where, I don't see shit here." The thing was directly above him, but it wasn't doing anything. Just sitting there. The markings on its back dull and still. Maybe it was sleeping. Or dead. Could it have given birth to those cocoons and then died? That's what happened to the spider in that book *Charlotte's Web*.

Ace spun around. "What the fuck, you little shit? Where's the weed? You fucking with me?"

"No, no, it's over there. I swear I saw it."

Ace shook his head, spun, and with a lightning-fast motion smashed his fist into Pete's surprised face. There was a crunching sound that echoed deep into the back of Pete's skull, then a rose of pain bloomed behind his eyes as a torrent of hot blood poured from his nose. Stunned, he stumbled back and fell down.

Ace pushed up the sleeves of his flannel shirt. "Kid, I'm going to mop the fucking floor with you." And that's when the creature struck.

Four nimble insect legs shot out of the shadows, clamping onto Ace and yanking him up into the darkness, stuffing him into that hungry mouth that fed into another universe before he even had time to scream.

—

"Can I have Ace's room if he never comes back?" Pete asked his mother as she stumbled into the kitchen in a dirty bathrobe and poured herself a glass of Kool Aid from the fridge.

It'd been over a week since Pete had taken his brother to the abandoned K-Mart. Since then he'd also taken Maggot and Stumpy to see the beetle-thing. The Queen Mother as he liked to think of her, for the cocoons had cracked open, adorable little baby bugs squirming out and snuggling against her. It was a beautiful and marvelous thing to see.

Pete's mother lit a cigarette and splashed some gin into her Kool Aid. "The fuck is wrong with you, Petey? Your brother's run off and all you think about is his room? Don't you miss your brother? Don't think he's coming back? What kinda way to be is that?"

Pete just looked at his feet, delicately touched his still-sore nose, ran a finger over the new ridge where it now went out of line. His mother took a long sip of her drink, then swatted him across the back of the head, hard. "Hey, I'm talking to you, boy. I said, 'Don't you miss your brother?'"

"Yeah, Mom. I miss him."

"Besides, if that kid ain't around and the social worker shows up, my welfare could be in trouble. We need to find him."

"You know, sometimes kids go to the old K-Mart on the other side of town to hang out."

"Yeah? Would you go there for your momma? Go find your big brother and bring him home?"

"We could go together. I could take you there. I . . . I heard they still got stuff in there." Pete's mind raced. What would it take to lure his mother to the old K-Mart? "I heard there's still jewelry in the cases."

"Jewelry?"

Pete smiled. "Yup. Jewelry and all kinds of stuff. Things you wouldn't believe!"

"Yeah? Maybe you ought to take your old momma out there for a looksee. You're a good boy, Pete."

"Thanks, Mom," Pete said, smiling and thinking of the Queen Mother in her nest, those pink lips to other worlds so hungry.

Finding her was the greatest thing that'd ever happened to him. Ace's room and all his stuff were a sure bet for him now!

NEST OF SALT

I'd saved up all summer for the dress: a pink Betsy Johnson baby doll. A special dress for a special night with a special boy.

I knew my mother would never approve of the lowcut and lace ruffle trim, the way it hung from my slender shoulders like a nightie or negligee, so easy to slip out of. She'd probably say something crazy, like it was demonic or the devil's dress and make me get down on my knees and pray with her.

So, I'd had to hide it from her. First stashed in the cellar with the board games we stopped playing after Dad died, then into my school backpack, where I planned to secret it away to my BFF Brenda's house, and finally get to wear it.

Brenda and I had been friends since we were little girls, she only lived a few blocks away. Ever since I can remember, I'd been skipping and running through those streets of Myrtletown, over the cracked sidewalks and past the crumbling Victorians and the little corner market to Brenda's house.

That day, the early-autumn sun high and bright, the first fallen leaves littering the sidewalks, my mind was just a swarm of butterflies, so wrapped up in thoughts of the pink dress in my backpack, and my date with Robby Jenkins that I didn't even see Pastor Willard standing there on the corner—wearing his three-piece baby-blue polyester suit and daisy yellow button-up shirt, a large wooden crucifix hanging on his neck from a leather thong, hair slicked back from his

long slanting forehead, staring at the sky and whistling—
until I nearly slammed into him.

"Why, Gretta," he said, catching hold of my left hand.
"So good to see you."

Mother had joined his congregation when dad died.
After the funeral she'd gone kind of Jesus crazy. Said my
sister and I need Lordly direction without a father to guide
us.

"Hello, Pastor," I said, startled and pulling back. He
gripped my hand harder, his thumb creeping down to my
fingers, resting there on my ring finger and easing itself back
and forth.

"I see you're not wearing your purity ring, Gretta."

Mom had forced my sister and me to take part in this
ridiculous chastity ritual where we married ourselves to
Jesus and swore to stay chaste until marriage. Afterward
they gave us these stupid silver rings that had *PURE IN THE
BLOOD OF THE LAMB* engraved on them.

I thought it was nonsense: it was the nineties not the
fifties.

Out of all my friends I was the only one who was still a
virgin, and I was nearly eighteen and going to graduate in the
spring. No one wanted to graduate high school a virgin.
Robby and I had been going steady months now,
unbeknownst to my mom, and I was ready. The ring, my
crazy religious mom, it was a total embarrassment. I slipped
the stupid ring off my finger every morning as soon as I got
on the school bus.

"Yeah," I said. "I had to take it off for cheerleading
squad. We're not allowed to wear any jewelry during practice.
Must have forgot to put it back on. I've got it right here," I
swung my backpack off and as I pulled my hand free to reach
into the zippered front pocket where I kept the ring, he
snatched it back and yanked me hard towards him.

I gasped and he said, very slowly, "You know, Gretta, I
understand what it's like to lose a . . . *family member.*"

I could smell him. Not the cologne he stunk of, but
him, a rotten unwashed odor like the locker room in the gym.

And when he talked, although his front teeth were square and white and perfect, I could see that his molars were craggy and black, rotten to nubs.

"And I want you to know," he continued, "I am here if you ever need me. Feel free to look upon me as a . . . well, as a father." He let go of my hand and I fell backwards a step, then fumbled for the ring, finding it in a clutter of pencils and erasers and slipped it onto my finger.

"Yes, yes," he said, licking his lips. "You must wear your ring. In sexual sin we violate the sacredness of the God-given body, the body that was made for God's love, not man's. A body made for the pleasure of The Lord, not those dirty boys sniffing around like stinking dogs." He lifted his hand and caressed my cheek. "Can I get an 'Amen,' Gretta?"

"Uh, amen?"

"And a 'Hallelujah'?"

"Hallelujah," I whispered.

"Hallelujah," he whispered back. "I'll see you in church on Sunday, Gretta. Be a good girl. Be not tempted by the demons of Babylon. Go with Jesus, in the blood of the lamb."

He plucked up the wooden crucifix that dangled from his neck, puckered, and brought it to his lips.

—

"That pastor is, like, so creepy, I can't even take it," I said as I smeared a streak of baby-blue eyeshadow across my closed left lid. Brenda sat cross-legged on the silly princess canopy bed she'd had since she was ten, Sasha Macfadenburgh laying on her belly beside her flipping through a glossy, thick-paged copy of *COSMOPOLITAN* and smirking.

My mom thought I was having a sleepover there, but I was really just waiting for Robby Jenkins to pick me up for our date. I was wearing my new dress and feeling very pretty as REM purred about losing their religion on the radio.

"It says here to give both him and you a thrill, get his dick cold with a piece of ice!" Sasha said, turning her face to Brenda. "Oh. My. God. Can you imagine? It'd be, like, all cold and stuff when it's inside you." She made a pinched face and shook her head, her blonde pigtails bobbing crazily.

Brenda laughed and looked up at me, catching my eye in the reflection of the mirror. "Hey, *Gret-ta*," she called—that's how she said my name when she was going to tease me, two syllables, not the breathless *Gredda* she said when she needed to talk or wanted something from me, or the cheerful and plain Gretta she used when she would call to see what I was up to, had been that way ever since we were little girls. "You going to use the ice on Robby Jenkins tonight, *Gret-ta*?"

I hated the way she acted around Sasha. All grown up and know-it-ally. Mocking everything, including my virginity. Another reason I was ready to lose it.

"Gross," I said, wiping the eyeshadow away with an alcohol pad, thinking that blue was much too garish. Something plainer would bring out my eyes. Maybe a light gray. I glanced at Brenda and Sasha on the bed together, giggling, the two of them blonde and perfect beneath a huge purple and yellow Backstreet Boys poster, exchanging knowing looks, and a pang of jealousy and loneliness rippled through me. Both Brenda and I had been towheads as children. There are all these pictures of us together in kindergarten and first grade, both with shimmering platinum locks, but while hers had patinaed and thickened into a golden yellow hue as we grew into teenagers, mine had thinned and dulled into a mousy brown that matched my eyes.

"But you are going to go all the way with him, aren't 'ya, *Gret-ta*?" Brenda asked, giggling away and burrowing into Sasha like a playful kitten.

"Ohhh, tonight's the night is it?" Sasha said, raising her eyebrows up and down, giving a little shake of her head that set those pigtails in motion again.

Heat rose up into my face, but it was a good feeling. I felt ready, I wanted to do it, to be like them. Stupid chastity pledge.

"Maybe," I said teasingly, turning to the side and

looking at my reflection over my shoulder, admiring how the light-gray of the new eyeshadow really did highlight my eyes, which I always thought had a beautiful, sleek shape to them, even if they were an ordinary mudpuddle brown. "But we won't be using ice or anything gross. I want it to be romantic."

"Romantic!" Sasha shouted before they burst into thick peals of obnoxious laughter, so hard the bed bounced.

"Yes!" I said, twirling before the mirror, making sure there were no wrinkles in my dress. "Romantic."

"I heard Robby tell his football buddies where he's taking you, sure sounds romantic," Sasha said, unwrapping a sliver of mint gum from its foil wrapper and curling it into her mouth.

"What's that supposed to mean?" I asked, her words worming their way into my blood and turning it cold.

"Nothing, it just sounds romantic," she said, smacking the gum beneath her molars, eyes focused on her magazine now, giving the page a careless turn.

"Well, where's he taking me?"

"It's a surprise! I can't tell. You'll love it, though. Trust me."

I shot a look at Brenda, she just shrugged.

The REM song ended and there was a brief moment of silence, punctuated by the low grumble of a car rolling to a stop outside the house, before three quick bursts of a horn ripped through the night and a Spice Girls song sprang to life, startling me so that I that gave a tiny shuddering jerk.

Sasha caught my unease, grinned, and winked. "Looks like Prince Charming is here in the romance vehicle. You ready, Princess?"

—

"Where are you taking me?" I asked as Robby eased his Mustang off the pavement and down a twisting dirt road.

He grinned that squinty-eyed smile of his, his head a

big square on that thick jock neck. "Someplace special. You'll love it."

The sky was cloudless and star filled, the moon fat and bloated and bright, and in the glimmer of that moonlight you could see the leaves of the tall oaks that lined the road turning yellow and curling in on themselves, some tumbling into the wind. Robby turned up the radio—*The Cure: Robert Smith crooning how the raging sea had stolen the only girl he ever loved*—and tapped a beat on the steering wheel with his fingers as he stretched his arm out so that I could curl into him, ensconced in his warmth, his man/boy smell of jock sweat and Polo cologne, and rest against the slow rise and fall of his breathing as the world swam by outside. The trees grew taller as we drove, oaks giving way to redwoods that obscured the sky with their dark silhouettes and there was a moment of almost utter darkness as their branches loomed out above us before the sky suddenly opened up revealing ocean.

A tiny private meadow tucked away above the sea.

It was magnificent.

Robby eased the Mustang to a stop as the road puttered out into a thin path that curled down to that grassy spot, a hidden little enclave overlooking the black lapping waves.

Robby squeezed my shoulder, turned off the engine and removed the keys. The hot engine ticked against the cool ocean air. "You like?" he asked.

"It's magical."

Everything was perfect.

He reached behind him and pulled a stack of folded blankets from the backseat. "Come on, let's go sit by the edge."

We trotted down the path and to the field, spread a blanket out by the rim of the cliff and curled up against each other, laying the other blankets over ourselves and staring up at the impossible depth of the stars, the pregnant moon reflected in the tall waves that crashed on the rocks far below us.

He leaned towards me and we kissed for a moment. Softly and innocently, tongues darting out for just a moment to playfully taste each other. Then pulled away and gazed into each other's eyes. I took a deep, shuddering breath, smiled and laid back against the blanket, my head upon the cold earth as he lay beside me, the sky so vast and open above us.

He nuzzled my neck, kissing softly upwards to my ear, making the hairs on the back of my neck go stiff and my insides soft and hot.

"Do you know why I chose this place?" he whispered.

"No, why?"

"Because a girl was murdered here."

"What?"

"Yeah. Back in the fifties. Forty years ago this night, actually. I thought it'd be neat. Kind of romantic and scary."

"Robby, you're not serious."

"I totally am. They called her the Lady of the Rocks, 'cause, like, after he killed her, he threw her over the cliff, thinking the water would carry her away. Only she landed on one of those real tall rocks, and just laid there till someone noticed her a few days later. They never did find out who murdered her."

"Stop. Just stop it." I pulled away from him and sat up.

"What? It's local history! It's interesting. I thought you would think it was cool. You like all that history stuff."

"It's scary. If it's even true. And you're freaking me out with it. I don't like it."

"It's supposed to be scary. I figured if you were scared, you'd want me to protect you. You know. Be close to me. Isn't that romantic?"

"Taking me to where a girl was killed? How is that romantic?"

"Well, how's it not romantic?"

"Robby, was a girl really killed here?"

"Yeah, October 13th, 1956. Forty years ago today. I told you. The Lady of the Rocks."

"Okay, I want to go. Take me back to Brenda's."

"Aw, come on, don't be that way."

"I just don't . . ." but I was interrupted by a moaning sound above the crashing of the waves. Almost like a fog horn, but more human. More feminine. "Did you hear that?"

"No. What?"

Again, this time a whimpering that seemed to come from behind us and to the side. "There it is again! It's like a crying sound."

"I don't hear nothing. Probably just the wind."

I stood up and peered around, shivering against the cold air. "It's cold, Robby. Come on, let's go back to the car."

He put his hands behind his head and kicked his feet out. "I ain't going nowhere."

"Robby, come on! I'm going back to the car." I stormed away towards the path.

And that's when I saw her.

A girl, not much older than me. Lying there battered and naked in the tall sea grass, smears and splashes of black blood covering her pale skin, her eyes turning up to look at me. She reached an arm out, a blood drenched hand, and murmured, "Help me."

Wounds, like black toothless mouths, gaped across her bare breasts and down her side, oozing dark liquid, before a shadow rose up over us, blocking out the sea and the stars and the moon, making everything but me and her darkness, as if we were caught together in some other plane of existence, some dream realm, suspended in time, and then the roof caved in. That darkness, that black shadow that had captured us, came crashing down with a heavy *whoompf*, knocking the air from my lungs, sending me falling back onto the wet grass breathless and dazed. I gasped for air, and when I found it began to scream.

Robby was beside me in an instant, kneeling in the grass to grasp my shoulders, flustered, asking, "What is it? What's the matter?"

"I . . . I saw something. I . . ."

"What? What'd you see?"

I looked around. There was nothing there. Nothing but grass shimmering in the blue light of the moon. Not even an indentation that someone had been there.

"I . . . I don't know."

Tears welled up from my gut, I tried to catch them, stop them, but a dam burst inside me and suddenly I was crying uncontrollably.

"Take me back to Brenda's, Robby," I managed between sobs. "Please, just take me back to Brenda's."

—

By the time we got back to Myrtletown I was calm, though I felt sick to my stomach.

"You okay?" Robby asked as he pulled up a few houses shy of hers, in the shadows of a couple tall, swaying palm trees.

"Yeah, I'm just . . . feeling mixed up."

"Look, I'm really sorry. I know you wanted this night to be special. But we can go somewhere different. It's not too late. Someplace you'd like to go to."

"I just want to go lay down."

"Come on, baby. It's still early. Let's go get a hamburger. Relax."

"Sorry, Robby, not now."

"But I thought tonight was the night."

"I don't know if I feel that way anymore. I'm not sure I still even want to go there."

"But why? You were so ready."

My mind was reeling. I stuttered, looking for any excuse I could. "I . . . I promised Jesus, Robby. Okay. I just don't think I want to do it anymore."

"You promised Jesus? Are you fucking serious? You told me that was all your mother. That you didn't believe any of that crap."

"Yeah, well, maybe I do," I shouted, swinging open the door, totally lying because I just wanted out of the car and any excuse would do. "Goodnight, Robby," I said, slamming the door behind me as I got out.

He stared at me a moment through the window, shaking his head, then slammed his palms against the steering wheel and took off, tires spinning and leaving black smears and a rank smell of burning rubber behind.

—

The next day, a storm rolled in.

I watched from my bedroom window as the dark clouds gathered in the gloomy distance, herded by the wind like black sheep, then roiling over the neighborhood and breaking open into a deluge of pouring rain, so transfixed that I started when the phone rang and my sister called up to me, "Gretta, phone!"

I went downstairs. My mother sat mesmerized and slack-jawed before the television, watching a preacher pace across the stage, waving a bible, sweat streaming over his pink, angry face. "De-mons, are real! They are not some metaphor to teach you a lesson. They are evil at work, try-ing to burrow their way into your godly soul."

My sister Trish sat smirking in the kitchen, dangling the receiver by its cord. "It's a boy," she said in a teasing, singsong voice.

"Just give me the phone, Trish," I said, grabbing it from her hand and slinking down the hall as far as I could stretch the cord.

"Hello?"

"Gretta, hey, it's me. Robby."

"Hi, Robby," I whispered, cupping my hand against the receiver to shield my voice from the spying ears of my mother and sister.

"I'm sorry about last night."

"It's okay," I said, though I was still a mess. I couldn't get the image I'd seen out of my head. That girl, naked, covered in blood, reaching out to me and pleading for help.

"But, look, I've been thinking. Maybe we shouldn't see

each other anymore."

The air turned to ice and my lungs froze. "What do you mean?"

"Well, I like you a lot. I do! It's just, you know, not really working out. Is it?"

I didn't know what to say and found myself opening and closing my mouth uselessly, finally managing to get out, "It's not?"

"No. And the way we're always sneaking around, afraid your mom is going to find out about us. It's a pain."

"Robby, I can change. I'll tell my mother about us. I'm not afraid. I—"

"Gretta, look, I've got to be honest with you. Last night, after you left, I . . . well, I was kind of upset, and a little hurt, and I . . . I really don't know how to put this, so I'll just say it. I hooked up with Sasha McFaddenburgh. I didn't mean to, didn't plan it. Neither of us did. It just happened. And, well, we're going out now."

I clasped my eyes shut, feeling the bitter sting of tears. *That slutty bitch.*

"Gretta, you there?"

"Yeah, I'm here."

"You okay?"

"Uh huh, I'm fine. I . . . I, uh, I gotta go. My mother needs me."

"I'm sorry, Gretta. I—"

"It's fine. That's fine. I gotta go. I'll talk to you later," and I was back in the kitchen hanging up the phone, struggling to breathe, an emptiness lurching open in my belly.

"Who was that boy?" my mother asked from the sofa in a monotone voice.

"Nobody, mother. Just a boy from school asking about homework."

—

Monday at school was a nightmare. My heart felt like a fragile

Sitting before the television, bathed in its projection-tube-blue light, an old quilt draped over my head, I watched a thin scarecrow of a man ride a pig about the screen, one eye a milky cataract-blue, the other brown like mine, moaning how some of them want to use you and some of them want to abuse you.

My sister came down the stairs and slipped up beside me.

"The big game's today. Aren't you supposed to be cheerleading?" she asked.

"I quit the squad."

"You quit?!"

"I don't want to talk about it."

The bare-chested scarecrow withered and snarled, the low notes of the dark melody filling the space between us, before she finally asked, "What are you watching?"

"Marilyn Manson."

"He is so ugly."

"I think he's beautiful," I said, reaching out to touch the screen, relishing the feel of the electric static tingle my fingertips.

"Gross. How can you say that?"

"There's something true about him. He's not a fake. A phony. You wouldn't understand."

"You know, Mom says we're not allowed to watch this channel. She says MTV is strictly off limits."

"Yeah? What are you going to do? Rat me out?"

"Not if you let me watch Beverly Hills 90210."

I laughed, stood, and tossed her the remote. "Be my guest," I said, heading to the door.

"Where you going?"

"To the library."

—

Down in the dusty depths of the library basement, I scrolled through microfiche. A blur of headlines and dates stream by on the screen. I slowed, October 10th 1956, October 11th,

12th, 13th and then, there on October 15th, I find what I'm looking for: The Lady of the Rock.

Missing teenage girl found murdered north of Clam Beach . . .

It was all true. Everything Robby had said.

Mary Mack, sexually assaulted and stabbed to death, tossed from the cliff's edge . . .

Below the article there's two pictures, side by side.

One is of an oval-faced girl with high cheek bones and a shy smile, hair a perfect black and shiny bob. She's showing off a what looks like a new dress, a leg kicked back teasingly in a pirouette, lifting the hem with one hand and waving the other. She looks so alive and happy.

The other is a grainy picture of a blurry figure atop a black rock jutting up from the ocean. Nothing more than a pale smear against darkness, really. But I peer closer, trying to make out just what I'm seeing. Though the details are impossible to make out, she's obviously naked, arms flung out to either side, her legs crossed and slightly curled, so that she almost gives the illusion of a mermaid, a thing of the sea unnaturally washed to the shore. I try to make out the features of her face, to tie this abandoned body to the picture of the happy girl beside it, but it's just grain, a few thick black dots implying shadow that seem to slowly spin as I stare harder and harder, willing my mind to make sense of the image, to find clarity in it, and I'm growing dizzy, my head feels gaseous and bubbly, effervescent like a soda pop, and then I'm falling, falling, falling to the ground in a heap and the librarian is there, asking me if I'm all right, if she should call an ambulance.

"I'm fine," I tell her, standing up and brushing myself off. "Just fine."

—

After midnight and swirling black water snaking around the sink as I rinsed my hair, quiet, quiet quiet so as not to wake my sleeping mother. Then the scissors, cutting it off above the shoulders, curling the ends to get that perfect bob. Rit dye into the washing machine with my Betsy Johnson dress. Black, black, black. And afterwards, blacking each bit of lace with a thick permanent marker, the industrial scent of its ink making my head feel hazy and distant.

—

"Oh my God!" Sasha says as she and a couple other cheerleaders pass me in the hall. "Halloween's not for three more weeks!"

I just ignore them, their laughter and squealing, their long swaying hair and whispered insults of *freak* and *Gretta the Frigid*. I've got my headphones on and I just concentrate on the Nine Inch Nails song on my disc player, thinking Brenda had a head like a hole. Supposed to be my best friend and now she doesn't even look at me. Pretends I'm not there.

I swing open my locker. There's a mirror hanging in there, and I stop and stare at my reflection: my Egyptian eyes framed in a now shimmering black bob of hair, my ebony dress with the blacker-than-black lace which makes my shoulders and neck look so bare and pale and soft.

I feel perfect.

I lift a pallid hand and lay a finger on the reflection of my face, as if to test if it is even real, a reflection and not a window.

For the first time in my life I feel like I am perfect.

I am the person I'm meant to be.

And I think, fuck this place, fuck these people. They could never understand me.

I take that black permanent marker and coat my lips in stinky ink. So perfect, kissing the mirror, leaving a flawless stain of puckered lips.

The bell rings shrilly, an awful sound that signals first period has begun, and the last stragglers duck into their classrooms. The hall is now empty. I just let my text books tumble from my fingers to the floor, and walk away, locker door open and swaying as down the hall I go and out the heavy industrial doors to the outside world.

—

That ocean facing meadow was easy to find, even if it did take me hours to get there.

My legs aching, calves on fire and blisters swelling on my feet, I sit on the cliff edge, watching the surf lurch out and smash against the rocks only to be pulled back frothing into the sea again. The squeal of seagulls and the dank salty scent of the ocean, and I could feel her there with me, shadowlike. An ephemeral presence, a kind of static lingering behind the sounds of the sea and the wind, like fingers of fog falling down the crevices of the surrounding hills she's behind me, placing a hand upon my shoulder.

"I've been waiting for you," I said.

"I know," she replied. "I'm sorry I scared you. Sometimes it's hard for me to . . . communicate."

"That's okay," I say, and she's sitting down beside me, wearing that same black dress I'd seen in the microfiche picture. She's flush with life, cheeks rose-colored, lips ripe and crimson, raven hair clean and shiny. We stare out at the horizon for what feels an eternity before she holds out her hand to me, and I take it.

—

I remember certain things.

I remember secrets told and promises given. A nest there in the tall sea grass. Me swearing I would avenge her, and her promising she'd never leave me, that we'd be together for eternity. I remember the taste of sea salt on her lips. Her hands running through my hair, her arms holding me as we rolled in the matted grass and the sun tumbled into the Pacific with a murmur of purple fire and the black of night fell upon us, the stars spinning like mad and my head alive like a circus, a calliope of exploding sensations as her hand slipped up between my legs, her curious fingers finding my secret places and her mouth on my chest and her eyes always boring into mine, hungrily watching my reaction to her touch, and we were together and one in every sense of the word.

—

They found me wandering along the road that night. Lost and disorientated, my black babydoll dress dirty and torn, mumbling to myself, not making any sense.

At least that's what they told me.

I don't remember any of that. I only remember waking up in my bed, feverish and nauseous. My first thought was wondering why I was wearing this ridiculous, long white nightie—the kind I used to wear when I was a little girl—not the oversized T-shirt I usually slept in. I looked around, dazed, my mother was beside me in a chair looking frantic.

"She's awake again," my mother said. "Gretta, Gretta is that you?"

"Careful," a deep voice called out. "It could be the demon again. Identify yourself."

I blinked and there was Pastor Willard at the foot of the bed, wearing some kind of weird purple robe over his tacky leisure suit, that big wooden crucifix dangling from his neck on its black leather tong.

"Mommy," I said. "What's going on?"

The pastor held a battered black bible towards me. "I said identify thyself!"

"Pastor, it's me, Gretta. What is going on?"

"Oh, thank God," my mother cried, taking me in her arms and rocking me, her chest hiccupping with sobs as she stroked my hair. "I was so scared. Scared I lost my little girl."

She was whimpering and squeezing me, suffocating me, and I could feel the snot from her nose dripping onto the top of my head.

"Jeeze, I'm fine. Stop." I said, pulling away.

"You are not fine. Look at you. Your hair, what happened to your hair?"

"It's black. I like it this way."

"Trish told me you were watching the MTV. You must have gotten a demon from that terrible television. *What* was I thinking letting them attach that cable to the house? *A cable straight to Hell.*"

The Pastor cocked his head and pointed at me dramatically. "And out in cars with boys sinning. We know what's been going on. Sneaking around full of lust. You've strayed from the herd and been tempted, let a demon into your heart. Now we must cast it out."

My head was pounding and I was dizzy. "You don't know what you're talking about. I didn't do anything with Robby Jenkins. Can you guys just leave me alone? I don't feel well."

"Leave you we will not."

"Why are you talking ridiculous Yoda shit," I laughed. "Seriously, I feel like I'm going to puke, so just leave me the fuck alone. Okay?"

"Hear the profanity? It's the demon!" the Pastor shouted. "Demon! Thing of sin! Leave this girl's body!"

I thought about Mary and laughed. "I know who you're talking about and she's not a demon. She's my friend and I love her."

"I can see the lust in your eyes, fornicator!"

"Listen to you, *Pastor*, you don't think all the girls see you eyeing them up? Staring at our tits. That we don't see the bulge in your pants when we're too close to you, see you sniffing at us like a dirty dog?"

The Pastor stepped back, his face twisted in anger and revulsion. "Foul beast. Liar. Whore of Babylon. Let us pray."

My mother fell down to her knees, hands clasped before her, head bent, and mumbled while the pastor stretched out his arms to either side and tilted his head skyward, saying loudly, "And all who dwell on earth will worship it, everyone whose name has not been written before the foundation of the world in the book of life of the Lamb who was slain."

Then suddenly I remembered. Like waking up from a

dream, it all came back to me and I remembered all the things Mary had told me about the night she was murdered. All the hot whispering in my ear about who had done it and how I was to avenge her.

"It was you!" I shrieked. "You killed her. Raped and killed Mary Mack. Didn't you?"

He thrust his bible at me again. "And they have conquered him by the blood of the Lamb and by the word of their testimony, for they loved not their lives even unto death."

I turned to my mother, kneeling at his feet, rocking with her hands clasped before her face. "Mom! Don't listen to this guy. He's sick. He's a killer. He killed a girl forty years ago."

He's leaning over the bed now, shoving his bible right into my face. "King of lies! Your web of deception mocks you. I'm only forty-five years old. How could I have killed someone forty years ago?"

"Bullshit. Utter bullshit, you fucking hypocrite!" I scream. Bolting upright, I bat the bible out of his hand and shove my palms into his chest as hard as I can. He stumbles back, a look of surprise crossing his stupid face, trips over his feet and falls onto the floor as I bound from the bed after him in my best cheerleading leap, using the footboard as a vault so that I'm so high in the air above him my black hair brushes the ceiling. I come down hard, landing with my knees on either of his arms. I can feel a creak as his shoulders give and both his arms dislocate. He bellows in pain and I cackle in his face.

"Dirty shaman, I know what you've done."

And I can feel her there with me, beside me, guiding me, her breath hot in my ear. "Do it. Do it! *Do it!!!*"

And I can hear my mother behind me, screaming, "No! No! *Nooooooo!*" as I lift the wooden crucifix hanging from his neck—that same cross I'd seen him press his foul lips to—bring it up over my head, and slam it down into his left eye, squirming it back and forth so that it sinks deeper and deeper. Blood and bits of eye spray up as he writhes helplessly, and my mother is pulling at my shoulders, screaming at me to get off of him, tearing my stupid nightie as she claws and yanks at me.

I swing out an arm and backhand her across the face, knocking her away, then bring my palm down with all my might onto the top of the crucifix. It sinks in with a cracking sound, propelled like a hammer-driven nail through his eye socket so that a deeper, darker, black blood gurgles out now, the horizontal beams snapping off the crucifix and Jesus falling free and one more time I bring my palm down on that wooden spike and I can feel it burst into the soft tissue of his brain and he erupts into spasms, his legs kicking and arms flailing briefly, before he is suddenly still and silent.

My mother sobs hysterically, curled fetal-like, hands clasped in prayer. *"Worthy is the Lamb who was slain to receive power and wealth and wisdom and might and honor and glory and blessing."*

The pounding of the cross has caused a wound in my palm and I prod at it a moment, watching my blood spill out and mix with that of the Pastor's, before slowly rising. I step over my mother and through my bedroom door, the nightie now gore-streaked and hanging from my aching frame in tatters, my black hair—damp with sweat and blood—cascading down over my eyes. Walking down the dim hall I see my sister's door ajar, catch her eye peering from behind it, watching me, ready to slam the door shut.

I smile at her. "Don't worry about telling on me. It's okay. I love you." And then I'm down the steps and out the front door and into the night.

—

Mary's waiting for me, in our nest of salt, by the cliff's edge.

I run to her, laughing, crying with joy and sorrow and the knowing of the abyss. We're spiraling about, arms around shoulders, hands in our hair and our lips together and tongues entwined. Below us the surf crashes black against the jagged ancient volcanic rocks. She looks at me, the infinite ceiling of stars reflecting in her eyes, and says, "Now we can be together forever."

We turn and look out over the ocean, where the night sky meets the sea, the forever of the horizon beckoning and winking.

THE PET

When he placed the order, Devon Newton thought of the pet as an early Christmas present to himself. It had been expensive, he'd blown his whole savings on it, converting the money to bitcoin to perform the transaction, and now he didn't have money for rent. A part of him wondered if it was a rip-off scheme, it did sound too good to be true, and he nervously questioned if the pet would even arrive. But a few days later, he got a message from the shipping yard: a crate had arrived for him.

In order to pick the pet up from the shipping yard, he had to borrow his mother's pickup truck. He had arranged to meet her at noon in the greasy-spoon diner where she worked as a waitress. He swung open the door to the Redwood Café and was greeted by the din of forks scraping over plates, muffled conversations, and rattling coffee mugs.

He was a big man, over six feet with a sizeable girth around his middle, but he stooped—bent at the back—and hung his head low, so that he appeared much smaller than he really was. He pushed his thick, Coke-bottle glasses up his nose and shuffled up to the counter where his mother was setting a side order of glistening sausage links in a puddle of grease down before a customer.

"There you are, Devon. Late as usual."

"Hello, Mother." He absent-mindedly dragged a finger under the back of his ear, brought it under his nose where he could take a quick sniff of the musky-cheesy aroma.

"Quit slouching and stand up straight, Devon. And for God's sake stop sniffing your fingers. It's a disgusting habit."

only tell that her eyelids had been stitched together over her sightless eyes if you looked really close and saw the fishing-line sutures holding them together.

He pushed up his glasses, ran his index finger back and forth over the back of his ear, and put his thick, sausage-link finger under his nose, inhaling deeply and marveling at his new pet. She was beautiful, with long raven-black hair and delicate skin the color of coffee with only half a spoonful of cream. He lifted her from the box and sat her beside him on the bed. She began to make terrified gurgling noises and to flail her stumps, but he stroked her back and soothed her. "It's okay. It's okay. I won't hurt you. You're home now. You're nice and safe." This seemed to calm her and she actually leaned into him and cuddled against him. He wrapped his arms around her and cried. It was the first time he had ever held a naked woman.

Before the crate arrived, he had imagined tying the pet up. Maybe suspending her from the ceiling somehow with a ball gag in her mouth and a dog collar on her throat, like he had seen in all those BDSM movies. But now he knew he would never do something like that, for the emotions that ripped through his heart were awe, pity and love.

Devon had always wanted to be a slave master. That's why he'd started searching the deep web for a pet. He frequented all the BDSM websites and even put some ads up on Craigslist as a dom looking for a sub. He got a few replies but only one woman—a pretty, older redhead—had agreed to meet with him. They had met at a coffee shop but after five minutes of talking to him she had started laughing and stood up.

"Sorry, honey, but you're no dom," she replied before walking out and leaving him with the check.

Of course, he fucked the pet occasionally. That's why he bought her in the first place, after all. But their relationship was not one built on sex, but rather tenderness. Most of the time he spent with her was brushing her lustrous hair till it shone and glimmered, delicately applying lipstick and eyeshadow to her winsome and arresting face, singing softly to her as he spooned soup into her mouth and changed her diaper, and just holding her in his arms at night while he slept, happy and content for the first time in his life.

"Cassandra," he said, his eyes brimming over with tears. "That's what I'll call you. Cassandra. My sweet, sweet Cassandra."

He began to walk taller and stopped slouching. Got a real job at the hardware store: stocking shelves with hammers and drills, boxes of nails and screws. One day he found himself canceling his membership to all the BDSM sites and packing a big box with all of his pornographic magazines and DVDs, hauling it to the dump. He didn't need that stuff anymore. In fact, it made him sick.

Then, Christmas day, sitting in church beside his mother, the sunlight shimmering down purple and blue from the tall stained-glass windows, he realized that the pet had been a gift from God.

Look at all Cassandra had done for him. She had turned his life around and made him whole, given him meaning and purpose. He smiled and looked out at the congregation. He wanted to give the pet a gift, to show how much he loved her, how much she meant to him. He would get her a companion, someone to be with when he wasn't there. Yes, another pet. A pet for the pet. This time, maybe he would just make his own.

A TRUE CHILD OF WODEN

A breath of autumn wind, heavy with the salt and scent of the sea, blew up the cliff face as Kvasir led his younger brother Baldr down the steep path to the hidden cove where the Faining ceremony was to take place.

Tonight was the night Baldr would officially be taken into the sect and made a member of the Frenrir's Wolf tribe. A night of great auspiciousness, promising immense ceremony, wonder and awe.

The ocean spread out below them as infinite and blue as the sky which stretched out above, and their leather boots fought for traction in the sandy earth as they made their way down to the beach. The fresh tattoos on Kvasir's face—runes that marked him as a man of knowledge—stung from the salty sea air.

As they traversed the path along the cliff edge, past the shimmering green lupines and clumps of gum weed, Kvasir noticed a possum rotting in the sun to the side of the path, two ravens picking and pulling at its glimmering guts. The birds cawed at them briefly, tugging on a ropey strand of intestine, before beating their glistening, black wings and taking flight. Kvasir turned to his brother.

"This is a good omen, Baldr. They are Huginn and Muninn, pets of father Woden. They will bring him word of your acceptance into the sect."

Baldr nodded gravely.

Though they were young— Kvasir sixteen and his brother only thirteen— the boys were tall and lean. Their hair was as pale and yellow as the sandy shore that lay beneath them.

They finally stepped down onto the beach: the secret cove Geirskogul had told him of. The surf beat loudly and rhythmically against the land, a few fishing boats dotted the horizon in the distance. It was a magical place where earth, sky and sea met. A place where the mysteries of Asatru would be revealed.

"All of this you see," Kvasir explained to his younger brother, "all of Midgard, was once Ymir, born from venom. Father Woden made the earth from the flesh of Ymir and the ocean from his blood. We truly are the sons of Woden."

Baldr nodded his head solemnly, his blue eyes staring out at creation.

Kvasir couldn't really remember his real father. His earthly father who had left over a decade ago on a voyage and never returned.

Kvasir could remember him in a foggy and nondescript way, a memory of a memory.

He could remember the dirty Caterpillar baseball hat he always wore, the scent of menthol cigarettes and liquor. The funny drink he made: Seagram's 7 and Mountain Dew, how he called it a Hillbilly Highball. Kvasir could remember being held on his lap and cradled in his strong arms, back when Kvasir's name was Kevin. He could remember his father telling him tales of his travels as a long-distance truck driver. The voyages to distant lands. Places with exotic names like Kentucky and Mississippi. He would tell him tales of a great salt lake and mountains that stretched up a mile into the sky. And Kevin would curl up, pressing himself against his father's big barrel chest, feeling safe and loved, and drift off to sleep. His little brother, then known as Brian, gazing over the edge of the bassinet at them, eyes wide in wonder. Now it seemed a time before time. A dream nearly forgotten.

—

It was still early and the rest of the sect would not arrive on the beach until the sun had set. It was October 9th, Leif

Erickson day: an auspicious and important day. Kvasir sat his brother in the sand and explained the importance of this day.

"You see, brother, most of the world thinks that Christopher Columbus was the first European to find this great land where we dwell. But that is a lie. Leif Erickson was here five-hundred years before Columbus. They tell you this lie because Columbus was Catholic and a worshiper of Jesus, the king of the Jews, while Erickson was a worshiper of Woden. Christianity has erased our heritage, our old true culture. Erased the world's true cultures wherever it spread. Christianity is the root of all evil. You understand this, right? You understand our mission?"

Baldr nodded his head. "I understand, brother."

The surf beat against the beach, sea birds screeched.

It was hard to believe it was only months ago Kvasir had discovered Fenrir's Wolf. How different life had been back then. How different he had been.

Just a skinny, sixteen-year-old black-metal fanatic, wearing his black-metal uniform: overcoat hanging limply off his shoulders like sad raven's wings, a belt made of sharp bullets, spiked wrist bands. Ubiquitous VENOM T-shirt with the sleeves cut off. He dyed his long hair black and let it hang over his face. He sometimes wore corpse paint: white-and-black makeup to make himself look lifeless and dead. Often he used his own blood to adorn his forehead with an inverted cross.

He loved European bands like Bathory, Mercyful Fate and Celtic Frost, but his favorite shit was the Norwegian stuff, like Darkthrone, Gorgoroth and Mayhem. Cold. Grim. The grinding guitar and other-worldly, screeching vocals, like something from a nightmare. A sound like the bleak darkness he felt in his heart.

He kept a poster of Mayhem's bootleg album *Dawn of the Black Hearts* above his bed. On it was a grisly photograph of the singer Dead after he had shot himself in the head. At night, when he heard his mother stumble into their apartment, drunk from a night at the bars, the sounds of her fucking some stranger reverberating through the thin walls, he would put on his headphones, his Walkman drowning out the moans and grunts, and stare at that poster, his gaze going from the black spiderweb of inverted crosses in the band's logo, to the dark spray of the singer's blood on the wall, to the fat, bright-red puddle of brains where they'd fallen out of his skull and onto the pillow before him, and he'd always end up fixating on that mysterious look in Dead's lifeless eyes, a searching gaze, as if he was looking past something, through the veil, and Kevin's mind would churn in darkness, reveling in it and wondering what death was really like.

But everything changed the night he saw Fenrir's Wolf play.

While Mayhem had brought him only thoughts of death, Fenrir's Wolf brought him life.

—

It was a typical black metal show in the basement of the Veteran's Hall in Eureka. He'd been to lots of them, the little apartment complex where he lived was only a few blocks away. There were a bunch of bands on the lineup. A couple local ones, one big one from Seattle. And this band he'd never heard of before: Fenrir's Wolf.

Everyone was milling around in their black attire, lots of corpse paint, Doc Martens and spikes, and then he saw what at first looked like a couple of dreadlocked hippies getting on the stage and setting up big goat-skin drums.

Dreadlocks and anything even slightly colorful stood out that night, but only a quick glance showed these were no peace-loving hippies but some kind of strange crust punks. They wore knives. Big ones, bowie knives. And they had tall, mud-splattered work boots, like a lumberjack would wear, and there was something fierce about them, their movements and their tattoos. Their arms were intricate patchworks of ink, and they had tats on their faces as well. Each of them had a line of markings below their eyes. Triangular, letter-like patterns he would later learn were *futharks,* runes signifying their places within the tribe.

The lights dimmed and the two drummers, standing shoulder to shoulder, began to pound away on the tall upright drums with large wooden mallets. They wore homemade-looking vests of patched together sheep's wool and leather, banging out this tribal rhythm, like the sound a galley slave would beat in the belly of a ship, as a muscular, bare-chested man, black-leather gauntlets clamped on his swollen forearms, a thick dread-locked beard spilling down over his chest, stepped to the microphone, croaking out a demonic-sounding chant through the mane of knotted hair that cascaded over his face and shoulders like giant spider legs.

Thus it is well seen that Sigi has slain the thrall and murdered him; so he is given forth to be a wolf in holy places, and may no more abide in the land with his father; therewith Woden bare him fellowship from the land.

An acidic roar, a cacophony of noise, erupted as a woman on the side of the stage plugged a battered electric guitar into a Marshall half-stack with a burst of feedback and ran the side of her pick over the strings. And then, there it was: that graveyard sound he loved so much. That buzz-saw tremolo of guitar, the notes coming so fast they sounded like one screeching noise, a sound like an engine revving or a million black insects beating their wings at once, her right hand playing lightning-quick plucked notes while her left's fingers snaked up and down the neck to let out an eerie, satanic-triad riff.

So dark, so powerful, and coming from this blonde goddess.

She turned from the amp and strode slowly across the stage, her steps sure and graceful, the guitar and her like one being, this awesome, evil noise just spilling effortlessly from her. She wore tall suede boots that reached to her knees, a short skirt of animal pelts, and a leather corset secured with dozens of tiny brass buckles.

And my god how she was beautiful.

Like something beyond this world. Both ethereal and majestic, fierce yet lissome. The sides of her head were shaved short, the rest of her thick blonde hair hanging in long ropey dreads that fell past her waist, and as the dim light caught her, Kevin could see bits of bone and rock sewn in there. She strutted to the microphone, eyes ablaze above the row of ancient symbols tattooed across her cheeks, and let out a ravishing war cry that made the hairs on Kevin's arms stand erect. Visions of Valkyries and banshees filled him.

The music was like a revelation: a combination of this new, stark, black-metal sound with the ancient and tribal, pure and primitive. How the drummers were even keeping up with the wicked guitar tremolo was a mystery, their mallets a blur as they replicated the double bass pounding most metal drummers used their feet to produce. The singer growling strange poetry, and like a shaman, hunching and drawing up spirits, then throwing his arms up and head back with a howl and releasing ancient ghosts into the night.

Kevin stood in rapt awe their entire set, utterly mesmerized.

Afterwards, the lights up, the air cooling as the crowd thinned out, he wandered over to the little merch table they had set up in the back shadows. The two drummers sat there on folding chairs, looking bored and ignoring him. They had a couple T-shirts for sale, that typical black-metal style of spasmatic tree-roots spelling out their name. They also had some cassette tapes, which Kevin really wanted, but had no money for. He wouldn't be getting paid from his part-time job at the record store till tomorrow. He'd paid to get in the show that night with change he'd managed to save, embarrassingly having to count the seven-dollar entrance fee with quarters and dimes.

Then a voice came from behind him, "How'd you like the show?"

He turned, and there she was: the Viking guitar

goddess. He was struck dumb for a moment, unable to form or even conceive words. She was even more gorgeous and fierce there in the light before him than onstage. A face like an angel, adorned with leather and bones and tribal tattoos. It was as if he was walking in the forest and came into the presence of a true wild thing, a bobcat or wolf. It was exhilarating yet scary at the same time. But she had a kind smile, and warm eyes that sparkled when she squinted, giving him a sense of inclusion and security, as if they were both in on some amusing inside joke.

"It was . . . amazing," he stammered.

"Oh yeah?" she said, cocking her head, as if she wasn't sure she believed him. "You wouldn't just say that, would you?" Her voice had a slightly foreign lilt to it and he saw what looked like a hawk's skull woven into one of her thick dreads.

"No! Totally amazing. I mean it."

"Then why don't you buy a shirt? Get a tape? If you thought it was *so amazing.*"

Kevin let his long black hair fall down over his face. "I totally would. I'd love a tape actually, but you know, I'm fucking broke. I don't get paid till tomorrow."

"Yeah?"

"Yeah. I work at the record store in Old Town. The Works."

"Ohhh, in the music business, huh?"

Kevin laughed and kicked at the ground with the toe of his Converse All Star. "Yeah. I just mainly sweep up and unpack boxes."

"So glamorous!"

"Yup. Quite the glamorous life. I'm hoping to make the big move from scraping gum off the floor to stocking used disco albums."

She threw her head back and laughed. She smelled of sweat and earth and woodsmoke and exotic herbs. "I like you. What's your name?"

"Kevin."

"Nice to meet you, Kevin who works at the record

store." She held out her hand. "They call me Geirskogul."

"Geirskogul. Very cool," he said, taking her hand and glancing quickly from her sparkling eyes and back to his shoes before letting go.

"Here you go, Kevin." She reached over and grabbed a cassette and a couple stickers, held them out for him. "Since you're in the music business and all."

He took them, shaking his head in gratitude, casting timid glances, a humble smile cracking his face. "Stoked on this. Thank you so much. I really loved the show."

"Yeah? Well, here," she snatched a flyer off the table, pressed it into his chest with a smirk. "We're playing on Saturday. At a campground in Orrick. It's a free show, so you don't need money, but, you know, donations are appreciated."

She gave him a sly wink and, feeling himself flush from his feet to the top of his skull, he ducked his head, studying the black-and-white flyer, hoping she wouldn't see how flustered he suddenly was. He didn't recognize any of the bands, but it looked metal as fuck with a very Nordic vibe: axes and horned-helmets, shields and spiked hammers.

"Cool," he managed. "I'll try to make it."

"Hope to see you there, Kevin."

—

The tape was beyond his expectations. Something about those drums and that black-metal guitar sound that was absolutely mesmerizing. So raw and primitive, yet structured and complex at the same time. The sound hollow and cold but rich with a thick primal essence.

And the haunting low growl of the singer. Completely and utterly terrifying and menacing.

It was difficult to make out the words, but from what he could decipher they were epic poems of Norse gods, the eternal struggle of life and death, trickery and magic, Loki and Thor. He'd loved Vikings when he was a kid and his dad used to entertain him for hours with tales of Scandinavian mythology.

He listened to that tape nonstop for the next three days and begged his mother to let him borrow the car. Begged, pleaded, cajoled. Nearly got down on his knees and cried.

She just sat at the kitchen table, eating scrambled eggs and smoking Kools, complaining about her hangover.

"Please," he said. "I'll bring it back full of gas. I promise."

"Kevin, you already said you'd take your little brother to the movies on Saturday. Remember? Now what kind of mother would I be if I let your brother down?" She put the butt of her Kool to her lips and sucked on it, shaking Tabasco sauce out, over her eggs. "Christ, my aching fucking head. They say protein and peppers are a hangover cure, you know."

"Look, Mom, I'll take him Sunday. That's cool, right, Brian?" he called to his brother who lay on his belly in front of the television, his chin nestled in the crook of his palms, watching Beavis and Butthead. "Cool if we see *Curse of Michael Myers* Sunday, buddy?"

"Well, I kind of wanted to see *Judge Dredd*."

"Okay, *Judge Dredd*. Fine. Just Sunday, not Saturday. Okay?"

"Yeah. Okay with me."

"See, Mom?"

"I don't know. This weird music you like, always dressed all in black. Ever think of wearing some colors? You were such a cute little boy. Now you look like some kinda zombie monster."

"Come on. I'll fill up the tank, *and get you a pack of Kools*."

"Pack of Kools, huh?"

"That's what I said."

"Tell you what, two packs of Kools and you got yourself a deal. But don't forget about taking your brother to the movies Sunday. And that tank better be full, mister!"

later learn were brothers from Australia who went by Skuld and Skogul.

It was as if the rain couldn't touch her, had no effect: she stood with her head cocked and chin up, one hand on her hip, the other grasping the handle of sticker-covered guitar case, booted feet planted firmly in the mud.

He inched up beside her, reached across and rolled down the passenger window. "Hey, what's up?" he shouted over the clack of the windshield wipers. "I heard the show was cancelled."

She turned, tossing her long, wet dreads over her shoulder, and ducked her head into the station wagon window, her face lighting up into a big smile when she saw him.

"Kevin! You made it. Yeah, sorry to say: show's cancelled. First some fuckers called the cops complaining, now this." She held her face up to the rain and stretched out her hands, like, *what can you do?*

A heat rose over Kevin at the thought that she recognized him and even remembered his name, and then the singer of the band was strutting up through the mud behind her, shirtless in the cold and rain, water dripping from his long, dreaded beard. He placed his arm around Geirskogul's waist and she looked up at him.

"Any luck?" she asked.

He shook his head grimly.

"Maybe Kevin here can help. Kevin, this is Gungnir. Gungnir, this is Kevin who works at the record store. *He thinks we're amazing.*"

Gungnir nodded and raised his palm. "Hail and joy to you, Kevin."

She ducked her head back into the window, rested her elbow on the sill and put her chin on her palm. "So," she said, raising her pretty eyebrows up to stare straight into his face. "We're in a bit of a pickle. Our friend's band Black Plague, well, their ride broke down. So we're helping them haul their equipment, and now there's no room for all of us in our van. One of us needs to find a ride back to our squat in Honeydew." She gave him a sly grin and a half wink, bobbed her head. "What do you think? Could you give a girl and her guitar a lift down the road aways?"

How amazing was this?! He'd drive to the depths of hell and back for this girl, this black metal guitar goddess. "Yeah, I guess. Sure. No problem," Kevin said.

She pulled open the door and tossed her guitar in the backseat, but as she bent forward to get in, Gungnir placed a hand on her shoulder, stopping her. "No."

She turned to him, "What's up?"

"You go with Skuld and Skogul. I'll go with Kevin."

"Yeah?"

"Yes."

"All right," she said, giving him a kiss as he impassively stared down at Kevin, face like an ancient chiseled monument.

She glanced at Kevin, "You boys have fun. I'll see you in Honeydew," then trotted off into the rain.

Gungnir slid into the passenger seat. He was a large man and looked cramped there, all muscles and dreads and beard, tattoos slick with rain.

Kevin put the car into gear, looked both ways into the storm before pulling out. "Bummer the show got cancelled," he said with a furtive glance. "Was really looking forward to seeing you guys again. Show last week at the armory was fucking insane good."

Gungnir just grunted, squinting ahead.

There was a cop in a light-blue poncho at the end of the drive, standing in the rain and directing the cars to turn around. Gungnir twisted slightly away, hiding his face. "Fucking pigs."

They turned, headed back out the twisting dirt road in silence, and soon were on the highway, coasting along 101 South through the redwoods.

Finally, Gungnir broke the awkward silence. "How do you know Geirskogul?"

"I don't really. Just met her at the show last week," Kevin said awkwardly.

"You like her, huh?"

Kevin glanced over at the huge man. He was staring straight ahead, somber, but Kevin could see his wide nostrils flaring. "Uh, yeah. You know. She's cool."

"Cool, huh?"

"Uh, yeah."

"You just seemed a little upset when I got in the car instead of her, is what I'm saying."

"What? No, man. As a matter of fact, I really wanted to meet you. I got your tape and I've been listening to it non-stop. I fucking love your voice and how you sing." Kevin pressed play on the tape player, grinding guitar and savage screaming came ripping out of the speakers. "See?"

"Mind if I ask you something personal?" Gungnir asked, turning to face him for the first time.

"No problem. Ask away."

"Why do you have that Jew's cross on your fucking head?"

Kevin coughed. Swallowed. Tried to focus his attention ahead. "The cross? The black cross on my forehead?"

"Yeah, the cross of the Jew Jesus."

"Well, it's inverted."

"Uh huh. Yeah? It's still a symbol of a Hebrew Messiah."

"But it's upside down, so, it's, like, satanic, man."

"Satanic? As in praising Satan?"

"Uh, yeah."

"Did you ever think by giving praise to Satan you are recognizing Christianity's Abrahamic domination over you? You're not really rebelling, but just giving them more power by acknowledging their gods."

"Huh. I don't know. I guess I never thought about it that way."

Then went back to silence. Headlights came up behind them, slipped past, trees silhouetted in the storm darting by.

"What is it that you like about metal music, Kevin?" Gungnir asked. "About black metal music in particular?"

"I don't know, man. I guess, like, the hardness. The

intensity."

"Exactly. The intensity, the *purity* of it. You like it because it's pure. There's a distilled essence to it. No bullshit. That's what you like, isn't it?"

Kevin thought about it, staring out at the storm, slipping through the tunnel of dark trees, and nodded. "Yeah, I guess so. It's stripped down, bare, no bullshit."

Gungnir smiled and gave his shoulder a friendly squeeze. "I thought so. You're a seeker of purity, Kevin. Just like me. But you've gotten sidetracked in their web. That's how thick their bullshit and dominion is: by trying to escape it you risk being tangled even further in it. I know. I've been there."

Kevin nodded. He couldn't deny what the guy was saying. Worshipping Satan *was* giving credence to Christianity, when he thought about it. He relished the rebellion and evil creepiness of it all, but it was really just the back of the same coin.

The tape ended with a squeal of haunting guitar feedback and then there was only the sound of the rain slashing down and the wipers softly clacking and squealing. The little town of Rio Dell slipped by them on the right, pointed rooves poking from the fog, and then they were passing Pacific Lumber, mountains of redwood logs waiting to be turned into lumber for decking and lawn chairs.

Gungnir ran a hand down his beard. "Us . . . we seek purity by going to the ancient religion of our own blood. Woden and Tiwaz, the European gods of old. This is our *true* origin, what that blasphemous Christianity wiped out. And the pure essence of that . . . is nature." He held a burly hand out, palm upwards, to the redwoods and ferns speeding by outside. "We find solace in the trees and the forest. But not in some bullshit hippie way. The forest contains multitude of darkness. It's a place of wonder, but also of struggle, of blood and bone. But where the true essence of life reveals itself. Turn off here."

Kevin slowed and took the Honey Dew/South Fork exit, the Eel River twisting below on their left, and veered onto a thin strip of blacktop snaking its way into the redwoods.

"My dad used to tell me stories about the Vikings," Kevin said.

"Really?" Gungnir asked. "Well I'd love to hear them!"

"I can only remember little bits now. He died when I was eight."

"I'm sorry to hear that, Kevin," Gungnir said, placing a hand on his shoulder. "I'm sure he was a good man."

They bumped along over the cracked asphalt for a while, and then Gungnir directed a thick finger off to a dirt road slinking up into the foggy hills on the right. "Up here. The road without a name!" The old station wagon bounced and heaved over the ruts, groaning up the steep incline.

"How far we going?" Kevin asked.

"Don't worry, you'll be home for dinner tonight."

They bounced along the muddy road, through the tall trees, past passages of clear cut, over hills.

"Easy," Gungnir said as they slid into a turn, then slipped past a busted-up gate and shotgun blasted sign, up a long driveway and down through tall alders and a tangle of whitethorn and to a tiny redwood-shingled cabin on a small flat surrounded by hundreds of black-plastic containers. Green garden hoses and thin lines of black tubing lay everywhere in a thick spider's web.

"Old pot farm," Gungnir said. "Owner gets busted, then never pays the land taxes and the county seizes the land, leaves these little cabins to just sit here and rot. Lots of 'em around ready for the squatting. Come inside a minute, kid, there's something I'd like to ask you." The big man winked at him before cracking open the door and lumbering out.

"Sure," Kevin said, as he shakily killed the engine and darted out into the rain after him. Gungnir hulked bear-like across the muddy abyss and to the cabin door, throwing it open and waving Kevin in.

It was musty and dank inside, lit only by the gray light breaking through the dirty windows. Gungnir stepped in and shut the door behind him, motioning to a tree stump by a wooden table of rough-hewn redwood slabs. "Have a seat. And here," he threw him a towel, "Dry off. You might want to wipe that shit off your face, too, it's wet and running everywhere." As Kevin toweled off his hair and scrubbed the corpse paint off his face, Gungnir went and squatted by the woodstove in the corner and began to make a fire.

Kevin looked around, there were candles and animal skins stretched everywhere. Drums and tambourines. An altar-like shelf of stones and amulets and a large steers horn. Jars of beans, bags of rice stowed in the corner beside a pile of Army field rations, pumpkins and odd-shaped squashes, big five-gallon glass carboys filled with cloudy liquid. Soon the fire was roaring, filling the place with warmth and strange shadows.

"Nice, huh?" Gungnir said. "People just use these places to grow weed and make money, not realizing they're living in paradise. What do you need money for if you can live here in nature, surviving off the land?"

Gungnir produced two mason jars from a shelf, pulled the cork from a large jug with his teeth, and filled them with a thick amber liquid with bits of plant matter floating in it. "Mead, made from local honey. Infused with damiana I harvested myself down in Texas." He lifted his glass with a beefy hand, the nails chipped and dirt crusted. "May Woden's wisdom light your pathways and part your shadows. Skål!"

Kevin nervously raised his glass and tapped it against Gungnir's, who let out a deep, growl-like laugh and tilted his glass up, swilling the elixir sloppily, liquid spilling down his thick beard, before slamming the jar down and filling it again.

Kevin sipped his cup cautiously. It was very sweet and fruity, but with a strong herbal flavor to it: minty and spicy, hickory like. He smiled at Gungnir. "It's really good. Thank you."

"You're most welcome, Kevin. And thank you so much for the ride, which is what I wanted to talk to you about. So, you have a valid driver's license, I assume?"

Kevin nodded.

"All up to date?"

Kevin continued to nod.

"See," Gungnir said, "problem is: none of us do, and some of us have some certain legal, ah, . . . issues we're dealing with it, making law enforcement a thing we're to avoid, if you know what I mean. So we could really use a driver. Someone to help us haul equipment. We can't pay you much, but you'd obviously get into all the shows, travel, meet a lot of girls, hear great music. But we offer you more than that, Kevin." He set his elbows on the table and leaned his big square forehead close. Kevin could smell his sweat and the fruity tang of the mead on his breath. "We offer you brotherhood. We're a family, but our beliefs are no joke. I must warn you, to us Valhalla, Woden these aren't just metaphors, they're real. And you must adhere to our ways if you decide to travel with us. Do you understand?"

Kevin nodded and swallowed, overcome as he realized something like this is what he'd craved ever since his father died. To be a part of something, accepted. To have a man like Gungnir to guide him. Someone to look up to.

Rain pattered against the roof and the fire crackled as the logs shifted, the room very warm now, the mead hot in his belly and gaseous and light in his brain.

Suddenly the door burst open and Geirskogul, Skuld and Skogul came barging in, laughing and screeching, rain drenched, water dripping from their dreads.

"Kevin!" Geirskogul shouted, her face lighting up when she spied him, holding up a dead racoon by the tail, shouting, "Behold the road kill-blessings Woden has bestowed! Found this poor little fellow on the side of the highway. He'll make a lovely stole!"

"Well, all right, the mead's already out!" Skuld exclaimed grabbing a glass, Skogul following suit.

Geirskogul had her big bowie knife out, and was sawing away at the tail of the racoon, tearing it loose, and wrapping a thin leather string around the fleshy base. "Come here, Kevin. I got something for you."

Kevin awkwardly got up from the table, pausing as she got down on her knees before him.

"Turn around," she said. "Go on, I'm not gonna bite ya."

Kevin turned and she pushed aside his cape, grasping his bullet belt, pulling him to her before winding the leather thong around the belt, yanking it taunt so that it hung down between his legs, then using her teeth to knot it off.

"There you go," she said. "Now you're a wild thing!"

Kevin beamed, the tail sprouting from him like something he was born with, and vowed to never take it off as long as he lived.

—

Kevin began driving their van for them, helping haul their rudimentary equipment up on stage, set it up and tear it down, working their little table selling merchandise.

Their shows were more like tribal gatherings than concerts, drawing Woden worshipers from throughout the Pacific Northwest, with a cross section of crust punks, goths and black-metal heads. It was a very underground scene, but surprisingly large. A huge network of different pagan communities that would come together for all sorts of festivals, parties and gatherings. They would play in the woods when they could, at National Parks, campgrounds or old hippie communes, and when they couldn't do that they'd play at Bowling Alleys, bars and community centers.

They started calling him Kvasir, taught him about the Gods of old. The Norse and Germanic Gods: Woden, Freyja, Frigg and Baldr. A change overcame him. He no longer thought of death and the devil anymore. He felt positive and full of life. He took down the black and white posters of the Norwegian black metal bands and replaced them with colorful images of nature and the gods of his new religion. Woden and Frigg. Thor, Loki, Balder, and Heimdall. He cut his long dyed-black hair to where it was growing in pale and golden.

Skuld and Skogul came to him one evening with some carved wooden drums, rawhide tops bound and stretched taut with thick rope and steel o-rings. "Oi, come with us, mate," Skogul said, offering him a small black hand drum.

They took him deep into the forest, over moss-covered logs, and down a ravine thick and downy with ferns. They sat by a running creek, and to the sound of water slipping over stone Skuld began to pound out a rudimentary beat, Skogul joining along, nodding his head in time. Kevin followed, slapping his hand against the percussive hand drum on each downbeat, letting his eyes slip shut as the rhythm filled him. Soon Skuld and Skogul were doing little rolls, filling the empty spaces with flourishes they traded back and forth, the sound like a giant creaking insect, echoing through the shadows of the tall redwood trees and Kevin was transported away to a primordial time and place.

They started taking him out with them all the time to get lost in their weird tribal rhythms. Sometimes to the beach, sometimes they'd hike high up into the mountains.

He really liked Skuld and Skogul. They were quiet, seemed to speak more with their eyes and their drums than with their mouths. But there was a sense of kindness to them. They never left each other's side, and their sense of brotherhood and the simple and obvious endearment they had for each other moved Kevin.

He began to gain a respect for the concept of family and a feeling of affection began to swell in him. He tried to spend more time with his own brother, take him places and talk to him more. He grew kinder to his mother and helped her by keeping their tiny apartment clean.

One day Gungnir approached him and laid one of his huge hands on his shoulder. "Kvasir, finding you was a great blessing, you've been such a help, and I want to thank you." He slipped him a few hundred-dollar bills. "Let this plunder be a token of our affection and gratitude," and he wrapped Kevin in his bear-like embrace, patting his back affectionately.

It was the most money Kevin had ever had at once. A

month's-worth of work at the record store. He spent the entire thing on groceries for his family. He felt so proud bringing them in the door to their apartment, setting those brown paper bags filled with food on the counter. He cooked them all green beans stewed with garlic and slivered almonds, pork chops fried in garlic butter and brown sugar-- smothered in a jar of homemade apple sauce Geirskogul had given him--his mother happily exclaiming about how his father had loved to cook just like him. He put a big metal tin of Hawaiian Punch on the table, punched a triangular hole in the top with a church key, and told his brother he could have as much as he wanted.

That was an amazing night, pride swelling in his chest as he watched his mother and brother feast on the bounty he'd brought home.

His mother licked grease from her lips and sat back in her chair, a beatific look of satisfaction on her face as she lit a Kool. "I have to admit," she said, "I like the direction you've taken this summer. Whatever you've been up to its been making you a good boy. No, not a good boy. A man. A good man. Your father would be proud."

Those words rang in his ears, reverberating like some great bell, and when his brother slurped down the last of his punch and let out a long deep burp, they all burst out into glorious laughter together.

—

It was a heady time.

Fenir's Wolf recorded an album in a dingy little basement studio and had a thousand compact discs burned. They made the covers themselves, Geirskogul drawing an amazing black-and-white picture of deer's skull, the antler's twisting into a tree-like maze of fractals that had Fenir's Wolf hidden within it.

The drawing spoke so much to Kevin, how the name, like the band itself, was hidden and only those who knew where to look could find it, puzzle out the mystery. It made such perfect sense: this music was only for the worthy. The initiated who could understand it for the magic that it was. There was a secretive, outlaw spirit to the whole thing, with a palpable sense of menace.

It was Kevin's job to fold each CD cover and slip it inside a plastic case with an oak leaf they'd gathered from the forest. He was sitting at the redwood table in the little cabin they squatted in, sweating as the fire blazed in the woodstove, a mountain of plastic CD cases on his left, a mound of xeroxed covers and a pile of oak leaves on his right, when the entire band somberly walked in the door, staring daggers at him. He was used to Gungnir's grumpy-bear demeanor, but it was odd to not have Skuld and Skogul smiling and waving at him, affectionately calling him brother in their thick Aussie accents.

"Hey, guys," he said, trying to sound casual. He pressed a folded paper cover into the plastic guides, tucked an oak leaf on top, shut the case and set it on the pile and reached for another as they circled him, faces stern: Gungnir in the center, massive arms folded over his swollen chest, Geirskogul beside him in a pale-blue peasant's gown, Skuld and Skogul to the side in their furry vests with bone buttons.

"Kvasir," Gungnir said, his voice grim and betraying no emotion. "We have talked amongst ourselves of you and it has been decided. We want to make you one with the tribe, officially bring you into the fold."

Kevasir's breath caught in his throat, and he felt a great smile break across his face.

Gungnir lifted a palm-facing hand. "Be not glad yet, young one. You will be tested. There will be a ritual which you cannot fail. Do you understand?"

"Yes," Kvasir said, knowing he must speak the affirmation.

Geirskugul narrowed those alluring eyes of hers and grinned devilishly. "A sacrifice of blood and fire is demanded. Prepare yourself."

—

very good, Kvasir," her hand against the back of his neck, fingers snaking up seductively into his hair for the briefest moment before slipping away.

Skuld's playful voice, tinged with that Australian accent, "How did Loki appease the vengeance of Skadi, then, eh?"

"With laughter. He made her laugh."

"Righto, he did."

And finally Skogul asking, "And how many days did Father Woden hang from the cosmic tree Yggdrasil?"

"Nine days. Woden hung upside down from Yggdrasil nine days with no food or water."

There was clapping and cheers and his blindfold was ripped from his face.

Kevin blinked into the night. They were standing in the middle of a dirt parking lot before an old white-clapboard church. Kevin stared at the rickety, paint-peeling steeple looming up into the stars, a vertiginous sensation filling him. His mind swam in a puddle of mushrooms and mead. It was as if everything was embroidered on some slowly turning tapestry, the moon and stars, the earth, the church. Then the leering faces of Fenir's Wolf were everywhere as they closed in, thrusting a squirming, struggling rodent-like creature at him.

Gungnir grasped the thing's two front paws, spreading them apart so that its soft down chest bloomed like a white flower. Skuld and Skogul each yanked on a leg, stretching the wriggling beast out to its full length.

Geirskogul sidled up beside him, pressing her body against his, reaching down to grasp the handle of her knife and slowly sliding it free of its sheath. "Spill its blood," she said, taking his hand and pressing the knife handle into his palm, gently closing his fingers over it. "Kill it."

A slow chant of "Kill it, kill it, kill it," went up amongst them as Kvasir slowly lifted the knife, the sharp edge shimmering in the starlight, and held it poised above the squirming creature.

It was a rabbit. A big old jack rabbit with long ears and

huge yellow eyes that blinked fearfully into the night as it jerked its head back-and-forth. It wrinkled its nose as it turned its face and looked at him, eyes narrowing. Its tiny pink tongue darted out, licking its lips, and then it spoke. "What are you doing?" it asked as it craned its neck to peer at its captors with those strange yellow eyes. "You don't really trust these people, do you?"

Kvasir blinked and ground his teeth.

"Don't listen to the rabbit," Geirskogul said, her face fierce and eerie in the strange light of the weird psychedelic night. Reality seemed to be slowly melting around her, dripping in molten droplets like hot candle wax, spilling to the ground about her feet. "Do it," she said, eyes half shut, her full lips wet and parted. She laid her open palm against his chest, pressed. "Do it. Stab the bunny. The Blot Ceremony demands a blood sacrifice."

His heart hammered beneath her outstretched fingers and the scent of her wafted up, filling his nose and face—sweet and fruity, yet savory and raw, deeply sexual and filled with pheromones and musk—and an electric jolt surged through him as he gripped the hard shaft in his sweaty palms. He shuddered and thrust the blade down into the soft furry belly of the bunny. The pink skin parted easily and the knife slipped into the warm wet insides. He gasped and with a moan jerked the blade free, then brought it back again, the rabbit thrashing and jerking. And again he brought the knife down, and again, until finally the bunny went limp and still, head and ears hanging flaccid and lifeless.

Geiskogul squealed with delight and ran her hand over the gash, slipping a finger inside the rabbit. Pulling her blood drenched finger from the belly, she smiled seductively and touched it to her tongue. "Welcome to the tribe," she said to Kevin and smeared a streak of rabbit's blood beneath his eyes.

"Oi, welcome to the family, mate!" Skuld said, giving him a hug before grabbing a red-plastic gasoline can and skipping towards the church.

"Welcome, brother," Skogul said, smiling his funny

crooked grin and wrapping an arm around his shoulder.

Gungnir produced a thick wooden branch, its end wrapped tightly in gas-soaked cloth, pressed it to Kevin's chest. With the strike of a match the torch burst into flame. "Now, as a symbol of erasing the false god forced upon us, in veneration of Woden, our true ancestral father, we will burn this church to the motherfucking ground. Go ahead, brother, go forth and set it alight."

Kevin looked up to see Skuld splashing gasoline against the church door and spilling it around its foundation.

He took the torch, the world swirling about him, and stalked to the church, the earth upending itself and melting around him. He stooped and touched the flame to the black puddle before the church's doorway and a ball of flame erupted from the stillness of the night, roaring and knocking him backwards into the arms and laughter of Fenir's Wolf who danced and cheered as the fire crackled and embers spun upwards into the dark skies.

And it was all howling and singing and crazy feral frolicking and mead and mushrooms and comets and black rainbows to other lands beyond our own.

And then they were back at the cabin. Candles flickered about the small room like dancing fireflies, constellations throwing off amber waves of light and shadow as Gungnir took the ceremonial horn from the shelf and filled it with mead.

Kevin was perched up on a tall chair like a king upon a throne, blood running down his face, Geirskogul curled on his lap, one hand pressed against his chest, the other tapping an ink-stained needle into the flesh below his eyes.

Skuld and Skogul were smoking a joint—the earthy, skunky scent like that of a primordial forest, a land beyond time—and the pale smoke hung like antediluvian mists, curling about them.

Gungnir raised the sacred horn vessel in a toast. "To Kvasir, who is now one with us. Welcome."

Skuld and Skogul lifted their fists, bellowing with agreement, "Here! Here!" and emotion washed over Kevin, his eyes growing hot and swollen, tears spilling down and mixing with the ink and blood.

"Does it hurt?" Geirskogul asked, craning her neck to look into his eyes, her face so gorgeous, her lips so close to his.

He shook his head. "No, it doesn't hurt at all." And she smiled, dipped the tip of the needle in a pot of ink and pierced him again, and he wondered what it would be like to kiss her. Taste the lips of this fallen angel, this earthly Valkyrie, so wild and feral and pure in her beauty. If he could kiss her, just once, he felt he could maybe die happy, that all the suffering and bullshit of this shitty life would be worth it.

—

His mother cried when she saw the tattoos.

She was at the kitchen table reading a tabloid and drinking coffee. He came in with an arm full of groceries, set them on the counter, and she looked at him, coffee mug frozen halfway to her mouth. "Tell me they're not real."

"They're real, mother."

She let out a hiccupping cry and, sobbing, ran from him and to her bedroom, slamming the door behind her.

But his brother liked them, popping up from his position prone on the rug before the television and running over. "Cool!" he exclaimed. "Do they mean something?"

He showed Brian what each symbol meant, the björk symbolizing spring and new life, the reio symbolizing his journey, how together they deemed him a poet and wiseman, and watching his brother's rapt face, eyes wide with wonder, he realized that for so long in trying to replicate his father he'd only been trying to replicate the hole in his heart his father had left. He'd been trying to give more emptiness instead of filling the void. He understood that now, and yearned to heal that wound, to be there for him.

As they sat there at the kitchen table, he told his little brother all the ancient tales of the old gods and their drama and ways, just as their father had once told the tales to him.

He felt whole and complete, keeping a culture alive and being the conduit for scriptures and esoteric histories. This sense of completeness and sentimentality filled his eyes with heat and tears and, overcome, he grabbed his brother and wrapped his arms around him, pressed his cheek against the top of his brother's head and told him how much he loved him. Told him things were going to be different from now on, and that from now on Brian would be known as Baldr.

And then he told him everything else, things he had promised he would never tell another living soul.

—

It wasn't the first time he had asked that his brother be taken into the fold. He'd mentioned it before and the response had always been the same: No. He was too young.

Apparently, they'd debated over whether to even bring Kvasir into the tribe. In the end they said it was his passion and love of music that had convinced them, but he was as young as they were willing to go. Anyone younger couldn't be trusted with the secrets of the sect. Their rituals and hidden ways. But this time Kevin felt emboldened to push it further, to give his plea more strength. He was, after all, now an official member of the tribe, the scabs on his face still fresh and painful.

They were sitting around the woodstove, Gungnir drinking mead, Geirskogul lying beside him, strumming a small lyre, Skuld and Skogul in the shadows, tapping their feet and passing a joint back and forth.

"We've told you before," Gungnir said. "Your brother is too young for the tribe. Let it be, you are disturbing the tranquility of the mead hall."

"But I've taught him well. He knows all our beliefs and customs. Everything."

"Everything?" Gungnir asked, his face hardening as Geirskogul stopped playing and set the harp aside. Skuld dropped the roach he was hitting and crushed it with the toe of his boot. Kevin hesitated and for a long moment there was only the sound of the fire crackling, before Gungnir spoke again.

"I asked you a question, boy."

Kevin looked at his shoes, scratched his leg. "Yes. Everything." The implication was clear. He'd told of that which was not to be mentioned: the burning of the churches, their most sacred rite. But it wasn't to a stranger. It was to his own brother! His own flesh and blood. They had to understand that.

Gungnir began to tremble. He stood, went to the shelf and placed the horn upon it, his nostrils flaring. Fear and doubt flooded Kevin's blood. *Was telling his brother a mistake?*

But then Geirskogul sat up and spoke. "Hasn't Kvasir always been loyal? Hasn't he been true to the tribe. I say we bring his brother in, give him what he wants." She strode to Gungnir, rested her hand on his shoulder and whispered into his ear.

Gungnir nodded, arms crossed across his broad chest, fair-haired Valkyrie whispering in his ear, his eyes locked on Kevin. "All right. We will discuss it amongst the band, and let you know when we come to a decision. Until then no more talk of it."

Geirskogul smiled at Kevin, her eyes sparkling, but brows and lips sharp, predatory and hawk-like.

"Thank you," Kvasir said. "Thank you."

—

Kvasir didn't hear from them for a couple days and began to grow worried. *Had he gone too far?* They wouldn't kick him out of their tribe, *would they?* Or maybe just abandon him?

He knew they could pack up and leave at any moment, it was their nature. They often talked about all the different places they'd lived and left— Austin Texas, Telluride Colorado, Madison Wisconsin— and there had been talk of them hitting the road again. The thought of them leaving him behind made his heart grow cold and still.

But then his mother was telling him he had a phone call and Geirskogul's heavenly voice was telling him congratulations, he was going to get what he wanted. There was going to be a big party, an Althing Gathering, with other tribes of Woden worshippers coming from all over, and for the blot ritual there would be a goat they would kill and roast. It was to be on a secluded beach, far up the coast, in Southern Oregon. He was to come early. And bring his brother.

—

Kvasir and his little brother sat waiting on the beach, watching as the sun slipped down into the ocean, a brilliant ball of molten red melting into the vast waters. As darkness crept over the cove and there was still no sign of anyone, he worried for a moment that they were in the wrong place, that he'd somehow misread the instructions Geirskogul had given him, but then he heard the faint beating of distant drums and saw a procession of torches slinking down the cliff-side trail.

They were led by Geirskogul and Gungnir who marched with the noble manner of royalty, Skuld and Skogul following behind beating a somber dirge on dark drums hanging from their shoulders. There were many others that Kvasir did not recognize, a dozen or so, bearded men, women in peasant blouses and leather pinafores. As he and his brother rose, they encircled them. Two five-gallon carboys of mead were placed in the circle, long torches stuck in the sand illuminated the scene with orange and red coruscating light. The pounding of the drums ceased and an eerie quiet fell upon them, punctuated only by the crashing of the waves.

Gungnir stood arms crossed with his stern, bear-like demeanor, while Geirskogul paced back-and-forth before him.

Her beauty always unnerved Kevin and made him feel foolish and childlike, but tonight there was a very intense fierceness to her, a cold and grim look in her eyes that chilled him deeply. He tried to appear strong, lifted his chin and spoke steadily. "Heil og sael, Geirskogul,"

"Heil og sael, Kvasir," she murmured back, slowly unsheathing her knife.

"Where's the goat?" he asked. "I thought we needed a blood sacrifice for the Blot."

"Oh, we have our goat," Geirskogul said, spinning forward and stretching an arm out, the knife point mere inches from his face. "Kvasir! Do you remember the nine noble virtues?"

Was this some kind of test? He could sense his little brother growing uneasy beside him and placed a hand on his back to reassure him. If this was a test, he would pass. He was Kvasir, the wise one.

"Geirskogul, chooser of the slain, the nine noble virtues as stated in the Havamal are courage, truth, honor, fidelity, discipline, hospitality, self-reliance, industriousness, and perseverance."

"Correct," she said, leering, her white teeth catching the light of the torches and staining her mouth an orange and amber hue. "But what is the greatest commandment in the law?"

"The greatest commandment is the proscription of oath-breaking."

"Very good, Kvasir. Very good indeed."

Kvasir felt relief. *Had he passed the test?*

Geirskogul stepped back and continued pacing, gently slapping the belly of the knife against her palm. "So, Kvasir, did you not take an oath of loyalty to this tribe?"

"Yes."

"Did we not make you part of our family?"

"Yes."

"Did we not name you and mark you so that you were reborn as one of us?"

"Yes."

"When you wanted to bring your brother into the tribe did we not tell you, 'No'? That he was too young? That he couldn't be trusted with the secrets of our sect?"

"Yes, but he's no stranger, he's my—"

"Shut your mouth, traitor!" and she flashed out her knife and nicked his cheek. The cut stung and a trickle of blood wept out. For the first time he felt doubt and real fear flood through him.

"But you insisted, she continued. "You were sworn to secrecy and you told him of our doings. An outsider! You have broken your oath!"

Kevin struggled not to weep, but could feel the tears and snot rising up in him, and he wondered if maybe he should throw himself at her feet and beg forgiveness. Mercy. But no, he had to be strong. Had to adhere to the ways of Woden, be a warrior. This had to be some kind of test. They were testing him. He had to remain steadfast and stalwart.

"But he's not an outsider. He's my brother. My blood. My family."

Geirskogul was shaking her head sadly, testing the tip of her knife against her finger. "Family, huh?" she said, and laughed, cocked her pretty head so that her dreads streamed down behind her like a cloak. "*We're* supposed to be your family. I'm just curious, you know. What the fuck were you thinking? How could you have done this to us? Forced us to this point? Wasn't I pretty enough for you? Weren't Skuld and Skogul brothers enough for you? Wasn't Gungnir enough of a father for you? I found you, I cultivated you. I tried to make you one with us. But what do you do? Revert back to your family? Your mommy and little brother? We're supposed to be your new family! Us. You took an oath and made a bond. And you know, Kvasir, I blame you for this.'

"For what?"

"For what's about to happen."

Brian began to shake and whimper now. "Kevin, I want to go home," he said. "I'm scared."

"It's okay," Kevin replied. "This is just a test."

"Oh, it's a test all right," Geirskogul, said. "But it's also a Blot Ceremony demanding sacrifice and blood." And she shot out a hand, grasping Brian by the wrist and pulling him to her as she brought her knife to his neck, holding it threateningly there. Kevin lunged forward, desperate to do something, anything, but Gungnir was there, holding him back with one of his massive hands.

"Help me, Kevin," Brian whimpered.

"Silence," Geirskogul said, slipping a hand up over his mouth. "There's going to be a sacrifice. An outsider has been told our rituals and must die. Now, Kvasir, you can either participate and live, or fight it and join him. But either way he dies. So, what's it going to be?"

Gungnir pressed a bowie knife into Kevin's hand. "Do it, Kvasir. Slay the rabbit."

"Come on," Geirskogul whispered, grasping Brian tight and licking her lips. "You know you want to do it. Just like the bunny. And then we'll be together forever. Nothing can break a bond like that. Do it for me. Do it to prove you love us. Your new family."

Kevin looked about at the leering faces all around him. Searching for any glimmer of sympathy or kindness. He saw Skuld there, but he just nodded his head as if to say, "Go on, then," and started a slow beat on the drum. Not knowing what else to do, Kevin stepped forward, tears streaming down his face, and shakily raised the knife. He stared at his brother's heaving chest, avoiding his wild pleading eyes, and with a grunt struck out, slicing Geirskogul across the wrist of her knife hand.

She cried out in surprise, dropping her knife, and Brian struggled free.

"Run, Brian, run!" Kevin screamed, spinning and slashing at Gungnir, who stepped back and laughed at him, batting the knife away.

"Good for you, Kvasir!" Gungnir said, a huge smile plastered across his bear-like face. "A noble and unwinnable fight is a sure way through the gates of Valhalla."

Then Kevin's nose exploded as Gungnir's fist slammed squarely into it, sending him sprawling into the sand. A million hands reached out, everyone grabbing him and hauling him off the ground, spinning him so that he was upside down, and he watched in horror as Geirskogul came dragging his brother screaming down the beach towards him by the hair.

She knelt in the sand and grabbed Kevin by the face, squeezed his cheeks, blood and snot streaming and bubbling from his shattered nose. "Oh, you stupid, sad little boy. I brought you in and it looks like I'm going to have to take you out. But first, I want to give you what you wanted." She pulled Brian closer. "You want your brother to know our ways? To grasp the mysticism, understand the scripture of the All Father? Well there's a price to drinking from the well of Urd."

"No," Kevin pleaded, gurgling through all the blood and phlegm. "Please don't hurt him. I'll do anything."

"It's too late for that, Kvaisr," she said and with a gleeful glint in her eye she jerked her knife up, the tip catching Brian's left eye, and dug it in. Brian howled and shrieked, desperately clawing at his face as she laughed and carved, pulling the orb free, grasping it up and slicing away the deep-red muscles and tendons. She stepped to one of the big bottles of mead, leaving Brian in a weeping ball in the sand, and plopped the eyeball into the vessel. It bobbed and floated there in the oily liquid, a trail of nerves and tendons hanging from it. "Now hang him from a tree. Let him experience Yggdrasil and the connection of the nine worlds. Then he will know our ways."

"Sorry, mate," Skuld whispered to Kevin as he and Skogul grabbed Brian up, "just the way it goes." They dragged Brian screaming across the beach to where a massive Cyprus tree jutted from the rock and sand. Kevin could see them, shadowy figures, duct-taping his squirming brother upside-down in the tree's branches like a spider wrapping a struggling fly in its web.

"As for you, Kvasir," Geirskogul said, wiping a streak of blood from her knife with a finger before running it down her tongue. "Oh, wise one, since there are no questions you cannot answer, your sacrifice will be to the Mead of Poetry, so that the tribe may drink of it and share in your knowledge."

She grabbed a fistful of his hair and jerked his head

MALL SANTA

Fuck that bitch, Trish thought as the light changed from yellow to red. She stomped on the gas, sending her Civic careening through the intersection, horns blaring. Her wheels skidded on the ice and the little car lilted out of control. Undaunted, Trish downshifted, cranked the wheel, and swerved through the light. Chomping on a stale piece of gum while hanging her middle finger to all the honking assholes, she whispered over her shoulder to Jenny—bundled in her car seat in the back, yanking at the hair of a naked Barbie doll.

"Don't worry, honey, I'll get you there."

Trish had to get her to the mall before Santa left.

She screeched into the Bayshore parking lot, a busy hive of headlights and shoppers. The fan to the heater was broken—Ronnie insisting he'd be the one to fix it, like being a technician assistant at Auto Lube made him a master mechanic—so it was freezing in the car. Her breath came out in pale, wet clouds as she eased the vehicle to a crawl, and began searching for a spot that wasn't a fucking mile away from the entrance. The clock was ticking.

This was her chance at a new beginning. She'd already posted on Facebook that she was on her way, and she'd be humiliated if she didn't get there on time. Becca, Annie, and Monica had already posted pictures of their toddlers on the lap of the mall Santa, and the amount of likes and comments they had received was fucking nuts. A good picture of Jenny on the lap of jolly St. Nick could give her a big boost, get her the respect she deserved from the other mothers at the preschool. Snobby bitches.

And then, right by the main entrance, a shiny minivan pulled out of a spot.

Rock star parking!

Trish waited, clacking her gum against her back molars, fingers nervously tap-tapping on the wheel to the beat of a Lady Gaga song, when—*motherfucker!*—an SUV cut in front of her and stole the space.

Fucking bullshit!

She slammed her palm against the horn and flipped her off, and as the yuppie-wannabe, bleach-blonde cunt pulled out her own toddler from the backseat, the stupid bitch smiled and shrugged, blew Trish a kiss.

—

The festive red-and-green Christmas lights of the mall bloomed like an oasis of light against the night as Trish hustled across the frozen parking lot. Jenny was perched on her hip, little arms clutching her neck. A small flurry of snow fell from the sky, glowing in the tall lights, dusting the rows of cars. People were leaving in droves and she had to push her way through them to get in the entrance.

When the first parent—Jessica Knicks, a quiet mousy lady—had asked to be her friend on Facebook, Trish thought nothing of it. She hadn't thought much about the other mothers at the daycare. But then more requests began to trickle in, and the other mothers' posts started appearing on her feed, and she'd noticed something, a sort of hierarchy of who had the cutest photos, who looked the nicest. Her own posts got a distinct lack of likes. And sometimes an odd comment could be taken so many ways: a simple "nice," no capital letters, no exclamation points, no emoji. How was she supposed to take that? She didn't know whether to like it, give it a heart, or what.

One morning when she was dropping off Jenny, another mom—Angela—said to her, "I saw your party on Facebook. Cute photos," and there was a tone to her voice. The other mothers sounded fake as shit, all the time, because they were, but this had a tone of cattiness she hadn't heard since high school. And then later that night, curled up on the sofa with her phone, sipping a Bud Light tall boy, Trish went through her own posts with a new eye, and, *damn*, some of her shit was tacky. Not only blurry and out of focus, but down right trashy:

—Ronnie and his grease monkey buddies sitting around a keg, Ronnie crazy-eyed and probably high on meth, holding up an overflowing red-plastic cup, head craned so that the SS lightning bolts tattooed on his neck took up half the frame.

Delete.

—Ronnie's mom in a fringed Iron Maiden shirt, grinning crazily and missing more than a couple teeth as she swings a terrified Jenny by the arms.

Delete.

—Jenny sitting in the homemade baby pool Ronnie had fashioned out of an old refrigerator in their yard.

Definitely delete.

That's when it all began, the need for the perfect shot, one that conveyed the right amount of class, sass, and cuteness:

—Forcing Jenny to sit cherub-like on a tree branch, yelling at her, "Smile! A *real* smile, you're just grimacing!"

—Posing fashionably by a lake.

—Sitting childishly by a mound of raked-up autumn leaves.

—Gleefully putting a carrot nose on a little snowman.

It grew into an obsession.

Trish began to plan future posts. Lying in bed at night, staring at the water stain on the ceiling, she'd imagine Jenny in a pretty dress, planting nasturtiums and marigolds, swimming in a gleaming-blue pool in a new bathing suit—not hanging out of a broken-down refrigerator in one of Trish's old Guns N' Roses shirts.

The back end of the mall was dark. Only the dollar store remained open. The rest of the shops—Borders, Sunset Video, Pretzel Company—had all gone out of business.

When she saw the tree and lights and Santa atop his throne in the distance, she thought of her father and her heart did some weird thing: pounding in her chest and filling her face with heat. It was her father who had always taken her to see Santa as a little girl. She could still remember his logger smell of gas and trees. And her parents had always put that picture of her on Santa's lap on the refrigerator door, every year.

Something clicked. It all made sense. Facebook was like the refrigerator door, a place to pin what you wanted others to see.

Jenny was getting heavy and so she put her down.

The little girl yawned, rubbed her eyes, and said, "Mommy, I'm tired."

Trish licked her thumb and scrubbed at a smear on her daughter's cheek. "I know, baby. We just gotta see Santa real quick." She then took her by the hand and tugged her along the final thirty feet to the North Pole.

A small gaggle of parents waited in line between two giant candy canes, Santa waiting upon his throne. As Trish strutted up to the other moms, dragging Jenny along behind her, a tall, redheaded teenager-looking dude—wearing an elf suit much too small for him—stepped up and clicked a frayed-velvet rope barricade across the entrance.

"Sorry," the douchebag said with a hideous bucktoothed grin. He wore thick glasses, a Band-Aid on his chin. "Eight o'clock, no more visitors tonight. Santa has lots of work to do!"

Really? Trish thought, putting a hand on her hip.

She cocked her head, snarled at the gangly ginger elf and said, "What? You gotta be kidding me. Come on, dude, let me in."

"Sorry. Can't. See, the cash register's all locked up and shut down for the night. We open again at eleven tomorrow morning."

"Yeah?" Trish asked, waggling a finger. "Well, I can't be here tomorrow. Some of us have real fucking jobs. Unlike *you* people."

The elf frowned and squinted. "Us ... *elf* people?"

Trish was about to respond—to throw down some hardcore shit on this stupid elf-ass motherfucker—when she spotted the bleach-blonde bitch who had stolen her space. The woman stood just ahead of her in line. And the bitch was looking right at her, smirking, lifting a hand and giving her a tiny wave before turning her back on her.

"Fuck you, cunt!" Trish screamed, rage exploding within her like a lit-up gas-soaked rag.

"Ma'am, you're going to have to leave," the elf said, his stupid freckled face looking all serious and concerned.

"What the fuck are you going to do, you stupid ginger?" Trish ground her teeth, spitting the words out from a clenched jaw. "You gonna tell Santa on me? Put me on the naughty list?"

She could feel Jenny hiding behind her, clutching her leg.

"Mommy, what's happening?"

"This pea-brained ginger elf won't let us see Santa. That's what's happening, sweetie."

The elf crossed his arms and stood up straight. "If you don't leave right this instant, I'm calling mall security."

"Yeah, well *fuck you*, elf boy. I'm going, okay? I'm going."

She scooped Jenny up by her armpits, tucked her against her shoulder, and glared at the elf, then turned on her heel, striding away.

But then her ankle bent all wrong, her foot slipping sideways across the slick linoleum floor—wet from the melted snow. She tried to right herself, over compensated, and pitched forward. She hung in the air with both feet off the ground a moment before she fell, watching horrified as Jenny propelled from her arms. Her daughter floated upward and away, then slammed down squarely on the top of her head with a gut-wrenching *crack!*

Sprawled on her belly, Trish screamed and crawled to her.

Blood oozed from her daughter's head and into her curly locks of pale hair, her eyes blinking once then closing.

"Jenny? Jenny? Are you okay? Jenny?"

The little girl gave a low moan, but her eyes remained shut.

Trish looked about her at everyone slack-jawed and frozen in place: the gangly ginger elf, the bleach-blonde bitch, the other parents in line, even Santa up on his throne in his red cloak, white-bearded and god-like, everyone staring.

She shrieked, her breath hitching in her chest and coming out in sharp bursts.

"Isn't anyone going to help me?"

As if awoken from a daze, the elf jerked, then yanked a phone from his pocket and began frantically swiping a long pale finger across the screen.

—

The ambulance ride was like some strange dream, everything happening both too slowly and too quickly: Jenny strapped to a gurney, neck in a brace, still unconscious, but muttering under shallow breaths, the sound of the siren, the spinning lights reflecting patterns on everything outside the windows, the antiseptic and sterile smell of bandages and solutions, the paramedics' questions about past illnesses, allergies, previous surgeries, tetanus.

Then Jenny was on a stretcher, wheeled into the hospital, ushered through a maze of crowded halls, and put into a big machine to examine her head. They were looking for dark spots and bruising in the brain, fluid, swelling, inflammation, hemorrhaging, and other crazy things she didn't understand which sounded terrifying, *hydrocephalus* and *ventricles*, like strange words from science fiction movies.

Waiting for the doctor to return with the test results was agony.

Trish sat in that tiny white room—Jenny laying there with her mouth slightly open, head wrapped in bandages—with her mind racked with worry, brimming. She blamed herself for causing the scene, for being so careless, for being so obsessed with fucking Facebook and how she appeared to other people and what others thought of her. And she vowed to change, to be a better mom, to be a better person ...

But then the doctor returned, smiling, telling her that the MRI looked fine.

Relief flooded through her with a physical force, like a great rush of water cascading through her, then leaving her weightless as Jenny opened her eyes, blinking and asking for her.

"Am I all right, Mommy?"

Trish grasped her daughter's hand and smiled.

"Yes, you're fine," she said. And it was a fine moment. A beautiful moment. A tremendously heart-breaking moment. One of the greatest moments of Trish's life. And Trish thought to herself, *I should take a picture and post this on Facebook.*

THE HAPPIEST MAN IN THE WORLD

It was supposed to be a standard drug bust.

Your average pill-mill situation: corrupt croaker doctor handing out scripts of OxyContin and Xanax for cash and favors. The Sheriff's Department, where I was a deputy, were to assist the DEA—which was protocol since it was originally our case, and also a courtesy since we were the ones who had alerted them to it in the first place. I was sent mostly to observe, that and help catalogue and transport all the evidence, which was bound to be a huge haul. Word was there were piles of cash and pills laying all over, stacks of pre-signed prescription pads waiting to be sold, boxes of files. Every item was going to have to be catalogued. The doctor was apparently using too, and the place was supposed to be a real mess.

And then there was the basement.

Of course, we'd been warned about what might be in the basement, what horrors we might find, but it was more horrible than any of us could imagine.

The basement was where the abortions were performed. You see, it was a pill mill by day and unlicensed, underground abortion clinic by night. Mostly women in the third trimester with nowhere else to turn. The desperate and poverty stricken. Or very young girls, hiding their predicament, scared and alone. We'd heard the rumors and whispers. Nasty stories of hastily performed operations with dirty instruments, of how he'd give near term women Cytotek and have them miscarry in the toilet. How he'd scoop the squirming fetuses from the dirty water and snip their spines with a scissor.

I'd only been a sheriff's deputy a few months at that point. It'd been a tough few years for me. After Amanda's death, I'd been in a dangerously dark place. Still so painful to think about, yet it's never far from my thoughts. Lingering there like a festering kernel of lead in my brain, causing a gangrene of the soul.

Fuck, how it haunts me. That terrible head-on collision with that damn drunk asshole (three previous DUIs on his record, if the crash hadn't killed him, I swear to God I would have found him and done the job myself) on that horrible, horrible winter night, leaving me a widower at thirty-two.

The doctors all agreed it was a miracle I'd lived.

I can remember lying there in the hospital, surrounded by ticking machines, tubes and wires running everywhere, my body wrapped in bandages and held fast by armatures. Lost in a morphine drip, I just kept thinking, *Why? Why spare me? Why couldn't I have been killed, too?*

The shit I'd been through as a soldier, the chances I'd taken, walking through minefields and facing sniper fire in godforsaken desserts, only to come home and have my wife and unborn son taken from me by something as mundane as a car accident.

I didn't want to live without her. And for a while I seriously contemplated ways to remedy that situation. Going back to the house was hell, all the pictures of Amanda and I together, so many of her pregnant and showing off her bulging belly. I couldn't stand to look at them, and I couldn't bear to take them down either, to touch them. I'd been in the heart of battle, seen unimaginably horrible things, but nothing was worse than staring at a picture of Amanda with her swollen belly, me beside her, but not me, a former me, the me I used to be.

I'd avoid them when I could, but if one caught my gaze, I'd find myself staring for hours, imagining those wonderful times, reverie and nostalgia like a physical weight atop me, like one of those lead-filled blankets they drape over you during an X-ray.

Our golden retriever Daisy, (named by Amanda because her golden coat reminded her of the center of that simple yet lovely flower) was some consolation. Her warm, kind eyes, so obviously thrilled to see me, tail thudding against the floor in such a happy beat. But even she could be difficult to look at times, so filled with memories she was. It was hard to see her and not think of Amanda.

About a month after I got out of the hospital, my Uncle won his bid for sheriff. Won in a landslide, actually. The last guy had been wrapped up in some scandalous shit. Uncle Ross took pity on me, took me on as a full-time deputy. Not that I wasn't qualified. I was more than qualified. Former first-class officer combat veteran having served in Falujah and Kabul. But pity on me in that it was no secret I'd suffered a long series of trauma and tragedy, both on the battlefield and off, and bore the effects.

You hear it called the hundred-yard stare. Shit, I had that before losing Amanda. My stare had gone infinite.

It was like I was trying to see between things and beyond things: part of me trained to be aware of everything at once, part of me desperate to retreat to nothingness and give it all up. A conflict of will I carried burden-like on my shoulders and in my hard gaze.

Before anyone had a chance to even scream or holler a warning, he had the barrel of that gun up against his temple and was squeezing the trigger. The gunshot rang out like an explosion in that cramped office. He fell to the floor and the blood made an awful sluicing sound as it squirted up, out of his head, splashing the walls.

Pandemonium broke out. The secretary was screaming hysterically, the junkies running to the door. There were cries to call an ambulance, agents and sheriff's deputies racing about frantically. I was oddly calm, enveloped in an eerie sensation of detachment and curiosity, as if I was watching the chaotic scene from a distance. Time stretched and slowed, the hurried motions of the people around me playing out frame-by-frame as a high-pitched ringing filled my head, and I found myself wandering away from the madness of the front rooms and down a long corridor.

A rangy tabby cat mewled up at me as I slipped down the hall, an otherworldly push leading me into the depths of the clinic.

It was a confusing maze of passageways and rooms, medical waste bags strewn everywhere, flies swarming and buzzing over puddles of brown liquid on the floor, splatters on the wall, random boxes filled with cat shit and shredded paper. I came to a big industrial refrigerator, opened it and peered inside. More medical waste bags, an apple, yogurt containers, a half-eaten sandwich, and several tall glass jars filled with tiny white feet floating in a milky liquid.

Yes, feet. No bigger than the nub of your pinky, but perfectly formed: little ankles and toes. Dozens and dozens of them. All left. It was so surreal and disgusting. I gagged, but still felt this desire to keep moving and explore.

Onward I went, that crazy buzzing tone growing louder in my skull, past piles of trash and broken, discarded medical equipment, past a doorway where in a dark, tiny room a young girl lay on a gurney, groaning softly. She turned her head to me, a dazed-and-pleading look in her eyes. She held out a hand. But I kept walking.

Finally, I came to a black door adorned with a small, innocuous sign: BASEMENT.

I did *not* want to go down to that basement. The rational part of my brain was howling against it, but some strange force compelled me. Barely conscious of my own movements, in a foggy daze like a sleepwalker, that ringing in my ears rising a notch in tone, I pulled the door open and started down those dark steps and into the shadowy cavernous chamber.

The muffled cries of women moaning echoed from back rooms, and a new scent hit me, both antiseptic and sour, like cleaning products and death. Drawn forward, I passed stainless-steel tables where I saw unspeakable things in the pale-blue scintillating fluorescent light: piles of little body parts, fetuses like miniature, pale, discarded baby dolls, dismembered and sewn back together, some missing heads, some with their arms and legs switched and backwards. It was truly awful, beyond anything I'd ever seen in war.

And then . . . then I was before a small red door with an ornate brass handle.

I knew I shouldn't be down there. That I could potentially be polluting or even destroying evidence, that this was more than a crime scene, it was an abomination against nature and all that was good in the world. But a compulsion I couldn't name or control drove me to try and open the door, to twist and tug on the strange knob.

It was locked.

The door wouldn't budge, and I actually breathed a sigh of relief. For I didn't really want to go back there at all. In fact, I wanted out of that terrible dungeon of a place and my mind was screaming, "Get out! Get out! Get out now!"

But just as I stepped back from the door there was a creak, and I gasped, nearly choking on my own breath, as the door cracked open.

Out of no volition of my own, I reached out, opened the door, and found myself staring into the vastness of deep space: planets and stars, galaxies spiraling throughout luminous nebulas of purple and orange.

I wavered under the enormity of it, remembering myself as a child beneath the gaping maw of the planetarium, staggered by the vastness, and later as a soldier staring at the infinite desert sky, the constellations scintillating and glimmering, melting together.

But blinking, I realized it was just hundreds of candles. Yes, hundreds of candles in a dark room with black-painted walls. I took in a deep breath of air, let it slowly out through clenched teeth, jarred by that ringing which seemed to fill my entire body now, curling my toes and straightening the tiny hairs on the back of my neck.

My eyes adjusting to the dim amber light, I saw there was a star-shaped pattern painted on the floor in red, with strange writing and symbols around it, and before it an altar of sorts rose up, draped in black cloth, lit with elaborate steel candelabras.

I stumbled forward, the terrible feeling of being a living-marionette percolating inside me, and there, up on that black alter, lying deathly still in a pan of oily liquid, was a tiny pale fetus. Yeah, a little human baby fetus, all curled up in that iconic way, like the space baby in that movie *2001 A Space Odyssey*.

Some sick fuck had tattooed the little thing. Weird markings, triangles and crescent moons, writing in a bizarre alphabet. I was filled with a terrible sympathy for it: Such an innocent, cute thing, misused, tortured, left dead here in this strange chamber. It was beyond sick. I thought of Amanda and the child that had swam in her. My child. And suddenly I was choked with tears.

Sobbing, I stared down at it, and to my amazement, it stretched its arms—tiny hands curled into perfect fists—then yawned, as if awakening from a nap! It turned and looked up at me. It was alive! A fucking miracle.

Impulsively, I reached in and scooped it up. Once in my hands it appeared bigger than it had in the pan. More like an infant than a fetus. There was a weight to it, a heftiness and heartiness. It nuzzled against my palm and let out a soft coo. My heart throbbed with heat. It was a girl. A little girl. And, yes, she was much bigger than she had looked, filling both my hands.

A craziness filled my head. I don't know how else to describe it. A strange insanity. For I took her.

God help me, I took her.

—

At the time it seemed I was guided by empathy, by love. That it was my desire for a family that drove me to try and save her from the media and scientists and cops and Feds.

But I know better now.

Then, it felt like destiny: How I was so easily able to slip up the stairs, through those godforsaken halls and out that open door, with her cradled against my chest, hidden behind my thick Sheriff's coat.

No one even glanced at me.

But it wasn't destiny. That thing was controlling them, just as surely as it was guiding me.

By the time I made it to my patrol car the infant had tripled in size. More. I took off my parka and lay it on the passenger seat, nestled her there, wrapping her in the folds. Purple veins crisscrossed the tiny pale body and I could see dark fluid pulsing within them, and those weird tattoos gave off an unworldly glow. I noticed then, for the first time, that its eyes were yellow, with rectangular pupils, like a goat, its lips glistening and black.

How had I not seen that before?

Suddenly I didn't feel too good about this whole situation.

What the fuck had I done?

—

There was an old-fashioned basinet in the garage, a hand-me-down from Amanda's parents. A heavy, wooden thing from the sixties when they built things to last, covered in white frills and lace. I hauled it out, Daisy at my side, panting, her kind eyes curious, and put it in the spare room that was meant to be a nursery.

Placing the creature in it, it looked blasphemous there. Obscene, that tiny, ugly thing, skin like a green-and-yellow bruise, in that cute frilly bed made for a human baby.

Daisy approached, ever curious in that canine way of hers, sniffed at it, then whined and backed away, ears flat against her head, tail curled between her legs, and again I wondered, *just what have I done?*

A feeling of loathing settled over me, a sense of doom, the creature just staring at me blankly, its black lips sullen, yellow eyes cold as the depths of space. For the briefest moment I was actually filled with the urge to kill it, but then something inexplicable happened: it bat its huge eyes, and smiled warmly at me, cooing with laughter.

My heart lifted as the infectious giggles filled me and before I knew it, I was laughing too, bending down to stroke its cheek with the pad of my finger. It gave a soft, contented sigh, turned its head, and grasped my finger, kicking its pudgy little feet.

It's like a drug goes off in my brain and I'm awash in some kind of opiate high. I think, I have to name this thing, this glorious creature. It's like I am pierced with a radiant light, like a spear from a different dimension, and there's a name in my head. It just comes to me. Later I will learn what it means, but then I was ignorant. Alnilam: the brightest star in Orion's belt.

—

The next day I called in sick to work. My uncle answered the phone.

"What happened to you yesterday?" he asked in his gruff voice. "You just disappeared."

I told him that the clinic, the whole scene, just brought back so many memories of Amanda being pregnant that I had to leave. Just couldn't bear to be there. I apologized, said, "My anxiety is at maximum and my therapist says I should take some time off to try to work through this." Truth was, I hadn't seen my therapist in months. Hated her smugness and condescending attitude. It made me feel weak.

"Take as much time as you need," he told me.

—

She won't eat.

I've tried formula and milk. Warmed it and tried to feed her with a bottle. She just turns her little face away. Tried spooning baby food of all types into her mouth: vegetables, fruit, meat, from jars, tubes, little pouches, homemade recipes I researched and put in a blender. She just spits it out and clamps her lips shut. In desperation I tried bits of hamburger, doughnuts and cake. Even pizza. Nothing's worked. Not even a nibble. I don't know what to do.

But she's plump and healthy-looking. And keeps growing. No longer the size of a newborn, she's now a hefty infant. She's able to sit up, hold her head high and look around. She even squirms on her belly as if any day she'll begin to crawl. She even smells healthy, that fresh, clean, intoxicating baby smell.

I keep her in diaper. Though there's really no need, she hasn't once peed or had a bowel movement. Which also worries me.

—

Christmas.

I think she may be feeding on me somehow. Draining me. I feel weak and listless. My hair has begun to fall out, clumps coming loose from my head in the shower and clogging the drain. My gums ache and bleed.

This morning I lost a tooth. A canine on the upper right side. I could feel with my tongue that it was loose. When I jiggled it with my finger it slipped right out of my skull, long and slender, slightly yellow and dotted in blood. I was turning it before my eyes, studying it, a weariness deep in the center of my bones, when I heard a thudding crash followed by a high-pitched yelp.

How to explain the horror I saw after racing to the nursery? I don't know how. Alnilam, the baby, *that thing*, was out of her crib and on the floor, spilled out on her belly like a white puddle, gripping Daisy's snout in her fat little hands, pudgy legs kicking.

Daisy was still, but trembling slightly. She had gone completely white, unnaturally white, as if bleached, and a strange purple mist sluiced out her mouth and nostrils and into Alnilam's gently parted lips. The strange markings that adorned her body, *those weird tattoos*, glowed with a pulsating green light as she slurped the mist up, lifting her unearthly eyes to mine and grinning.

I screamed, pressing my palms against the sides of my head, as if my skull might crack apart if not held fast by my hands.

Alnilam burped and a giggle escaped her as she tossed the dog aside. I dropped to my knees, tears welling up, and took Daisy's head in my hands. Her lips were shriveled and dry, mummified, her eyes hollow and blank. She was stiff, and incredibly light, as if devoid of substance. I pulled her into my arms, rocking back and forth, clutching her to me and weeping.

Alnilam lifted herself up, cocked her head, and pointed a fat finger at me. "Da da. Da," she said, her voice a sweet singsong. Those words hit my heart like a wrecking ball and everything seemed to change.

Da da. Those elemental and ancient sounds. She saw me as her father. And when I looked at her, Christ, it was *so* easy to look beyond the preternaturally-pale shade of skin, the black lips, goat's eyes and glowing markings, to see a sweet, fat-faced baby girl. A cute little thing grinning innocently, clapping her chubby hands.

And how could I be upset? How could I be angry?

—

But later, digging Daisy's grave, wearily cracking open the cold earth with a mattock, beyond the strange influence of that baby thing, I made a grim decision: I'm going to kill it.

She was an abomination. Evil. She had to die.

Daisy was the last connection to my old world. To Amanda. To normality. Slipping her into that dark pit, spilling soil over her emaciated and bleached form, I realized why I was chosen. It was that empty part of my heart. That place Amanda had emptied with her death. That hollowness that yearned to be a father, a husband, to have a family.

That's why Alnilam had chosen me.

She needed someone wounded. Someone vulnerable to be her keeper. Someone desperate enough for a sense of family that they'd accept a demon into their life. She was using my hurt, my festering inner-wounds.

Yes, she had to die.

—

I approached the nursery slowly, my service revolver clutched in a trembling, sweaty fist, finger on the trigger. I had to be swift, without hesitation. I stepped into the room and raised the revolver, centering the sights on her.

She turned her strange goat eyes to me, those black lips yawning upward into a terrible grin, and my finger froze, locked, unable to squeeze the trigger. My hand quaked as she tilted her head, commanding me. I was helpless, under her complete control, as she demanded I lift my arm and put the barrel of the revolver to my head, pressing the cold metal to my temple.

And, yes, I admit, I found some peace in the thought of death. Welcomed it. I shut my eyes, took a breath, and gave in to her.

But she wouldn't even give me that condolence. She needed me and wouldn't let me die. Worse yet, it was then she let me know what she wanted. What she needed. What she feeds on. She had no need for flesh and blood as sustenance, no. She wanted souls. That's why she didn't want formula or baby food, dead stuff, pieces of meat and vegetable, fruit and milk. She needed something living, something with a consciousness and self-awareness. She craved to devour spiritual essence, and had taken mine to the brink.

And Daisy had a soul. That glint of love and empathy you see in a dog's eye, that's what Alnilam fed on, leaving nothing but a shriveled white shell, a worn-out body drained of life.

But what was the innocence and affection of a mere dog compared to that of a human child?

—

I found the first one standing just outside the park, staring forlornly towards the playground swings, a dripping ice-cream cone in her chubby hand.

She was a fat little thing in a pink sundress, with bushy-blonde ponytails bobbing on either side of her head, lapping sullenly on that vanilla cone. She couldn't have been more than four, her mother yapping away to a group of other young women in a gossip circle. Didn't even notice me take her by the hand and lead her away.

—

We've had to stay on the move. From California to Arizona to New Mexico and now Colorado. Looking for places where tourists come with their children. Living in cheap hotels beside third-rate amusement parks. I'm weary of the road, but constantly moving is the key to remaining undiscovered. Jurisdiction to jurisdiction, leaving no links, nothing for law enforcement to put together.

—

She's sick! My poor little Alnilam. I'm in an utter panic.

She's fevered, burning up. She just lays there moaning and there's something terribly wrong with her back. Her little shoulder blades have these nasty boils on them. They started as tiny welts, but have been growing and swelling, weeping a foul-smelling green puss. And I can see a weird movement in them, the swollen skin fluttering, as if there's something living inside them.

Can I take her to a hospital? Call a doctor?

Are these options even possible given our predicament?

I feel so helpless. She's all I have now. The thought of losing her is beyond soul crushing.

—

WINGS!!! SHE HAS WINGS!!!

This morning those nasty blisters on her back split open and out unfurled slick, slimy, beautiful black wings! All leathery and bat-like. Her fever was instantly gone and she was immediately back to her old happy self, laughing and giggling, flapping those wonderful new wings.

Oh, what a relief. My soul feels as if a terrible weight has been lifted from it. Thank God. Thank God my little Alnilam is all right.

—

She can fly. Actually fly. It's so amazing. Such an incredible sight.

I brought her back a toddler I found wandering around by the fountain at a shopping mall. A chubby little boy in OshKosh overalls with big blue eyes and a double chin. I led him into the room, and as soon as I shut the door behind us she spied him from the bed, lifting her head, those beautiful yellow goat eyes studying him as he plodded around clumsily.

Her pupils narrowed and those black wings fluttered to life and rose, beating softly, lifting her gracefully upwards. The little boy saw her and grinned, pointed a fat finger, mumbling nonsense, a bit of drool dripping off his bottom lip as she circled, as predatory and beautiful as the most American of bald eagles.

Then, in one swift and calculated motion, with the precision of a striking snake, she swooped down, catching his surprised face in her hands. He staggered back, nearly falling, but she held him fast, pulling him towards her, sucking his spirit from out his nose and mouth in a stream of purple mist. The little boy's ruddy complexion went pale, his rolls of fat shriveling and drying up, his wide eyes going blank and empty.

Then she released her grip and he toppled gently, nothing but a little husk of a child now. Alnilam laughed and swept across the room as I clapped my hands and whooped for joy, tears of happiness swelling in my eyes.

She's so amazing. The greatest daughter I could ever have asked for. An answer to my prayers. And I know within my heart, we have nothing but wonderful, wonderful days ahead of us. I'm just sure of it.

A NOEL IN BLACK

The doors to the homeless shelter shut in ten minutes, but Caleb needed another drink. It was Christmas Eve 1970, and he was wandering the streets of Eureka, California in a tattered and filthy Santa suit, crimson hat perched atop his head, dirty beard pulled down around his neck, a streak of vomit running down his left leg.

When the Salvation Army gave him the costume, days ago—how many now? Three? Four?—it had been brand new and shiny clean, but he had gone AWOL as soon as he had begged up enough money for a good drunk. He couldn't believe how easy it was to get money begging in a Santa Suit during the holidays, especially when people thought they were giving to the Salvation Army. Too bad, he thought, that the racket had to end tonight. Fuck it, he was headed to the nearest bar and had a pocket full of money.

Bells on bob-tail ring, making spirits bright. Oh what fun it is to sing a sleighing song tonight.

Finally managing to make eye contact with the ape-faced bartender who was absent-mindedly pushing a dishtowel up and down a pint glass, Caleb waved a twenty in the air, a wry smile of *what the fuck?* on his face. Red and green Christmas tree lights flickered over the bottles and mirrors and off in the corner the Ghost of Christmas Past grinned its horrid smile. The bartender nodded acknowledgment and strutted over.

"Yeah? Whaddya want?"

"Beer and a whiskey."

"What kinda beer? What kinda whiskey?"

"The cheapest."

The bartender got him his drinks, took the twenty, and left his change in front of him on the bar.

Sipping the bitter medicine, Caleb noticed a woman a few stools down trying to draw his attention, a jet of blue smoke issuing from her cherry-red lips as she raised and lowered her thickly-pencilled eyebrows. He could tell she had done her best to look good tonight: lots of eye makeup, newer, hipper-looking clothes, but he could see the age in her face, recognized her need like a bad smell. Battered, needy women gave off a stink of desperation he'd learned to recognize over the years. Those years since he'd been back from the war. He'd had his fair share of these types. Always good for a warm bed and a hot meal, but too crazy to spend any real time with.

"Hey there, Santa. Buy a girl a drink?"

"Sure thing, honey." Caleb glanced at the barkeep. "Give the lady what she wants."

She slid down next to him as the grim-faced bartender mixed a rum and coke, speared a lime with a tiny sword and dropped it in the glass. "I've always had a thing for Santa," she whispered. "Coming in late at night to punish the naughty and reward the nice."

"Yeah, and what are you, darling? Naughty or nice?"

"I've always thought I was a little of both."

"Ha. What's your name, baby?"

"Sandra. They call me Sandy around here. But I think of myself as Sandra."

"All right, Sandra. What's your story?"

"Just a local girl, been in the same place too long. What about you, Santa? Don't you gotta lot of work to do tonight?"

Caleb laughed, that deep, reassuring laugh he'd mastered over the years, to put people—women especially—at ease. They talked for a while. Then Caleb ordered a pitcher of beer and a couple more shots and they moved to a corner booth. Sandra talked on and on, chain smoking Salems while he drank his beer and sipped his whiskey, watching as the room began to spin in slow, psychedelic and nauseating circles.

"You're awful quiet."

"I've been told that before."

"How'd you get them scars on your neck?"

Caleb put his hand to his neck, let it drift down to the dirty fake beard, and pulled the knotted grey and black mess of hair over to cover his throat. And that wicked Ghost of Christmas Past with sunken eyes and yellow teeth whispered, "Tell her." And so Caleb did.

"In the war."

"You were over in 'Nam, huh?"

"Yeah, two tours."

"And then what? You come back to have these damn hippies spitting at you? I feel for you, sweetie. My daddy died in France fighting Nazis. Now my brother is in the Navy while this country goes to shit. You got these bastards like that dirty Abbey Hoffman saying to steal everything. And this Charlie Manson Family killing movie stars." She laughed, shook her head and sipped her drink. "It's enough to make you sick."

They grew quiet. "So, you going to tell me about those scars, or what?"

"Well, I was a Kootchie Kootie. A tunnel rat. You know what that is?"

"Oh, yeah. You were one of those guys that go down in those gook holes?"

"Sure was. Infantry. 1st Reconnaissance Squadron." He sighed, not wanting to get into it, but once he started it was hard to stop. "I was working three clicks west of Duc Pho in the Quang Ngai province. I was down in a tunnel. Just me, my .45 and a flash light. Looking out for booby traps and rats and spiders, and this animal. . . it came out of nowhere. Fucking attacked me. Just latched onto my shoulder and wouldn't let go."

"Oh, baby. You was attacked by an animal down in

one of those tunnels?"

"Yeah. But when I killed it, when I shot it . . . " He couldn't tell her the rest. He couldn't tell her how after he had shot that thing, the muzzle blast a blinding light, the report deafening, after he had filled that monster full of holes and watched it drop, it had looked just like a little girl. Just a tiny, raven-haired girl, all shot up and bloody, when moments ago it had been a beast: a mess of lurching fangs and drool.

His mouth moved up and down silently. He couldn't say anything. Then, with an incredible effort, what he had managed to say was, "I think I brought something back with me. I . . . I . . . I don't know."

"You brought something back with you? You mean like that Agent Orange stuff, honey?"

"No, something different. Something, something. . ."

"What? In your head?"

He wanted to say, no, something in my blood: I brought back something in my blood that makes me a monster; but instead, he just nodded yes, his face a knot, visibly fighting to not break down in tears.

"Oh, baby, oh, baby, I understand."

The room was twirling now at a breakneck speed. He was going to be sick. He pulled away from her and vomited on the floor.

"Son of a bitch!" the bartender shouted. "Who's going to clean that up?"

Caleb hung over the edge of the booth, retching and dry heaving.

"Fuck you, Sam. He's a veteran! He fought for this country, got attacked down in one of them gook holes. What the fuck you ever done?"

"I don't care if he was on the beach at Normandy. Get him the fuck out of here!"

"You're a piece of work. A real piece of work, know that, Sam? Where's your sense of Christmas spirit?"

The bartender stomped up to her, eyes bulging, an accusing finger extended. "Get your cheap-whore ass out of here, bitch, and take your Santa Claus friend with you. Got me?" he grabbed her face in his hand and jerked her chin up so that he could look her in the eye. "This bar ain't no place for you anymore, Sandy. You make my customers sick. Everyone who's wanted to has fucked you, and none of them's too proud of it either. You'se don't belong here. Find some other place to haunt, you cheap skank." With that he tossed her head aside and stormed back behind the bar.

We wish you a merry Christmas. We wish you a merry Christmas. We wish you a merry Christmas and a happy New Year.

Sandra walked Caleb back to the motel room she rented by the month, holding him up the whole way while he leaned against her mumbling and pointing to ghosts she could not see. Once they were back at her room she helped him out of his Santa outfit and got him into the tub. In the heat of the steamy water he regained a semblance of consciousness, came back to himself. When he looked up he saw her through the mist, leaning in the doorway, staring at him. She had changed and was now wearing nothing but a silk kimono. He had to admit she didn't look that bad.

"How you feeling, Santa?"

"Good. I feel . . ." he paused, unsure what to say, how he actually felt. "Good."

She knelt down beside the tub, ran her finger over the surface of the water. "Thirsty?" she asked, holding up a tumbler of Scotch and water.

"As a matter of fact, I am."

Taking the glass into his hands, he took a sip. Handing it back to her she gave him a penetrating stare that he found hard to decipher and then leaned in to kiss him. She tasted of whiskey, cigarettes and peppermint. But it was good, the way she gently ran her tongue over his upper lip before she pulled away, and Caleb felt himself growing aroused.

"Now that you're all cleaned up, why don't we get you

to bed."

"Sounds good, baby."

"Dry yourself off. I'll be waiting." With that she disappeared out the door.

He got up from the tub and dried himself the best he could with the cheap, tiny towels the motel provided. When he entered the room she was already on the bed, prone on her back and naked. She may have had a butter face but her body was to die for, and she knew how to flaunt it. He started towards her but she held up her hand, palm out toward him, and exclaimed, "Stop right there, mister. The Santa suit. Put it on."

He gave her a questioning half grimace and then smiled. "You serious?"

"I told you: I gotta thing for Santa."

Smirking, he pulled on the dirty jacket and set the conical hat atop his head. "Better?"

"Oh, yeah, baby. I've been so naughty. I need to be punished."

With that she burst out in playful laughter, turned over onto all fours, and stuck her ass into the air, whispering over her shoulder, "Come and get it, Santa."

He approached the bed and, still standing, he pulled himself into her. She let out a deep moan and he began to move, slowly. He was still drunk as hell and the room was spinning slightly but he could feel that primal urge within to rock and rotate. He began to lunge faster, and faster, and then, suddenly, it was happening again.

Fuck. No. No. No. It was happening *again*. He could feel himself beginning to change as he thrust against her. A part of him wanted to run away, to bolt through the door and into the night so that he wouldn't hurt her. But another part of him wanted this. It felt good. It felt *so fucking good* to let go and let the animal inside him take over. Still pounding, Sandra moaning beneath him, he watched in wonder as his fingers—tightly gripping her bony hips—became claws and a thick mat of fur began to weave itself up his arms. Thrusting against her with all his might he lifted his face and began to howl as his mouth filled with sharp, gleaming fangs.

Here comes Santa Claus, here comes Santa Claus, right down Santa Claus lane!

Margaret Ashton was the manager of the Lone Pine motel. She had been across the street visiting with her daughter and grandson in their two-story, cookie-cutter house, and was just walking back to the motel office when she heard the screaming in room 308. It was that cheap-tramp Sandy's room. Margaret had been waiting for an excuse to evict her and marched up to the door, ready to throw her out, Christmas Eve or not. But as she grew closer and heard the urgency to the screams, the gut-wrenching terror of the squeals, she grew hesitant and stopped.

The screaming stopped and the window exploded outward, showering her with glass and splintered wood. She fell back and slipped to the ground, watching in utter disbelief as the craziest thing she had ever seen in her life of fifty-six years came tumbling down atop her.

A wolf.

A huge monster of a wolf, with a snarling mouth of bloody fangs and drool. And it was wearing a red coat lined in white fur with a Santa cap perched atop its head.

From his bedroom window her grandson Tommy watched the entire thing.

Later that night homicide detectives would interview the little boy. Tearfully he would relate how he had seen his grandmother ripped to shreds by some kind of beast in a Santa suit. One of the uniformed officers standing idly in the background would then turn to his partner and whisper under his breath, "Looks like grandma got run over by a werewolf, walking home from his house Christmas Eve."

Oh Tannenbaum, oh Tannenbaum, lovely are thy branches.

God, the Easter Bunny, and the Ghost of Christmas Present watched as two-year-old Annabelle toddled out the door of her street-level apartment and onto the sidewalk, a thumb stuck in her mouth and dragging a Barbie doll along by the hair.

God looked like the guy from the Dos Equis commercials: an incredibly good-looking older gentleman with white hair, perfectly coifed, and a nicely trimmed beard, in a tuxedo. The Ghost of Christmas Present looked extremely bored and kept yawning. The Easter Bunny was an out-of-work writer who needed a shave, dressed in a pink bunny outfit.

"Cute kid," the Easter Bunny commented.

"I wouldn't get too attached," the Ghost of Christmas Present replied, disinterestedly stifling a yawn.

Annabelle's parents were fighting again and their voices echoed out from the apartment.

"Christ, how many Quaaludes did you take? You can't even look at me. Wake up, bitch, I'm talking to you."

"Fuck off, Henry. You always were a bore."

"You dumb piece of shit. I oughta slap the stupid right offa your face."

When the wolf came galloping down the middle of the street in its blood-soaked Santa suit the Easter Bunny turned to God and said, "You gotta be putting me on, man."

God rolled his eyes.

The wolf snatched the baby in its fangs and threw the child up into the night sky where she hung suspended in the moonlight for a moment, tiny arms and legs kicking, and then tumbled down, landing on the street with a thud. The beast leapt at her, sinking its sharp teeth into her neck and thrashing its head side to side until the tiny figure ceased to struggle and lay limp in its mouth.

"It's probably for the best," the Ghost of Christmas Past said.

"What? Why?" the Easter Bunny asked, scratching at the stubble on his face.

"You want to tell him, God? Or should I?"

God gestured with his hands, as if to say, "Go ahead. It's all you."

"If Annabelle had lived through this night, after being molested by her stepfather and stepbrother, she would have become a heroin addict by fifteen and a prostitute by sixteen. She then would have gotten picked up by a notorious serial killer who after raping her for days would finally kill her by trying to give her a lobotomy with a cordless drill. Her life taken like this, quickly and mercifully, is a blessing, a thing of joy. A Christmas miracle."

"Is this true?" the Easter Bunny asked God.

God grinned and nodded.

"You don't say much, do you?" the Easter Bunny asked God.

God just shrugged.

Deck the halls with boughs of holly, fa la la la la la la la la.
'Tis the season to be jolly, fa la la la la la la la la.

Father Mulligan was cleaning up after midnight mass when he heard the click-clack of claws on the wooden floor. He paused, chalice in one hand, ciborium in the other, and listened.

"Hello?" he called out, his voice echoing throughout the empty chapel. "Who's there?"

Beneath the pounding of blood in his ears he distinctly heard panting, like that of a large dog.

"Hello?"

Deep in the dark recess of the hall something stirred, moved, and then came slinking out of the shadows: a large creature walking on all fours, its eyes alight and flickering like yellow flames. The beast came forward slowly down the aisle, Santa hat drooping down one side of its head, a dead baby hanging limply in its mouth. The wolf approached the altar and came so close that the priest could smell it, a feral odor of blood and musk. It spit the baby to the floor where it landed with a horrible smack.

But the priest didn't run. He stood his ground, murmuring prayers beneath his breath. He knew why the beast was there, why this spawn of evil had come. It was here to punish him. Punish him for the things he had done to all those little boys. So many. First in Ireland when he had just been doing what had been done to him when he was an altar boy. Then, after coming to America, in Philadelphia, where for years the urban darkness of poverty and city life had let him run rampant. Not yet here in California, where he had been sent quickly by the diocese so as not to cause a scandal. But he had his eyes on a few of the boys in his congregation. Some of the poorer ones who he thought wouldn't tell.

Seeing the monster here was a blessing and death would be a mercy. He fell to his knees, kissed his stole, and lifted his neck to the beast. But instead of taking him by the throat, the beast spun him around by the shoulders so that the priest fell face first to the floor. With one quick jerking motion the monster shredded the priest's pants and mounted him. The priest cried out in pain and surprise as the wolf forcibly entered him and warm blood began to trickle down his leg.

God, the Easter Bunny and the Ghost of Christmas Present stood at the back of the chapel watching. The Easter Bunny had taken off his hood of rabbit ears and was puffing on an e-cigarette and furiously tapping away on an iPad mini. "Been blogging about this whole thing, and, yeah, a lot of people see that as offensive. I mean, what the fuck? You got a werewolf dressed like Santa Claus raping a child-molesting priest on Christmas Eve?"

The Ghost of Christmas Present laughed heartily. "Well, I hate to say I told you so, but . . ."

"You got nothing to say about this, God?" the Easter Bunny asked, momentarily looking away from his iPad.

God tilted his head to the left, his thin lips bending into a sad frown, and, raising his eyebrows in an, "Oh, well," manner, shrugged again.

Joy to the world, the Lord has come. Let Earth receive her king!

Gravy Brain Jane was out of her mind on LSD and had nowhere to go. She had a thousand tabs of purple sunshine on her but the connect had never shown and wasn't answering the phone. Exasperated and befuddled, her vision a swirling cyclone of light and darkness, she stumbled from the Greyhound Station to a small clearing in a copse of woods. She sat leaning against a tree, the branches dripping and melting around her, the sky a miasma of spiralling stars and galaxies. She giggled and mumbled her strange mantra. "No sense makes sense. No sense makes sense. No sense makes sense."

Charlie had sent a message from prison that she should deliver the acid here. If Charlie said it would work out, it would work out. She was sure of that. She had thought the other passengers on the bus would have been startled and scared by the X that Sandy and Squeaky had helped her burn into her forehead with hot bobby pins, but no one had noticed at all.

The Easter Bunny, who wasn't even wearing his rabbit outfit anymore, and was now just dressed in his usual black jeans and t-shirt, was pacing back and forth irritably. He turned to the Ghost of Christmas Present and asked, slightly argumentatively, "Well, where's God?"

"Oh, he couldn't make it. Had a concert to catch."

"A concert? What are you talking about?"

"Well, it was Skynard and you know how he loves 'Free Bird'."

"Typical."

Gravy Brain Jane giggled when she saw the beast slowly creeping towards her. She had been taught to love coyotes when the family was in the desert of Death Valley. Back on the ranch Charlie had taught them to break down the final walls society imposed on them by having them fellate the stray dogs.

"Hey there, beautiful," she said. The wolf just stared at her with its unblinking yellow eyes.

From their glimmer and spark she knew just what the creature wanted. It wanted what all men want and she had been taught the ways of a free love society. Giggling she squirmed from her panties and lifted her skirt with a vacant grin. She knew that in love there is no wrong. That submission is a gift and that you should never learn not to love. Charlie had taught her well.

She spread her legs and the beast crept up to her and lowered its snout to her and began to lap at her in quick, greedy, licks. She gripped its ears tight, her head thrown back, and thought about how groovy and sexy it was to be pleasured by the beast, to have death and life so close, to lay your hands upon the monster and be free in love. As she bucked and lurched and felt herself climax she thought about how the Son of Man had taught her that death is only another orgasm, that everything in the universe is in-and-out and in-and-out in a cosmic orgy, babies coming out, galaxies sinking into black holes, knives plunging in, blood pouring out. *Wow! Talk about the Big Bang!*

The beast crawled atop her and slipped itself into her. When it shuddered and released itself inside her she knew within her heart that she would be with child. This was a happy moment. A glorious moment in time. Another Christmas miracle. Oh, joyous night. She would name this child Steven, Steven Kirby, after her grandfather.

Afterwards, the beast lay against her, spent. She stroked its fur with her nails and gently kissed its blood drenched snout. In this way the beast kept the girl warm through the coldest hours of the night.

Silent Night. Holy Night. All is calm. All is bright.

Free in the moonlight as snow began to fall, bathed in the stink of congealing human blood, the taste of flesh and woman fresh on its lips and tongue, the lycanthrope ran, the stars above him a smear of spilled milk, the moon a cataract eye aglow in malignancy.

On the First Day of Christmas my true love gave to me. . .

Caleb awoke in the morning naked and freezing, enveloped in the scent of the Douglas fir and redwood. He shivered and looked about. Snow was falling heavily, blanketing the earth in white. Beside him lay his tattered Santa costume, by some miracle the hat still clung to his head.

He glanced above the towering tree tops to the shelter of the sky and saw there a light both majestic and bizarre. Seemingly fake, like a bad special effect from a cheap television show. And in that glaring gleam of white, he saw a black figure descend: The Ghost of Christmas Future who spoke in a deep and sultry voice while extending out a hand, "Do you wish to come with me?"

In his mind all he could hear was Bing Crosby crooning *I'm Dreaming of a White Christmas*, and a million worlds passed before his eyes. Birthday cakes with only a few candles to blow out. His mother's smile as she tugged on thread, sewing patches on a Cub Scout sash. Playing catch with his dad who bought him that special glove for little league and would oil it with him in the falling sun of the suburban evening. Watching Kennedy's skull explode on television, Jackie screeching and trying desperately to crawl away. The Howdy Doodie show. Lee Harvey Oswald grimacing in pain and turning as Ruby put a bullet in his side. That gnarled old apple tree in the backyard, how that ancient tree would fill with tiny white blossoms in the spring so that you could not tell how old and bent it really was, its age hidden in its blooming. How those tiny petals fell in early summer, glistening in the amber light, a shimmering rain of flowers cascading down and lying white as snow on the ground. Sweat streaming down his brow as he pushed a lawnmower, that smell of fresh-cut grass, such a vibrant green it made his head hurt. Behind the baseball dugout with Betty Connors on a warm summer night: his first kiss. How she had moved away soon after and he had never seen her again. His draft card: that plain and innocuous envelope of a pale-yellow color that they'd all dreaded and all expected. Telling his father, "Guess I'm going to war, pops." And his father just nodding back stoically. His gal Sally, with her beehive hairdo, who wouldn't let him fuck her no matter how hard he begged and pleaded, telling her he didn't want to go to war a virgin. The ancient apple tree in autumn, loaded with ripe fruit. The bumpy ride over the Pacific in a military transport plane. The Vietnamese whore who spread her legs for a single American dollar. Paddy fields burned and incinerated so that no water stood within them and the rice stalks withered. January 1968. Tet: The New Year, a time to worship ancestors. An intricate barrage of hellfire. Medivac choppers stuffed with bloody men and boys. Fire fights, flares illuminating the night, the thunder of mortars and sparks of muzzle flash. A landscape of smoke and exploding ordinances. Those mornings when the bombers flew in and the ground shook like jelly. Seeing men he knew dancing and screaming in flames. Splintered, broken trees, smoke billowing in the distance. The Pickle Switch and canisters of napalm. VC bodies dressed in black lying in horrible piles. A rifle on the ground with a stream of ammunition dripping out of it. "I dare you to pick up that dead man's gun." "Yeah, right." The tunnels. And the idea of winter, just the concept of it in that hot, hot land where all is hidden from you, taken, and there is nothing to believe in or hope for, but you imagine that tree back home nonetheless, barren and without leaves and fruit, draped in snow and frozen. The way the men whispered when they found a dead body, till all you hear is whispers of body, body, body. Then the beast appears who is really only a little girl. How could you have thought that a little girl was a monster? There was no monster, just a little girl, you made everything else up. But now there is a monster, just as sure as there are ghosts, an Easter Bunny and a God. It's you. You're the monster. You're the beast. And you think to yourself, *What have I done? What did I do?* Then, as you face this ultimate truth, the cold takes you. And when would spring come again? Certainly not in this lifetime, and not on this earth. So, "Yes," you say to the cold and the winter. To the Ghost of Christmas Future who holds nothing forth but death. "Yes. Take me. Just take me away and let me be free." An affirmation to end the rest of your negations.

And you let go of that aching, awful, agonizing pain of being a man of flesh and blood, the cold slowing down your heart, and give in to death.

And as you slip away, into the embrace of the Ghost of Christmas Future, you wonder, "Was it real? Was any of it real at all?"

And in the heavens a laughing God finally breaks his silence and answers: "There is no such thing as real. It's all just a dream within a dream."

PUBLICATION CREDITS

A WITCH'S YULE is new to this collection.

THE GYPPO'S CLOTHES is new to this collection.

THE TALE OF THE FEARLESS VAMPIRE KILLING BROTHERS was originally published in a slightly different form on Creepypasta.wikia under the name THE FEARLESS VAMPIRE KILLING BROTHERS in April 2015.

BLIND CLOWN CHAOS was originally published in *Body Parts Magazine* #8, Spring/Summer 2017

CHARYBDIS is new to this collection.

NEST OF SALT is new to this collection.

THE PET was originally published in *Infernal Ink Magazine* Summer 2017

A TRUE CHILD OF WODEN is new to this collection.

MALL SANTA was originally published in the collection UNDER ROTTING SKY in April 2019

THE HAPPIEST MAN IN THE WORLD is new to this collection

A NOEL IN BLACK was originally published in *Collected Christmas Horrors Vol 2* by KJK Publishing in September 2018.

ALSO BY MATTHEW V. BROCKMEYER

KIND NEPENTHE: A Savage Tale of Terror Set in the Heart of California's Marijuana Country

UNDER ROTTING SKY: Stories

BLACK THUNDER PRESS